EVERY
PICTURE
TELLS
A
STORY

Previous books by Gregory Dowling

DOUBLE TAKE
SEE NAPLES AND KILL

EVERY
PICTURE
TELLS
A
STORY

GREGORY
DOWLING

ST. MARTIN'S
PRESS NEW YORK

DESIGN BY DAWN NILES

Library of Congress Cataloging-in-Publication Data

Dowling, Gregory.
  Every picture tells a story / Gregory Dowling.
      p.   cm.
  "A Thomas Dunne book."
  ISBN 0-312-05815-2
  I. Title.
PR6054.0862E94   1991
823'.914—dc20   91-4489
                                                                      CIP

First Edition: July 1991
10 9 8 7 6 5 4 3 2 1

AGAIN FOR PATRIZIA

FOREWORD

My sincere thanks to Chiara Maida of the Accademia Gallery, Venice, and Jess Wilder of the Portal Gallery, London, who both gave me technical suggestions and help which I can only hope I have put to good use.

All the institutions, establishments, and people described in any detail in the novel are imaginary. Venice, on the other hand, may seem so but is not.

1

WELL, they noticed me, there was no doubt of that. When I entered the gallery at eight-fifteen and handed my coat and shoulder bag to the lady at the door, a definite murmur ran around the room—a frisson even.

I don't suppose everyone in the room had instantly recognized me, but enough people had done so for the message to start moving and it was still doing the rounds, together with the frisson, as I walked toward George, whose exhibition it was. He greeted me coldly from behind his Old Testament beard, pointed out where I could get a drink, and then turned back to the true believers gathered in a mystic circle around him.

I picked up a glass of wine and looked around the room oh-so-casually. I found my eyes meeting other sliding eyes everywhere: and then a few seconds later there were just backs of heads, and the murmur was the usual low-pitched one of discriminating appreciation as they studied the paintings or chattered in little clustered knots. The knots all seemed to be pulled extra-tight, and I didn't know any of the people outside the knots well enough to start up a conversation with them.

So I'd just have to look at the paintings. What had I expected anyway?

Then Adrian Limpett appeared, popping out from what had looked like a granny-knot of clustered Chelsea dames. "Martin!" he cried. He was wearing his usual earnest gray suit, earnest gray mustache, and glasses, but his expression was almost exuberant for once: that murmur of recognition as I entered had obviously been all that he, as owner of the gallery, had hoped for.

"Oh, hello, Adrian. Thanks for the invitation."

"Not at all, not at all. Glad you could come. Do you know everybody?"

"No, but they seem to know me, even without the ball and chain."

"Oh, Martin. People forget these things. The past is the past, you know."

"Then why do you keep asking me to do a picture of Wormwood Scrubs for my show?"

"Well, there's no point pretending it didn't happen. In fact there should be a lady here from the *Evening Standard* who said she'd love to ask you one or two questions." He looked vaguely around the room. "Hmm, she doesn't seem to have arrived yet."

I swilled back some wine. "Adrian, you do realize that I'm yesterday's story as far as the newspapers are concerned. Okay, so people turn and stare when I enter a room: that doesn't mean they're all dying to read my views on prison reform."

"Prison . . . ? No, I'd suggested 'True Forgery' as a headline to this lady."

"For God's sake—"

"You've got to understand, Martin, that publicity is part of the name of the game nowadays. Your show is in three weeks' time. You say they've forgotten about you, so we've got to remind them. Get them talking about you. And, well, let's face it, forgery is one of the things you're known for. So talk to this lady about it. Frankly and fearlessly. It'll be a chance to set the record straight."

"My record is irredeemably crooked. It's myself I've got to

think about getting straight. But what the hell, put her onto me if she comes. It'll be nice to have *some*body to talk."

He patted my arm and then set off toward George, probably to reassure him in case he was getting jealous.

Well, it had been too much to hope that I'd been invited for my charm.

It was almost enough to make me try and look at the paintings—the last thing one comes to a private view for. But a mere glance around myself convinced me that this would be a hopeless task. All I could see were occasional chinks of color through the wall of people. This told me that green was this year's color for shapeless blobs (chromatic abstractionism, according to the catalog); I was quite prepared to be satisfied with this knowledge.

I'd have a go at mingling, I thought. After all, they weren't actually going to walk out on me. I started walking round the gallery.

I realized I'd completed a full circle and still not met any eyes, so I snatched another glass of white wine as a tray went by. I might as well take what consolation I could there. I could see two bubbles rising from the bottom of the glass; well, that made it more sparkling than the conversation around me. It was about the same temperature as the two pints of beer I'd swilled before coming in—somewhere between blood and urine.

I kept circling, listening to little snatches of conversation here and there—"Oh, I *so* agree"; "Do you *really?*"; "Oh, yes, I *do* think so"; "*Such* a nice man"; "Oh, *isn't* that just *too* exquisite." I'd not heard such italicized conversation for ages. Nobody had talked like that at the Scrubs—maybe that had been one of the few pluses of the place. If I drank too much, I'd probably find myself parodying the tones. If not pulling faces at the speakers.

I was on my fifth glass before anybody talked to me. I was staring at a painting and wondering if the fact that I could see blobs hovering outside the picture frame was a proof of what the catalog said about George's works "deconstructing the formal limits of the confined surface area and thus giving rise to a new spatial awareness, a new dialogue between the container and the contained," or whether I was just plastered, when a blond girl with a breathy "upper-crust" voice said, "May I have a look?" She was pointing at my catalog.

"Of course," I said.

"Thanks." She flipped through it perfunctorily, then said, "You're Martin Phipps, aren't you?"

"Yes."

"I—I've always loved your works."

"Thanks."

"I mean, they—they *really* seem to say something about the state of Britain. You make a real statement."

"Ah. I thought I made paintings." My no-nonsense Kingsley-Amis style this.

She smiled a bit nervously at this. "I suppose your next exhibition will be—will be even darker in tone."

"Pitch-black. You won't be able to see a thing." This was stupid. How could I hope to get people chatting to me, particularly a really pretty girl like this one, unless I opened myself up a little more welcomingly? I put on a sweeter smile and got ready to say something nice about containers and contained. Then I saw her make a little grinning turn of the head to the other side of the room where another girl was watching, her hand clapped over her mouth to suppress the giggles. I clammed up.

The blond beauty said, "Gosh, well, I—I can't wait, goodbye," and then turned and almost ran to join her friend across the room; she at once exploded in a fit of quiet giggles herself. She'd obviously won her dare.

I looked around for another glass. There was none in sight.

Adrian came up again, bringing with him a bemused-looking young man, obviously foreign, whom I'd earlier seen him leading over to talk to George. "Martin," Adrian said, "this is Signor—Signor, er. He's from the *Corriere della Sera*. Their art correspondent. I'll leave you to have a chat."

"Yes, sure."

4

Adrian walked away, no doubt still in search of the *Evening Standard* lady. The Italian, a thin man of about thirty with a nervous face, looked after Adrian rather forlornly, and then at me, even more forlornly. I waited for a second or two and then as he still hadn't opened his mouth, I said in Italian, "Do you know this place?"

His expression changed to one of surprise. "You speak Italian—*cioè, lei parla italiano?*"

"*Un po'*," I said, with bashful modesty. "I've often visited Italy. I've even lived there for a while." I like to think of my Italian as fluent rather than correct—which means I babble away and let the details sort themselves out in the rush. And it's always better when I'm drunk—or at least it seems to me to be so.

"You speak very well," said the young man, as if bearing me out.

"Are you from the Veneto?" I said. I was interested in placing his accent. And in showing off, of course.

"Venetian. That's very clever of you."

"Thanks. Do you cover all the exhibitions in London?"

"Well, only the ones I think interesting. You're an artist, yes?"

"That's right." I saw Adrian looking at us from the other side of the room as if hopefully trying to lip-read the word *forgery*. Or perhaps he was going to mouth it at me.

"But you're not exhibiting here now?" the Italian said.

"No. This is all George's work."

"George?"

"Yes. The man you were talking to a moment ago. The one who looks like Michelangelo playing Charlton Heston. His name's on the invitation card. Didn't Adrian explain?" He seemed a singularly vague journalist.

"Ah. I'm not used to the first name, you know."

"Is George well-known in Italy?" I'd never thought of him as being well-known much beyond the Old Brompton Road.

"Not *very* well-known."

"So why are you here?"

"I—I, well, in fact I hoped to meet some people from the London art world, you know. For a story." He paused in thought, and then as if on sudden impulse, and lowering his voice, said, "Do you know a Signor Osgood?"

"Vaguely." I looked at him curiously. Because Osgood—Harry Osgood—was one of the crookedest art dealers in London—and I, as they say, should know. (He was also probably the fattest, but that was by the way.) He had never actually been had up for anything definite as far as I knew, but everybody in the art world knew that honestly acquired paintings made up about ten percent of his business. "You could get a good story out of him, I'm sure."

"Yes, I hope so. But please, keep it quiet." He was looking around himself in a manner guaranteed to arouse suspicion. "I was told he might be here tonight."

"Really? Adrian doesn't seem to have nailed the paintings to the wall."

"Sorry?"

"No, nothing. Silly joke. So you're not really covering George's show then."

"Well . . ."

"Don't worry. I won't tell him. So long as you promise to cover mine. Shall we ask Adrian if he knows when Osgood's coming?"

"No, no, please not. Il Signor Limpett is—is a friend of Signor Osgood, I think. I don't want . . ." He tailed off vaguely.

"Ah. So what's the story?"

"It is complicated. Tell me, what do you paint?"

"Forgeries. Hundreds of them. For money. Lots and lots of money. And for sex and drugs when I can." I said all this in English and loudly. Suddenly all other conversation stopped.

The Italian looked alarmed. "Ah, I see, I see." He too spoke in English. "I think I must go to see some paintings." He gave me a quick smile of salutation and made toward the nearest visible blobs.

I looked at Adrian. He was the only one still looking at me;

6

everyone else had gone back to fierce consultation of catalogs or close examination of paintings. The conversations had started up again, with extra-urgent but hushed italics. Adrian's expression was one of earnest concern: I suppose he was trying to decide where the borderline lay between Good Publicity and Unacceptable Scandal.

He came over to me. "Martin, are you feeling all right?"

"I won't drink anymore, if that's what you mean." Just one of my many comic turns, I tried to suggest.

"Well, maybe you should slow down just a little. . . ."

"Yes, yes. Any chance of the drink at my do having more bubbles? So people can watch them pop if they get fed up with the paintings."

"What? Oh, er, well . . ."

"Look, sorry, Adrian. I'm in danger of making a fool of myself. I mean even more of one. Maybe I'd better go."

"Well, er, perhaps, if you'd feel better . . ." He'd obviously given up all hope of the *Evening Standard* lady. "I'm sure people will understand."

"Yes, I'm sure." I realized he was walking me slowly to the door: not exactly pulling me or even ushering me; just leading the way. We passed the two giggling girls; they were listening to a young man whose suit suggested merchant banker and whose face suggested berk; he was probably here looking for sound investments. I heard him say, "Of course they say the jails are riddled with drugs—they spend all their sentences on a permanent high."

I stopped. "Excuse me," I said to him, not quite so loudly as before but loudly enough for most people to stop talking and listen in. "Can I just add my little contribution to this sociological assessment of the prison situation?" I felt rather proud of this sentence—particularly at having pronounced all the words correctly—and was tempted to repeat it. But I went on: "Because maybe you don't know it, but I do have firsthand experience of the problem."

"Well, yes, actually I did know," he said, smiling and

adopting a casual arm-folded pose that revealed the Wall Street braces on his trousers and said to the room, Look at tolerant me, hobnobbing with an ex-con.

"Oh, you did? Jolly good. Well, it's true some of the lads do get hold of a little hash or coke or whatever. But would you believe it, I didn't even know what marijuana smelled like until I went to the Scrubs?"

"Really." No, I wouldn't believe it, his Michael Douglas smile said.

"And in case anybody thinks otherwise, at this moment I am drunk—simply drunk, inebriated, pissed, flown with wine—or warm fizz. I have never touched bloody drugs in my whole life." This was addressed to the whole room. Adrian's fingers were now on my arm, almost tugging.

The room was silent. Because, of course, they all knew: they'd seen the headlines—DRUGS IN FORGERY CASE, or FORGERY IN DRUGS CASE, depending on which crime the newspaper thought the more sensational.

"I was imprisoned for forgery and nothing else. Clear? Clear?" I'd intended this little banter to be a supreme Oscar Wildean put-down, but the way it was coming out, I'd have done better to yell "yah boo" and stick two fingers up in passing.

"Crystal clear," the merchant-banker type said. He was standing as if to protect the two young damsels. The blond girl must have been feeling pretty smug; her dare was definitely rising in story value.

"And I'm ready to sue anyone for libel or slander or defamation who says any different. Or tweak their bloody braces."

"Come on, Martin, come on." Adrian was now unambiguously tugging.

"Yes, all right, all right. Sorry, everybody. Interlude over." I walked to the door. The chattering broke out again, the italics extra-excited. George was standing by the door, looking just like Charlton Heston eyeing the debauchery under Mount Sinai. "Sorry, George," I said. "That was unforgivable. Your show. I'm a bastard. Come along and smash mine up in three weeks' time."

"A pleasure." I couldn't see what his mouth was doing way down below the beard, but he didn't *sound* as if he was smiling as he said this.

"And sorry to you too, Adrian. Not even any journalists present—unless you count the Italian bloke."

"Never mind. Go along and get a good rest. Don't worry about anything."

I put my coat on, picked up my bag, and stepped outside. The January wind swishing down the road sliced through my anorak, pullover, shirt, and skin, so that even the wine finally got chilly inside me. I started off in the direction of the Gloucester Road tube station.

I wasn't so very drunk, I realized. I'd been trying to pass off the outburst, even to myself, as the result of my lower toleration level of alcohol since prison, but I realized that my reasoning faculties, if not brilliantly lucid, were far from being out of control. The proof was that I was fully aware of what a bloody fool I'd made of myself.

So what *had* slipped the reins inside me? It must have been a sudden low toleration level of ostracism: I just hadn't been able to take the role of outcast.

That prison made you different I'd long known: different from what you'd been and different from other people—and not just in little things, like getting drunk more easily, or never throwing anything away without first thinking of its possibility as barter, or expecting other people to open doors for you. But I'd always preserved, somewhere in the deep medicine cupboards of my heart, the little hope that sooner or later it wouldn't matter: I'd get closer to other people or they'd move closer to me. Tonight's social occasion had made me feel that the divide was permanent: my cell bars had been replaced by unbreakable reptile-house plate glass; I lay slobbering behind it for all to look and shudder at, with a big sign around my neck, PICTORE CRIMINALIS STONED-OUT-OF-MENTE.

This was postprison blues getting me, as any experienced

con could have told me: you spend your last few weeks in the nick suffering from what they call gate fever—you lie in your cell, counting the days, and you play little mental videos of yourself running through daisied fields in slow motion, standing on sunlit mountaintops with the wind, invigorating and lung clearing, in your hair and face, or even just going for a walk down the High Street, drinking a pint in a pub, going to the loo with a book. The very thought lifts you like a lyric from Shelley or a 1960s rock opera. And for the first few days when you're out, all these things really *do* feel good, and you really *are* able to block any onset of gloom by saying, "Just think, if I were in prison at this moment, I'd be . . ." And then . . . very soon you get your first funny looks from the neighbors—or from anyone who knows—and you realize, banally but inescapably, that freedom is a pretty relative thing. And all that comes to mind, day in, day out, is that simple child's cry: "It's not fair."

Tonight I'd embarrassed people by shouting it at the wrong place, on the wrong occasion.

I heard running footsteps behind me. I turned and saw the somber Italian loping along. He was holding a briefcase in one hand and with the other was attempting to hold his flapping greatcoat closed. He drew to a halt beside me.

"Hello," I said. "So you want my story after all?"

"I, er—" I suppose it was a difficult thing to say no to. He said, "Well, I was wondering . . . er, who are you?"

"I'm Martin Phipps, the notorious forger and drug trafficker."

"Drug trafficker?"

"So everybody believes. You might as well tell the Italian public so as well."

"But it is not true?" His English was precise and only lightly accented.

"It is not true. I was arrested for doing forgeries—"

"Of what?"

"Oh, the usual things. Renoir, De Chirico. Modigliani; you know, the things everybody does. I had a good line in Dutch landscapes too."

10

"You must have been very clever."

"Not so clever. They found me out. Though not, mind you, till four years after I'd stopped doing them." Four contented years of success, doing and selling my *own* paintings—my *real* work. Four years during which those forgeries had become in my mind nothing more than a juvenile prank—though a prank that had admittedly raised me a few bob here and there.

"So where do the drugs come into this?"

The Ancient Mariner compulsion was so strong in me at that moment that it hardly occurred to me to wonder what I was doing recounting all this in the back streets of Kensington on a cold January night to a young Italian I'd only just met.

I went on: "Well, it turned out that the guy who'd started me off doing forgeries was a drug peddler. He was arrested for that and then they discovered paintings of mine in his house, and out it all came." My defending counsel had continued to repeat that I was on trial for "obtaining a pecuniary advantage by deception" (about £760 all told, but only I knew this) and for this crime only, but the message had never got through to the papers—or, it turned out, to the judge. "Things got a bit confused," I said.

"Ah." He nodded seriously.

"So you're going to write this up?" I said. "At least put me right with the Italians?"

"Well . . ."

"You *are* a journalist?"

"Yes, yes. And I want to find Mr. Osgood, as I said to you earlier, for a story."

"So, go to his gallery."

"This is the point. I cannot find it. He is not in the telephone book. He is not in the Yellow Pages. So I came to this show because I had heard he might come."

"You're right. I remember now. He's just changed premises." I'd heard this from Adrian only a few days earlier in a gossipy lunchtime chat. "And of course he doesn't generally need to advertise his whereabouts."

"Ah. So where is he now?"

11

"You seem very anxious to see him. What is this story?"

"I'm afraid I can't tell you that." He shifted his briefcase to his left hand and put his frozen right hand in his pocket. He still hadn't done up his coat, and had to hold his arm across, Napoleon-fashion, to keep warm.

I could have offered to hold his briefcase, I thought, but didn't. Nor did I ask him for his press card, if only because I was sure he hadn't got one. Instead I just told him the address Adrian had mentioned, north of Oxford Street, not, however, adding Adrian's comment about the Wallace Collection now having to be a little more careful about locking up at nights. Then I said, "Are you selling or buying?"

"I told you, I am interested in a story."

"Well, I'm not. I suppose you're selling. For a friend, no doubt."

"Please, it doesn't matter. Here I will leave you." We'd reached a side road and he was preparing to turn down it. A little like a rabbit into a burrow. I doubted whether it really was his route home. I said, "Okay, *ciao*. Best of luck."

"Thank you, good-bye." He walked quickly down the road, still hunched up in his coat. I stayed watching him for no particular reason. As he passed a pub two youths came out of it, and one of them, a big lad with even bigger boots, deliberately slammed his shoulder into the Italian. It was the kind of puerile loutishness which, if you're the size and build the Italian was, it's best simply to ignore. He, however, instantly retaliated by swinging his briefcase into the youth's stomach. But this was obviously not meant as some kind of bravado challenge, because the next thing he did was run.

The two youths seemed mesmerized by surprise for an instant, and then with no more than a vicious nod at each other they took off after him. I saw the Italian look around as he ran, and in the lamplight his face seemed all mouth—wide open and noiselessly moving. Seconds later one of his pursuers—a youth who seemed at this distance and in this light to be wearing a sculpted model of the Alps on his head—grabbed his shoulder.

12

The Italian was now stammering, "*ma—ma—*" It meant "but," but was only an *m* away from a whimper for his mother.

It could still be mere horseplay, I thought wishfully, moving forward as if through treacle. After all, this was Kensington, not the Bronx.

But the next moment the Italian was on the ground. I saw their boots drawing back and, well, I just had to run. Toward them. I give the wine all the credit for the direction of my run.

2

I SUPPOSE it was responsible too for the manic howling sound I came out with, which surprised them if nothing else. (It surprised me as well.) I saw their faces swing round.

I too had my bag, a shoulder bag containing a sketchbook, three pencils, some loose change, and a library copy of an Iris Murdoch novel. I think it must have been this last that connected with the nearer one's head as I whirled the bag by its strap in his direction. I'm sure the Dame had never been so lightning-quick in her effect before. He was on the ground a second later.

The boy with the Alpine haircut was already moving in on me—and I saw his right hand drawing back with something metallic in it. I was still tottering from my mad swing and could only think, this was it, when my assailant staggered, his hands clutching and flailing at my coat, and the knife slipping from them. The Italian was clasped around his knees and I found myself saying, "Bite him."

I kicked the knife, so it scuttered across the pavement and dropped into the road—and then felt my own legs clutched. A second later we were all down there, among the cigarette stubs and sweet wrappers.

Then there were voices farther down the road—a male voice saying, "Oh no" rather stupidly and a female voice saying, "My God." The two thugs scrambled to their feet. The one whom the Italian had first hit with the briefcase gave the Italian a last savage kick in the ribs and then they both ran.

"I think we won," I said to the Italian. We were both still on the ground; I was more or less in a sitting position, while he was kneeling bent forward like a figure two.

"I say, you all right?" It was the stupid male voice I'd heard a moment before and I looked up to see that it came from a stupid male face. Stupid but solicitous: a short-haired young man with a frizzy blond girlfriend. They had presumably just come out of the pub. She said, "Did they take anything?" Their accents were more what one expected of the area than the thugs' boots had been.

"No, we're okay," I said. I looked at the Italian, still bent forward. "At least, I am."

"I say, are you all right?" the short-haired man repeated. He seemed rather pleased at having found the correct question.

"Yes, yes, yes," the Italian said in three quick pants. He looked up now, first at our two succorers, then at me. "Thank you, thank you." He was frighteningly pale. He looked around himself with sudden panic. "My case—"

"Here it is," the short-haired man said, stepping toward where it lay behind the Italian. Its catch must have given in the struggle because as he picked it up it jerked open and papers slitheringly cascaded to the ground.

"No!" yelped the Italian, snapping out of helplessness and diving forward to arrest their flight, as the wind fluttered them.

We all bent to help him, the young couple obviously relieved at having something definite to do. They were mostly typewritten pages, which I hardly glanced at; my attention was taken up with the large color photograph—about eight by ten inches—I found myself holding. In the lamplight the color had naturally attracted my eyes. I was just turning it the right way around when suddenly it was jerked out of my fingers. I looked up to see the Italian thrusting it fiercely into the black depths of the briefcase.

15

He looked defiant for a second, and then turned away to accept the papers offered him by the couple.

I rose to my feet and dusted myself off a little and the Italian did the same. The short-haired man said, "But I say, are you all right?" and the Italian nodded vehemently. "Yes, yes, yes. Thank you, thank you." He backed away saying, "I'm—I'm fine now, good-bye, good-bye." He turned and started walking quickly down the road, still busy fumbling with the lock of his case.

I nodded to the couple and said, "I'll go and see if he needs any help." I followed him down the road. I heard the short-haired man say as they walked off in the opposite direction, "I say, I hope they're all right."

"Listen," I called to the Italian, "you're obviously still shaken. Let me buy you a drink or something."

He turned around and shook his head. "No, no, I'm fine, fine. Thank you, thank you." His mouth was twitching and his pallor seemed to have increased.

"No, you're not and you know you're not. And suppose those two are still waiting farther down the road?"

"You don't think—"

"Well, no, but let me buy you a drink anyway."

"I don't drink," he said.

"Okay, I'll just walk with you until you feel calmer."

He looked at me with a sort of resigned despair and gave a shrug—or it might just have been another twitch.

We walked on in silence in the direction of Earls Court. After a while I said, "What made you hit him back like that?"

"But I—I didn't know—"

"Didn't know what?"

"I thought—never mind." He was far more shaken than I would have thought warranted. And even now, as we turned into a relatively busy road, he was looking nervously from side to side.

"What *did* you think?" I said.

"Please never mind. I didn't know who they were."

This struck me as a rather odd thing to say. "Well, of course

16

you didn't." Then a moment later I said, "Do you mean, you thought they might be someone else?" I saw that instant retaliatory swipe with the briefcase in my mind again, and it struck me that it must have been due to equally instant and overwhelming panic.

"What?" He was caught off guard and looked quickly at me with frightened eyes. Then they jumped away again to look at the traffic. "No, of course not."

I was sure I'd guessed right—and equally sure that aggressive questioning was only going to shut him up. I changed tack. "So what *are* you doing in London?"

He seemed to breathe slightly more easily. He said, "Research. I'm finishing a—a thesis."

"What on?"

"On the ballad form and protest in the literature of the Industrial Revolution."

"Oh." This was a bit of a conversation stopper for me, but I did my struggling best. "So shouldn't you be in Manchester or somewhere?"

"The documentation is all in London."

"Was that your thesis that nearly got scattered all down the road then?"

"Yes."

"That would have been a pity."

"Yes."

"And, er, the photo? Was that part of your documentation?"

"Yes," he said for the third time—and it was the flattest one so far. I glanced sideways and saw him looking ahead—rigidly, as if he were having to fight to stop his head turning to see my reactions.

"I see," I said. My eyes had been on that photograph for less than a second, and it had been upside down; and yet, when it had been snatched from my fingers, a kind of subliminal afterimage had lingered in my mind: I saw a frameless painting apparently attached to the ceiling of a room. Logic told me that my impression of this unlikely position was due to my having seen the photo upside down, and presumably the painting had in fact been standing on the ground, propped up against a wall; as for the subject of the painting I could only recall the vague mass of a Madonna and Bambino, and I couldn't make even the vaguest guess at the painter—nor even his nationality or century. There was just one niggling memory of something large and white and sinuous in a corner of the painting. Niggling, because it reminded me of something—or suggested something—that I had seen somewhere, sometime. Somewhere on the earth, and sometime in the thirty-four years I'd been on the earth. "I see," I repeated, and indeed I was doing my damnedest to *see* that photo more clearly in my mind's eye. Could I just try asking to see it again with my real eyes?

"Well," he said, "I'm all right now. You needn't come farther with me."

"Are you sure?"

"I'm sure. Good-bye, thank you very much, you've been— you've been kind. Good-bye." We'd reached another side road and he was preparing once again to do his white-rabbit disappearing trick down it. I couldn't think of any further excuse for continuing to force my company on him. He wasn't, I imagined, likely to take up a hint for a cup of coffee and he didn't seem in the right mood for a chat about his thesis or Venice or Italian cooking—or Italian art. So I said, "Well, so long. You'll be careful, won't you?"

"Yes, yes." Rather unexpectedly he shook my hand; despite the cold it felt like a just-used tea bag. He gave me a last quick smile and then set off down the street.

I watched as he scuttered along in front of the tattered terraced houses, his head twitching pigeonlike to left and right as if on the lookout for lurkers within the pillared porches and his right arm clutching his briefcase like a shield—or teddy bear. I could almost hear the words "Oh, my ears and whiskers . . ." Then he turned right around and saw me still standing there, and with a—well, a flounce of irritation, he started walking even more briskly.

18

I turned and started back to the tube station—and then stopped again. I wanted to know where he was going—where he lived.

Why? What the hell business was it of mine? Okay, so he was probably trying to flog a hot painting; but why should I stick my already burned nose in? I should be trying to keep my nose under the permanent cold cream of honesty—or indifference.

But there was more to it than just a hot painting. There was his whole paranoid behavior, as if the Mafia were after him. And there was—there was something else. . . .

I stood and scowled at the traffic and tried to think what the something else could be. And then I knew: it was that white sinuous shape in the corner of the painting in the photograph. *That* was what was stimulating my curiosity.

I knew—at least my determined striding legs seemed to know—that that shape meant something important, and I was going to have to find out what. I reached the side road just in time to see the Italian turning off it in the distance.

I reached this next turning within seconds and, glancing down it, saw him mounting the steps of a house some twenty yards away. He was looking around himself as he did so, and his eyes again fell on me. Fortunately I was nowhere near a lamppost, and that fact, together with the distance, made me unrecognizable, I reckoned. I kept walking briskly across the road—and this in itself was a disguise, when compared with the drunken slouch he'd seen earlier. Seconds later I was out of sight.

I waited a minute or so and then cautiously went along the road to note the number of the house he'd entered. There could be no hope of remembering it without the number the next day; the houses in the terrace were otherwise only to be distinguished by the peeling gaps in their stucco. Anonymous houses inhabited by anonymous people; bedsits and boardinghouses and cheap hotels; few people, I imagined, ever stayed in any of the houses long enough to receive a letter.

The number was barely legible, as if it hadn't been repainted since the terrace went up. I had to go right up the steps to read

19

it. While I was there I looked at the doorbells. There were four bells and only one bore a name. I went back down the steps, and at the bottom just glanced up casually. Somebody was staring down at me from a window on the first floor; there was no light on. The figure at once stepped back into the darkness of the room.

It could easily have been the Italian: it would match his paranoid behavior to tiptoe across to the window before turning the light on, for a last lookout. I wondered if he'd recognized me. Again there was no lamppost nearby. I hurried away, my head buried deep in my coat. I felt just a little foolish.

I reached home some forty minutes later. Well, home . . . not mine. It was a narrow two-story terraced house in Acton belonging to a friend who was in America for a year, as tame campus artist in a midwestern art college. I was there to keep vandals out and redirect his mail.

When I'd come out of prison I'd gone and stayed with my mother for a week or two in Totnes. She had looked after me as solicitously as ever, continually making me cream-teas and giving me hot-water bottles (the only two pleasures of the flesh she tolerates), but the recurrent theme of "I always knew it would end like this" (by "it" she meant not only my taking up the profession of artist but my going to live in London and, worse still, abroad) had me hankering for the big city and its freedom. So I'd been delighted to get Jim's phone call offering me the flat at a minimum rent.

The house had seemed just what I'd needed; Jim too was a painter, and the front room, spacious with large north windows, made a good studio—apart from a tiny kitchen, it was the only room on the ground floor. He was about as tidy and house-proud as Attila—or myself—and this made things much easier, of course. There would be no question of living for a year on tiptoes.

But it was still Jim's flat. Almost nothing in it was mine, in fact. There were still all his pictures, his photos, his books; there were his cooking stains, the springs in the chair he'd broken, the glasses he'd chipped, the loo chain he'd snapped, the cupboard door he'd wrenched off the hinges, the lampshade he'd allowed to burn. . . . My few belongings—my clothes, some art books, my painting equipment—hung about in odd corners of the rooms, like interlopers—like me, in fact.

I made myself a cup of coffee in the kitchen; this had been a policy decision, my first instinct having been to open a can of beer. Plumping for coffee meant that I had decided to keep on thinking about the events of the evening, rather than keep on going down the road to carefree mindlessness and leglessness. I sat stirring the sugar and pondered another decision: whether to have the coffee there or in the studio. (The studio possessed the only armchair in the house and so served as a drawing room as well.) I decided on the studio, even if it did mean depressing myself by staring at my paintings.

The phone rang. I took my coffee over to it. "Hello."

"Ah, Martin."

"Oh, hi, Mum. I've just got back."

"How did it go?"

"What?"

"Well, your show. You told me the other day you were going to a little party at the gallery."

"It wasn't my show today." My mother is incorrigibly vague on the details of my working life. As she hardly ever leaves Totnes to go farther than Exeter, she has never seen an exhibition of mine. This is a source of relief to me, in many ways—but, consequent on this, a source of guilt. These two feelings, unfortunately, are at the basis of all my doings with my family—my mother and my three elder sisters (my father, a part-time housepainter and part-time Baptist minister, died when I was three). I had never felt so relieved as when, at the age of nineteen, I left Totnes to go to art college in pagan London. Finally I had made that longed-for break with the family and the chapel and gameless, joyless, Bible-reading Sundays. I can still remember the thrill when I entered my first pub on a Sunday and downed my first pint of beer. It was a dreary little place in Kilburn and the beer had tasted horrible, but I'd nonetheless savored the experience as a glorious moment of defiantly hedonistic decadence. And then . . . well, then of course the guilt feelings had set in, and I'd felt duty bound to ring home and ask how the family all were and how their Sunday was being passed. Throughout my college career and beyond I made regular phone calls to let everybody know that I was enjoying the parks and museums and riverside walks of London, with never a mention of pubs or parties or nightclubs—or even cinemas.

"Oh, I see," she said. "Well, I'm sure it will be one day, Martin, don't let it worry you."

"I wasn't. My show's in two weeks' time. I'll let you know how it goes."

"Yes, do. Everyone sends their love."

"Oh, thank you."

"You're eating properly, are you?" she said. "And you're being careful who you talk to at these parties?"

"Yes, yes. Or they're being careful about talking to me."

A few more reassurances on my part, a few questions about Totnes life, and we both hung up—both no doubt feeling relieved. And then both no doubt feeling guilty.

I suppose if I were ever to try to offer some kind of excuse for my crime, it would have to be based on the classic and feeble lines of what a mixed-up kid I'd been at the time, what with the family background I'd had. Not that I'd been deprived or cruelly treated: it was just that it had been kept from me which century I was living in. When I'd gone up to art college I must have been the most out-of-place and out-of-date student that the place had ever seen, with ideas about *la vie de bohème* that were practically neolithic. A strict Baptist upbringing isn't designed to keep one *au fait* with the latest fashions, and even rebellion against it therefore is likely to take an antiquated form. So as far as I was concerned, the artist was nothing if not a romantic rebel, intent on shocking the bourgeosie. (It's only to be wondered at that I asked for beer and not absinthe on that first visit to the pub.)

22

Some of this anachronistic and shallow "defiance" got knocked out of me of course during art college, but obviously not enough. So when one of the restorers for whom I worked after college put it to me casually one day that as I was so good at imitating the styles of painters when "retouching" them, maybe for a few extra pounds I'd like to have a go at doing a De Chirico all of my own—"just for the fun of it"—I don't remember having more than the vaguest of moral qualms about it. If any at all. After all, the people who were going to be fooled (and it wouldn't be me telling them that it was a De Chirico—I'd merely painted the thing) were the enemies of all that true art stood for, weren't they? People who put paintings into bank safes or treated them like investments in a company. And I had to live.

Of course none of this gets around the fact that I was making money by deceiving people, however far I was from the actual handover of the finished painting. (And I was far enough away to be satisfied with the peanuts that the restorer gave me for my cut—but that was stupidity on my part, not restraint.) However much I argued with myself about the whole business when in jail, I couldn't get away from that fact—and that therefore I deserved punishment.

I don't know whether I deserved the Scrubs. But then I don't know whether *anyone* deserves that.

I went along to the studio where I was confronted by the usual chaos. The easel in the center bore the work in progress—a view of tower blocks in Stepney. The paintings chosen for the exhibition were propped against the walls all around the room, so that I couldn't help seeing them, whichever way I turned. Views of Thames mud, of rubble-strewn waste ground, of uncompleted motorway bridges in the rain, of railway sidings, of car scrap heaps. . . . All with my usual predominance of browns and grays, with just here and there a vandalized phone box or workman's DANGER sign to add a splash of brightness. And then above these, tacked to the wall, Jim's postcards: almost every square inch of the plastered surface was covered with minuscule reproductions of paintings he liked; a riot of clashing colors to

23

rebuke the drab tones below. They were put up with defiant lack of order and logic and taste: Manet next to Vermeer next to Duccio next to Hockney next to Masaccio next to Stubbs. . . . Daunting company.

I sipped the coffee and stared at my paintings and found I wasn't as depressed by them as I had suspected I might be. No, tonight I was just indifferent. I knew them so well by now that I found it almost impossible to judge them. Sometimes a wave of confidence would go through me and I'd think they were really good: technically excellent and imbued with the "spirit" of the city. Other times I'd think they were all surface cleverness and gimmicks. As the opening day of the exhibition approached, the latter feeling had begun to predominate, and I just hoped that the buyers would like my cleverness and gimmicks.

Five years earlier, while I was still working for the restorers, I'd caught a little of the world's attention—a fluttering thread of its sleeve—with my cityscapes. After months of traipsing from dealer to dealer with portfolios of my work I had finally got a phone call from one of the few who had agreed to look through a selection of slides of my work—a selection I'd prepared after being told for the tenth time by a dealer, "We don't see artists"—as if artists were some particularly repellent kind of beggar. The dealer had a gallery in Knightsbridge that specialized in rather romantic landscapes, and I think he felt that my scenes of mud and misery would give him something to point to whenever anybody accused him of dealing exclusively in chocolate-box prettiness. Or perhaps he just wanted his other pictures to look so much the brighter by contrast. Anyway, for whatever reason, he offered me a two-week personal exhibition. My pictures must have caught a particular mood of the time because I suddenly got noticed. Even a reviewer from a posh Sunday paper dropped by and gave me a pat on the head. Not all my paintings were cityscapes; I'd included a few portraits and even an abstract or two to show the full range of my genius, but the only ones that got the attention were the London scenes in London rain: comparisons were made with Doré and with

George Scharf (whom I'd never heard of), and dinky things were said about my tonal values and color harmonies (I'd never heard of them either). And during the week all the cityscapes got sold. When I was offered the chance of another show a year later by the same gallery, I took the line of least resistance and exhibited only cityscapes, with just a couple of pictures of Dartmoor to break the monotony. They all sold except the ones of Dartmoor. And the most depressing cityscapes (rubbish tips, sewage works) sold the quickest. I became briefly fashionable: I was invited to parties, I met pop stars, I was asked to describe my room to the *Observer* magazine. (I often thought of that "room of my own" when bedding down with my two cellmates and their chamber-pots.) This kind of spotlit attention didn't last of course; the thread was twitched from my fingers as the world passed on to other painters, other sculptors. This didn't mean I starved, of course; I no longer held cocktailing court to packed "private views," but my paintings still sold in a fairly steady, unflashy way: so long, that is, as I went on painting the kind of works I'd been granted my fifteen minutes' fame for: my pictures of high-rise misery and industrial squalor obviously still came to mind when people found a few spare wall inches in their Knightsbridge flats and Richmond villas; but that was all. The pictures of Dartmoor I sent to my sisters—one of my periodic and guilt-ridden attempts to keep in touch with the family.

And then those foolish forgeries came to light—and what light, a throbbing glare of flashbulbs outside the courts each day, thanks to the scandalous trimmings of the case, and I was sent to darkness: the inspissated gloom of Wormwood Scrubs.

When I came out and found myself turned down by my old dealer, Adrian had at once seen his chance. He was hoping that "Martin Phipps, the Return of" was going to get as much coverage as "Martin Phipps, the Removal of" had in its time. So, I suppose, was I.

When Adrian had approached me I'd thought that this could be a turning point; I'd no longer paddle in picturesque squalor, I would truly plumb the depths. I'd make pictures of prison life that would match Doré's drawings of Newdigate—the boredom of cell life, the oppression of metal corridors and doors, the degradation of "slopping out". . . every humiliating detail.

But it seemed I was no plumber. Whenever I actually tried any of these subjects, the result never reflected what I felt. It remained surface cleverness, no matter how deep the chasms inside me. I remembered too some of the more scornful experts at the trial ("How anybody could have been taken in . . ."), and I saw them all waiting to pounce again at the exhibition, with retrospectively wise cries of words like *imitative, derivative, thirdhand, third-rate*. So I decided to stick to what was definitely my own territory, where nobody could accuse me of trespassing or pilfering, and where I couldn't accuse myself of high-wire trickery over the abyss: and if anybody wanted to see developments, well, they could note postprison Dostoyevskian depths in the extra dogshit and piss puddles in the paintings.

You could call it a sage acceptance of my limitations—or you could call it playing safe.

That evening, as I sat slumped staring at the easel and recalling my youthful ambitions, I called it yellow-bellied chickenhearted jelly-legged flabbiness.

But the painting should still sell, I thought. It was okay. Clever stuff. I wondered whether to add a few sea gulls to the rubbish tip in the foreground. Something that people would pick out against the grayness and be able to comment on: "Note, Camilla, how those few spots of white give life and movement. . . ." Another little gimmick.

"Hey!"

I shouted this out loud, spluttering coffee all over the floor. And I found I'd stood up. My hand miraculously still held the coffee cup in a more or less horizontal position.

I couldn't have done other than get up. It was only surprising that I hadn't tried to fly. Because even as I thought of the sea gulls another white bird had suddenly reared up before my mind's eye—vivid, unmistakable. And I saw the painting in the Italian's photograph clearly, as if it were hanging on my wall.

26

A Madonna and Bambino, seated in a meadow with gentle hills and a castle behind them, and in the foreground a swan.

La Madonna del cigno. A painting by Cima da Conegliano that I'd seen in a village in the Veneto on one of my first visits to Italy.

I sat back down on the arm of the chair, closed my eyes, and thought back to the day I'd gone to see that painting: the village was some miles from Treviso, a few straggling houses around a church rebuilt in the dullest eighteenth-century style, in the middle of the flat Veneto countryside. I'd hitched and walked, in the steamy July weather, the sun an oppressive yellow smudge in a soapy sky. The coolness of the church had been particularly welcome; just a few old ladies muttering the Rosary and the Cima there on the side wall—the simple peasant Madonna, the sunlit landscape under a blue sky—cool cool blue—and the swan floating in the most deliciously rippling water of any painting I'd ever seen. I had almost felt like stripping off there and then. Instead I had gazed for some minutes while my shirt dried, then I'd gone for a beer in a bar opposite the church, and then returned to gaze some more.

I got up off the chair and went upstairs to the bedroom where a bookcase held the flat's library—art books and thrillers. Jim's books were to the left; he went for books with plenty of reproductions and minimum text ("Most of what people write about pictures is such balls"); my few filled the empty space on the right and were mostly on minor artists—bought on the principle, patently false, that I knew the major artists so well that there was no point spending money on books about them. (And the minor names looked more impressive too on the book-shelves.) So I had studies on such people as Garofalo, Tibaldi, Thomas Girtin . . . and Cima da Conegliano.

I sat on the unmade bed and flipped through the book until I found a black-and-white reproduction of the painting. My memory of it was pretty well perfect. The only thing I'd forgotten was the convincing babylike way in which the Bambino twisted around to stare up at the Madonna. And there, preserved next to the text, was a folded yellow cutting from a newspaper, with the penciled date of June 1978.

"In the past week there have been three separate art thefts from churches in the Veneto (the province around Venice in the northeast of Italy). In all three cases the churches were in small villages, and the thieves broke in at night. Only one painting was taken from each church, but in each case it was the church's greatest treasure." There followed a list of the three villages and the paintings: *The Madonna of the Swan* by Cima da Conegliano, *The Crucifixion* by Alvise Vivarini, and *The Annunciation* by Palma il Giovane. "The police are convinced that the thefts are the work of a skilled team, probably acting on commission."

That was all. I remembered cutting the piece out; it had caught my eye only a few days after I'd bought the book on Cima. Three weeks' beer money it had cost me and this made Cima a personal concern: anything touching him touched me. And in particular, the theft of a painting that I'd sweated miles under the sun to go and see—a painting that probably only the parishioners of the church, the author of the book, and I knew about—well, I'd felt almost a proprietory pang at its loss. Cima was *mine*.

I suppose at the time I'd cut the article out, I'd intended to follow up the developments of the case, but if there had ever been any, I'd never heard of them. Until tonight.

I put the book away. Could I be *sure* that that was the painting I'd seen in the photo? Yes, I could. It was the only explanation for the way that white shape had niggled at the corner of my mind. And even as I thought about this question the photograph leaped into limpid blue and green and white detail.

I went down to the studio, and as I entered my foot kicked something. I looked down to see my coffee mug, its contents spreading rapidly over the paint-flecked lino. Well, that decided things. I went to the kitchen and opened a can of beer. I was about to return to the studio bearing this, but then on reflection took another two cans from the fridge as well. Might as well save myself another journey.

I went back to the studio and settled myself in front of the easel. I was going to add those sea gulls. For some reason I felt myself surfing on a surge of sudden confidence. The painting was going to be damned good. And I was going to save that Cima.

For the moment the beer would help me bring about the first prophesy (or at least make me feel it to be true). As to the second, well, the morning would show. I'd go and call on Osgood.

I picked up the palette. And what if instead of sea gulls I put in a swan?

In bed that night I woke with a throbbing head and fur-lined mouth and a nagging question. Who had the Italian thought might be trying to attack him? And why had he been so wildly terrified of whoever it was?

3

I LEFT the house the next morning—well, it wasn't lunchtime yet—without going to see the result of my night's work in the studio. I didn't want to depress myself. I was no longer riding the crest of that confidence wave: it had shattered and slithered scummily down the shingle of my hangover.

I was in Oxford Street by one o'clock and I made my way to Osgood's gallery. His name, in fact, did not appear on the sign; it was named after the road it was on. In the windows were a few nineteenth-century English watercolors (the sort of thing that every Victorian traveler did on his walking tours), an extremely boring Dutch landscape, and a more than usually lascivious Alma-Tadema.

I entered, and the young lady behind the desk at the far end of the gallery gave me a mere flicker of a glance before returning to her work. She was either considerately refraining from being pushy or was just assuming that I was a mere looker.

I approached her desk and asked, "Could I speak to Mr. Osgood?"

She looked up. She was a Burne-Jonesian heroine with a

diaphanous hair-drifting beauty and Laura Ashley clothes. "Well, actually, sir," she said, in a breathy voice with syllables as long and languorous as her eyelashes, "he is just about to leave for luncheon."

"Luncheon?" I repeated. I couldn't help it, I swear. Well, I suppose any meal that contributed to Osgood's considerable girth deserved the dignity of the unabbreviated word. I said, "He wouldn't have time for even a quick word?"

"Well," she said (and this one word took her almost as long as my whole sentence), "I could go and ask him." Her brow was furrowed with the effort of thinking this possibility out.

"Could you really?" I said.

"Yes, if you would wait just one moment. What name must I give?"

"Martin Phipps." It wouldn't bring him running, but it might just make him curious.

She rose and floated to a door in the corner of the room. I think she opened it before passing through, but it hardly seemed necessary.

I looked at what she was working on: the *Guardian* crossword. I heard her fairy voice in a distant room being answered by an ogrelike rumbling and then footsteps approached. His, of course, not hers.

Osgood appeared at the doorway. He was larger than ever and I wondered whether he always hesitated before passing through a doorway. He was all generous curves, like the hills around Totnes, and tall with it. His face, with its Orson Welles graying beard and its great Boreas-puffing cheeks, radiated joviality and bonhomie. The pale blond girl hovered behind him, and together they seemed to make a rather too obvious Wattsian allegory of the flesh and the spirit.

"Martin," Osgood said, extending his two sausage-balloon arms to me.

We'd never been on first-name terms before. Indeed, I'd only met him once, at one of my flashier private views—before the Fall. Maybe he was showing that he was no snob. Or just accepting me as a partner in crime. "Harry," I said, taking him up on it.

"To what do I owe the extreme pleasure of this visit?" His voice was as large and rotund as his figure and his jowls jumped jollily at each roly-poly syllable. "You're not looking for inspiration?"

I said, "No, no. I was just curious. I'd heard on the, er, grapevine that you might have a rather interesting Cima, or at least might know something about where one could be found."

"A Cima?" Extra lines of puzzlement appeared amid the creases and rolls of his face.

"Da Conegliano. With a swan, so they said."

"Good Lord, you're not talking about the *Madonna del cigno*?"

This came rather too quickly, I felt. And although his face was still generally jovial, there was a watchful expression in his eyes. I said, "Could be. *Cigno* means swan, does it? That must be the one. You don't know anything about it then?"

"Wish I did," he said. "Wish I did." He chuckled at the idea of possessing such delicious knowledge. "Just where did you get this curious information?"

"Bloke at a party. Oh, well, Harry, mustn't keep you from luncheon."

"Bloke at a party." He glanced at the Lady of Shalott, still hovering there with an expression of sweet incomprehension. She, I suppose, helped the image: how could a business with anybody so ethereal in its front room have anything to hide? He said to her, "Melinda, would you just go and tell His Grace that I'll be along in two ticks."

"Yes, Mr. Osgood." She melted away to confront His Grace with hers.

"Now, Martin," he said, wheezing conspiratorially now, "I'm sure you're aware that the *Madonna del cigno* by Cima is a stolen painting. Eh? Yes, of course you are. So you do see that an allegation that I know anything of its whereabouts is slanderous. No joke for a fellow like me. So, well, I really have to ask you to tell me who said such a thing."

"Honestly, Harry," I said, smiling fatuously, "I just got talking to a bloke at a party. Never met him before."

For the first time a frown appeared, and he lifted a pudgy hand to his beard. "You're being rather foolish, if you don't mind my saying so. I really have to take this very seriously." I knew the words that were coming next: "My reputation, you know. Very important in my line of business."

Here I suppose I could have put a finger to my nose and said, "Oh, come off it, Harry," and dug him in the ribs—or thereabouts. Instead I said, "All right, I understand, you've got nothing to do with it. I'm sorry. I'll have to be more careful who I speak to at parties."

He tut-tutted. "So you're not going to tell." He took out a packet of fruit gums and popped one into his mouth, without offering them to me. He smiled and said, "I understand you're to have a little exhibition very soon." He stressed the word *little* with genial indulgence.

"Yes, please come along."

"You won't want any trouble, I suppose." Still smiling.

"You're going to send the boys around?" I said.

He lifted his hands in a gesture of mock horror at this crudity. "Dear me, dear me. Your recent experiences must have taken you into another world from mine. The boys indeed. I simply mean that you no doubt hope that your exhibition will put you back on a—how shall I put it?—respectable footing." He liked this phrase and said it again, sucking on his fruit gum with relish: "A respectable footing. Once more the bright young artist and not the drug-running forger."

"I never had anything to do with drugs," I said, probably too quickly.

"Perhaps not, if we're being pedantically accurate about details, but whoever is about such things?" This seemed very comical to him; his eyes were squeezed tight in a little wheezy chuckling fit. "But anyway, you're hoping that all this will be forgotten and Martin Phipps will be judged for his works and not for his scandals. Well, just remember there are many other ways for a man of influence to act, besides sending in the boys,

33

as you call it. And I am a man of influence. Still, all the best. If you're not going to tell me the source of this slander, you're not going to tell me. Let me just say that I don't want to hear any more of the same nonsense." He patted me on the shoulder, which had me flinching. Then, with a little snorting and wheezing, like an ocean liner maneuvering out of port, he turned and left me.

So as not to seem too browbeaten, I hung around in the gallery for a while, looking at the watercolors. Melinda came back into the room and stood looking at me, with her head on one side so that her hair poured down Rapunzel-like. Maybe I was supposed to grab my sketchbook.

"His Grace okay?" I said after a pause.

"Oh, yes. Mr. Phipps, you may not remember me."

I'm senile enough to know the only thing in these cases is to look frank and say, "No."

"I was on a course you taught at in Venice. Two years ago."

"Ah." Another reminder of my halcyon days before the Fall. One of the little perks that had come with fame and fortune had been an invitation to teach on an art history course in Venice for two weeks every year. The teaching was an hour a day, and the expenses—flight and hotel—were all paid, together with a fairly generous wage for the ten hours' work. Well, *very* generous, considering the improvised impressionistic impudence I passed off as lectures. I had been invited by the organizer of this course, a certain Mr. Robin, to talk on contemporary art but had straightaway declared my inability to give anything like a fair assessment of the scene and had chosen as the title for my lecture series, "A Painter and His Predecessors," which gave me license to talk on just about anything. Which, with the help of slides, I did. The students wouldn't have noticed if I'd talked each lesson about the previous day's slides: they were in a land of cheap wine, without school discipline, and that was all they cared about. Just so long as I stuck a nude in every so often and made a vaguely blue joke they were happy, and this meant that Mr. Robin invited me back year after year—until, that is, my

34

accommodation arrangements c/o H.M. Government made it impossible. The course was defined as pre-university, and the students were all fresh-faced lads and lasses straight out of public school, whose parents obviously didn't care much for the novel idea of having them full-time at home and so willingly paid the exorbitant fees Mr. Robin charged for keeping them in Venice from January to April. The parents were happy, the students were happy, I, and the other teachers, were happy, and Mr. Robin was happiest of all. (Those fees must have been *really* exorbitant.)

"Melinda. Ye-es," I said. Well, there had been about fifty of them every year for five years, all with names like Melinda and Camilla and Charlotte—or Piers and Nigel and Charles. I could recall very few of them individually—generally the Melindas and Camillas rather than the Pierses and Nigels. And only one really well.

"I was on the course with Lucy Althwaite," Melinda said.

"Oh yes." Lucy Althwaite was that one. "You didn't have your hair like that then, did you?" I said. I'd surely have remembered her if she had.

"No. I had it short then. How clever of you to remember. I must confess I didn't recognize you when you came in. Not until you gave your name, and then it only clicked when I was out in the corridor."

"The new haggard look, I suppose."

"Oh, no," she said with the same breathy earnestness. "You look exactly the same really. It's just been such a long time. Two years. Do you still see Lucy?"

"I haven't done for nearly a year."

I expected her to look embarrassed and say, "No, of course not," or something like that, but instead she said, "Oh, what a pity. Why not?"

"Don't you read your newspaper?" I said, glancing at the *Guardian*.

"Well, only the women's page and the crossword," she said with a smile of sweet candor. "Oh, and that cartoon thing—

Doonesbury." And with an even candier smile, "And I never understand that. Why, has Lucy been in the news?"

"No. I have."

"Oh, really?" she said. "How exciting."

I took a decision. "Would you be free for a drink?"

"That would be nice. In fifteen minutes. I usually have lunch at the pub on the corner."

It was difficult to think of her doing anything so fleshly as eating. I said, "Are we likely to meet your boss there?"

"Old Ozzers? Oh, no. He always goes to a restaurant."

"Okay. I'll see you there then."

I left the place, had another lecherous look at the Victorian pinup in the window, and then strolled along to the pub. It was already fairly full, so I stood by the door drinking bitter and thinking bitter. Bitter, bitter thoughts about Lucy.

Yet again I mused over the background to our last few days together. Yet again I indulged in the bitter bitter pleasure of feeling like Humphrey Bogart as he tossed the rain-streaked note from Ingrid Bergman onto the departing Paris platform. Yet again I imagined to myself the scenes at the Althwaite household: Daddy Althwaite must have put his foot down and Lucy had said meekly, "No, of course we don't want a jailbird in the family, how right you are, Daddy." And I hadn't tried to win her back. Not a single plaintive word. If that was the way she wanted it.

Still, she could have at least sent a letter, or even just a postcard. But no, nothing. Oh, well, water under the bridge, I said to myself—and this cliché instantly summoned up a scene from our past: our first kiss on the bridge by the Arsenale in Venice. Complete with moonlight on water. Just like the ice-cream advertisements.

I had fallen for her simply because she had been a few years older than all the other students on the course and so had been the only one capable of talking about other things than memories of hockey matches or midnight dormitory feasts. And she for me for the same reason. There had been nothing more serious or deeper than that in the whole thing. A mere shipboard romance.

I wondered idly how Melinda had got to know of the affair; at the time, Lucy and I had been discreet about the whole thing, which had meant many sudden dives into back alleys and *sottoportici*, and avoidance of the more popular bars and *trattorie*.

Melinda arrived. "A lager and lime, please. Oh, and could you get a pork pie and some crisps too?"

I was more taken aback by the earthiness of her appetite than by her assumption that I was buying her lunch as well as a drink. I smiled, however, and pushed my way through the masses to order these dainties. A half or a pint of lager? I was asked. Well, maybe it would be a male-chauvinist assumption on my part to order a half, so I bought her a pint, which caused her eyes to open to Bambi extremes when I made it back. She had found two seats at the end of a table—probably by fluttering her eyelashes and looking likely to swoon picturesquely.

"So why were you in the news?" she said after an eager sip at the lager and a finger-fluttering nibble at a crisp.

I satisfied her curiosity on this business and then forcibly changed the subject. "How do you get on with Osgood?" I asked.

"Oh, he's not too bad, so long as you know which way to rub him."

I decided not to contemplate the gruesome vision this conjured up. I said, "But presumably you know something about his reputation."

"Oh, yes. He's always talking about it."

"Well, I mean what other people say about it. About him."

"That he's a crook?" she said, her blue eyes as large and untroubled as ever.

I looked around myself instinctively. "Well, that he—that he has sometimes been said to be involved in some rather, er, shady um . . ."

"Flogging hot paintings. Oh, yes, I've heard all about that. It doesn't bother me really."

"No?"

"No. The art market's all such a dirty business anyway. Lots of people really don't deserve to own their paintings. I mean, it's absolutely wicked to keep works of art as investments."

"But you can't just—"

"Anyway, that's what you said on the course. I've always remembered it."

"Oh, I see, so I've corrupted you, have I?" I said, looking at her serene countenance. "I didn't actually mean you all to set up as thieves."

"Well, I'm a bit of an anarchist actually. You see, I don't believe in private property."

"Osgood doesn't believe in other people's private property," I said, "but I think his belief in his own is pretty fervent."

"Anyway, I don't have anything to do with any of that side of Osgood's dealings. I'm really just a secretary."

"So you've never seen or heard anything of a painting by Cima da Conegliano called *The Madonna of the Swan?*"

"Cima? Wait a moment: he was the one with that Baptism of Christ with the little ducks in the background. I remember you pointing out the ducks. But a swan—no, I've never heard of anything with a swan."

I was rather touched by her memory of one of my more enthusiastic but less "relevant" lectures. "Oh, well, I just wondered. How about a Vivarini Crucifixion or a Palma il Giovane Annunciation?" The two paintings that had been stolen at the same time as the Cima.

"Oh, gosh, yes, the Palma il Giovane." (She pronounced it "Giovanni" in fact.) "There was quite a to-do over that."

"Oh, really?"

"Yes. Don't you remember when that gang boss got killed— what was his name? Mike La Rocca. About a year ago. And the police found lots of paintings in his house. It seemed he collected Annunciations."

"How very devotional."

"Most of them he'd bought regularly but this Palma il Giovanni was one of the hot ones. And Ozzers actually got questioned by the police about it. They'd found some evidence of his having had dealings with Mike La Rocca some years beforehand—about the time La Rocca had acquired the painting."

"I see." I didn't remember any of this. "How many years beforehand?"

"I remember exactly because I had to go through Ozzers's records for the police. It was in 1979."

"Ah." Almost immediately after the theft—if it was the painting in question. And this was by no means certain. Palma il Giovane was one of the most prolific painters of all times; there's hardly a church in the Veneto without a couple of his works—and usually not just miniatures or sketches: huge altarpieces or wall paintings; he probably turned out Annunciations as Barbara Cartland does novels. "You can't remember any details about the painting?"

"Why?" she said—not suspiciously or even curiously. Just said it.

I was thrown for a little. "You don't need to worry on account of your anarchist principles," I said. "I'm nothing to do with the police. I'm just curious. I heard something about a Cima and got interested. For Cima's sake. So can you tell me anything about the Palma?"

She accepted my far from exhaustive reply. "Well, it came from somewhere near Venice."

"Yes." A Palma il Giovane was pretty well bound to. "Not a place called Fregazze by any chance?"

"Yes, yes, that was the name, I'm sure. And it showed the Virgin Mary and, um . . ."

"Don't tell me—the Angel Gabriel."

"Well, an angel," she said seriously. "And it was quite a little work." She made gentle gestures with her piece of pork pie and glass of lager, indicating a rectangular shape of about two feet by one foot. "But the police couldn't find any evidence about Ozzers." She licked a fleck of pastry off one finger's end. I realized that by some mysterious ethereal process she had finished off all the food—without offering me a single crisp. "Mmm. I could do with a Yorkie Bar," she said. "And a Crunchie."

Well, I'd paid for girls with more expensive tastes, I thought. I went over and bought this final course. While she unwrapped the Yorkie Bar I said, "Has a young Italian been in today? About so high, rather nervous, dark hair and eyes, speaking pretty good English?"

"Oh, yes. He came as soon as we opened up. And wanted to talk to Ozzers."

"What about?"

"I don't know. They talked in private. But when he left I think I heard Ozzers saying something about meeting for dinner at Ciro's."

"Where's that?"

"It's a restaurant in Soho. Ozzers often goes there because it's near the other gallery."

"What other gallery?"

"The Blue Moon. Ozzers has an interest in it."

"Do you mean he finds it interesting or—"

"Oh, he's got shares or something, I think," she said with the sweet vagueness of one who lives on a higher plane. "And they sometimes do some cleaning or restoring for him. It's quite an exciting place. Lots of the latest really important movements. Always on the go, you know."

"Did you say it was an art gallery or a discotheque?"

She looked puzzled and said, "They have had dance-related exhibitions actually—you know, the whole performance-painting movement."

I didn't know. Go to jail for a few months and you miss a whole movement of contemporary art.

I felt I'd got as much out of her as I could without making her too suspicious. I said, "Well, it's been a nice lunch. Er, I know as an anarchist you won't give a damn about what your boss thinks, but still maybe I should point out that if you tell him about your friendly lunchtime chat with me, it won't actually help you get into the Blue Moon."

40

"Oh, no, of course I won't say anything. Thanks for lunch—and thanks again for those marvelous lectures in Venice."

"Oh, well, you know . . ."

"We all agreed about them, you know. We said, he might not know much about the facts, but gosh, can he enthuse."

"Thank you." I took our empty glasses back to the bar. She'd drunk the full pint—and when I returned was putting the last morsel of Crunchie in her mouth.

We said good-bye in the street and she kissed me on both cheeks. Well, we'd been talking about Italy, I suppose. I gave her an invitation card for the private view and told her I'd see to it that crisps and Crunchies were laid on. I watched her shimmer off down the road, somehow making January London streets look like June meadows.

But Lucy, I suddenly thought, had been able to make January *feel* like June. By just being there.

But only in Venice, I then answered myself back, breaking into a vigorous and sentiment-squashing stride. Nowhere on the real earth.

4

I TOOK the tube back home. I wondered how that bloody Stepney swan was going to affect me when I opened the door of the studio; a masterpiece of transcendent dazzling pith or a messed-up piece of trivial Disney kitsch. Maybe it would depend on whether I had another drink before opening that door.

I got off the train at Earls Court. One more piece of procrastination. I went along to the house I'd seen the Italian enter.

I pressed the second doorbell, which presumably corresponded to the first-floor flat. After about forty seconds the door was opened by a large woman with badly dyed blond hair. She said, without taking the cigarette out of her mouth, "Yeah?"

"I'm looking for the Italian man who lives on the first floor."

"He's gone."

"Oh. You don't know when he'll be back?"

"Not coming back."

"What?"

"Not coming back. You deaf?"

42

"No. Um, when did he leave?"

"What's it to you?"

"Well, he's a friend . . ." I trailed off under her contemptuous stare.

"Had about enough of it," she said after a few seconds.

"Of what?" I said.

"All these bleeding questions." Each clipped remark seemed to be thrown down as a deliberate challenge: Let's see if you can work that one out.

"I've only asked two," I said carefully.

"Yeah. *You* have." Then, after another defiant pause: "So far."

"So who else has been asking questions?"

"You'd like to know, wouldn't you?"

"Well, yes."

"Well, this ain't Russia, is it?"

I worked on this one for a couple of seconds, then said, "No. Two pounds?" This was Thatcherite Britain.

"Ten."

"Five."

"Okay." But she just stood there, the cigarette unmoving in her mouth. I got out a five-pound note and handed it to her. She pocketed it carefully then began, "So first off he just comes and tells me this morning he had to go, at around eight o'clock, I mean, what a time, I wasn't dressed even, and he didn't even give no reason, but I told him he had to pay till the end of the month anyway, 'cause I mean, fair's fair, innit? and he said okay, and then off he went, I mean talk of being in a hurry. Then about an hour later along come these other Eye-ties who say they're his friends, and they wouldn't take no for an answer when I said I didn't know where he'd gone, I mean, bloody cheek, who do they think they are, that's what I want to know." It was like a dam burst.

"I see. What name had he given you?"

"Tony."

"Tony what?"

"How should I know? Tony Spaghetti or Tony Ravioli, I expect. I mean we don't go much for second names here."

"And these two who came along? They were definitely Italian?"

"Well, they talked funny like Tony did, and they said they were his friends, so what do you expect me to think?"

"Did they say why they wanted to see him?"

"Just said they were his friends. But the one of them, a little bloke with a beard—well, they both had beards—but the little one, I can't imagine him being nobody's friend. Dead creepy. His eyes didn't move once. And wouldn't take no."

"And they didn't—"

She interrupted me, "That's a fiver's worth." And slammed the door.

Back home I made myself a cheese sandwich and then went along to the studio clutching a can of beer—not too desperately, I hoped. I opened the door.

Well, nobody could say the swan wasn't noticeable. It occupied about one-fifteenth of the canvas but dominated the whole picture. Dominated the whole room. I'd portrayed it as rearing up from the rubbish heap, its wings half-open, its neck and head straining to the sky. Probably it was all wrong ornithologically—didn't they have to take off from the water? So maybe I could call it something ironic like *Wasted Effort*. Like my morning.

No. That title would be too much like a gift to any critic looking for a cheap crack. *Homage to Cima*. And on an impulse I took up a fine brush and painted this title in one corner of the work. There. I hoped Osgood would hear of it. Then he'd feel—well, if not small, less enormous.

Except he'd probably be bigger—as a result of huge meals paid for by the proceeds of the Cima sale. He might even offer to buy my *Homage*. That would be the kind of crushing joke he'd enjoy. And if he offered enough, I'd possibly even sell him it. That would be the kind of crushed worm I was.

Oh, well. I phoned Adrian. I apologized again for the

44

previous evening, told him not to expect anything in the *Corriere della Sera,* and then said, "Listen. I've just finished a real winner. And I mean a winner. Something quite different."

"Oh, dear. That is—ah, how interesting. I'd love to see it. Well, I'd like another look at them all in fact. Suppose I pop over tomorrow morning?"

"That would be fine. Er, not too early. After ten."

"I understand. And, um, you're not going to phone back in half an hour and say the painting's terrible?"

"Adrian."

"Well, it wouldn't be the first time. Just don't destroy it, that's all. Good-bye."

"Good-bye." That last warning was not really necessary. I had my ups and downs, as he knew, but I hardly ever reached the point of doing anything so decisive as destroying a painting. There might always be somebody prepared to pay for even the worst tat.

I spent the rest of the day just tinkering with my canvases, pretending I was adding finishing touches or improving them generally. I tried not to drink too much, as there was a danger I might wake up the next morning and find a bloody great swan on every single painting. When it was clear I was merely wasting time—when I found myself picking paint off the easel—I went out and bought a Cornish pasty and some tomatoes and a yogurt: a three-course meal. I also bought an *Evening Standard.*

I read the paper over dinner. There was no mention at all of my performance the previous evening. So even my notoriety was a failure now. I drank another can of beer and then I went back to the studio. I put the paintings in two stacks leaning up against the wall. I had decided I could no longer stand the all-surrounding eyeful of gloom every time I entered the room. Also it meant I would be able to show them one by one to Adrian, and see his reaction to each painting individually. I left the swan on the easel.

I read one of Jim's thrillers until about eleven-thirty and then started up the stairs to bed.

The front doorbell rang.

I turned back down the stairs, but as my fingers reached out for the latch my irritation changed to wariness and I thought, Hang on. I called out, "Who is it?" There was no answer. I peered through the letter box. There was nobody there. Obviously just kids who ought to be in bed.

And then there was a tinkle of broken glass from the kitchen, at the back of the house. Stupidly I still thought, Bloody kids, and I moved in that direction.

And somebody, not a kid, came out of the kitchen holding a gun.

"What?" I said in blank amazement. I wasn't even scared yet.

Then, one and a half seconds later, I was. My hands were already pointing to the ceiling, without my being aware of having raised them. The same probably went for my hair. I was now saying something like "But but but but" and I went on doing so till my mouth dried up.

The somebody was in darkness, at the other end of the unlit corridor, a large unmoving figure holding a large unmoving gun. Somebody else came out of the little kitchen behind him, a smaller suppler figure. As he moved toward me and into the light that seeped from the top of the stairs I had a nasty shock: his face was dead white and featureless. Then I realized he was wearing a mask: one of those blank plaster masks for the whole face that they sell everywhere in Venice, with just eyeholes. The explanation didn't comfort me any.

"Who are you?" I said. Probably a foolish question.

"Silence." There was something horrible about the way this came from a nonexistent mouth. He frisked me with deft gloved hands. The larger figure moved closer. He had the same kind of mask, which again looked extremely sinister above his turned-up greatcoat. Why couldn't they wear something traditional like stockings over their heads?

The smaller one straightened up. He was dressed in a leather jacket and jeans. A brown polo-neck sweater was visible where the jacket was open at the top.

46

You might think these sartorial observations were an odd thing to be indulging in at the time, but half of my business is looking at things, and I couldn't see their faces. My looking, however, didn't tell me anything that answered any question my mind was asking. All I could guess from the clothes was that there was something foreign about them. And even that had perhaps been suggested by the one word spoken so far—wouldn't any English person say "Shut up" or "Be quiet"?

"Go in there," the smaller man said, and the foreign accent was obvious now. He motioned me to the studio.

"What the hell is all this—"

"Go," he repeated, and the other one flicked the gun.

I went, my hands still foolishly raised. I moved into the center of the room by the easel and the smaller man found the light switch. He turned the lights on and looked at the windows to check that the curtains were drawn. They bloody were of course.

"Sit on that chair," he said, pointing to the armchair.

I sat in it. I supposed the chair hadn't been chosen for my comfort, but because it was the lowest, the one that made me most vulnerable. He took a length of cord from his pocket and told me to hang my arms down the side of the chair. I did so, still wondering furiously what the hell all this could be about. Were they just local thieves? The gun seemed a little excessive in a bit of housebreaking around here. After all, what would they expect other than video machine, compact disk, and the rest? Hardly worth risking the extra charge of armed entry for. Were they Osgood's boys? But no, why would he have foreign thugs? In fact, would he *really* have thugs at all? So were they Italian? The Italians who'd been asking after Tony? The masks suggested Venice. So it seemed possible. And one of them was little, as the woman had said.

The cord was pulled painfully tight and I gasped: it was released a millimeter or so. I looked at the man with the gun standing by the door—and I gasped again. The man laughed; a single derisive "Ha," and his colleague finished tying his knot and looked at me. "Ah, you have seen."

The big man threw the gun onto the ground, which it struck with a feeble clack. I'd been terrorized by a child's toy.

"But now is too late, no?" the small man went on, and the blankness of his mask took on an extra sinister touch, since it was obvious he was smiling behind it. I looked at his eyes, which were a pale green, and did not flicker as they met mine.

That's what you think, I should now say, and burst out of my bonds, kick him in the teeth, and then dive for the gun—no, wait a minute. . . . "You bastards," I said.

The big one now drew a cosh from inside his greatcoat. Not a toy this time. The real original blunt instrument. He stood there tapping it into the palm of his hands, looking like a cliché of dumb violence from a horror comic. But a cliché I wasn't going to argue with straightaway.

The small man looked at the paintings against the wall—or, at least, that's the way his mask was pointing. "An artist, I see."

"Thank you."

"An artist pretending he has a social conscience."

"Where?"

"The degradation of the proletariat exploited to make pretty pictures for the *borghesi*. Such tenderness of conscience."

"Not many proletarians living on that motorway flyover, I should think," I said, referring to the picture he was standing in front of.

"So you have also the ecological conscience. A green who thinks the world's problems will be solved by bicycle paths and the prohibition of aerosol sprays."

"Look, I'm sorry if you don't like my paintings, but I didn't invite you in and—"

"Silence." He didn't bark it out, just said it in a voice as expressionless as his mask. His eyes returned, unblinking, to me.

And I won't invite you to the private view either.

"We want to know where is Toni Sambon."

"Who?"

"Alfredo, hit his left hand. I'm sorry," he said as Alfredo approached, swinging the cosh. "These are not the methods I would choose, but we have no time to waste."

The sudden blow made me yelp. He'd merely tapped the cosh on my knuckles, but it felt as if he'd shattered every bone in the hand.

"That was your left hand. As an artist you will not want that we are harder with your right hand. So where is Toni Sambon?"

"The only Toni I know is I don't know where. I mean I don't know where the Toni I know is." I was babbling in undisguised panic. I forced my voice back to steadiness. "I don't know."

"Another hit I think, Alfredo. The same place would probably be best."

"No!" I yelled as Alfredo drew the cosh back.

"So speak."

"Look, I don't know anything about this bloody Toni. I just got talking to him in a gallery yesterday and that's all I know."

"Alfredo, you will probably have to hit him again. But wait a moment. First I will try to make him reason."

Alfredo, who obviously understood English perfectly well, said in Italian, "These types never reason." A northern Italian accent.

The small man said, "We know you went to Toni's flat this afternoon. You were seen. And this afternoon when you went out we entered in your flat and—"

"You what?"

"—and we saw that painting." He pointed to the swan. "And we saw the title. So please do not pretend you know nothing about Toni."

Oh, hell. I'd got myself into a right mess. Why hadn't I called it *The Ugly Duckling*? Why hadn't I painted a bloody sea gull? I grabbed at an irrelevance. "How did you get in?"

"The window in your kitchen. We had to break it this second time, I'm afraid."

I remembered now that I'd closed it on coming back from the shops. I was always leaving it open to get rid of cooking smells—well, burning smells. "Why did you ring the bell?" Another procrastinatory irrelevance.

49

"We wanted to be sure we would find you downstairs."

And at their mercy—at the mercy of the toy gun, that is.

"Now, please," he went on, "answer to our inquiries."

I was now sweating all over, watching that dangling cosh, watching the obscene blankness of their faces, the unnatural fixity of the small man's pale eyes, unable to force my mind to anything like constructive thought. I remembered tales of men under torture who shat their trousers and then suddenly that was the only thing in my mind: God, don't let me foul myself, don't let me—

The smaller man must have seen my lips moving. "What?"

"Nothing. I—I—"

"You see, you are frightened. It is natural. Nobody likes pain. I don't like to see pain myself. As I said, this is not our usual method. It is a question of efficiency. We require the information you have and this seems the quickest way of obtaining it. We have little time, you understand. Alfredo, another hit so he doesn't forget how it is."

The hit came and I hadn't forgotten. I burst out with a torrent of the foulest language I knew: against them, against myself, against the pain. It was either that or tears. Or shitting myself.

"It is not pleasant," the smaller man said. "But please don't make too much noise. Or we will have to silence you."

"And then how will you get the information?"

"It will take more time, it's true. But it will be even less pleasant for you, so I don't think it is in your interest."

"Does he do everything you tell him?" I said, nodding toward Alfredo. These questions were all a way of keeping myself calm—from fouling myself.

Alfredo made a menacing step forward, saying, "*Stronzo*," and the little man said, "We have no hierarchy. But he is obviously more suited to the muscular work than I am. Again a question of efficiency. True, Alfredo?"

He replied as usual in Italian, "True. But why explain things to this *borghese* shit? He doesn't want to understand."

"We are wasting time, true. Where is Sambon? And where are the paintings?"

"Paintings?"

"Yes. Another hit unless you start to—no. Paintings. I have a better idea." He went over to the stacks against the wall and picked up a small work. *Chelsea Wharf: Homage to Whistler.* He picked a corner of the canvas, pulling it away from the stretcher. Then he took out a cigarette lighter and flicked open a flame.

"No!" I yelled in undisguised panic.

"Ah. You get the point. Please speak."

"But look, I really don't know anything. . . . I got talking to Toni at this gallery last night and then on the way home, and I just happened to see a photograph of this Cima painting in his bag, and I got curious. . . ."

"You just happened to see. I require more truth." His flame caught the corner of the painting, and spread as a tiny blue ripple across the Thames. He kept the cigarette lighter there, feeding it. I could only repeat, "No, no, no," as I watched the flame curling up the canvas, catching the wooden stretcher as well. "You filthy bastard."

He trod on the last burning fragment, reduced it to ashes. "That was to convince you. I hope it was sufficient."

Alfredo laughed briefly, slipped the cosh into his pocket, and picked up a painting himself. *Waste Ground in Wapping.* He didn't want to be out of the fun obviously. He took out his own lighter.

"Look," I said, and my voice was close to a sob, "you can surely see I'm telling the truth now, how could I not be? I don't know anything. That photograph fell out of Toni's bag in the street because we got involved in a fight, I happened to recognize the painting and got curious, today I went round to his house to ask him about it, they told me he'd gone. That is all I bloody know. All. Please put that painting down."

Alfredo wasn't to be denied any bit of fun that his friend had had and fire swept across Wapping. I think I may have screamed at the same time, I don't know. I was scrabbling in the chair as if I could feel the flames licking at my own body.

Alfredo dropped the last bit of flaming canvas with a curse as he got scorched—and I didn't even get any satisfaction out of that—and kicked it away from him.

The smaller man said, "That's enough. Let us hear this story again. You recognized the painting. It is of course so famous."

"No, of course it isn't. But I like Cima de Conegliano. I once went to the church in Treganzi to see it there and—"

"And perhaps it was then you decided it was a good painting to have."

"Look, I was a student at the time, a poor bloody student."

"Poor." He didn't snort. Just repeated the word. "You don't know what it is, poverty. But this isn't the point. We know Toni had a contact in London. Or that Toni's Venice contact had one."

"What the hell do you know about what I know or don't know," I said. "What the hell do you know about my life." I wasn't clear why in the midst of all this savagery this point should have angered me so particularly: maybe because this cool assuming arrogance seemed to be the clue to his whole behavior—that and the fact that he was a bastard. While Alfredo was obviously just a bastard, *e basta*, as they say in Italian.

With the same arrogance he ignored this question. "Toni obviously came to London to meet this contact. Someone in the art world." He waved a hand around the studio. "This, I suppose, is the art world."

"Toni spoke to me for the first time in both our lives in that gallery last night. We were nearly all from the art world there: what do you expect—bloody footballers?"

He picked up another painting, looked at it at arm's length. A car scrap heap: one of my better works; beautifully played-down chaos of colors; I saw it through a haze of sudden tears—the colors swam, it became a piece of chromatic abstractionism. I said, "Please, I'm telling the truth—" I was about to say, "Not that one," but stopped myself in time; it would hardly have helped.

"Let us try another question," he said. "Who is Toni's agent in Venice?" The lighter was already on, the little flame a steady glowing menace.

"Oh, God, I don't know I don't know I don't know!" A crescendo to a scream.

The car scrap heap became a furnace. Then ashes.

"You see how stupid this reticence is." He now strolled to the easel. "The agent's name in Venice. Where is Toni? Where are the paintings? Three questions. Three answers. Then we go. We leave you to tidy up. Paint those little pictures again." He bent to look at the swan—his sinister blank face next to the swan's sinuous white shape. "Not bad. Cima must be an inspiration."

"What are *you* going to do with the Cima?"

"We have a buyer. The source of the money is not clean, but the money is necessary."

"Necessary for what? Who are you?"

Alfredo spoke quickly in Italian. "He's asking too many questions. Don't answer him."

The smaller man said, speaking in Italian too, "Don't worry. He knows anyway. And he understands Italian too, I'm sure." The eyes turned to me: it struck me that what was so disturbing about them was not that they were penetrating or shrewd but that they were as unmoving and expressionless as the mask; they suggested that the mask was his natural face.

"Are you going to answer these three questions?" he said in English.

Maybe I should invent answers. "The agent in Venice is called Scarpa," I said slowly. Scarpa is one of the commonest surnames in the city. "Toni is now in Scarborough with the painting." I had an aunt who lived in Scarborough.

"Where?"

"Scarborough, in Yorkshire."

"Why there?"

Because my aunt lives there. Because of the fair. "I don't bloody know."

He jerked his lighter at the corner of the painting.

"No!" I screamed, struggling in the chair. The flame caught hold—a spreading blue and yellow wave. Suddenly the rope jerked open—he was obviously not a skilled knot tier—and I leaped toward the easel just as the swan became a phoenix—but a phoenix which, like the swan, wasn't going to rise. Wasted Effort. Alfredo grabbed at my left shoulder and whirled me around. My fist flung out and connected with his mask. Then I was on the ground, on my back. Alfredo was standing over me with the cosh out. The mask had slipped, so his head looked sickeningly askew, but all I could see of his real face was a black beard. The easel was a flicker of light to one side. I made another squirm toward it, and the smaller man shoved the whole thing to one wall where it collapsed in a flaring heap.

"Oh, my God—no—" I saw the flames catch the nearest stack of paintings.

"*Andiamo*," said the smaller man. And suddenly they were out of the room. This obviously looked like it was becoming too public an affair. The front door opened and closed, but I was hardly aware of it. I jumped up and ran to the curtains and tugged. They came down in a velvety slither. When I turned, the whole stack was ablaze. I took one step forward and trod on the end of the curtain and fell flat again. I found myself fighting with the curtains: the whole thing would have been a scene from a Laurel and Hardy film if it hadn't been my future flaring up there. I struggled up again, saw that the other stack was alight too. I threw the curtains over the flames.

Half a minute later it was clear I'd saved Jim's house. And a minute later it was clear I'd saved one and a quarter of my paintings. *Rain over Clapham Junction* and a few stranded oil drums from *Thames at Low Tide*. Too damp to catch alight.

5

THE bell rang repeatedly and I suddenly realized who it was. "Oh, hell," I said, and got into my dressing gown. "Coming," I yelled.

"Ah, up bright and early as usual, I see," Adrian said facetiously when I opened the door. And then seconds later: "Martin, are you okay?"

"No. Come in. Out of the rain." It was pouring down. Even Adrian's earnestness was a little bedraggled. He turned and waved to a taxi and the taxi drove off.

"Told him to wait until I was sure you were in," he explained.

"I said I would be."

"Yes, I know but—Martin, what's the matter? You look terrible."

"It's not a hangover. At least not only." Of course I'd got smashed. What else had there been to do?

"Oh."

"Let's have some coffee and then go—oh, bugger it, let's go to the studio and then have some coffee. You'll need it."

He took off his coat and hung it on the bottom of the banisters, looking at them anxiously as if suspecting them of being about to collapse. Then he followed me into the studio.

I had cleared up nothing. The ashes, the charred curtains, charred canvases, the broken easel, the toy gun all lay exactly where I'd left them as soon as I'd ascertained the extent of the damage. *Clapham Junction* and *Thames Mud* lying against the wall did nothing to cheer the scene up. Even the coffee stain from the kicked cup of two nights before was still there.

The only relief was to keep one's eyes on the upper half of the wall and enjoy the colorful riot of Jim's postcards. I wondered whether to suggest this to Adrian.

"Martin, what have you done?"

"I had a bit of a funny accident. Dropped a cigarette end and *whoosh.* . . ."

"But you don't smoke."

"I know. That's what makes it so funny."

"What do you mean? Are you being funny—facetious, I mean?"

"I'm being a riot. All right, it wasn't just a cigarette, it was a joint. So I deserve all I got."

"Martin, Martin. What made you . . . ?" He shook his head.

"It was a bloody accident. I've just told you." It had taken me only five minutes' thinking the previous night to decide not to go to the police. After all they most likely wouldn't believe a word of it. And if they did believe just half of it, they'd end up convinced for the other half that I'd wanted to get my hands on the Cima for my own nefarious purposes.

That had been about the full extent of my logical thought; then I'd started on the whiskey—and at a later point the tears. Well, they'd diluted the whiskey.

"So there's going to be no exhibition?" he said.

"Well, unless you think those two are enough," I said, pointing to the one-and-a-quarter scenes of forlorn dampness. At about two A.M. I'd been thinking of putting a foot through *Clapham Junction.* Why hadn't I? It had probably been too much like effort.

56

"Martin, it *was* an accident, wasn't it?"

"Why should I do such a self-destructive thing deliberately?" As I said this I kicked the curtain so that it covered the toy gun, which he hadn't spotted yet. I couldn't think of any explanation for that.

"Because it *was* self-destructive perhaps?"

"Let's have some coffee, Adrian." When he just stayed there, staring at *Clapham Junction* and *Thames Mud*, I said, "Coffee, I promise you, not cocaine—or cyanide."

"It's a nice picture," he said, pointing to *Clapham Junction*.

We went to the kitchen and I put the kettle on. After a long silence I said, "Well, at least nobody'll be able to say I did it for the insurance."

"Because you weren't insured."

"Correct." The kettle boiled and I poured the water into the mugs. "So I suppose they'll just say it was a publicity stunt." I gave him his mug and he stared into it as unenthusiastically as if it were the mud of my painting. I began to elaborate on my accident story. I had at one point thought of telling him that local thugs had broken in just for the hell of it, but then thought that Adrian would probably insist on calling the police, so accident it had to be. "No, it wasn't a joint. I don't smoke anything, as you know, but you might as well use that as a story to tell other people; they're bound to believe I was high on something. The truth is I was burning a little charcoal and a bit fell on a rag on the floor and I just didn't notice. And I'd stacked all the paintings up against the wall and . . ."

He didn't pay much attention. At the end he said, "So you weren't smoking a—a joint."

"No."

"But you see, you deliberately choose a self-destructive story to tell me." Again he shook his head slowly. He finished his coffee and put the mug down with the look of one who has carried out an unpleasant duty. "What are you going to do now?"

"Tidy up, get dressed . . ."

"You know what I mean. Your future."

"Become a sculptor. Working with asbestos or something."

"Seriously Martin."

"Get down to bloody painting again. What else can I do? Though I might try for a teaching job as well." I was inventing on the spur of the moment. "Either that or join a monastery."

"I'll make you an offer."

"What?"

"I'll give you three thousand pounds for that painting in there—I'll buy it myself. Now. If you promise to get down to work again. Get an exhibition ready for the end of the year."

I thought about this. "It's very generous, but . . . I can't accept it."

"Why not?"

"Well, not quite like that. I'm going to get back to work, of course I am, but not straightaway. So it wouldn't be right to take the three thousand on those exact terms."

"Why? What are you going to do?"

"I'm not sure exactly, but I might be going away for a little." This was as much news to me as it was to him—but as soon as I'd said it I knew it was right.

"Of course, take a breather. You haven't been on holiday once yet. My offer still stands."

"And suppose for some reason I don't manage to get a show together by next year?"

"You must. But all right, let's say that in that case, and if I still haven't sold that painting for a sum superior to three thousand pounds, you'll take the painting back and repay me."

"Okay."

And there, on the kitchen table, between an empty yogurt carton and a beer can, he wrote out a check. He then rang for a taxi and we went back to the studio.

"And was that painting you rang me about really good?"

"Yes," I said, "it was."

"Oh, Martin."

"Oh, Adrian. Look, I appreciate the sympathy but do you think you could cut down on the slow sad headshakes?"

"Sorry. Where will you be going?"

"I'll let you know with a postcard."

We made some rather artificial chat about other topics—the weather even—until the taxi came. I suggested he leave the picture until a sunnier day but he just glanced at the charred mess on the floor and said, "No, I think perhaps, er . . ."

I thanked him again for his generosity and then I was left alone to my thoughts.

I looked around the studio. Just *Thames Mud* left to console me now. I shook my head—but quickly, firmly—and walked out of the room. I'd break down again if I stayed staring at that mess any longer: I went to the kitchen and stared at the check instead.

That lifted me slightly: pulled me out of the mud—the slough of despair. It wasn't only the money, welcome though it was; it was the confidence that it showed Adrian had in me. I had to build on that, if I didn't want to sink down into another miasma of misery and hopelessness—like last night.

I had no chronological awareness of what I'd done or felt or thought after the thugs left. It was all a confused nightmare: I'd got drunk and I'd raged; I'd been haunted by visions of blank faces around me, over me, masked figures holding coshes, wearing judges' wigs and jailers' uniforms. I'd heard the clunk of my cell door over and over again; I'd groveled in the ashes, and then, after knocking the bottle over, wept into them—indeed, my only certain memory was that the whole nightmare had ended in deliquescence: myself unable to rise, weeping over *Thames Mud*, and a sludge of whiskey-soaked ashes, and listening to the rain outside. And all this with the curtains open—or rather, absent.

I picked the check up. It crackled between my fingers with a reassuringly crisp, dry sound. I gazed out of the window but I wasn't seeing the gray rain now but the sunlit meadow and pool of the Cima painting. Suddenly I found a new determination for the future: I was *not* going to give up on that painting; I was *not* going to let either Osgood or those two bloody thugs get their hands on it. I was going to be personally responsible for the return of the picture to its church. The previous day I'd let myself get involved in the mystery of the picture through a desire to do something for art that didn't have the doubts attached to it that my own works did. Well, now all I had of my own works were the doubts, so there was all the more reason not to let the Cima matter drop. No, this would be one unwasted effort: this swan would take flight.

A new crisis calls for a new purpose, and this purpose felt good to me. It was nearly enough: and when I added to myself, "*And* I'm going to get those two bastards," I knew it was fully enough. It meant I wasn't going to play safe any longer.

I tidied the house up to the accompaniment of a cassette of Beethoven's Pastoral Symphony, after which I set out for central London again. It had stopped raining.

On the tube I tried to think a little more concretely about the whole business. First of all, who had the painting? presumably Toni Sambon. He (and perhaps his agent in Venice, whoever that might be) was/were trying to sell the thing to Osgood. Those two masked thugs knew he had it and had traced him to England, but had got to his flat just too late to nab him. Toni, judging from his extreme terror of the previous night, knew that someone was after him: maybe, come to think of it, it had been because he'd seen me apparently lurking around the house last night that he'd moved off the next day. Even if he'd recognized that it was me, the fact that I was keeping tabs would have been enough to scare him, or at least make him very wary. If so, I'd saved him—saved his life perhaps.

Now those two thugs: just who were they? From some of the language they'd used I'd guess they were political thugs—terrorists. (And probably this meant that the name Alfredo was just an assumed "combat" name.) So what did terrorists want with a Cima Madonna and Bambino? Hardly the sort of thing to inflame the passions of the oppressed masses. Well, they'd said they had a buyer, so the answer must simply be money. Terrorists were always carrying out bank raids to finance their operations, and no doubt a suitable buyer would pay enough for the Cima to make it worth their while to come to England after it—and do over a lonely London artist or two along the line.

I'd have to find out somehow who had taken the thing in the first place: why hadn't I followed up the case at the time? All I knew was that one of the other paintings stolen at the same time had passed through Osgood's hands very shortly after the original theft: the small Palma il Giovane—perhaps because it *was* small and thus more easily smuggled. Toni had only had a photograph of the Cima, so perhaps that was still in Italy.

One little point: if they were terrorists, why had they had toy guns? Again, perhaps a question of smuggling; they might not risk crossing borders with their real guns. So it would probably be wise of me to try to keep my dealings with them in this country.

But I realized I was already relishing the idea of a journey abroad. To my favorite foreign country—and my favorite foreign city, which had been mentioned a few times so far: it was Toni's and Palma il Giovane's and Alvise Vivarini's hometown, and Cima's adopted town, and it was where Toni's mysterious "agent" was. And anyway I wasn't playing safe any longer, was I?

In fact it would be nice for "abroad" to have a thrill of daring about it once again—just as it had always had in the past, when taking my holiday on the Continent had been another act of rebellion against the family (though always followed up by my usual guilt-assuaging presents of Perugina chocolate and souvenir tea towels on return).

So, first of all to Osgood again, and a few rather more pointed questions this time: his threats to queer my reviews would sound a bit silly now. I thought of the fact that I hadn't mentioned his name to the thugs the previous night. Well, it certainly hadn't been in order to protect the poor man; I suppose there just hadn't seemed to be any advantage in giving his name away—and perhaps it had been the first indication of my new role as savior of Cima da Conegliano from the barbarians.

The Alma-Tadema was still there in the window, giving the come-on to all passersby. Melinda gave me a rather less fleshly welcome as I entered. It was just the word *Hello*, but breathed forth like a mystic enchantment.

"Hi," I said, "Ozzers in?"

"Oh, no, he's gone."

"How do you mean, gone?"

"Gone to the Continent. For a couple of weeks."

"What? I mean, did you know—that is, when?"

"Well, when I say he's gone, he's going. His plane leaves this afternoon. He just came in this morning and announced his decision and I had to book him on the earliest plane." Which would still be a lower plane than the one she lived on, her dreamy tone suggested.

"Kind of sudden then."

"Oh, yes. But he's often like that. He was planning to go very soon anyway. I just had to anticipate everything."

"And where he's going exactly?" I said, guessing the answer.

"Paris."

I'd guessed wrong. "Oh."

"And then a few other places. Ending up in Venice, I think."

Not so wrong. "When's he getting to Venice?"

"I'm not sure. He only got me to book the first part of the journey. But I suppose after a week or so. He mentioned Lyons and Milan as well, you see."

"And I suppose you don't know where he'll be staying in Venice?"

"No. He usually calls us from each place and lets us know his number then, in case of anything urgent coming up. Is it still this Cima you're interested in?"

"That's right. The man with the ducks. Osgood didn't say anything about it, did he?"

"No. He never talks to me about the pictures."

This seemed odd in a picture gallery. "And you don't have any idea what he's going to Venice for?"

"No. You *do* promise that you're nothing to do with the police?"

"Do I look like it?"

"No. You haven't got that fascist aura."

"At heart I'm an anarchist too," I assured her. Well, I felt like one that morning anyway. "I'm just curious. I'm trying to trace this picture. So you've no idea what he might be doing in Venice?"

"Well, I suppose he might be going to see Zennaro."

"Who?"

"He's a painter in Venice that Ozzers is interested in. He sometimes sells through the Blue Moon."

"Ah. Any good?"

"We-ell . . ." Her face puckered into unwonted frowning lines. "Rather traditional sort of stuff. Not *really* a Blue Moon artist, if you know what I mean. I don't know why Ozzers is so fond of him."

"Well, thanks for all your help—and, again, it would probably be best not to mention anything to Osgood. Oh, where in Soho *is* the Blue Moon? It sounds a place I should get to know."

She told me and I thanked her. "Oh and by the way, I'm afraid that invitation for the private view is no longer valid."

"Oh."

"No. I had a bit of a fire. Lost all the paintings."

"Oh, what a shame," she said, as if I were telling her of how I dropped a Yorkie Bar down a drain. "Well, better luck next time."

"Thank you." I said good-bye and she returned to her newspaper. Judging from her look of concentration, it was Doonesbury she was now reading.

As usual in the daylight, Soho looked a little apologetic for its sleaziness. The doorman at the strip club next to the Blue Moon invited me in as I walked by, but without much conviction. The photos in his window weren't anything like as sexy as the picture in Osgood's window. The Blue Moon looked even sleazier and more apologetic than its neighbors: the window needed cleaning and the final *n* of the name on the signboard was dangling by one nail, so that it looked like an overlarge comma. I passed under it quickly.

I peered through the glass and saw a window display of what looked like upturned brooms of varying sizes, all of which were sprouting large colored wings. There was a title below: *Angels of the House.*

I walked in. At first sight the place looked like a secondhand shop for domestic appliances. There were ancient Hoovers, mops, brushes, clothes racks, coat stands, shelf brackets. . . . But then one saw the strange position or color or decoration of each object—the Hoover upside down embedded in concrete, with a knotted scarf around its roofward-pointing nozzle (*Char* was the curt title to this one), the clothes rack draped with shredded pieces of Union Jack, two coat stands leaning toward each other with their pegs turning into entwined tentacles (*Desire*). . . . A plump man in a black shirt and tight jeans was sitting with a copy of *Time Out* in a wicker chair next to the Hoover.

He did no more than glance at me, so I kept pottering around. The whole of the front room of the gallery was given over to this jumble. But there was another room beyond that was full of paintings. They were in various styles, each labeled with an artist's name and a number. No prices. None of it was my sort of stuff. I looked around for anything with a Venetian subject, but it was difficult to recognize any subject anywhere: then I saw the name Zennaro next to what looked like a geometrical problem from a math book that had been colored in by some bored pupil. Staring hard, I realized that the shapes bore a kind of diagrammatic resemblance to some of the more famous buildings of Venice, like San Giorgio Maggiore, the Rialto Bridge, the Bridge of Sighs. They were all superimposed on one another and painted in the brightest oranges, purples, greens. . . .

I went back to the broom-cupboard half of the gallery and approached the man in the wicker chair. He looked up and said, "Hi."

64

"Er, hi. I'm interested in that Zennaro painting. Do you have any more of his stuff?"

He didn't curl his lip at my taste, but it took him a second or two to put his look of professional interest on. "Oh, yeah, Zennaro. Up-and-coming. We don't have anything else just at the moment. He's getting a name over here. If you're interested in that one, it's going for two hundred and twenty."

"Ah. Well, no. I'm not too keen on the colors there, but I like the style. I'm thinking of my wallpaper, you see. It would clash."

"Yes, of course." He relaxed in his chair, perhaps realizing there would be no need to bother pulling out any jargon on me.

"It was Mr. Osgood who put me onto this man Zennaro," I said.

He definitely blinked in surprise, but then his face went professionally smooth again. "Oh, yeah? Well, he put you onto a pretty good thing, I reckon. Definitely up-and-coming."

"It was a bit of a surprise to me," I said. "I didn't know Mr. Osgood dealt with this end of the market."

"Yeah, well, in fact he only comes to us for a bit of cleaning now and again. We do some cleaning and restoring in the back room there. Sideline like." He indicated a closed door in the far wall.

"Oh, so Osgood's got nothing to do with this gallery in fact."

"No." He said it a shade too vehemently. "Well, call again. We'll probably have a Zennaro you'll like sooner or later."

"I don't suppose I could have a peep into the cleaning room? I'd be awfully fascinated." I found I was slipping into an upper-class-twit role. Anything to persuade him I was harmless.

"Afraid not." His tone was quite firm. He didn't offer any explanation and I didn't press for one. To be fair, very few restorers would welcome observers while they worked; all trades have their secrets, and the art trade more than most.

"Oh, well, it was just a thought," I said. "I'll pop by again to see if you've got a Zennaro that would tone in nicely."

"Yeah, sure." He returned to *Time Out*.

"Well, good-bye and thanks awfully." I just managed to stop myself adding "toodle-pip," and then when I reached the door I thought, Why not? and turned and said it. After all, I wasn't likely ever to return—certainly not to see the paintings.

6

I TOOK the train to Venice. I wanted to *know* that I was traveling, *feel* the miles that I was covering. And my journey on the 14:30 from Victoria was unambiguously a journey: a choppy Channel crossing; the lights and bustle of the Gare du Nord and then Gare de Lyon; fitful sleep in the couchette with the mysterious SNCR nappy-liner sheets and the heating on too high; standing out in the corridor with other bleary-eyed passengers, watching Lago Maggiore and its islands slip by under a steady drizzle; the fascist architecture of Milan station, and the noise of Italy and Italians. And then the last three and a half hours to Venice with occasional glances at the hazy Po plain and occasional reading of an Agatha Christie novel.

I was feeling good—or, at least, I was feeling certain that I was doing the right thing: the right thing to get me on the road to feeling good.

Even the last-minute phone call to my mother hadn't left me as guilty as it usually did. She hadn't given me the line about my only ever calling her to tell her I was going away, and she had actually finished by telling me to enjoy myself. Of course I hadn't filled her in on any of the background reasons for the trip.

67

After Mestre I put my book away and just watched as blocks of flats gave way to oil refineries on the right, and to mud and river on the left, and then as both these gave way to the lagoon, an almost rippleless expanse of olive-oil green, hazing away to gray on the horizon. It must have been two years since I last enjoyed this spectacle, this unparalleled sense of arrival. And as I came out of the station with my rucksack on my back and saw the Grand Canal there in front of me, I asked myself that corny question, why should this saddest of cities have the power to lift the heart so?

For I felt great. It's a case of true love between me and the city. At least it is on my part; the Serenissima, of course, is a two-faced old bitch—but, as with Cleopatra, that's half her charm.

I first came to the city when a student (that same holiday during which I saw the Cima in fact). I'd been hitching up and down Italy and was already half-drunk with the country and with the beauty of the art and the women; Venice—even in August, with the hordes of trippers and the inflated prices and the mosquitoes—was the final cup. I just floated around the place in a sort of ecstatic dream: I was my own gondola. I know I spent one whole night wandering the empty streets, finally watching sunrise come up over the Lido from the Punto della Dogana, and feeling, as I felt now, besotted.

In later years I had shamelessly pulled strings to get a job each year on that pre-university course, and my love for the place only increased with each visit. All this of course lays me open to the scorn of those who point to the city's artificiality, its debased role as museum cum funfair, its tattered gaudy beauty, like that of an old whore with cheap crowd-pulling clothes and makeup. But I feel that what such people are really bugged by is Venice's too-accessible beauty: they usually go on to profess a preference for some out-of-the-way place like Bassano or Feltre, as one might claim to prefer Balakirev to Tchaikovsky, Morisot to Renoir. You have, in fact, to make a very conscious effort at resistance to be scornful about Venice, and I see no reason to. I just swoon straight into her clammy arms.

I took the vaporetto down the Grand Canal and sat out front in the cold gray air, the only person foolish enough to do so. As so often in winter, it was quite a bit colder in Venice than in London. By the time we reached St. Mark's I was frozen, with my ears likely to shatter into ice splinters if touched.

As the boat pulled out again into the lagoon, with me still foolishly sitting there, admiring the glimpse of the greatest square in the world, and noticing they still hadn't put the winged lion back on the pillar at the water's edge, somebody tapped my shoulder. I glanced around and saw a uniform. I fished out my ticket and offered it.

"*No, signore, documenti, passaporto.*"

I realized it wasn't a ticket inspector but a carabiniere—complete with gun hanging on his shoulder. I fished out my passport from my anorak pocket. "Why?" I said.

He made no answer but looked through its pages. I looked back down the boat and saw another carabiniere passing down the cabin. He too had a gun at the ready.

The one standing over me handed me back my passport. "*Turista?*"

I explained I was going to a hotel near Via Garibaldi. He nodded and left. I noticed the resigned faces of all the passengers as they proffered their documents. The carabinieri got off at the next stop, San Zaccaria.

I got off at the stop after that, the Arsenale, and I made my way through the various stalls and attractions of the city's winter funfair to a small cheap hotel I'd stayed at on a couple of occasions when my accommodation wasn't being paid for by others. I got a single room without a bath, from which I could, if I leaned far enough out of the window, see a strip of lagoon. Otherwise I saw a blank wall about six feet away.

It struck me, as I looked around this completely anonymous room—bed with coverlet well turned down, hard chair, never-to-be-used wardrobe, sink without a plug, and chipped water glass—that it felt more comfortable to me than Jim's house. Maybe, despite all my half hankerings for a home, I was naturally a cheap-hotel dweller.

I stripped, washed, and put on clean clothes and then set out. It was already dusk, and cobwebby mist was creeping up on the city, swathing even the funfair in its forlorn embrace. The children clung to their damp miniplanes, cars, and trains with scared-looking faces; the lights of the various stalls all glowed fuzzily, distantly. The only real life was to be found in the arcade of the videogames—a barrage of buzzing and crashing and bleeping and squealing; but the people using the machines were all grim-faced and mute.

I looked at this scene and suddenly found myself accepting the invitation of the fog to indulge in exquisite melancholy. Instead of turning right toward St. Mark's, the natural direction of all feet on their first day in Venice, I turned left toward the Public Gardens. I walked on past the last stalls, and then there was just the steady dull clanging of the fog-warning bell somewhere out in the lagoon and the occasional mournful hoot from a boat. To my right the lagoon was a gray blur. There was hardly anyone around. I reached the gardens and walked along its gravelly paths, with just the cats and statues for company—and of course my memories. I stopped at a damp bench near a bust of Verdi and sat down. The bush that hid him from a bust of Wagner hadn't been trimmed, I was pleased to note. I found myself humming *Celeste Aïda*.

On our very first entwined walk Lucy and I had sat on this bench, in very similar weather, and among other things Lucy had taught me some tunes from *Aïda*—it was, she'd explained, Verdi's warmest opera. She had been shocked to learn that I'd never been to or heard a single opera of Verdi's. (I still haven't, but I know every word of the aria *Celeste Aïda*: it became our song.)

This was really stupid, I suddenly told myself. It was certainly not the way to forward my purpose: Okay, Venice might not be the best place for forward thinking—even the vaporetti sometimes seem to go backward—but there was no need for me to aid and abet the city by wallowing in its mushy memories, and getting rheumatism in addition. I got up and made firmly back down the Riva.

70

I caught a number-five boat and was taken through the Arsenale to the Fondamente Nuove, and from there made my way to a small square nearby, where the Britannia School was situated. The school occupied a fair-sized palazzo with a Gothic frontage. It was originally just a private English-language school for the citizens of Venice, one of the many in the city, and then one year Mr. Robin, its director, conceived the idea of hosting an art course for English students on his premises as well.

The courses took off well. Indeed, it was owing to their success that he was able to move his school from what by all accounts had been a very run-down building at the other end of Cannareggio to this rather impressive four-story Gothic palazzo. The language school occupied the damp, sometimes even flooded, ground floor and second floor, while the pre-university course (generally referred to as the Derek Robin Course) occupied the more imposing first floor: the *piano nobile*. The third floor was Mr. Robin's own flat—an inviolable sanctuary.

It was to the *piano nobile* that I now made my way. I entered the large reception room from the staircase at the side and looked around its marbled magnificence—polished floor, decorated oak beams, faded bucolic frescoes. The furniture was a bit of a letdown, consisting as it did of rows of lightweight gray chairs, all facing a white hanging screen on the end wall. There was no one around. I crossed the room and tapped on the door marked *"Segreteria."* A voice said, *"Avanti,"* and I entered. The school secretary was sitting at the other side of a huge desk, which was mostly occupied by the Venetian newspaper, *Il Gazzettino.* She recognized me immediately: "Mr. Pheeps!"

"Ciao, Luisa."

We went through a long-time-no-see routine, by the end of which I had taken in the following facts: she had put on weight, she still hadn't married her long-standing *fidanzato,* she knew all about my Fall. All of these facts I had deduced from visual evidence. She hadn't asked me a single question about the last two years other than how I had been keeping, but there was a whole flood of them waiting to burst through the dam of her

71

decorum. I concluded our little reunion with the question "Mr. Robin in?"

"He's upstairs in his flat."

"Oh. I'll just pop up and knock on the door—"

"Well, no," she said immediately.

"Just joking, Luisa." Mr. Robin had never been known to invite anyone in, even for a cup of coffee. I suppose he wanted to make sure that his flat didn't turn into the school canteen, but it led to speculation among the staff about opium fumes, lurid tapestries, naked concubines . . . or perhaps just china ducks on the wall.

She lifted the internal phone and buzzed him. He was down in half a minute, his usual elegant self. I always hoped one day to catch him out with some tiny imperfection in his appearance— say, the loops of his shoelaces not exactly equal circles, or one bristle outside the ruler-drawn borders of his beard—but as ever I was disappointed: he was dressed with immaculate geometrical precision. He wasn't even allowing any of his undoubted puzzlement to crease his brow.

"Ah, Martin. Very good to see you."

"And you. Yes, I'm out again."

He nodded. "Ah yes, I see."

I said, "And I've come to Venice for a holiday. But I thought I'd drop in and see how the course is going."

"Oh, just fine, just fine. Er, where are you staying?"

He was probably worried that I'd come looking for a job—and if so, he was right. I'd known that there would have been no chance of his offering me a post if I'd simply telephoned plaintively from London, but by turning up in person, I thought I might be able to win him over: at least it would be clear that I wasn't expecting my airfare to be paid. I was prepared to negotiate over the hotel too. "Little place on Via Garibaldi," I said. "Um, I was wondering if you, er . . ."

"We've got a very full course this year, you know," he broke in, as if apropos of nothing. "Some excellent teachers. We're doing quite a bit on architecture as well, with tours round some

72

of the villas on the mainland. That's where all the students are this afternoon."

"Ah. So there wouldn't be any chance of my doing my usual stint?"

"Well, nothing's been programmed," he said. I remembered now that nothing really existed for Mr. Robin unless it was first on paper: he lived his life by programs and schedules and timetables, probably visiting the loo only after official self-notification in triplicate. He was probably the only inhabitant of Italy who took any of the state's spaghettilike entanglement of red tape seriously. "And of course," he went on, "you have to remember that the course has, em, a . . ." He tailed off in an uncharacteristically hesitant way.

"I know. A reputation to keep up."

"Em—well, precisely."

"I wasn't sent to jail for white slavery, you know."

"No, but . . ." And he nodded significantly as if that "but" said it all.

"Look, didn't I always go down well with the students?"

"Yes, and I'm sure you would now. It's the parents I have to think of."

"Well, there you are, I'm not on the program, so why should they know anything?"

He frowned. I think the idea of getting a few extra lessons on the cheap probably appealed to him, but he was just naturally averse to anything improvised.

I persisted. "I've brought my slides, you know." There may have been a certain lack of dignity in my position but, hell, I needed the money. "And I'll slot in whenever you like."

Luisa, who followed English well enough, spoke up in Italian: "Remember that Signor Jones has had to cancel his lessons."

"Ah yes."

"If it would make you any easier," I said, "I'll call myself Mr. Jones."

He looked thoughtful for a moment, as if seriously considering the advantages of this both from the bureaucratic point of view and that of reputation. He said, "Well, we won't alter the program officially, but we'll slip you in there and explain to the students in person."

For him, agreeing to do something unofficial must have been like putting on an unironed shirt. I said, "Thanks. That's really kind."

"Not at all. Mr. Jones was to talk on Venetian choral music."

"Well, I'll stick to pictures, if it's all the same to you."

"Yes, yes." He seemed to feel that it was all concluded. He probably wanted me to discuss all other arrangements now with Luisa; after all, as I had accepted an unofficial status, I no longer existed as far as he was concerned. He said, "Well, I now have some paperwork to see to."

"Yes, well, thanks for bending things for me."

He almost winced. "Glad to have been of help," he said. He made for the door, but as he reached it he turned and said, "You said you're in a hotel?"

"What? Oh, yes, yes." Great, I thought, here comes the offer to pay the bill.

"Well, please remember, if you should move into any private accommodation, to register at once with the Questura."

"Oh, er, yes, of course."

"I make this clear to everyone every year, as you know," he said.

He did. You'd think he had shares with the stationers supplying the Questura.

"But this year," he went on, "we must be extra-careful. On account of these murders."

"These what?"

"Do you mean to say you haven't heard?"

"Remember I've only just arrived here."

"Well, Luisa will fill you in," he said, as if murders were a detail that went along with the timetable and the pay sheet.

"Oh, right."

74

"One other thing, Martin."

"Yes?"

"Please remember that you are here unofficially and try not to call attention to your presence."

"What, no sandwich boards?"

He considered this remark and obviously filed it away under the heading Irrelevant. "I mean, try and maintain standards of decorum, whether in or outside the school."

"Are you thinking of any specific slobbish episodes in my past?" I said, a little offended—well, quite a lot offended actually.

"I would just be happier if you avoided contact with the students outside your lessons."

Here was definitely the point to say in a cold and dignified way that if he was as worried as all that about my corrupting influence, I would do him a favor and withdraw my offer of lessons.

But I needed the money. So I said, "I see"—in a cold and dignified way of course.

"After all," he said, "they are only just out of school, you know."

"Would you like me to put my talks on tape so they don't even have to see me?"

"Well, no. We needn't go as far as that. Good-bye Martin."

He left me alone with Luisa: he must have decided she could look after herself.

I said, "Please tell me he's said the same thing to everyone."

She smiled and shook her head. "But you mustn't take him too seriously. He has to be careful. You know, last year a girl got pregnant."

"I have an unbreakable alibi," I said. I wondered whether it was only my criminal record that worried Mr. Robin. Could he, despite all our discretion at the time, have heard of my unteacherly relationship with Lucy? Some of the other students clearly had (witness Melinda), and word might have got back.

"Yes, it was a Venetian boy."

75

"And these murders," I said. "Was it Mr. Robin avenging the honor of his course?"

She laughed but then looked serious. "No, these murders are something horrible. The papers here have talked of nothing else." She pushed her *Gazzettino* over the table and I saw the headline: NO DEVELOPMENT IN RED KILLINGS. It had to be serious for a lack of developments to make the front page. Or else there was no other news.

"Who got killed?"

"There have been two killings, one in Castello and one in Mestre. They were both *terroristi pentiti*." That meant literally "penitent terrorists." But since the law was passed awarding significant reductions in jail sentences to terrorists (and then to mafiosi) who collaborated with the law, the word *pentito* has come to mean little more than "informer." "They were shot. But the horrible thing was that in both cases their tongues had been torn out."

"Oh, God, how sick. It's like something the Mafia does."

"Yes. That's what all the newspapers said."

"So who was it?"

"The BR, you know," she said.

I remembered that the first time I saw these initials in an Italian newspaper I'd wondered how British Rail had got involved in assassination—and then I'd thought of what Red Brigades would be in Italian. "So is that why there are carabinieri everywhere?"

"I expect so," she said.

"I thought the BR were all in jail now—or had all become social workers or ecologists."

"Yes, well, they think they're just a small group of *irreducibili*." The opposite of the *pentiti*—the hard-liner or psychopathic ones.

"I see. Small, but nasty. When were these murders?"

"One after Christmas, and one a week ago. In fact, only one was a real *pentito*, the other was just a man who'd given some information at a trial but who had never been accused of anything himself."

76

"I see. So an easy target."

We fell silent for a moment and I found my tongue was pushing up against my teeth, as if to remind me that it was still there. I said with forced brightness, "Well, what about the timetable then?"

She told me my hours—in the afternoon from five to six starting next Monday—and then we passed on to a little gossip about the other teachers, who were nearly all old friends or acquaintances, people who had gotten onto this freebie and had no intention of ever getting off it. Eventually she said, "Well, I must finish some accounts."

"I'll just go out and find a student to rape."

"Oh, Marteen." She shook her head. "You mustn't think too much about what Mr. Robin says. Ever since last year he's been very worried about the reputation of the course. This year, in fact, he has a—well, he calls her a nanny." She used the English word.

"A what?"

"Oh, a lady who is there to look after the girls." On an afterthought she added, "And the boys. Just to be on hand if they have, you know, emotional problems or things like that. Maybe you know her. She did this course some years ago."

"How many years ago?"

"Two or three."

"She'll be a kind of young nanny, won't she?"

"Well, she was a little older than the other students then. I think she's about twenty-seven or twenty-eight now. Her name's Lucy."

"Lucy Althwaite."

"Yes."

"Well, Mr. Robin can feel secure. I'm sure the students will be protected tooth and nail."

7

I GOT out of the building and into the fog. It was drifting lazily and heavily around the square—and around my mind. I was full of hazy indefinable thoughts and feelings, about Lucy and about murderers. Just one thing was clear: Mr. Robin couldn't have heard of Lucy and me; he would hardly have offered her the job if he had. I started walking toward the Rialto; it was the natural direction to drift at that time of the evening. Venetians meet and chat in the square at the foot of the Rialto Bridge, Campo San Bartolomeo (or San Bortolomio, as I always take smug and knowing care to call it). On the way I bought a *Gazzettino*. When I reached Campo San Bartolomeo, full of young people contributing to the fog with their chatter in impenetrable dialect, I propped myself up against the railing around the statue of Goldoni and read the article through properly.

The investigations were in the hands of Giudice Menegazzi, I read. The note claiming responsibility for the second murder was undergoing analysis; although the investigators were taking seriously the claim that a new and more ferocious terrorist group called *Il Nuovo Fronte del Proletariato* was behind the murders, they had not yet discarded the idea that they might simply have been the work of embittered *ex-compagni*. In general the opinion seemed to be that the "years of lead," as the violent seventies were often called, were not making a comeback: these murders were the work of a violent and dangerous group of people, but they obviously had no chance of a popular following. Communism was not exactly *di moda* at the moment. And even the terrorists in prison, with the exception of one or two *irreducibili*, had declared their revulsion at the crimes.

Inside I found an article about the funeral of Gianni Boscolo, the second victim, which had taken place in the Church of San Francesco della Vigna that day. A photograph showed a wreath against a wall near where his body had been found: it looked like a piece of waste ground. The caption said it was near San Francesco.

I folded the paper and walked slowly up the bridge, my mind no clearer than before. I reached the top and went to the edge to stare out into the clammy blur that had replaced the customary view of the Grand Canal. I perched on the damp parapet. Another Lucy memory—are there any lovers in the world who have visited Venice without perching there? Well, there were none there that evening. Everybody was hurrying past, buried deep in coats or holding scarves across their mouths.

I got up off the parapet, the damp beginning to seep through to my skin. I started walking down the bridge. *Celeste* bloody *Aïda* had started up as a mental *sottofondo*. It had obviously been foolish of me to expect anything simple from this city; Venice might have been in origin a product of mercantile hardheadedness and shrewdness, but for foreigners the sole aim of the old charmer seems to be that of messing them up emotionally. She'd got me drifting in her natural tidal tug toward the past again, and I'd have to paddle damned hard to keep steady.

And right now where was I going in fact? My feet seemed to be taking me down the other side of the bridge, toward the market. Probably because there was a bar down there where

Lucy and I had often gone at this time of the evening. (Casanova had too.) I switched off *Celeste Aïda* firmly, pulled myself to a stop, and turned around. Wherever I ate tonight it would be far from Lucy memories—geographically at any rate. So why not San Francesco della Vigna? Right on the other side of the city, an area I'd never visited with her. There was a good pizzeria near the church where I'd occasionally eaten on my own. And it would be a way of proving to myself that I was getting down to *serious* business. I'd go and have a look at that waste ground. A glance at the scene of the crime seemed a logical way to start investigations: if only to prove to myself that the murder in fact had nothing to do with me and Cima.

After all, why should it? The only link I could think of was the fact that the murders were apparently acts of left-wing terrorism, and the two thugs the other night had used leftist-type jargon. This was not exactly hard evidence. Not like, say, finding spare tongues in their coat pockets.

But—and I remembered the short man's calm, flat voice and his unblinking pale eyes as he fired my canvases, or watched "Alfredo" doing so—I could easily imagine them tearing out someone's tongue. Very easily. Probably with some explanation about the extreme efficiency of the process.

I had a nasty feeling that I was going to find myself involved with these murders.

I crossed the city in my usual haphazard way, pretending that I knew the way perfectly, while Venice snickered up her damp sleeves at my presumption and proved to me yet again that progress wasn't her specialty. I kept getting entangled in dead ends and backward-twisting alleys, finding myself at the edge of black uncrossable canals, and coming out into dank courtyards where cats stared at me from wellheads. This of course would have all been very sinister in the drifting fog, if I hadn't known what a very low street-crime rate the city really has.

I reminded myself of this fact constantly.

I crossed the bridge toward the ex-Church of Santa Giustina with its pigeon-spattered Baroque facade, and for the first time in my walk there was no one at all around. I was now in the parish of San Francesco. I turned into the *calle* itself, at the far end of which the church's Palladian facade hung as a white haze in the fog: St. Francis of the Vineyard. The city's gasworks seem to have replaced the vineyards now; I could dimly see the skeletal metal shapes high above me to my left. And then on my right I saw an area of rubble-strewn waste ground.

I stopped and stared. I had never noticed—or had completely forgotten about—this patch of ground. The place was so desolate, with its indistinct masses of rubble, its bony bushes, its creeping wraiths of mist, that I half expected to see the corpse still there. I saw the wreath, slouching against the wall, like any other piece of litter. I picked my way over to it.

There was just the victim's name, Gianni Boscolo, hanging loose like a luggage label. Nothing about the manner of death. I put the wreath down again, and while I was still bending, somebody tapped me on the shoulder.

I did something like a leap from a Russian folk dance, which carried me forward, whipped me around, and straightened me up all in one. Very spectacular. Then the whole effect was spoiled by the fact that I landed on an uneven stone, slipped, and fell backward.

"I scared you, did I?" the shoulder tapper said in a thick Venetian voice. He was a tiny old man, in a long raincoat and a battered gray hat; he peered down at me with curiosity rather than solicitude.

"Surprised me." I got up, rubbing myself.

"Are you a journalist?" he asked. He said it first in dialect and then at once, as if suddenly taking in the fact that I was a foreigner, repeated it in Italian.

"Why?"

"Been a lot of journalists along here. They've all interviewed me. And the police. I live over there." He pointed to a house with windows overlooking the waste ground. "I found the body."

"Ah."

"Foreigner, aren't you?" Again he asked it first in dialect, then "corrected" himself with Italian.

"Yes. I'm English."

"From the BBC then."

"Um, er, yes, that's right." Well, why not?

"The RAI interviewed me, you know. I was on the news on RAI one and RAI two, lunchtime and evening. My grandson's got it on one of those video things. And then in all the papers. My photograph in the *Gazzettino* and *La Nuova*. And *Gente*."

"Oh, really. Would you like to tell me about it too?"

"Where's your camera?"

"Well, maybe I'll come back tomorrow and take some pictures. In the daytime, you know."

"All right. Well, I woke up at my usual time, around six-thirty." His voice suddenly fell into a kind of singsong recital, all in careful Italian, with only occasional slips into dialect. "And I looked out of my window as I was making my coffee and thought, That's funny, someone's left an old coat out there. So I came out to look at it—not for me, you understand, I've got plenty of good coats—but just to see. And I saw it was a body. I turned him over and there was blood everywhere. You've never seen so much blood. His face was lying in a pool of it. Only it was all dried up. And his mouth was sort of caked up with it—"

"Yes, yes," I said quickly. "I get the point."

"So I guessed there was something wrong then. So I went back in and I told my wife. And she went out and had a look. And she screamed. My God, how she screamed." He chuckled at the memory. "Well, you know women, don't you? So then we phoned the police. And they asked us lots of questions. Had we heard anything during the night. And I said no, but then my wife said that was funny they should ask, because around about four o'clock she'd got up—she often has to get up in the night—you know, got a bit of a problem, only she didn't tell them that, I did, I mean they like to have things accurate—so she got up and she thought she heard people running down the alley to the canal. She had a peek through the bathroom window and just saw one man in the distance. I mean, there were probably several men, but she could just see the one, running away. And she saw him from the back only. And then she heard a boat going off. The

82

police think they killed him in the boat and dropped him here, and then went off again. They didn't kill him here because we'd have heard the shots—and the yells perhaps—but they can't have killed him too far away because then he wouldn't have been bleeding so much when they dropped him. And he did bleed a lot. God, you should have seen it."

"Yes, I'm sure. Did you know him?"

"Well, not *know* him. But he lived near here, you know. At Celestia. He'd hidden guns for some terrorists in his flat and he gave evidence about it. Bad people at Celestia, you know. As bad as the Muranesi. He was buried today. I went to the church. A lot of journalists again. But they didn't seem to see me."

I asked, "When was the murder exactly?" This was, I suppose, a pretty odd thing for a journalist not to know, but he didn't seem to be a suspecting sort.

"Five days ago. Or six? Sunday night anyway."

And he was still looking out of his window for journalists. Well, these golden memories were probably going to have to keep him going for the rest of his days.

"I see," I said. "Thank you."

"Giuseppe Pavan," he said. "That's the name. Born in 1915. Always lived here. Worked as a caretaker at the Morosini school until I retired. You'll mention that, won't you? People like to know these things. So you'll pass by tomorrow to take some photos?"

"Yes, yes, if possible."

"If I'm not at home, try the bar in Salizzada Santa Giustina. Just ask for Bepi. They've got the *Gazzettino* photo framed, you know. There on the wall."

"Ah."

"Oh—and I found the tongue too. Didn't mention that, did I? Thrown over there it was." He pointed to a black clump of bushes. "Found it before the police got here. I suggested a picture of me holding it but nobody wanted to. And anyway the police had taken it."

I decided to change the subject. "You say your wife saw one

of them from the back. Did she notice anything of any use?"

"No," he said contemptuously. "I mean, she wouldn't. If it had been me . . ."

"Oh. A pity."

"They kept asking her, but he was right in the distance, and it was dark of course."

"Yes, of course."

We were silent for a moment. Then he said, "Actually she did say one thing to me, but I told her to shut up about it, or they'd think she was crazy or something."

"What was that?"

"Well, it was really stupid. She said this bloke just turned around once, to look back, and it was like he didn't have a face."

"What?"

"Just nothing. No face. An empty white head, was what she said. I told her she couldn't have been seeing properly and told her not to say anything so stupid to the police, so of course she didn't."

"No, of course not."

"I mean, I wouldn't want people going around saying I'm married to a madwoman. You won't say anything about this, will you?" he added in sudden alarm.

"No, of course not, if you don't want. She probably imagined it."

"Just wasn't looking properly. I mean, you know what women are like. Can't see a thing if it's staring them in the face. She'd have never seen that tongue, like I did. It was just lying over there, and I spotted it and picked it up, it was kind of dry by then—"

"Yes, yes. I understand."

"Well, I'd better get back. My wife gets nervous on her own."

"Of course, good-bye."

I stood there for a few seconds after he'd gone, and stared down the alley. I found I could imagine all too clearly the running figure, turning around and displaying its empty white face.

And no doubt its pale eyes. Like the man in the white mask who'd invaded my flat, roughed me up, and burned my paintings.

Once in the restaurant I didn't read the Henry James novel I'd brought with me—I've brought it to Venice with me now five or six times and never yet started it. Instead I took the line of least resistance and drank enough wine with my pizza to make my stumbling bumbling walk back to the hotel through the empty streets and alleys of Castello comical rather than sinister. And enough, I hoped, to ensure a dreamless sleep.

It worked. I woke up the next day at about nine-thirty. The weather had decided to lend a hand as well: when I opened the shutters I felt a wind like a scalpel slicing down the alley; my slight throb of a hangover was cleaned out at once and I found myself feeling ready for anything. Once I'd stepped out of the hotel I found that every last clinging cobweb of mist had been swept away as well and the air was left as bright and clean and cold as a Canaletto painting. I walked toward the Riva and saw the city spread out before me, flaunting her newly washed palaces and domes in a long lazy curve between dazzling sky and water. Delicious was the word that came to mind: the Church of the Salute, for example, looked positively edible—crisp and buoyant in the sunshine, a marble meringue. And the golden angel of St. Mark's perched on the cool mint-chip peak of the chocolate Campanile. (I was feeling hungry too.)

I stopped for a cake and cappuccino in a place just off the Riva; I had decided not to have the hotel breakfast but day by day work my way through all the *pasticcerie* in the city—just as I had, in younger, more fervent days, worked my way through all the churches. As well as being a good start to the day, it was one way of feeling a little less cut off from my family, since the *pasticcerie* were the only thing I could think of in Venice that my mother would really approve of. A pity one couldn't take the meringues home.

The place had a phone and phone book, I saw as I licked the last blob of *zabajone* off one finger's end. I got some phone tokens from the lady behind the bar and stickily flicked through the book's pages.

I phoned the Cipriani Hotel. No Mr. Osgood was expected. I phoned the Gritti Palace. He wasn't expected there either. Then the Danieli. He was expected there the next evening. Did I wish to leave my name or any message? I didn't. I put the phone down. Well, that was one thing established. I'd guessed that if Osgood was going to stay in a hotel, it wouldn't be any poxy four-star dive.

The arrival time of Osgood came as a bit of a blow. The idea behind my trip had been that I would seek out Toni Sambon before Osgood got here and I'd persuade him to desist from selling the painting to Osgood. Something along those lines anyway. I'd thought I would have at least a week: easily enough time to flush out anybody in the city. Well, it was not to be.

I scrabbled through the phone book with extra urgency, looking up the name Zennaro. There were five columns of them. And I knew nothing but the surname and the occupation. A glance showed me that none of the names was advertising itself as a painter.

I tried Sambon. There was just one: Marino Sambon. I made a note of the phone number and the address. The address, however, was the particularly unhelpful Venetian kind: just the name of the *sestiere*, S. Polo, and the number—a four-figure one. I could spend all day going up and down the alleys of S. Polo before I found it.

As I left the *pasticceria* and strolled on down the Riva I pulled out of my shoulder bag my Lorenzetti guide to Venice, now a much battered and bescribbled volume. On the off chance I looked up the name Sambon in the index—or rather one of the indexes—and discovered there were two palazzi of that name. It was by no means likely that either was still occupied by anybody called Sambon, but neither was it impossible. It would be worth going to see because the kind of questions I wanted to ask were obviously better asked face-to-face than over a phone. I looked through the book to study the details of the two buildings, having to use both frozen hands as the pages flipped and flapped in the wind. Lorenzetti, of course, gave no such prosaic details as who lived in the buildings now: he confined himself to architectural descriptions and dates of construction. One was a Renaissance building in the style of Coducci (frescoes of the school of Tiepolo inside) in the *sestiere* of Cannaregio, not far from the Ghetto, and the other was a Baroque building, attributed to Longhena (frescoes by Guarana and followers) in the *sestiere* of S. Polo—not far from Campo S. Polo in fact. Remembering the address in the phone book as I did, this latter clearly seemed the more logical one to try.

But even if I couldn't actually conduct my interrogation over the phone, I could at least save myself a totally pointless journey. There was a phone next to the boat stop of the Arsenale. I rang Marino Sambon's number.

A female voice replied, *"Pronto."*

"Signora Sambon?"

"Sono io." The calm emphasis of the word *io* sounded habitual.

"Good morning. My name is, er . . ." For a second or two I wondered whether I should give a false name, and then wondered why I wondered it. Then I realized that whatever name I gave, uncertainty about it was not going to help my credibility. I finished hastily, "Martin Phipps. I'm doing research into the painter Guarana and I understand that in your palazzo there are some rather important frescoes by the artist."

"That is correct."

"Now, I know you must get so many requests to see them but I was wondering whether—"

"When would you like to come?"

"Well, as soon as is convenient."

"Today at twelve-thirty." It wasn't an offer or a question; more like a command.

"Thank you, thank you. That would be fine."

"Good-bye then." She'd put the phone down before I had time to ask where exactly the palazzo was.

I looked at my watch: it was now eight minutes past ten. A vaporetto was just approaching the stop bound for San Marco. I bought a ticket and boarded. Again I sat outside, and reached San Zaccaria feeling as if my face had been flayed with a honed icicle. I got off there and made toward the Marciana Library. I read up on Guarana for half an hour; unfortunately the book I'd ordered referred only in passing to the frescoes of Palazzo Sambon. I also looked up the name Sambon in the general indexes of the library but could only find references to the palazzi of that name. The family had obviously never been in the Golden Book and had done nothing of any historical significance. I ordered a book on the palazzi of the city. There I discovered that each of the two Sambon palazzi was known as "Palazzo Sambon, *già*," some other name, which meant the Sambon family had bought them from some other decaying Venetian family. The one in Cannaregio was apparently unoccupied and in disrepair—nothing strange for Venice. The description of the one in S. Polo merely mentioned the Guarana frescoes, without even saying what their subject was, and then talked about the other art treasures preserved there, among which were two paintings by Francesco Guardi. If only I'd read this before phoning, I'd have been saved a lot of bluffing, because I really did know about Guardi. Oh, well, at least I'd ask to see them before I left the palazzo.

By now it was getting on for a quarter to twelve, so I set out, not knowing how long it might take me to find the building. According to the topological information given in the guidebook, which was not exactly of military precision, it was somewhere between S. Polo and Sant'Aponal, an area I'd never really got sorted out. Neither, I discovered when I was reduced to looking at the map (the shame, the shame), had the cartographers: they had made only the most impressionistic of attempts to reproduce the crosshatch of back streets and back canals; I felt it would have been more honest on their part to have drawn dragons or griffins there and left it at that.

I got to Campo S. Polo at five past twelve and it took me

another twenty minutes to find the building—or at least to find the entrance. At one point I found myself staring right at it, recognizing all the architectural details described by Lorenzetti—but across a canal. Grotesque stone faces leered down from the coping above the water entrance, one even poking its tongue out at me. I got the point.

I eventually found the entrance, a Gothic doorway at the end of a dark alleyway—a marked contrast with the arrogant Baroque facade I'd seen earlier. The doorbell, a white button held in the green teeth of a bronze lion face, had the name Sambon written above it.

I pressed it, wondering if the teeth were designed to snap shut if one rang for too long. The door was opened by a maid—a definite maid. She was even dressed as one.

"Buongiorno," I said, "I have an appointment to see over the palazzo."

She said, *"Ah sì?"* as one might say "Oh yeah?" and then asked my name. I told her my name and she shrugged her shoulders and motioned me in. We went through a courtyard with a well into a marble-paved hall with a watergate at the far end, and then up the sort of staircase beloved by Hollywood for acrobatic swordfights or for floating processions of drapery-linked chorus girls. We entered a room the size of a tennis court, with eighteenth-century chairs perched around the edge as if for fastidious linesmen. Fleshy gods and goddesses cavorted on presumably robust clouds in fresco above, and an enormous colored chandelier, like several upturned cornucopias of glass, hung from the center of the ceiling.

"Momento," said the maid, and left me.

I gazed around respectfully. At the far end of the room, where a vast array of arched windows gave onto the canal, reflected sunlight did an elegant gavotte on the ceiling, and the parts of the fresco thus tremulously touched took on something of the ethereality one guessed the painter had been trying for. I strolled down to see the view—and perhaps because drawn by the sunshine. The marble floor was like ice under my feet and my breath made little ephemeral imitations of the god-supporting clouds above. I felt quite sorry for the gods, who were somewhat scantily clad.

There was a cough behind me—a severe cough.

I turned. Signora Sambon, as I presumed her to be, was a tall lady of about sixty. She looked unbending if not actually unbendable. She was wearing a tight blue dress that proclaimed how well she'd kept her figure and, subtly but still quite loudly, how rich she was. Her shoes, necklace, bracelet, and expression also passed on the second message.

"*Buongiorno,* signora," I began, wondering how a simple cough had managed to make me feel like a trapped sneak thief. "It was most kind of you to receive me at such short notice."

"Not at all. I consider it part of our duty. We are custodians of these treasures, but they are to be shared as well."

I looked up at the frescoes. "His late period," I said. That was one hard fact I'd picked up.

"I believe so."

I walked up and down the room squinting and gazing upward. There was at least no risk of tripping over the furniture. I occasionally uttered comments on the color harmonies and tonal values and the influence of Tiepolo, and she nodded as if she'd always thought so. I needn't have been so scrupulous in mugging up on Guarana, I realized. "Are there only these frescoes?" I asked when I felt I'd stared enough—my neck was getting stiff.

"There are no other frescoes in the palazzo."

"Ah." I would really have to get on to a few more personal questions; but it was difficult to start.

"I understand there are some fine Guardi paintings here," I said.

"They are being cleaned."

The answer came like a pistol shot, as if I'd asked to stand on one of the chairs to get a better view. I was quite startled: had the Guardis been so dirty as to be a public scandal? I said, "That's a pity."

"Who told you about them?"

90

"I, er, I read about them."

She relapsed into silence. The temperature had dropped several degrees. "In fact," I added, "I first heard about these frescoes from a Toni Sambon in London. Would that be your son?"

Again there was no doubting that I'd asked the wrong question. She glared, then spoke. "I know nobody of that name," she said with firm conclusiveness—and then, after a careful dramatic pause, added, "No longer."

"Er, sorry?" I said.

"I know nobody of that name now," she said. She was obviously enjoying the effect of her cryptic remarks.

"Oh, I see." I paused. "No longer."

"No longer."

Well, this could go on for ages. I said, with an air of innocent academic bumbling, "Sorry, I don't think I've quite understood."

"Antonio Sambon was my son. He is no longer."

"Oh, I'm sorry. Is he—"

"He is not dead, if that is what you wish to ask. At least, not so far as I know. He is simply no longer a son of mine."

I heard a door open at the far end of the room: when I looked at it, it had already closed again. Somebody had heard what the contessa was saying and knew better than to interrupt.

"Ah, I see. Sorry I—"

"That is all right. Well, I imagine you must have seen all you wish to see now."

"Oh, yes, of course." So I was getting turfed out. As Toni had been, I suppose.

The maid appeared as if summoned by telepathy. She escorted me back down the stairs, across the courtyard, and didn't quite slam the door behind me. I set off briskly down the alley. I wanted to get into the sun.

I heard footsteps behind me and a female voice said, *"Scusi."* I turned and saw a slight girl in her mid twenties, with long dark hair framing a rather serious-looking face.

"Sì?" I said.

"Were you asking my mother about Toni?" she said in the careful English of one who has studied the language rather than spoken it.

"Yes, that's right, but—"

"I know, I know," she said, "my mother doesn't want to talk about it."

"But you do."

"Yes, I do," she said with simple gravity. "Shall we go to a place where we can talk?"

"Take me somewhere sunny," I said.

"Let's go to Campo San Polo," she said. She walked quickly ahead of me, with a firm decisiveness that I guessed she'd inherited from her mother. She was physically quite unlike her, being small—at least a head shorter than myself—and pretty, but she had some of her mother's bearing, and this meant you soon forgot about her size. She walked with her hands in her sheepskin-coat pockets and her head up, her hair bouncing to her steps. Maybe it was this bounce that made her attractive rather than Valkyrien like her mother, or maybe she was just attractive and her mother wasn't. She led me through the quiet twisting alleys and over a couple of bridges until we came out unexpectedly into the bright expanse of Campo San Polo.

"Would you like a drink?" she asked. "There is a bar here."

"Yes, fine," I said.

She led me into a bar on one corner of the square. I ordered a *prosecco* and she a fruit juice. We took our drinks over to a table. She sipped hers and looked at me with her dark, serious eyes for a second or two as if appraising me. Then she said, "I'm Francesca."

"Oh, ah, yes. I'm Martin."

"I heard you talking to my mother. I listened when I heard you say Toni's name."

"Oh, that's all right. There was no secret—"

"I wasn't apologizing." She said this very simply. "But have you news of him?"

"Well, not really. I met him in London and—"

92

"What was he doing? Where was he staying?"

"He was in a bedsit or something in Earls Court—do you know London?"

"Yes. But was he all right? Has he money?"

"I don't know. He didn't look starving. Look, maybe I'd better explain. I don't really know your brother at all well, and I'm afraid I can't give you any news of him. In fact I came here hoping the family might be able to give *me* some news of him."

"Oh." She looked more serious. "I'm afraid not. Then it isn't true that you are interested in Guarana?"

"Well, I—I'm an artist in fact. I like the Venetian *settecento*—"

"But you do not study Guarana?"

"No, I admit that was an excuse." She wasn't exactly browbeating me, but her direct, rather grave questions nonetheless made me feel a little embarrassed.

Then she said, "I think one would have to be very dull to study Guarana," and a smile alighted on her face for a second and I felt pardoned. She had a most illuminating smile; it reminded me, in its effect, of the tremulous sunlight on the ceiling in the palazzo, giving life and light to what had seemed still and sober—though this was probably the *prosecco* on the ceiling of my brain talking.

She said, "Why do you want to know about Toni?"

"Well, really I want to find him."

"Why?"

"It's very complicated. But I think he might know something about a painting that interests me."

She looked definitely troubled. "Not Guarana."

"No."

"But why do you come here? Isn't he in London?"

"I think he's come back to Venice."

"But he mustn't," she said, "he mustn't." And now she was almost agitated.

"Why not?"

"It is dangerous for him. Oh, surely he knows the danger."

"How is it dangerous?"

"You have heard of these murders, no?"

"Yes." I felt a sinking feeling. "So your brother's involved too?"

"You don't know then—you don't know who is he?"

"No. I don't know anything." I was beginning to feel this was almost literally true.

"Then you don't know why my mother was—was hard with you."

"No." I didn't like to suggest that it was probably because she was just hard.

"You must understand her. She has suffered much. Toni has been in prison. For five, six years. He was co-involved with terrorism."

"Ah," I said.

"You know the 1970s were a terrible period in Italy, *gli anni di piombo*, the years of lead, we call them. And my brother Toni was at university then and, well, he was co-involved in various bad things. But he was not bad really—not really. He made some bad choices. And he never killed anybody. Never. I am younger than him and I was too young then to know well what he was doing. But my mother did not want him at home when he left prison. So he went away, to England I think. And my father followed my mother. That is, he was agreed with her. So for a long time we hear nothing from Toni. I think he was lonely."

"I see. And he was a *pentito*?"

"Yes. And he was really *pentito*. He *really* renounced his past, but *really*. He didn't do it only to reduce his prison sentence."

"I see. He helped the police then, did he?"

"He had to. He had to do what he could to stop the violence, no? Or his *pentitismo* would be nothing but words. And that meant of course he had to give information. It wasn't an easy decision."

Though perhaps the thought of a few years off his sentence had helped, I said to myself. But I certainly wasn't going to condemn him for that. And anyway he was paying for it now.

"But why do you think he is coming back to Venice?" she asked.

"It's a bit complicated," I said.

"Never mind, go on." Her dark eyes stayed steadily on me.

I said, "He told me about a painting he wanted to sell and I got the impression the painting was here in Venice."

"He told you? When? You said you don't really know him."

"That's the point. He only got talking to me at this party because he thought he'd never meet me again. At least that's my guess. He met me at a private view in an art gallery and heard that I was an artist. So he wondered if I could give him advice about how to sell this painting." I thought it best to simplify things a little.

"And did you advise him?"

"Well, no. I was a little suspicious actually. I mean, I know the laws about the sale of works of art across borders."

"So why didn't you go to the police?" She had a disconcerting knack of going straight to the point.

"I suppose because I didn't know enough. And perhaps because I liked his looks." Maybe this last was even true. He hadn't struck me as an out-and-out rogue, just a rather helpless one.

"Yes," she said thoughtfully, "people generally like him. That has saved him perhaps more than once. And what was the work of art?"

"A Cima da Conegliano."

"*La Madonna del cigno*," she said. She wasn't asking.

"That's right. How do you know? Or rather, how does he come to have it?"

"In the 1970s he and his—his companions—stole three works of art from little churches in the Veneto. This was to help finance the group that he belonged to. They tried to obtain a—a *riscatto*?"

"Ransom."

"Yes, a ransom. But nobody wanted to pay. So nothing

95

more was heard. When Toni was arrested, they asked him what had happened to the paintings and he said he didn't know but he thought they had been destructed. He was sorry but he wasn't responsible."

"I see," I said, trying not to wince too noticeably as I thought of destructed paintings. "So maybe he was wrong and they were hidden away."

"You mean maybe he was lying and he had hidden them away." Her eyes were as unwavering as ever.

"Well, it looks like that, doesn't it?"

She was silent for a second and then she said, "I suppose so."

"And where would he have kept them hidden?" I asked.

"I don't know."

"Not in your palazzo?"

"Are you joking?"

"Well, it just struck me as a big place. Lots of room."

"Well, I can assure you they're not there." This was made as a statement of unarguable fact.

After a pause I said, "Er, how can you be so sure?"

She smiled. "I know the whole building very well. You see I have a shop—"

"A shop?"

"Yes. A boutique, near the Fenice Theater. And when I first opened it, I hadn't told my parents anything. It seemed best to—to wait. To let them see it as something accomplished, if you understand me. This meant that when I was getting ready to open it, there were many things I had to store in our house—in all the little corners—the attic and places like that. I tell you that there couldn't be even one painting hidden anywhere that I don't know about."

"I see. What about the other Palazzo Sambon? Does that belong to the family?"

"Yes," she said. "You don't know about—" She stopped.

"What?"

"No, of course. You don't know anything."

Well, there was no need to rub it in. "Well, I, er—"

96

"I mean, you don't know about Toni's arrest, do you?"

"No."

"When they realized he was—he was co-involved, he disappeared. They arrested some companions but he escaped. They thought he was perhaps out of the city, but in the end they found he was living secretly in the old palazzo. I think he was waiting for—for things to calm down so that he could leave the city without problems."

"Presumably they searched the building after they'd arrested him."

"Oh, yes. I think they found some guns or something. But nothing else. Nothing. It is completely empty now. It's since the 1950s that nobody lives there, you know. We would like to restore it but we have not the money." She looked at her watch. "They will ask themselves where am I. I should return for lunch."

"Yes, of course. Thanks for talking to me. So you haven't heard anything from Toni, I can conclude?"

"No."

"Who might have? Do you know anybody he might have gone to? Anybody he was close to?"

"We always thought we were close," she said. There was an awkward pause while I thought of and rejected various consoling remarks, and then she went on, "It's difficult to realize how little you know someone who has always lived with you. So perhaps he was close to his—to his *compagni*." She used the Italian word this time, with a note of contempt or rejection. The English equivalent would be "comrades." "And now—now, I think he must be very lonely."

"So nobody at all? Nobody at work—at the university?" I remembered that thesis he had claimed to be working on.

She smiled, but not the earlier transforming smile. A rather sad smile, bitter almost. "There was his great friend, his great *compagno*, Giulio Padoan. Now probably his great enemy."

"No one who was completely uninvolved in the whole business?"

She thought. "I can only think of two friends, two colleagues who are now teaching at the university in Rome." She mentioned two names and I made a mental but not very serious note of them.

I said, "Colleagues? He *worked* at the university?"

She looked puzzled. "Yes. Why, what did you think?"

"Oh, he mentioned research. I thought he was just studying."

"No. He taught also. In the department of Scottish literature. And I think he taught well."

"Good." She was obviously on his side, if things could be put in such crude terms.

She said, "Well, I must go now." She rose and took her purse out. I said, "No, no, it's on me," and she said, "Next time."

I said, "Okay," glad she was thinking of there being a next time. As we came out into the sunlight again I said, "Those people who were killed—"

"Yes?" Her voice was flat, toneless.

"Sorry, but they were connected with Toni? I mean, did he know them?"

"I think so. That is why he *must* stay away. Someone is—is taking revenge. If you find him, please tell him he must leave, he must go away again." She was standing close, looking straight up at me with such appeal in her eyes that I felt sure anybody looking would take me for a bounder deserting my pregnant girlfriend. And yet she was in fact the reverse of helpless: even her pleading was done decisively.

"Yes, of course," I said.

"And do you still think not to go to the police?"

"Yes," I said.

Again that *prosecco* smile. "Thank you. You are right. Trust how Toni looks because deep down he is not bad." She put her hand out and shook mine firmly. "And I think it would kill my mother."

Privately I thought not even a ton of Guarana frescoes falling on her head would do that. But I nodded. "I'll keep in touch."

98

"Yes. But perhaps not through my house. Come to my shop." She took a card from her pocket and gave it to me. It bore the simple name Francesca and had an address, phone number, and a tiny map showing the easiest route from St. Mark's and from the nearest vaporetto stop. "I am usually there in shop hours."

"Okay. Oh, one last question. Does the name Zennaro mean anything to you? Did Toni have any friends called that?"

She frowned. "I don't know. It is a common name but I—I can't think of anyone. Why?"

"Oh, I just heard this name. Apparently he's a painter."

"Toni wasn't very interested in painting really. But if I think of any Zennaro, I will inform you."

"Thanks. I'll drop by at your shop."

"And please inform me if you hear of Toni. Remember he *is* worth saving. You saw that when you met him, no?"

"Well, I—"

"And one must trust such instincts. It is thus that I trusted you. You *look* honest."

"Thank you."

"Because, after all, you could have been from the terrorists, looking for Toni to—to take revenge. But I decided, no. Good-bye again." One last smile, slightly sad, which even so put the sunshine to shame, and then she walked briskly away, her hands in her coat pockets for warmth.

8

ABOUT half an hour later I was in a small square in Cannaregio not far from the Ghetto. A large Renaissance palazzo dominated one side of the square. It was flanked on its left by a rather despondent-looking pensione and on its right by a narrow alleyway that led toward a canal. The square was quiet, with just a cat sunning itself by the wellhead and keeping an eye on things.

Palazzo Sambon was a beautiful but rather hopeless sight. It had arched windows on the *piano nobile,* while those at either side were rectangular, with colored marble disks above them to complete the harmony; a low balustrade with hourglass marble pillars ran the length of the central room. These details were noted by Lorenzetti. What he didn't mention was the way the pillars of the arches were chipped and blackened at the top, the marble was cracked, the windows either walled up or shuttered, and the whole place looked as if only indecision kept it from slithering in on itself as a rubble heap, like the campanile of San Marco in 1902.

The bottom windows at the front were not only shuttered but had bars across them. I walked down the side alley, still holding my Lorenzetti so as to look like a lost tourist. There were a couple of windows along here too, but again with bars. I reached the end of the alley, where the canal lay oilily still on a seaweedy step. There were boats moored to limpet-shaggy poles prow to bow all down the canal, so that it would be possible, if I so chose, to make my way along the waterfront of the palazzo. But I looked at the buildings opposite and decided that that might be rather too public a performance. And anyway the waterfront windows weren't likely to be any less shuttered or barred than the others.

I turned back down the alley. As I passed the window nearer the canal I gave one of the bars an experimental tug. It jerked away from the wall at the bottom with a powdery shower of rust: it was eaten through. Very little vigor was needed to accomplish similar results with the two adjoining bars. They came so easily I wondered whether I was the first to try it. They were now just dangling. I pushed at the shutter beyond and it opened with just a little scraping reluctance. Then, feeling a little unnerved by the noise, I pulled the shutter back and pushed the bars back into position. I set off quickly down the alley. Maybe I'd come back later with a torch and look around.

As I came out of the alley into the square I saw pigeons descending from the rooftops. A little old woman had come out of the pensione next to Palazzo Sambon and was throwing bread onto the ground. The cat by the well watched the busily bobbing birds with disdain: presumably he'd had experience of how hopeless it was to try to catch them unawares. Sea gulls flapped and shrieked above the pigeons, looking three times as beautiful and making three times as much noise, but not actually getting any of the bread. I saw the woman stare at me and I did my puzzled-tourist bit, studying my Lorenzetti and looking curiously at the buildings. Then, with a final shake of my head I picked my way through the squabbling gray hubbub and approached her. "*Buongiorno,*" I said.

She nodded. "*Buongiorno.*"

"Could you tell me, is this Palazzo Sambon?"

"Yes."

"I'm from the BBC. In England, you know." It had worked once, so why not again? "We're thinking of making a film about empty buildings in Venice and we're looking for ones with some kind of story behind them."

"Well, I don't mind, so long as you make it clear it's nothing to do with our pensione."

"Sorry, I don't—".

"We've always been very respectable. We take only the best people—not just anyone. No rucksacks, I've always said. And my husband agrees. And no southerners."

"I see. Do you remember—"

"When we took the place over, there were people who said it sounded like bad luck, a pensione next to a terrorist hideout, but I said, well, even if he was a terrorist remember he was a count's son. And we've always got on very well with the family." She threw another piece of bread out, with a gesture of aristocratic largess. Another low brawl broke out among the beneficiaries.

"I see. Do you often see them?"

"Well, not *often*. They've come once or twice with people thinking of buying the palazzo. The *comune*, for an infant school. The university." I got the idea that she didn't see much difference between the place being used as a university department or a terrorist hideout. "But these people talk talk talk, but they never buy. It's always the same in Venice. And meanwhile the buildings rot."

"Yes, I'm sure. But has the building been empty ever since they arrested this terrorist? Never been used for anything?"

"Never. Completely empty."

"Do you remember the arrest?"

"Oh, yes. Everyone in Cannaregio must remember it. We were living just nearby then. Policemen everywhere. And all with machine guns. And lights and megaphones." Not a nice memory, it seemed; well, probably a lot of the policemen had been southerners.

102

"And the terrorist surrendered?"

"Well, there was no shooting."

"I see. Are there any other stories attached to the palazzo?" I wasn't worried about the possibility of my inquisitiveness making her suspicious; she clearly welcomed any chance to talk.

"Nothing I can think of. Though sometimes we have heard noises in the palazzo."

"What? When?"

"At night. A few weeks back actually."

"What sort of noises?"

"Just like people walking around. Didn't think much of it. Could have been tramps or drug addicts." She added quickly, "Not that we get much of that sort of thing around here, you know. Mind you make that clear."

"Me? Oh, yes, of course." I'd momentarily forgotten my role. She hadn't. Despite her concern for her hotel's reputation she was obviously as intoxicated with the idea of herself appearing on the magic screen as the old man the previous night had been. "Did you tell the police?"

"No. No point. Nothing there to steal. Completely empty in there, as I said. Just rats. Rats the size of cats, I shouldn't be surprised."

My next call, after a lunch of oily snacks at an *osteria*, was the university. I made my way to Ca' Foscari, the university's main building, a magnificent Gothic palazzo on the Grand Canal. The land entrance took me through a courtyard decorated with political murals; they could only have been about ten years old, but they already looked as dated as Victorian *Punch* cartoons. A not very convincing attempt had been made to grow rosebushes over them. Young men and women in stylish clothes stood in front of these faded mementos, smoking and chatting in the bright cold air; another race, apparently, from the angry perpetrators of the murals.

I asked at the porter's lodge for the department of Scottish literature and was directed up to the first floor. I made my way up the marble staircase, reflecting on the fact that no matter what architectural marvels universities may occupy, they all look the same on the inside: doors with numbers, peeling walls, overcrammed notice boards, people hanging around with lost-hope looks. Italian ones perhaps have more forlorn queues than most. I've never found out what it is they're always queuing for.

At the end of a dark corridor I reached a gray door with a notice: *"Dipartimento di Letteratura Scozzese."* I knocked.

"Ah, finalmente," a voice called out. *"Avanti."*

Rather puzzled at the warmth of this welcome, I opened the door. At first glance there seemed to be no one in the room—just big glass-fronted bookcases reaching to the ceiling and tables covered with books and papers and magazines. Then in the far corner I saw a small bearded man, about my age, at the top of a ladder: he was reaching out at an impossible angle to a shelf by the side of the ladder. "Just in time," he said. "I'm stuck."

"Ah." I crossed the room.

"I thought of letting go of the ladder and hanging on the shelf, but then I thought it might break and I wouldn't know what to tell the librarians. Could you just move the ladder a little?"

I did so and with a sigh of relief he climbed down. I looked around the room as he descended: there weren't any stags' heads on the wall, or tartan rugs, just one photograph of the Walter Scott monument in Princes Street hanging askew on the end of a bookcase.

"I thought I might have to stay up there all day," he said. "Thank you." He looked back up. "And I still haven't got the book."

"Shall I get it?"

"Well, do you mind? I feel just a little bit strained."

"How long had you been up there?"

"Well, only ten minutes or so, but it was the angle. . . ." He went to a chair and sat down. He was quick and nervous in his movements, like some small animal of the bush: this similarity was heightened by his big dark eyes, which looked out of his face with an apparently permanent expression of alarm. But he was a creature of the bush who didn't much like climbing, it seemed.

"What was the book?" I asked.

"Oh, don't bother," he said suddenly. "I don't want it. I just wanted to check a quotation for an article I'm writing, but since no one'll read the article anyway. . . . I mean: 'Surrey's Indebtedness to Gavin Douglas.' " He gave this title in well-accented English. "Would you read it?"

"Er, well, since I've never heard of—"

"Never mind. The important thing is to publish it, with lots of footnotes and a few words like 'extra-diegetic' and 'analeptical anachronies,' and sorry this is most rude, can I help you?" It took me a few seconds to realize that these last words were a question addressed to me, as there had been no pause to mark a new sentence, nor any change in the nervous babble of his delivery. He wrapped a strand of beard around his finger as he looked up at me.

"Oh, er, well, I was wanting to ask about an ex-member of the department."

"Really. Who?"

"Antonio Sambon."

"Oh, yes?" He unwound his forefinger and started on his middle finger. "Er, why—if you don't mind my asking?" His big eyes stayed on me for half a second, then jumped away to cover when mine met his.

"Well, it's kind of complicated."

"Ah. Oh. Well, I suppose it's not my business." He started gathering papers together on his desk—in quick scrabbling motions, like a bush animal digging a hidey-hole in the sand.

"I'd just like to get in touch with him," I said.

"I see, I see. It could be difficult, you know. Er, you know Toni's history, do you?"

"Yes."

"Poor Toni," he said.

"Well, yes."

"Well, poor—" He paused, then said with a quick smile, "Poor Italy."

"Er, yes," I said again. "You wouldn't have any idea where he might be now?"

"Well, I—look, I don't want to be rude, but—um—why *are* you looking for him?" As if to distance himself from the question he asked it in English: nervous, jumpy English, with, I was interested to note, no trace of Scottish in the accent.

I replied in English. "I met him in London and—well, I lent him some money." I'd thought this tale out before I came: my first idea had been to say that I owed him money, but then I thought that a selfish story would be more convincing than an altruistic one; the story did perhaps cast an extra slur on Toni's character—that of the debt shirker—but his character was probably about as slurred as my speech had been at the private view the other night, so that one more could hardly make any difference.

"A lot of money?" he said.

"Well, no, not so very much. I mean I'm not wanting to make a fuss, but I thought that as I was in Venice, I'd try and look him up and remind him about it. I'm sure he just forgot."

"Yes, yes. So he was in need of money."

"I suppose so," I said.

"Poor Toni. When did you lend him this money?"

"He was in London—last week."

"So you needed the money back pretty fast." We were both speaking English now, and I noted that despite his jerky delivery he spoke idiomatically.

"Well, I only thought I was lending it for the evening."

"And you came to Italy for it?"

"No, no. I was coming anyway. I suppose Toni knew that."

"Ah, I see, I see." He flashed another smile. "So he's in Venice, is he?"

"Yes, I think so. But I don't know where he's staying. He doesn't seem to be with his family."

"Really? I thought all had been forgiven, if not forgotten, there."

"Well, not from what I saw of his mother. So anyway, you have no idea of where he could be."

He threw his hands apart in a gesture of ignorance. "I haven't seen him for at least five years, you know."

"And you don't know of any friends he might be with?"

"Toni's friends . . . they're mostly in jail now. And not so friendly now, I think, either. A terrible period, you know."

"Yes. Do you think it's over then?"

"Ah—these things." He threw his hands forward—a gesture of disgust this time. "Sick people, you know." Then he looked hard and sharp at me again. "You aren't looking for Toni for this reason?"

"What do you mean?"

"I—nothing. Look, I'm sorry, I know nothing about Toni at all now."

Something in the way he said this made me ask, "But at the time you did know him, didn't you?"

"At the time? The years of lead and all that?" He shook his head, but not in denial. "I knew him—and—and some of his companions. And now to tell the truth I have no desire to remember these things. Do you understand?"

"Yes." It was the snub direct. Well, fair enough perhaps. There was just something suddenly extra-nervous and evasive in his attitude that made me reluctant to leave at once. I pressed another question. "You've never heard of a painter called Zennaro, have you?"

"No. Why?"

"Well, Toni apparently knows him."

"Oh, yes? Well, I'm sure he didn't get to know him for his work."

"Really? Do you mean Toni wasn't interested in painting?" I was remembering Francesca's words.

"Yes. He once asked me if the Impressionists came before or after the Cubists. And he only asked because of a reference in a book he was reading, not because he wanted to know—I mean in the sense of add to his knowledge." As he recalled these things about Toni's character his attitude of wariness seemed to evaporate a little.

I felt I had to encourage this. "So he had no real interest in art? But he was a university teacher—in an arts subject."

"Toni kept to strict limits. He studied his subject, the

107

popular ballad, and nothing else. The same applied to his politics, I suppose."

"I see."

"But maybe he's completely different now. You could tell me." And again he suddenly confronted me with a sharp look.

"Well, I hardly got to know him. But I did meet him in an art gallery."

"Did you? My God." He jumped up and went over to a rather grotesque object at the end of a desk in a corner of the room: a ceramic shepherd boy clinging to a crooked staff that supported a lamp and frilly lampshade. "Toni was always complaining there wasn't enough light in here, and nothing ever got done, so one day he walked in with that. We thought it might have been a joke at first, but then we realized that for him, well, it was art." He switched the light on, and the shepherd boy's expression could be seen in all its painted pouting petulance. "I suppose we could have thrown it out, but we've got used to it by now."

I picked it up with some curiosity; I'd always wondered who bought these things, which are on sale all over Venice; they're kind of heavy as souvenirs. Underneath it was a tiny adhesive that read: *"Busetto. Antiquariato, Oggetti d'arte."* I put it down and switched it off. "I see. But he did help steal a Cima da Conegliano and a Vivarini."

"I believe so. But I'm sure not for himself. Look, I really must be getting on with this article. All those people dying to know about Gavin Douglas's influence on Surrey, you know . . ."

"Yes, of course. Sorry if I've held you up and thanks for your help."

He moved over to the ladder. "You know you may not be the only one looking for him, don't you?"

"Well, I—er, really?"

"But I hope you are. Toni was a bit of a fool and obstinate too, but he deserves some peace now, I think."

"Sure. I've no intention of disturbing it. You're sure you wouldn't like me to get that book?"

"No, no. This is a challenge I have to face myself. Good-bye."

"Good-bye." I left him gripping the ladder and staring up at the heights with an expression of grim determination. As I left the university I wondered whether I oughtn't to mention his possible predicament to the porters, but then thought they'd be bound to discover him when they locked up for the night.

I went out in search of Zennaro. It was the only path I could think of following. I started going around the galleries in and near St. Mark's Square, asking if anybody had ever heard of him. The name rang no bells—or at least none that chimed in accordance with what I knew of my Zennaro. I was offered a Zennaro who did sculptures in stainless steel, a Zennaro who lived near Belluno and drew mountain scenery, and a Zennaro who'd died in the 1950s and had painted religious works of sickly piety. But no Venice-as-colored-geometry-problems Zennaro. I traipsed on, trying galleries farther from St. Mark's, crossing the Accademia Bridge and going toward the Salute, and then back again to the area around Campo Santo Stefano.

After the fifteenth or sixteenth head-shaking answer (in a gallery near San Samuele exhibiting sexual organs sculpted in polystyrene) I decided I needed a break from contemporary Venetian art, and went to a bar.

I sipped a glass of *prosecco* and looked out of the window, letting the bubbles get to my brain and pop there brightly. I found myself staring at the name above a shop some way down the street, and I wondered why I was staring at it. It read: BUSETTO. ANTIQUARIATO, OGGETTI D'ARTE. What was so interesting about it? I was hardly going to find Zennaro's paintings there.

Then I remembered: Toni's pastoral lamp stand had come from there. I finished my drink and strolled down to Busetto's Antique Shop to see what other horrors he sold.

Through the window I could see a dim clutter of curlicued rococo shapes: there were chairs with arms of gilt wood that unfurled into floral fantasies, there were mirrors with trumpeting-cupid surrounds, there were vases with curling, looping handles, chandeliers with twirling, drooping pendants, and all around hulked statues in gilt wood of Negro torch-bearing contortionists.

And on a side wall there were two paintings by Zennaro: unmistakable—and unmissable. They were the only straight lines in the whole shop.

I entered and the door gave an old-fashioned tinkle. A man emerged from an inner room: he could only have been in his forties but he stooped noticeably—as if he were adapting himself to the whorled and coiled objects that formed his environment. His head pushed out toward me from his dusty gray jacket, like a tortoise's from its shell, and he peered at me over half-moon glasses. He seemed to be trying to assume the respectable if delicate appearance of someone three times his age—again like many of the objects in the room, I suspected.

"Signor Busetto?" I said.

"*Buongiorno,* signore." His voice had an infinite weariness in it. I wondered whether I should ask him to sit down. None of the chairs, however, looked very suitable.

"Tell me," I said, "how much is that painting there?" I pointed to the larger Zennaro, about thirty inches by twenty. St. Mark's and the Rialto Bridge superimposed and painted in green and purple with the help of a compass and a slide rule.

"Ah yes, quite amusing, isn't it? Two hundred thousand lire."

"Oh. That's a little too much. And the other one?" Towers and domes and gondolas, in orange and pink and blue.

"One hundred and fifty thousand."

"I see. They're rather unexpected things to find here, aren't they?"

"Well, yes, I suppose they are. But something unexpected in a shop isn't a bad thing, I always think. It livens the place up a little. Ha-ha." The laugh was about as lively as the creak of a disused door.

"Er, yes. Zennaro, aren't they?"

"That's right." His head, which had been moving in its heavy reptile fashion from me to the painting and back again, stayed on me, and I could see curiosity in the lizard eyes. Although there were little labels on the paintings, presumably with the artist's name, I was standing too far away to read them.

"I saw some of his works in London," I explained. "I liked them and thought I'd look out for them when I came here. Is this the only place he exhibits?"

"I'm not sure. I hardly know him."

"Oh. A pity. I'd rather like to get in touch with him." And then, since no gallerist can expect to welcome a customer's interest in the artist's home address, I added, "I'm a journalist." Not the BBC this time, I thought. "I work for the *Evening Standard* in London. We're doing a few articles on contemporary art in Italy. All aspects, from commercial and tourist art to the more serious schools." I thought it better not to try to pretend that I considered Zennaro the age's Michelangelo.

"I see. Well, I'm sorry. I'm afraid I have no idea of his address. I don't even know if he lives in Venice."

"How do you happen to be exhibiting him?"

"I can't—I can't remember. I think it was through a friend of mine. Now, are you interested in the works or not?" He was suddenly almost brusque—and what was more surprising, brisk. He obviously wanted me out.

"Well, possibly. I'd have to think about it." I walked over to one of the other more-to-be-expected paintings on the wall: an eighteenth-century landscape with cows and dancing peasants— or peasants and dancing cows; it was too obscured by dirt to see properly. "Zuccarelli?" I asked.

"School of." His head followed me around without his body moving. But he was no doubt doing an internal dance of fury at my refusal to leave the shop.

"Amusing. Through friends, you say?" I turned from the painting. "Antonio Sambon, by any chance?"

"What?" This really caught him. His head jerked back as if

he were going to close up shell. Then he said, recovering his slow dignity, "I have met Signor Sambon, and of course I know the contessa, but I would hardly say we were friends."

"Oh. So you wouldn't have any idea where he is now?"

"No. Why should I? Look, are you interested in buying anything? If not, I do have other things to do than answer your gossipy questions."

"I see. I'm sorry if that's what they seemed to you." I tried to think of a good *battuta* (wisecrack) to go out on—one that would leave him cringing amid the curlicues in nervous apprehension—but none came to mind in Italian. Nor in English. *"Arrivederla,"* I said, and left.

I went back to the bar for another glass of wine and another think about what to do next. I could hardly keep watch on the shop all afternoon in the hope of seeing Toni drop by. And if I just went away, I would be leaving the only lead I'd had all afternoon.

I gazed out at the darkening street, watching the last rays of sunlight on the chimney pots, which rose from the tiles like miniature parodies of Tuscan hill towns, all tottering towers and spires and domes and chalice tops. I thought of such towns: Cortona and San Gimignano and Montepulciano—and I found myself thinking how simple and soothing it would be just to slip off and forget the whole business. I could take the next train down to Tuscany: that would be the perfect way to put the whole thing right out of my mind. Leave the slippery city and go pottering around steep stony streets, quaffing Chianti and studying frescoes, undisturbed by even the thought of terrorists or Cima da Conegliano.

The lights went off in Busetto's shop. I looked at my watch. Just gone five. There were at least two hours until the usual closing time of shops. Busetto came out in an overcoat and pulled a metal shutter down over his window. He came down the alley in the direction of the bar. I turned away from the window and retreated a little. Out of the corner of my eye I saw him walk on past.

112

I paid the barman and stepped out into the street. I could see Busetto in the distance walking in the direction of Campo Santo Stefano. I started following him.

He was walking a little faster than one might have expected from seeing his shop manners. I stayed about twenty yards behind and he didn't look back.

We came out into Campo Santo Stefano near the church and he crossed diagonally right. This was good. It meant he was probably going to take the alley that leads to St. Mark's, which is always fairly busy; even if he were to look around, he probably wouldn't spot me. Of course it also meant I would have to be careful that I didn't lose sight of him.

When he reached Campo Santa Maria del Giglio, he turned sharp right. I knew the alley led only to a vaporetto stop on the Grand Canal—not a very busy stop either. There was no way I could follow him down there without being spotted.

I thought a little. He was presumably going to take the boat in the direction of St. Mark's and the Lido; if he had been intending to go the other way, he would have walked from his shop to the Sant'Angelo stop. I started walking briskly—and then, a few seconds later, running—toward San Marco, the next vaporetto stop on this side of the Grand Canal.

Of course it was possible he was going to call on somebody in that alley and not get a boat at all: it was also possible he was going to get the boat but then get off it at the Salute, the very next stop on the other side of the canal. But you can't cover every eventuality.

I came running down the Calle Vallaresso with my heart pounding and my lungs bursting. I reached the San Marco vaporetto stop and saw the boat on the other side of the Grand Canal, just pulling away from the Salute stop. It was of course impossible at that distance and in that light to see if he had got off there or not. I sat down, letting my breath get back to normal, and I listened in to a group of Americans who had obviously just come out of Harry's Bar.

"I tell you it was Jackie Collins."

113

"You reckon? And the guy with the beard?"

"I didn't see no beard."

"Oh, come on. The guy who ordered the Michelangelo or whatever it was."

"Titian."

"Yeah, that. Wasn't he someone? I mean, you know, someone?"

"Like Hemingway, you mean?"

"No, I don't mean. I know Hemingway's dead."

"No, I mean someone like him. Like a writer."

"Like Jackie Collins."

The boat pulled in, bumping up against the *pontile.* I moved with the rest of the people toward the chain barrier and peered into the dimly lit cabin. All I could see was that the boat was pretty full; the windows were too steamed up for any faces to be recognizable. I stepped on last and stayed outside, standing to the right of the driver's cabin. There were no more stops on this side of the boat, so there was no reason why Busetto should see me here, and I would be able to peer around at the descending passengers fairly unobtrusively. The only risk was that of frostbite, I thought as the wind slashed into me, and I pulled my head down into my coat and shoved my hands deeper into my pockets; if Busetto wasn't on the boat, or if he was going all the way to the Lido, by the time we got there I'd probably have coiled and congealed enough to be a suitable object for his shop.

We reached San Zaccaria and he didn't get off; I hadn't expected him to. One could just as quickly walk that far from Santo Stefano. We pulled out again toward the Arsenale. I watched the last daubs of a departed sunset over the Salute and tried to gather warmth from the sight, without much success. I thought how suitable it was that Venice's public transport system should be named after a sneeze (ACTV, pronounced Atcheeteevoo). Busetto was not among those getting off at the Arsenale either.

The boat moved off again. It suddenly struck me that despite the cold, for the first time that day I was really feeling

114

good. It was extremely satisfactory to be doing something. I knew in fact why I had refused at any point during the frustrations of the afternoon to take the easy option of saying "Screw Cima" and going off to Tuscany: because I knew I needed that sense of purpose. Without it despair would ambush me. Wherever I might be, in whatever Romanesque church of whatever picturesque hill town, the blues would come at me like a cosh-swinging mugger. Worse than the blues—the blank blank blanks of emptiness.

The boat moved in toward the Giardini stop, and as the engine noise changed a great crowd of people came out of the cabin. I saw Busetto among them, clutching the door with one saurian hand. The boat pulled in, I heard the iron swish of the railing being pulled back, and the crowd moved forward. Busetto was one of the last, which made things a little difficult for me. I waited till the descending passengers were all off and people had started to board, and then with a few *scusis* and *permessos* on my part and a few dialectal grunts on the boarders' part, I elbowed my way off.

Like most of those who'd got off, Busetto was going down the tree-lined avenue that leads toward Via Garibaldi. Half of these people then took the first right; Busetto kept walking. I kept following. At the end of the avenue he passed to the right of the monument to Garibaldi; with fiendish deviousness I passed to the left. The little pond around the monument was covered in icy scum, and the lion at Garibaldi's feet looked decidedly peaky under his mossy mane.

Via Garibaldi was as animated as ever, with people casually shopping and busily chatting. Busetto walked to the right, past the groups of men standing around outside the bars that seem to outnumber the shops at this, the market end of the street. Beyond the market Via Garibaldi effectively ends in a canal, with just two narrow *fondamente* continuing along either side of it. Busetto was now walking along the right-hand *fondamenta* and had just skirted the shoppers crowding around the vegetable barge moored at its very beginning. I hung back a little as the crowd thinned out here, and I saw Busetto in the distance turn and cross the second of the bridges over the canal. At this point I ran: it would be easy to lose him in this area, which I didn't know at all well.

The bridge led into a narrowing alley on the other side of the canal and I reached it just in time to see Busetto take the first turning to the right. When I got to that turning, however, Busetto had disappeared.

This alley ended in the wide canal of San Pietro and there were no turnings off it, so he had obviously entered one of the houses. I walked back down, looking at the names on the doors. There was no Zennaro, which proved nothing. There were some bell pushes without names at all. I noted the name of the alley. Calle S. Ana (dialect spelling for S. Anna).

It would be impossible to keep a discreet watch anywhere in the alley, so I walked back over the bridge to the *fondamenta* and then proceeded up alongside the canal, looking at the houses opposite, in the vague hope of seeing Busetto in one of the windows. It was a long row of three-story houses rising straight (well, not so very straight) out of the water, with simple square windows at regular intervals and high square chimneys at irregular intervals. Occasional patches of flaking paintwork mottled the crumbling brickwork. Most of the windows had shutters across them. The houses ended where the *fondamenta* ended, in the canal of San Pietro.

A long wooden bridge supported on piles crossed to the island of San Pietro. I walked over it and then turned left. Just past a small group of houses was the entrance to a boat yard from which there was a perfect view across the canal of Calle S. Anna. A man was working by the light of a gas lamp shaving a plank of wood. I wondered if in this light I could convincingly say that I'd like to sketch the view.

Then at that moment I saw the light of a door opening onto the Calle opposite. Busetto's unmistakable shape came out. The door looked about halfway down the Calle.

The man shaving the wood looked up at me and I moved away. I walked back to the wooden bridge feeling that I was probably getting somewhere, but first of all I had to get something warm inside me. I remembered noticing a *pasticceria* at the beginning of the *fondamenta*: I could do a little prebreakfast research there.

As I put my hand to the glass door of the *pasticceria* I saw Busetto on the other side of it doing the same. I stepped back and let him out.

He came out onto the pavement and stared at me, obviously taken aback. Then he said, "You've followed me."

"Why should I do that?" I said. Then: "My hotel's just down at the end of the road."

"Don't lie to me." It must have been the shock of the moment that was making him speak out so wildly. I was *definitely* onto something, I thought exultantly, and glanced across at the houses on the Rio S. Anna.

He caught this glance and said, "I order you to stop bothering me." He almost drew up straight.

"I tell you, I happen to be staying in a hotel here. And anyway what have you been doing that you're so scared of my knowing about?" This was the sentence I intended to say at any rate, but I got a bit confused toward the end and I think what I actually said was something like, "What have you done that comes so much fear to you about me?"

He said in a low venomous tone, "Leave me alone." Low, because one or two interested faces were staring at us from the *pasticceria* by now. Venomous, because that's the way he was.

"Yes, all right, but—" And foolishly I put a restraining hand on his arm as he made to leave me.

Only guilty panic can explain his next action: I didn't think about such explanations, mind you, until quite some time later. I was rather too concerned with the immediate result.

He turned and shoved hard at my shoulder. We happened to be standing next to a flight of steps down to the water, and thus at the one point on the *fondamenta* where there was no railing. I just had enough sense to break off my yelp and close my mouth before I hit the water.

For a second or two nothing went through my brain but

shock: physical and mental shock fused into one sudden explosion. Then the physical shock resolved itself into the intensest feeling of cold I'd ever experienced: I was lucidly aware that death was not an impossibility. My clothes all seemed to be on death's side, particularly my shoes, and I felt myself to be in battle against them as I struggled up to the surface. My shoulder bag was obviously out to throttle me; I was either too panic-stricken to think of shaking it off, or too farseeing to want to lose it (it had my wallet); it stayed around me. My head emerged and heard a great babble of voices—but about a mile away. I couldn't take in a single word. Helping hands stretched down toward me.

I came up the steps, but I have no clear recollection how—whether pulled or pushed or carried. I know there was one moment when my foot slipped on the seaweed and I almost fell back, tugging a helper in with me. But some seconds later I was on the *fondamenta,* a dripping shaking huddle. The various obscenities that came to mind couldn't get beyond their first consonants at my lips. I saw that three or four people were restraining Busetto, who was looking extremely flustered. I began to take in some of the voices. Everyone was talking in dialect of course, but I got the gist. Those closest were talking about the police, somebody near the bar was talking about an ambulance, and those at the periphery were explaining to those who had just arrived, and these then formed a new explanatory periphery for the next arrivals.

Nobody seemed quite sure what to do about me, until a barrel-bellied man ushered me into the *pasticceria.*

" *'Na graspa,*" my escort shouted.

"*No, un brandy,*" countermanded another.

"*Un whisky,*" a third voice put in.

Now was the time for me to put in a truly English request for a cup of tea. I didn't. I took the first glass that came and swigged it gratefully. It was brandy, I think. Miles down in the frozen depths of my body something improved: the tip of a tiny stalactite thawed. I might not die then, I thought for the first time.

118

"Shall we call an ambulance?" an unshaven man asked me in dialect.

I somehow got out the word *no*. I drank some more of the brandy. Another stalactite snapped off. "I'm at the hotel down there," I said, pointing. Every movement seemed to paste the icy clothes further into my skin. I was still shivering and it seemed unlikely I'd ever stop.

"But did you swallow the water?" someone else asked—and pointed at his open mouth with his finger in explanation. They'd gathered I was a foreigner.

I didn't have the energy to worry about this aspect of my condition as well, even though I knew this was one of the most putrid canals in the city: walking past it earlier, I'd noticed how the mere rocking movement of the vegetable boat wafted up a wave of sewage stink.

There was a bustle at the door and Busetto was pushed and pulled in. A man with an authoritarian-looking gray mustache was flapping an identity card: "I've got his name."

"*Bravo, Gianni.*" The barrel-bellied man told me, "Gianni was a *vigile.*"

I was glad about the past tense. Then I heard somebody say, "Let's call the police."

I spoke up. "It was an accident." The last thing I wanted was to end up in front of the police, on whichever side of the law.

"I saw it," protested a young man with an earring. "*Wham!*" and he mimed the shoving action.

"I slipped," Busetto said.

This was greeted with general contempt.

"Shall we slip this time—with *you* at the edge?" The young man with the earring again. There was an approving murmur at this, and Busetto looked around desperately.

I'd have happily done the shoving myself if it hadn't been for that tiny still-reasoning part of my brain that told me that the less public trouble there was, the better. And an act of clemency might give me a hold over him later. It was a pity I was in no condition to use the advantage now. I said, "Let him go. It was an accident."

119

The man with the earring obviously didn't like the idea of the affair ending so tamely. This might be all the excitement that Saturday night was going to offer Via Garibaldi. "And if you die?" he said to me. "You'll want him arrested, won't you?"

"I won't die if I just get back to my hotel and change clothes. Quickly. Forget about him." I don't know how much of this chattering rush of words they understood, but my desire to get away was clear enough.

"Poisoning. That water would kill anyone."

General agreement was expressed with this. The barrel-bellied man had his remedy. "Another grappa. That kills the germs."

I took it gratefully enough. It was in fact brandy again. Busetto said, "Excuse me," and pushed his way out; I think he wanted to look coldly dignified, but his stoop was against him; he unmistakably slunk. A mutter of contempt mixed with disappointment followed him. This was one *pasticceria* he wasn't likely to return to.

I put my hand toward my shoulder bag to get my soaked wallet out, but the barman put up an imperious hand. "Thank you," I said. It was a kind gesture on his part—though possibly he just didn't want sewage-soaked bank notes in his till.

I left the bar with everybody continuing to inform me about the various diseases I could have caught. The *ex-vigile* seemed to be on the point of asking me for my identity card, but then obviously thought better of it. Four or five people accompanied me down Via Garibaldi, vying with each other in the telling of horrific hospital cases they'd heard of. When we got to the hotel, the man with the earring came in with me, reassuring me that if I did die they'd make my assailant pay for it. He started to explain things to the man at the desk, whom he obviously knew, and I went upstairs with my key, leaving them to it. "What, Rio Sant'Ana?" I heard the deskman say. *"Che schifo!"* How horrible.

120

9

A LITTLE under an hour later I left my room and locked its door with great care: my money was hanging over the edge of the chair near the radiator to dry, together with a notebook and—though I had little hope for them—my Lorenzetti guide and the Henry James volume. My skin shone a scrubbed pink and my hair ponged of apple shampoo. I was wearing just about all my spare clothes and was at last feeling fairly confident that I wasn't going to die—of cold at any rate. I'd have preferred to stay crouched next to the radiator for another nine or ten hours, but that would have meant spending Sunday without a coat, so I had eventually forced myself to my feet. I had about forty minutes to get my coat before the shops closed, but probably only about five before my bloodstream stopped moving. And I had to find a laundry too. All my sodden clothes were in my rucksack, which I was now holding adangle from my left hand: I didn't want them pasted onto my back again.

I burbled an apology to the lady I found busily cleaning the staircase which I'd turned into a momentary extension of the Rio Sant'Anna, and she waved a cheerily dismissive hand at me, as if nothing else was to be expected on a Saturday night.

I bought an anorak and a scarf in a shop that accepted credit cards, almost opposite the hotel. They weren't elegant, but they weren't expensive either—and they weren't, I thought, *noticeably* inelegant; I wanted nothing about me that was noticeable. The shopkeeper of course knew all about the "accident." Well, he had probably seen my dripping and escorted arrival at the hotel.

The laundry was off Via Garibaldi, but the man there expressed no surprise as he took the clammy bundle from me. I wondered how many bridges the news had crossed by now. He made out a little ticket for me while the clothes dripped and oozed over his counter. It struck me that they looked exactly how I'd felt a few nights before in London.

Things had changed since then, I told myself as I walked down the Riva degli Schiavoni, huddled in my cuddly new anorak and scarf: I'd got my Purpose and I was getting places. Tomorrow I was going to go to that house in Calle Sant'Anna (I couldn't do anything like that this evening—not down that end of Via Garibaldi) and I was going to catch whoever was there doing whatever he was doing. So long as the aliens in my guts didn't get to me first.

I realized I was near the Church of San Giovanni in Bragora. There was a chance it might still be open.

It was. I entered and breathed its familiar charm. Nothing spiky or even soaring about its Gothic architecture: a "homely" Gothic almost. There was just one very small old lady cleaning a candle stand. I went up to the high altar and dropped a coin into the light machine: the Cima Baptism of Christ appeared out of the gloom, in all its glowing serenity: the calm figures, the calm landscape with its hills and towers, the river, the boat, and the ducks, Melinda's ducks. I stood and gazed. The afternoon's frustrations and worries dropped from me. And then the years. I was twenty and had never been to prison.

"Hello," said a quiet voice behind me.

I heard the voice but didn't leap. It almost seemed inevitable. I turned around and saw Lucy. "Hello," I said.

"I just knew it had to be you," she said. "No one else looks at paintings so restlessly."

"Was I? I was feeling really calm."

"You kept moving up and down, to and fro."

"Oh, yes." I suppose I had been. That's how I look at paintings—big ones anyway. I had felt still, however. Warm even.

The light on the painting went out.

"Let me," she said. She walked past me and dropped a coin in. She hadn't changed, I thought. The same long straight hair, the same long gray coat even. And when she turned around, the same natural laughing eyes and lips.

She looked at me too. "You look well," she said.

"So do you."

We were both standing about a yard from each other and we were both, I think, aware of the fact that we'd made no move to kiss—not even a formal cheek peck. She turned to the painting. "I suppose if I was going to bump into you, here was as likely a place as any."

"Yes?" And I'd been thinking, of all the churches in all the towns in all the world, she walks into mine.

"I remember your talk on Cima," she said.

"Don't tell me: the ducks."

"What? Oh, yes, aren't they lovely. No, I was remembering how you finished, 'Cima is the tops.' I've only realized now it's a bilingual pun."

"Yes, well, trust me for a smart-ass punch line."

"At the time we all thought it really strange. Everyone went round saying, Tintoretto is the tops, *vino rosso* is the tops. . . ."

"Oh, yes?"

"Well, maybe it wasn't so hilarious."

We were both silent for a few seconds and the light machine ticked away. The old lady bustled up from the back, jangling what I guessed were keys. We didn't turn around, both determined to get our money's worth of aesthetic delight.

"And you said Bellini copied it."

123

"Took some suggestions from it," I said. "Not a bad testimonial for Cima."

"*Si chiude.*" The little old lady was standing be- hind us.

"*Ci scusi, signora,*" Lucy said, "*andiamo via subito.*"

"You've learned Italian," I said as we left the church.

"A little," she said.

We stood outside as the lady pushed the door to behind us and turned a hefty-sounding key. Neither of us made a move across the square. I wanted to finish the conversation, rush off, and drink away my confusion. Surely now was the time to bring out my "Miss Althwaites" and formal bows? But no, that would be too ridiculous.

"Isn't this stupid?" Lucy said suddenly. "Both of us making careful comments about Renaissance art."

"What do you propose as a topic?" I said.

She gazed at me, her eyes widening and a laugh getting ready to explode. "What do I what? Oh, Martin." The laugh came—one quick burst. She squeezed my arm affectionately. "You don't change."

"You really don't think so?"

She looked at me hard. "Maybe that was silly of me. I expect you have."

"Yes, I expect so."

"Come and have a drink," she said. "Then we can find out just how much we've each changed."

"Well, I—I really ought—"

"Oh, come on, Martin."

This wasn't going on at all as I'd imagined (let alone planned) our first meeting would—or should—go. Where was my cold dignity? And where her lowered eyes and shuffling feet?" "A quick one," I said.

"Let's go to that place by the Arsenale. You remember?"

"Yes." Maybe she wanted me to start humming *Celeste Aïda*. We'd had our first long chat there—about the third week of the course—which was then followed by that entwined walk up to Verdi's bust. We'd talked about Renaissance art on that occasion too—as a starter.

124

"The *tramezzini* are still great," she said. She started out of the square with that quick impulsiveness I remembered so well. I followed. "So what were you doing in the church?" I asked, keeping things safely on the Renaissance.

"I'd just come to check a hotel booking at La Residenza for one of the lecturers, and then I remembered the painting—remembered your lecture in fact."

"Thank you. Down to its last punch line."

"Yes. We never saw the church together, did we?"

"No."

"The painting I most remember seeing with you is the Bellini in San Zaccaria. You said it was the one painting that could make you feel you wanted to go off and join a monastery or something. But that only seemed to last until you stopped looking at it."

"I don't think I'm likely to feel that anymore."

"Had enough of cells." She said this straight out, turning and smiling at me.

"Yes."

We walked down the narrow bending alley toward the Arsenale in sudden silence. As we crossed the bridge she said, "Was it awful?"

"Yes."

"I'm sorry."

We reached the bar on the corner of the Campo dell'Arsenale. I'd been through the square the previous evening but in too much of a huddled fuddle to take much notice. So now I greeted the place properly; I looked up at the massive Renaissance entrance with its posturing statues (some overkeen souvenir hunter has pinched Neptune's trident), and I said hello again to the four stone lions on guard outside; they range in size and dignity from the regal to the merely cuddly—the last one could be a baa-lamb. Up above the gateway St. Mark's lion shows off his wings and snarls sneeringly down at his earthbound colleagues.

"Why do all the guidebooks say his book's closed?" Lucy said, pointing to the winged lion. "The *all* do—all of them."

"Do they? Well, I suppose guidebooks copy guidebooks."

"Well, they only have to look at the thing," she said.

"It's quicker to copy," I said.

She looked at me as if about to say something—perhaps along the lines of "Is that your philosophy in life?" But she held back. That irritated me—probably more than the quip would have done.

We entered the bar and Lucy said, "*Ciao,* Livio" to the barman, who answered "*Ciao,* Lucy" back. I don't suppose she'd been there more often than I had. She turned and said, "Let me guess—a *prosecco?*"

"No. Tea. *Un tè con latte,*" I said to Livio.

"You have changed," she said. She ordered a spritz with Aperol for herself.

"I need something warm," I said. "I've not gone dry." I thought of the afternoon's main event and added, "Far from it."

There was a pause as our drinks were prepared and handed over to us. Then she said, "Derek told me you were here."

"Who?"

"Derek—Derek Robin."

"Oh, yes. He told me you were too."

"Ah."

"I hadn't known you would be," I said.

"No. I suppose—" She stopped. "How are the paintings? We heard from Professor Perkins you were having an exhibition."

"It's off. I had a fire."

"A what?"

"You know, flames, heat, *whoosh.*" I made quick quivering skyward motions with my hands. "They all got destroyed."

"Oh, my God." She put her drink down and stared at me, her eyes widening. "How on earth—"

"Forget about it. That's what I'm here trying to do."

"The Derek Robin course instead of the Foreign Legion."

"Well, Venice. Derek Robin only for the pennies." I changed the subject. "I'm going to have a sandwich."

"Me too," she said. "They're still the best in Venice."

We both took a *tramezzino* with tuna fish and mayonnaise: the bar's own homemade mayonnaise, I'd once been told. Like all good *tramezzini,* it swelled plumply with the filling, and two or three paper napkins were needed to hold it.

"So what are you doing here?" I said after a few oozing mouthfuls.

"Do you mean, 'Why haven't you got a serious job?' "

"I just asked."

"I'm sorry. I do get that, particularly from my brother."

Her brother was an accountant. We'd never got on. I went on quickly: "Tell me then, how did you end up with this job?"

"I hope I haven't quite 'ended up,' " she said. "It's temporary, until, until—"

"They offer you a starring role in *East Enders.*"

She smiled. "I've chucked in the whole acting idea. To the great relief of one and all at home."

"Why? I mean why have you chucked it in?"

"I was obviously no good."

"Oh." I'd been expecting the usual actor's spiel about the impossibility of breaking through the theater Mafia. I wondered if I was supposed to slap her on the back and say, "Oh, come on, Lucy. . . ." Instead I said, "So you got in touch with Mr. Robin."

"Well, you probably remember that my father knows him. That was how I came to be doing the course in the first place."

"Of course. Daddy."

She looked at me sharply, then said simply, "Yes, Daddy."

"Give him my regards—or perhaps better not."

"I will, if you want me to."

"Well, it might be kinder to let him think I'm still safely locked away."

"Oh, Martin. Why do you—" She broke off with a shrug.

I looked at my watch. "Look, sorry, Lucy. I really ought to be going. I'm—I'm meeting someone."

"Oh."

"So I can't stand here nattering on about the past. After all, it's kind of pointless, don't you agree?"

She said, "Well, if that's how you feel, I suppose it is."

127

"It is."

"Okay. Let me pay here."

I was about to refuse when I suddenly realized I had nothing but my credit card. I didn't want to say that next time it would be on me, so instead said, "As it happens I'm cashless, so thanks. I'll pay you back on Monday."

"Don't be so stupid."

"It's tidier that way," I said.

She said, "You bloody try paying me back. Just try it."

She was laughing, but I knew she was angry too. I knew all her moods still. I said, "See you on Monday then, 'bye."

I left abruptly and walked to the wooden bridge across the Rio dell'Arsenale. This was of course opposite to the way I'd been going earlier, but it was also opposite to the way she'd probably be going. I felt more or less pleased with the way I'd brought the conversation to a close. More or less.

I found a restaurant in between Via Garibaldi and Sant'-Isepo, where I had an excellent fish dinner and read a Dick Francis novel. And in between chapters I thought about Cima da Conegliano, *not* about Lucy. And if I did think about Lucy again, it was only because a tune on the radio reminded me of *Celeste Aïda*. I put her straight out of my mind again.

10

NEXT morning I discovered that my bank notes, though crinkled, were satisfactorily crisp to the touch. Lorenzetti and Henry James, however, remained thick wudges of indivisible sludge. It looked as if Dick Francis would have to be my daytime reading as well.

I dressed and went downstairs. The cleaning lady was at work on the stairs again. She looked up at me and said, "How do you feel?"

"Fine, fine, thanks."

Well, I'd soon test this out with my breakfast. The first question to decide was whether I should go to that *pasticceria* and try its cakes. But I soon decided I preferred to consume cream cakes in the comfort of anonymity, so I found a place in the Salizzada dei Greci where I had a rum baba, a meringue, and a cappuccino, and nobody looked twice at me. There were no protests from the murky depths either—just from my conscience.

I made my way back to Via Garibaldi, noting the little old ladies and the bambini straggling into the churches on the way. (These two groups seem to make up ninety percent of Venice's church-going population.) Would Lucy be going to one of them? I wondered. She was a Catholic (which was the main reason I'd never told my mother about her), though it had sometimes struck me that this was only to be noticed on a Sunday morning. And in England, where RCs can very rarely get much of an aesthetic kick from their church-going, it was hardly to be noticed at all.

I walked the full length of Via Garibaldi: very small children, dressed for the most part like Michelin men with their stubby arms almost at right angles to their bodies, were being paraded up and down by mothers in fur coats and fathers in greatcoats and scarves; how many fur coats, I wondered, would one see in, say, Stepney, which must be the social equivalent of this end of Venice?

I walked quickly past the *pasticceria* and nobody noticed me. I crossed the bridge and turned right into Calle Sant'Anna. The door I thought was the one Busetto had come out of had two bell pushes, and the top one had no name. That seemed my most likely bet. I was about to push it when I thought better. After all, whoever was there could simply refuse to let me into the building.

I looked at the lower bell: Trevisan. I took out my Dick Francis novel and wrote Piero Trevisan on the first page. I pushed the bell.

"*Chi xè 'o?*" a tinny female voice came from the grille.

"I found a book in the street, signora, with the name Trevisan." I exaggerated my English accent as I said this in careful Italian.

"*Cossa?*"

"I found a book."

"*No go capìo gnente.*" I haven't understood anything. The door clicked open and I entered. The staircase was of stone and dimly lit. I started up it, and heard a door opening above and a woman repeating, "*Chi xè 'o?*"

She turned out to be extremely old and frail looking, and she spoke only dialect. I explained that I'd seen this book on a bench in the public gardens and because it was English had picked it up to have a look at it. I'd seen the name inside and someone had told me that a Trevisan lived here. She looked at the book and shook her head, "No, that's not mine."

"I see. I'm sorry, signora."

"I only read *Famiglia Cristiana* and *Il Gazzettino*."

"Then I'll try somewhere else."

"My niece lent me a book once. I didn't like it."

"I'm sorry."

"She knew I liked flowers, so she gave me this one: the something of the Rose—but not a flower in it. All about monks. And not good ones either. Try next door. The son's at the university."

I said I would and went on down. I opened the front door and closed it noisily—staying on the inside, however. I then tiptoed to the storeroom next to the staircase: it was a window-less room, full of bottles, old mattresses, cardboard boxes, and other junk. I waited there for a minute or so. My eyes got used to the gloom and I noticed a bottle of rat poison in a corner. I felt my back go goose-pimply—and then my legs. Perhaps the beasts were hanging around to see if my legs really were fixtures and suitable for gnawing. I hastily shifted them.

A radio was turned on above, presumably by the old lady. A recent hit of Duran Duran was being broadcast. I had intended to wait a couple of minutes until my brief intrusion had been completely forgotten about, but this cover was perfect. I started up the stairs, without even needing to tiptoe. As I passed the flat I heard the old lady humming along with Simon Le Bon.

I reached the top floor. There was a tiny landing that contained a broken chair and a bulging plastic bag full of rubbish, tied with string. Next to the flat's front door there was a bell push made of transparent plastic that contained a piece of paper. A name was written there in faded ballpoint ink; in that dim light I had to screw up my eyes to read it.

Zennaro.

I felt a brief glow of triumph. I pressed the bell. There was no answer. I tried again. Still no answer.

So now what—shove off and come back later with another Dick Francis?

Downstairs the song ended and a disc jockey's voice babbled away the usual hearty inanities and then gave way to a hearty folk song. I looked at the edge of the door. I could see the latch. I got my credit card out of my crinkled wallet. This was something I'd tried on my own (Jim's) front door in London after locking myself out and in the end I'd had to break a window. (I'd shared a cell with a housebreaker for six months to little profit.) Should I? It would be my first definitely illicit action. But I felt so certain that I was onto something that I knew I couldn't just turn around and go back downstairs.

I slid the card gently into the crack, fumbled, fiddled, twisted, prodded—and I was just remembering that if I snapped it I'd go without dinner that night when I felt the catch easing back.

Gently, gently, gently . . . The door suddenly swung open under the pressure of my left hand. I listened again down the stairs but could only hear the steady rhythmical thump of the radio. I stepped into the flat. I was in a tiny entrance-hall-cum-dining-room and there were three doors off it, all open. The one straight ahead was a tiny kitchen, and the nearest one on the left was a bedroom and the farthest an artist's studio. I entered that. A rather stale but sweet smell hung over the room, swathing the more familiar smells of paint and turpentine. I didn't bother to stand and sniff in the hope of identifying it, but started looking around at once. There was a window onto the canal with dirty net curtains that presumably filtered the midday sun. The other room with north-facing windows, the bedroom, was obviously too dark for painting in.

The immediate impression was of general confusion; the second impression was of total confusion. But very colorful confusion. Zennaro's paintings, which were arranged all around the walls, assaulted the eyes: a raging battle of violent greens and oranges and purples and yellows and reds; the geometrical neatness of the pictures' lines and designs merely looked ironic amid the room's kaleidoscopic chaos. The floor was protected by old newspapers, which were now so paint-flecked they could be mistaken for works in progress. The walls were not so protected and were also flecked; the blobs of color took one's attention off the patches of damp and the peeling plaster. There were dirty rags tossed everywhere, even on the two rush chairs in the corners of the room; next to the easel, in the center of the room, was a table, again covered with old newspapers. It held all the painting equipment: tubes of paint, mostly squeezed from the middle, and some with the paint oozing out onto the newsprint, as if eager to join in the room's general riot. But the brushes, I noticed, had been washed properly and placed upright in jars and old tomato tins to dry.

I looked at the work on the easel; another geometrician's opium dream of the city, in red and green and white this time. Most patriotic. The lines were all sketched in in pencil, and it was half-painted. He was using a good-quality canvas, and the paints and brushes were Winsor and Newton—not cheap. It was just the work that was, I thought. Then I added to myself, And listen to who's talking.

In a corner of the room was an alcove, over which hung, by way of curtain, an old sheet. Everything here, it struck me, was makeshift and inexpensive except for the tools of the trade. Which was quite possibly as it had been in the young Titian's studio. I pulled back the sheet. There were more paintings stacked here. I pulled one out. It was not by Zennaro. It showed St. Jerome beating his breast in the desert, with the lion from the *Wizard of Oz* for company. Seventeenth-century Veneto, I guessed. Rather too old and rather too good to be the sort of thing one bought in junk shops just in order to have a cheap canvas.

I pulled out the next one. A Sassoferrato-style Madonna, hands joined, sweet sad Bambi eyes: not my favorite kind of painting, but again not junk—from the financial point of view. There followed a Nativity of the Bassano school: shepherds kneeling around the manger, their dirty soles toward the spectator, and the whole scene lit by the Bambino's own glow and an apparently exploding star above. Then another saint in the wilderness, apparently by the same painter as the St. Jerome: this time a naked Mary Magdalen, with Valkyrien tresses in blush-sparing dishevelment; the rocks and trees and even the curious birds were the same. Only the lion was missing.

These paintings were all unframed, and mostly in need of a good clean—or even a transfer of canvas. A charitable explanation of their presence here was that Zennaro made a sideline of cleaning or restoring old paintings. That was not the explanation that came to my mind. I went back to the work on the easel and had a hard look at the canvas. The back of the canvas was obviously new, but squinting at the side, I could now see that this was a mere fresh skin added to the real painting surface as a disguise. The join was cleverly concealed with extra-thick paint, but the double layer couldn't be hidden completely. He was clearly painting over an older work—just as I had heard of painters doing when they couldn't afford new canvases—but they would presumably be using, say, nineteenth-century rubbish, cheap family portraits or sentimental landscapes that nobody in the world would ever miss.

I'd found out what I'd come to find out and there was no point in hanging around waiting to be collared as a trespasser. I just needed some proof. Could I take one of Zennaro's smaller paintings with me? But there was no knowing that every one of his works hid another, rather better one. I screwed my eyes up protectively and had a look at the paintings along the wall—or more accurately at the canvases. Most of them seemed quite genuinely modern, but there were three clearly old ones, which hadn't even had a fresh skin attached to their backs as disguise. They were, however, all too large to be taken out unobtrusively. My hands were damp as they handled the works, I realized, and my shirt was beginning to feel as it had done the night before, only warmer. I had better go before the thumping of my heart made itself heard over the thumping of the radio. I went over to the table for one last look, to see what he was using to protect the painting beneath.

134

"*Ma!*" A sudden exclamation from the doorway, and I did that Russian leap of mine—backward, away from the door.

There was a man of my age, or a little younger, standing there, his face writhing with a mixture of emotions I wasn't cool enough to analyze just then. His right hand dived inside his shabby overcoat and produced an object, which with a sharp flick suddenly doubled in length; the new half glinted as he agitated it. I looked at the table to my side and couldn't see anything of any obvious use as a weapon, so stepped back around the easel. He came forward slowly, crouching, holding the knife out before him and waving it menacingly. I was very much afraid, from film memories, that this was the professional knife fighter's stance.

The trouble was that I didn't know what the professional knife victim's stance should be: I could only recall the words of my cellmate apropos of fights in general: "Get 'em before they get you." But how to get him? He was now on the other side of the easel from me, and obviously at the first defensive twitch on my part he would leap. The knife hand alternated dead steadiness with sudden glinting slashes through the air.

Finally I spoke—and my voice came out raucous, which was at least better than trembling. I said in Italian, "If you jump, I'll bring this picture down on you and you'll cut that as well as me." This could be the way to get him.

"Who are you?"

"Put the knife away and I'll tell you."

"Tell me now."

"Put it away."

"Tell me."

This dialogue was getting positively childish: but I was pleased to notice beads of sweat on his forehead and definite agitation in his eyes. He wasn't as coolly professional as his stance suggested. "Look," I said, raising my arms and opening my hands, "I am completely unarmed. Put—"

This had been a bit of a gamble, and as it turned out a rather unfortunate one. At that moment he leaped. I just saw the blade streaking up to my face and I hurled myself backward, crashing

135

against the wall and immediately falling to one side. At least I think that's what happened. I ended up on the floor at any rate. I rolled over as he threw himself down on top of me, and my right hand grabbed hold of a painting and swung it protectively. The blade went through this with a dull ripping sound and I felt him go suddenly rigid with shock; I profited by throwing him off me and again rolling away from him. Judging from his reaction it *was* the way to get him.

I grabbed another painting and pulled myself to my feet, holding it in both white-knuckled hands like a shield. "Okay," I said, "put the knife down."

He got to his feet and tossed the knife onto the table. *"Stronzo,"* he said with calm simplicity. "Who are you?"

"An investigator."

"Investigator for whom? Are you the police?"

I wondered for just two seconds whether I could say yes, and whether there would be any advantage in so doing. But first, he probably wouldn't believe me, and second, even if he did, he obviously wasn't the sort in whom the very word would instill a sort of religious terror.

I was at last able to make a reasonably cool assessment of what sort he was. Well, he was certainly nothing like his sharp-cut strident pictures: *faded* seemed the best word to describe him—like a watercolor left too long in the sun. His coat and the jeans below it were shabby and colorless; his hair was long, but the reverse of luxuriant, weakly straggling around his neck and receding at the top. He was more than unshaven, but one wouldn't have said that he had anything so definite as a beard. The only truly assertive note was a ring in his right ear, and this didn't exactly make him into Errol Flynn. His expression was sullen and watchful; now that I could get a calm look at him I could see that he was obviously no muscle man—but I would keep an eye on the knife all the same. There was no point in forgetting that he did know the correct stance.

After this pause of assessment I said, "Not the police, don't worry."

"So who the hell are you?"

"It needn't matter to you. I just want some information, and if you help me, you won't get into any trouble."

"Look, you broke into my flat, you're the one who could get into trouble."

"It's no use," I said gently. "I've seen what you're up to."

"What do you mean?" As he said this his eyes went straight to the alcove and the paintings I'd taken out of it.

"What you now have to say is, 'I'm restoring them.' And I then say, 'What, like the one under your painting there?'" I pointed to the patriotically colored work on the easel.

He shrugged. "Prove it."

"I could take this work along to be X-rayed. By the Sovrintendenza. Before it gets sent away to London. By Busetto."

He blinked, no more. "And why should I let you take it away?"

"Look, you can see I know the whole traffic. Busetto gives you the paintings to be smuggled out. You paint your pictures on them. And off they go to the Blue Moon Gallery in London, where some clever restorer removes your work and hands over the painting to Osgood. Am I right?"

He shrugged again. "I don't know where they go in London."

"So I'm right. I suppose works by living authors don't need any permission from the Sovrintendenza to leave the country— or just get a quick check. And presumably it's only one or two works in each batch that are actually hiding anything anyway. Of course there's always the risk of an X-ray checkup. What do you do—use a lead-based varnish?"

"Busetto knows someone in the Sovrintendenza." He obviously saw no point in further denials.

So his disguising of the works to be smuggled didn't have to be foolproof—just good enough not to be obvious. "Where do these paintings come from?"

"I don't know. I never ask. Busetto just tells me to come and pick them up at his shop. I go there with my boat. Look, who are you and why should I answer your questions?"

"Don't worry. I'm not concerned with getting you into

trouble. But just remember I could if I wanted. You say you don't know where they come from, but someone somewhere will. How long have you been doing this?"

"About two years. But it's only a sideline to my real work."

Oh God, I thought with a sudden pang: these were the words I had always reassured myself with when doing those "foolish forgeries." I should really be throwing my arm around this man and saying "Comrade." Except . . . except . . . there *was* a difference, though I'd sound a self-righteous prig explaining it: I had never been removing works from circulation. (Just other people's money, prosecuting counsel would riposte quickly here.) *And,* I added to myself unworthily but irrepressibly, my real work was rather better than his. I asked neutrally, "What started you?"

"I did some restoring and framing for Busetto. One thing led to another. He said he'd hang some of my works if I did a few little jobs for him."

"And why did you want them hung in an antique shop?"

"I wanted them hung anywhere. Nobody would take them. And he told me he could get them sold in London too. And he has done. People are really buying them there, you know. I may go there in fact. Here you can't even get a license to exhibit on the Riva degli Schiavoni. And you try doing it without a license. Your brother artists are the first to call for the *vigili.*"

He spoke with quick quiet bitterness, and it struck me that he must be entirely sincere in his vocation. Indeed, in the whole room—and as far as a quick glance had told me, in the whole flat—there was nothing that wasn't related to the job. A Spartan existence, it seemed, dedicated to his art. No concessions to pleasure—unless. . . . And I realized that the smell I'd noticed on entering was hashish. Well, Zennaro probably needed a good deal of consoling. And I found it difficult to believe he could ever get it from looking at his works.

"So you had a rather hard time of it at first," I said.

"Yes. And I'm not exactly living in luxury now."

"But do you mean to say you've never been to London to see how your pictures sell there?"

138

"No. Never had enough time or money."

"So you get paid everything through Busetto?" This was taking artistic dreaminess too far.

Another all-purpose shrug. "Yes. He pays for all the materials and gives me a regular down payment for each picture. I suppose I could check that I'm getting a fair deal. . . ."

I said, "If you're interested, two hundred pounds was the price quoted to me for one of your works in London—about four hundred and fifty thousand lire."

"What?" This had really opened his eyes. "The *stronzo* gives me fifty thousand a picture. And a hundred for the—the other ones."

"Go and get a plane. You may find you don't need to do those other ones anymore."

He was looking at his paintings and obviously making some calculations in his head. I suppose he had fallen into a passive acceptance of drudgery as his natural state. Then he said, "How much do you think they make on those other ones?"

And I'd thought I might be helping him onto the path of honesty. I said rather sourly, "You could go and ask the top man himself. He's coming to Venice today—and he's staying at the Danieli, so that'll give you an idea of the kind of money he's making."

"Look, who are you and how do you know all this?"

"I told you. An investigator. Let's say an art-loving investigator. My advice to you is to go and find out who's buying your pictures and set yourself up again without Busetto. Perhaps even set up somewhere else—do you have to be in Venice?"

Shrug. "That's what I paint."

"Couldn't you equally well paint, I don't know, Mestre?"

He looked at me with surprise. "What—Mestre? Oh, come on. . . ."

So he was just another soppy romantic. I was about to ask if he'd ever tried painting anything else but then took hold of myself; these questions were hardly pertinent to my real quest. "You've never heard of Toni Sambon?"

"Who?"

139

I repeated the name and he automatically shrugged but then said, "Wasn't he some kind of terrorist?"

"Well, he was involved. But you've never had anything to do with him?"

"No. Why should I?"

"Never mind. What about the paintings you've disguised. How much do you know about them?"

"I look at them."

Well, that was something.

He went on: "You know, I have to choose the best way of covering them. How many layers they'll need. I did a course in restoring. About the only useful thing I got from the Accademia."

"So you can tell me if you've ever covered over a Cima da Conegliano."

"No. Nothing that period. It's almost all this seventeenth-or eighteenth-century rubbish."

"Nor an Alvise Vivarini then?"

"No."

"A Palma il Giovane?"

"Hundreds of them, I expect. I don't always know the painters. Most of the time I don't care either."

"Do you mean you don't care who they are or you don't care how you cover them?"

"Oh, I do it properly. I don't know what they're like at the other end, taking it off, but I do my end properly. I suppose there are bound to be accidents sometimes, but I expect they can touch them up."

"Yes, I'm sure." I'd done a lot of touching up in my time: from replacing ships' rigging in Dutch seascapes that had been cleaned too vigorously to resupplying whole landscapes in eighteenth-century portraits. "How do they know which ones to clean off?"

"I always paint a little green circle on them somewhere."

I looked at the one on the easel. In the top left-hand corner there was a green circle. "I see. What's under that one?"

"A portrait of some Venetian nobleman. I don't know who by."

I said, "Why did Busetto call on you yesterday?"

He looked at me sharply, but then obviously decided he wasn't going to ask me how I knew that. He said, "I was supposed to deliver some of these paintings to him tomorrow. He came to tell me to wait a while. I don't know why."

Well, it was nice to know my visit had had some effect on Busetto. It didn't look as if this visit was going to have any effect on Zennaro—any beneficent effect, at any rate. I gazed at him and it crossed my mind that maybe if I hadn't had that freak success in my first few years, I too would still be a drudging attic artist, getting by with occasional forgeries the eventual sales of which I would be careful never to ask about. Then, as I looked at his faded coat, faded jeans, faded hair and beard, I rejected the thought almost with revulsion: no, I might have been an exploited fool as a criminal, but I'd surely never been quite so colorlessly unenterprising with regard to my own works: my success might have been an inflated one, but I'd sweated for it—and made sure I got a fair deal. Whereas poor Zennaro, for all the stridency of his paintings and for all his quickness with a knife, was obviously a born loser.

And then I laughed out loud: I was such a winner of course.

"What are you laughing at?" he said, at once ready to take offense—and to take up the knife too perhaps.

"At myself, don't worry."

"Look, I've had enough now. You'd better get out or there'll be trouble."

This was typically vague and not really very frightening but I thought maybe I should be generous enough to let him finish on an assertive note. "Okay," I said. Then I added, "I would take back those paintings to Busetto. Just tell him you've had enough."

He answered with a shrug. Even his gestures, it struck me, were faded noncommittal versions of what body language usually was in Italy.

"Doesn't it interest you in the slightest to know what happens to those paintings?" I asked.

"No, why should it?" I'd touched him on something he really felt about. "Why should I be bothered if one more crappy seventeenth-century painting gets lost or destroyed? There's too much bloody concern for dead art. What about us living artists? Look at the money that gets spent on museums and restoring old churches and all that while I can't pay the rent."

I walked to the door. Before I'd even reached it he was bending over the picture he'd stabbed. I felt no sudden rush of sympathy: the last thread of fellow feeling had been snapped by his little tirade, while I imagined the Frari church being pulled down to make way for a gallery of his paintings.

At the last moment, before closing the door, I asked, "Did you learn knife fighting at the Accademia too?"

"Military service," he said.

"I see," I said. Of course this didn't explain why he still carried a knife around in one of the most tranquil cities in Italy. Maybe it was just a way to make his criminal status feel big rather than just sordid.

I went down the stairs. Signora Trevisan was now humming to Lucio Dalla. I wondered whether she'd ever find out she was living under an international art smuggler.

11

AS I walked back down Via Garibaldi I felt a new surge of exultation. I was getting closer and closer to that Cima, I felt sure. I didn't need to feel so worried by time limits: I could hold Osgood off by threatening him with what I knew. I reached the end of Via Garibaldi and the view of the city spread out in splendor on the sun-dancing lagoon did its usual spirit-lifting job as well. I almost felt like painting it there and then, to prove my superiority to Zennaro.

Except of course I'd then be up against Carpaccio, Canaletto, Guardi, Turner. . . .

It was a shade hazier today—not quite the knife-edge clarity of the previous day: the Salute looked even lighter and crispier: as if one bite would reduce it to powdery flakes; it made me feel like going for another *pasticcino*. I resisted, however, and instead went over to the newspaper stand and bought a *Gazzettino*.

My holiday spirits evaporated pretty damn quickly once I'd opened up the paper. The front-page news had little effect on me: it was all about trouble in the Middle East and trouble with new tax laws in Italy: another world. I passed straight to the Venice section of the paper. I was crossing the bridge over the Rio dell'Arsenale when I suddenly realized I'd seen my name. It had leaped straight into my brain while my eyes were skimming over the page, and it took me a few seconds to locate where I'd seen it. It was in a brief article at the bottom of the page with the headline:

RISSA IN VIA GARIBALDI
Turista inglese cade in canale

"Brawl in Via Garibaldi. English tourist falls into canal." I read through the article quickly. It gave the facts with reasonable accuracy: it told of my fall and rescue, the aid given by the people on the spot and in the *pasticceria*. It gave my name, age, address (London, England), and hotel. It was presumably from the hotel that they had obtained the information. The article mentioned the fact that many of the onlookers claimed to have seen the man I was arguing with—Michele Busetto, 47—push me in. He had denied doing so deliberately, stating that he had merely slipped. Sig. Phipps himself had upheld this version of the facts. Sig. Phipps had refused any medical attention, merely returning to his hotel for a wash and new clothes, despite the temperature and despite the fact that the canal is one of the most polluted in the city.

How the hell had the *Gazzettino* got to hear about such a minor incident so quickly? Well, I suppose all Via Garibaldi had known, and ten minutes later most of Castello, and half an hour later the news was probably crossing the causeway to Mestre. You don't have to stay very long in Venice to realize that the city, as well as being the ex-bride of the Adriatic, ex-ruler over an empire that linked east and west, ex-center of all maritime traffic, and an architectural and artistic wonder of the world, is a village. Quite possibly the editor of the *Gazzettino* had been in the *pasticceria* himself. Or his wife. Or his next-door neighbor.

I made my way to the next newspaper stand and bought Venice's other paper, *La Nuova Venezia*. I wasn't in that. Its editor must have been in another *pasticceria* yesterday evening. I folded the two papers and put them under my arm and walked on down the Riva pensively. I had lost my anonymity, and all I had gained in exchange was Busetto's home address.

I looked at the other Venetian news. There was an article on the killings in both papers, but neither of them said anything more concrete than that the investigations were proceeding. Giudice Menegazzi had questioned several people suspected of having affiliations with extremist political groups. There was a photograph of him: he looked rather Edward G. Robinson.

By now I was getting closer to St. Mark's and at each bridge I crossed the crowds got thicker; well, on a sunny Sunday like this people flock into Venice from the mainland for a day out; the cold is no deterrent, but rather an excellent opportunity to flaunt fur coats. I suddenly got nervous about all these faces, all of them equipped with eyes—and I couldn't know whose eyes. I found myself yearning for Friday's evening fog, recalling it (quite untruthfully) as a kind of comforting cocoon that had provided a clammy but cozy anonymity.

And then I thought about the hotel: perhaps even now they were setting the booby-trap bomb under my pillow. I turned around and started walking back. I was going to have to move elsewhere.

When I told the young man at the desk that I'd decided to go on to Verona, he raised an eyebrow or two but made no problems. He said he would make out the bill while I got my stuff ready. He turned to my pigeonhole to give me my key and took out an envelope. "This was left for you."

"Oh, yes? Who by?" It bore my name in block capitals and nothing else.

"I don't know. I found it on the desk a moment ago when I came out of the bar."

"I see. Okay, thanks. I'll be down in a minute." I went up the stairs trying not to look too curious. As soon as I'd rounded the first corner I tore the thing open. It was written entirely in block capitals and in Italian. It read:

145

MR. MARTIN PHIPPS. KEEP OUT OF THIS BUSINESS. GO
BACK TO LONDON UNLESS YOU WANT YOUR NOSE TO FINISH
LIKE OTHER PEOPLE'S TONGUES. THIS IS NOT A JOKE.

A FRIEND

In fact I didn't feel like laughing.

I opened my door and it didn't explode. There were no
cobras under the bed either. I threw my things into the
rucksack—still slimy from the previous evening. Henry James
and Lorenzetti I put into the rubbish bin.

I paid the bill with the credit card and apologized for leaving
so abruptly and for any trouble I'd caused the previous evening.
Forty-five minutes later I left my luggage at the station deposit
(noticing that the English translation of *consegna* and *ritiro* was
still the wrong way around: it has been so since my first visit to
the city). This strategy left open the possibility of my sleeping
outside Venice, in Mestre or Padua—or Tuscany. Or in a
couchette on the train back to London.

But this was feeble defeatist thinking again. I left the station
and walked down the Lista di Spagna, with its tacky tourist
shops, all open even though it was Sunday. I had a look again at
Busetto's address according to the *Gazzettino:* Cannaregio followed by a four-figure number. Once again I cursed the Venetian
address system. Cannaregio extends from the station almost to
the Rialto and San Giovanni e Paolo. I looked at the numbers
above the shops: we were in the two hundreds here. It looked as
if I was going to spend another morning traipsing the back
streets of the city.

Well, there are worse ways of spending one's time. I was
glad too that it was Cannaregio, which in some ways is the most
soothing *sestiere*. It isn't so teasingly intricate in its geography as
most of Venice; it has no large bustling squares and offers no
sudden surprises—just occasional views of the lonely northern
lagoon. A good walk around it might calm me down a little.

I found the house about an hour later: it was a tall building
not far from the Church of the Madonna dell'Orto. He didn't

answer his doorbell. After the success of the morning, naturally my immediate instinct was to reach for my credit card, but a few seconds' thought deterred me. For a start there were six bells by the side of the front door, which meant there would be quite a high chance of someone walking by as I fiddled with the card on Busetto's lock; and then Busetto was no mere bum of an artist and would probably have a better lock than Zennaro; and finally I wanted to speak to him, not just rifle through his flat.

So I crossed a bridge over to the Fondamenta della Madonna dell'Orto. The church contains my favorite Cima: the first painting of his I ever saw and one of the greatest. I just had to hope Lucy wouldn't be there, perhaps combining Mass with a Cima crawl.

As I came into the open space in front of the church I saw an old tramp peering at the coat of arms by the side of the door. I recognized him: Professor Perkins, expert on Lorenzo Lotto and worst-dressed art historian in the world. Today he was wearing a coat that had apparently just been taken out of a tumble dryer, and trousers he had borrowed from Charlie Chaplin. He looked at me absently when I greeted him, "Good morning, Professor."

"Ah, er, yes." He had obviously recognized me, but without any enthusiasm. I'd never meant much to him ever since I admitted I hadn't read his article on the correct dating of Lotto's *Annunciation at Jesi.*

"Sight-seeing?" I said.

"Well, I . . ." His face showed intense distaste. "I was hoping to see the Tintoretto *Presentation,* but they're having some service or other."

"Well, it is Sunday," I said.

"Yes, I know. Worst day for seeing anything. Masses and suchlike in every church."

"Yes, thoughtless of them," I said. "Still we can always go in and look at the Cima." The painting is right next to the entrance door, on the very first altar.

"Well, yes," he said, again without any enthusiasm, "but I

particularly wanted to see that Tintoretto. Some American fool in the *Burlington* writing about organ paintings with some theory about musical symbolism. . . ."

He wittered on for a half a minute or so. As usual, he became incomprehensible after the first ten seconds, since he took for granted that you were not only up on all the details of *Burlington Magazine* controversies, but also knew all the little private nicknames that were in current usage among art historians. "So I decided I'd prove quite definitely that it couldn't have been painted with that in mind by going to the original contract for the painting, but then old Foulface came out with some nonsense about the painting not respecting certain stipulations anyway, so I thought I'd better check up on the foreground figures. And I find I can't get close to the thing after walking all the way over here."

"Let's go and look at the Cima anyway," I said. "That's worth any walk." Even a walk across boring old Venice, I decided not to add.

He followed me in again. I was pleased to see the painting was still there despite Busetto living so nearby. I hoped the lock on the church door was better than Zennaro's. Professor Perkins started up sotto voce about the fatuously incorrect identification of the buildings in the background on the part of another American, but I managed to blank out his voice as I gazed. John the Baptist and four saints under a ruined classical portico. A clear wintry light that seemed to come from the window of the church itself, and a sharply painted background of castles and hills. I felt a much-needed sense of calm come over me.

You can't look at a painting like this one and be agitated. After just a few seconds I felt all the tension go out of me. And after a minute I felt as if I'd done a full course of yoga. I was glad Mass was going on; otherwise Professor Perkins would certainly drag me over to see the Tintorettos, and for all my admiration for him (Tintoretto, not the professor) he was what I didn't need just then: his Last Judgment with its swirling turmoil of bodies and skeletons, angels and demons, would not sustain the mood of calm. (It sent Effie Ruskin running out of the church.) And I hadn't felt so good since—well, since the last Cima. The evening before. And this time there was no voice from the past to sound the last trump in my ear.

"Look at that owl," I whispered. "I'd forgotten about him."

"What about it?"

"Well, it's rather—rather nice."

He said yes, without any particular intonation. Then, with a touch more warmth: "There's some cretin of a Frenchman working on bird symbolism in altar paintings, but he's apparently completely ignored my work on the subject. You know I wrote a paper in '76. . . ." I blanked out his voice again. It struck me I couldn't remember him ever saying anything that showed he actually *liked* a painting, not even one by Lorenzo Lotto.

After another minute or so I said, "Well, I think I'll be off."

"Well, I suppose I might as well too. This man sounds as if he could go on for ages." He was referring to the priest who was preaching at that point.

We stepped out into the sunshine again. He said, "Are you lecturing then?"

"Yes."

"Thought you were having an exhibition in London."

"I was." I remembered that he knew Adrian—or Adrian knew him. Adrian knew most people. "But my paintings got burned."

"Ah." He thought this over for one and a half seconds and then said, "Do you know of any good restaurants round this area?"

"What? Oh, well, yes. There's one on the Fondamenta Ormesini."

"Right. That's over there, isn't it?" he said, indicating the bridge.

"Yes."

"Well, see you sometime, I suppose." He didn't ask me if I wanted to go and have lunch with him, and I didn't suggest it.

"Yes," I said, "I think I'll go to Burano for the day."

"What do you want to go there for?"

I gathered there were no *Burlington* controversies about paintings on Burano at the moment. "I don't know—it's picturesque."

He hmmphed and said good-bye. I watched him make his wheezing way over the bridge, and then I set off down the *fondamenta*. I had decided only that very moment that I'd like to go to Burano; a trip across the lagoon seemed like a good way to put things into perspective and stay cool.

I got off the boat at Mazzorbo about fifty minutes later and had lunch at a restaurant there, feeling the peaceful self-satisfaction of a tourist definitely leaving the beaten track. I thought as little about terrorists as possible, and a fair degree about Cima, wondering how I'd feel if I managed to save the painting and it was then put for safekeeping into a museum run by someone like Professor Perkins.

I took the next boat to Torcello. The cold seemed to have deterred most people from this usually popular Sunday-afternoon jaunt. A few young couples got off at Torcello with me, the girls huddled in their furs or sheepskins, the boys holding tiny transistors to their ears to hear the football commentary. The more reverent ones turned the radios off before entering the basilica. From there I crossed to Burano, which was as picturesque as ever: it's always a surprise when you hear the inhabitants speaking to each other instead of bursting into operatic choruses (well, in fact, their dialect is more singsong than in Venice).

My last visit to the island had been with Lucy, I now remembered. As I walked down one of the *fondamente* gazing at the brightly colored houses, flaunting their washing, I remembered how she had asked me, "Why don't you paint it?" We had just passed an English husband and wife, each doing an earnest little watercolor view. I had said, "It's too picturesque," and she had accused me of visual inverted snobbery. "I can see you love it as much as I do," she had said. "This painting of rubbish dumps and gasworks is a gimmick really, isn't it? Just a way of proving you're not an amateur dauber like them." She had been joking, but I think she realized how this thrust got home. She had at once changed the subject, suggesting a drink.

The sun was going down now and the air was getting chilly. I made my way back to the *imbarcadero*. On the way I stopped at a souvenir shop and bought a couple of lace doilies for my mother, trying to remember whether I'd bought her the same thing last time. I felt my usual twinge of guilt at not being able to think of anything else, apart from cream cakes, that she might like.

At the same shop I found a postcard with a reproduction of a nineteenth-century painting of the place. I bought it, thinking I could send it to Adrian, telling him this was the style I had now decided to model myself on, and thus throw him into a complete panic. I then continued on my way, refusing to think anymore about painting. It was a bit depressing when I couldn't even look at a picturesque view without starting to worry about my ability to make a picture of it. I repeated to myself that I was at least better than Zennaro.

And it was a bit worrying when I could only cheer myself up by comparing myself with hacks and daubers.

I hoped the sunset wasn't going to be too beautiful.

When I got out at the Fondamente Nuove it was already dark—and damn cold again. I made my way to Busetto's house. Still no answer. I went on to the station and picked up my luggage. I walked out of the station, pushing my way through the home-going crowds. I crossed the bridge over the Grand Canal and walked along to a hotel on the Rio Marin. I suppose I went there as a sort of act of reparation to Henry James, as I remembered someone telling me that *The Aspern Papers* (which I had dropped *splatch* into the rubbish bin) is set in a palazzo on that canal. I took a single room without a bath—and without breakfast of course: there was a whole new area of *pasticcerie* to explore here. From a nearby bar I rang the Danieli Hotel and was told that yes, il Signor Osgood had arrived, would I like to speak to him? No, thank you, I would call around in person.

Twenty-five minutes later I got out of the number two at the

151

San Zaccaria stop—directly in front of the Danieli Hotel. I was a bit disconcerted to see that there were two carabinieri on guard outside the place, holding machine guns. But I recalled that this was in fact quite a common sight, merely meaning that some politician or other was staying the night; the carabinieri were there to let the terrorists know where to attack.

I looked at my watch. It had just gone seven. This was about the time you might expect to see Osgood sauntering out for dinner, or at least a predinner drink, if he hadn't already. Well, I could lose nothing by hanging around for a few minutes to see.

I took a seat inside the _imbarcadero_, from where I could see the hotel's revolving doors. The minutes passed and each one seemed to drag the temperature down a few degrees. I looked at the sea gulls bobbing on the water's surface and took the same meager consolation that I had done with regard to Zennaro as an artist, that at least I wasn't them.

I was on the point of leaving when I saw Osgood squeezing through the revolving doors. He was dressed in a cream-colored suit and an open shirt, with no coat; the only concession he made to the weather was a rather flamboyant red scarf: either he was one of those who think that Italy never gets cold, or winter was just never long enough for the cold to get through to his bones. He set off down the Riva in the direction of the Piazzetta.

Well, no great skill was going to be needed in following him. I could probably do it by putting my ear to the ground—and he wasn't likely to slip away down a back alley since he wouldn't fit down most of them.

He walked on past the Piazzetta and along the front by the little Public Gardens, where the souvenir stalls were all closed up for the night. At the end he turned right and I could just see him turning again into the first doorway. Well, of course: Harry's Bar. Where else could he order a Bellini in a loud voice without the Sovrintendenza at once jumping on him?

So now the usual question: what next? Was I going to beard him here? If not, what had I followed him for? This place at least had the advantage of not being guarded by carabinieri. But- ... but ... it was quite possible that he was merely going to take an aperitif here and go on to dinner somewhere else. If he was in fact going to dine in the restaurant part upstairs, there was no hurry for me to barge in. And if he was going to move on, I might as well see where, and who with. After all, there was no knowing: he might have fixed up to meet Toni Sambon on his very first evening.

I walked about halfway down the Calle Vallaresso and there stopped and looked idly at the theater posters and at the shop windows. At that distance and in that light, I thought, I would be unrecognizable—though he of course would not be. I was looking in at a shirt shop and thinking that the prices weren't too bad when I suddenly recognized, in the window's reflection, the shape of somebody passing behind me: Busetto. I didn't move and he walked on past, obviously without having recognized me. I saw him enter Harry's Bar.

Harry's Bar certainly didn't seem his natural ambience; it must have been Osgood who'd decided on the rendezvous.

So now what? I definitely knew enough to make my side of any conversation we might have interesting enough to them, so maybe it was time to move in. But there was still the chance that they were going to move on somewhere else—to another rendezvous with Toni.

I decided to wait a little longer, firmly squashing the little voice that accused me of merely wanting to put off an embarrassing scene. I went back to my study of the shirts—and realized I'd missed a zero in my reading of the prices. I moved on to the next shop, my hands plunged deeper into my coat, and my feet beginning to curl up protectively in my insufficient shoes.

I suddenly asked myself whether I would recognize Toni if he should enter the alley from the far end, from the vaporetto stop. I started staring hard at the people as they turned into the alley—and then I saw a girl turn and put her hand rather hesitantly to the door of Harry's bar. She glanced down the alley in my direction but obviously didn't recognize me. She entered. I had recognized her, however: there was no mistaking that small upright figure. It was Toni's sister, Francesca.

I felt suddenly as if I'd been clobbered. Could this just be a pure coincidence? Well, of course it could—but the chances were that it wasn't. So just what could she be up to? Was she acting as a go-between for her brother? If so, all that anxiety she had shown for him must have been faked. I remembered those steady but troubled dark eyes: I couldn't believe it. That would make her a better actress than Meryl Streep. She had really been worried for him, I was sure.

I walked down toward the bar, but kept on past it, merely glancing at the irritating frosted glass panes of the door. I entered the *imbarcadero*. I'd get the story off her the next day. I was too cold and too tired to think properly—and too hungry. I'd catch a boat now and go and eat in a restaurant I knew over by San Giacomo dell'Orio, not too far from my hotel. I could take the number two and get off at Piazzale Roma. I sat down on one of the benches in the shelter and rubbed my hands together in a sort of self-exhortatory gesture. The nagging doubt remained that maybe I was walking away just when things were going to get interesting—but that doubt would probably remain even if I tagged along after them until they went to bed. I put it out of my mind.

A few minutes later the number two, the *diretto,* pulled up to the *imbarcadero,* and I, along with three or four of the other people waiting, boarded. At the last moment, just as the sailor was about to flick the rope free someone came running up the gangway of the *imbarcadero* and the sailor called to the driver, " '*Speta,* Gianni," and pulled back the railing. I was on the way down the steps into the comparative warmth of the cabin and so didn't see who it was until the boat had moved out into the Grand Canal and I had taken the one free seat next to the door. Through the dirty pane I saw her come down the steps, and put her hand to the door, but then she obviously thought better of it and moved to the small sheltered alcove next to the steps. She didn't sit down, which would have meant facing into the cabin, but stood with her back to us and her face to the window. I saw her hand go up to her face in a gesture of weariness or even despair, which she managed to turn into a mere retidying of her long dark hair.

I got up and stepped out of the cabin. I said, "Francesca—" and she turned around, startled. Her face was dead white in the gloom and her eyes desperate. I noticed her "petiteness" in this fragile state: there was something of the frightened child in the way she looked up at me.

"Oh," she said. *"Sei tu."*

"Yes." I couldn't pretend not to notice her state, so said, "What's the matter?" I spoke in Italian—I suppose because she had done so and also because it seemed gentler.

"Nothing, nothing." She had flicked her head so that her hair came down protectively over her eyes.

"Sorry, I don't want to—to interfere. . . ." I couldn't think of a word for *intrude.* "But is it anything to do with Osgood?"

Her face swung up in surprise, so that I saw her eyes darkly glimmering with tears. "What do you know about—" She stopped and switched to her slightly stilted English. "Please, it is nothing. Leave me."

"It's obviously not nothing. Please, I'd like to help."

"At the moment I am confused, that's all."

"Is it to do with Toni?"

"Yes, but—oh, I can't explain. That man—that fat man—he said such a thing. . . ."

There was disgust as well as despair in her voice. I said prosaically, "What?" but she simply repeated, "Leave me," and turned away from me, with her hands to her face.

I said, "Can I accompany you home?"

She said, still looking away from me, "No. I need to think. I get off at the Accademia."

"Okay." I said. Then, after a pause, "Do they know where Toni is?"

"No. They want to know. And they think I know. It is so very much complicated. I—I . . . Please, leave me now."

The boat was approaching the Accademia Bridge now. I said, "All right. But can I—"

She pushed past me to go up the steps. The boat wouldn't reach the stop for another twenty seconds or so, but she obviously wanted to cut short the conversation. At the second step she turned back to me, perhaps feeling a little more in command now that she was more or less the same height, and said, "Sorry, excuse me this—this confusion. Come to my shop tomorrow. I will try to explain." Then she went nimbly on up. I saw her hand go up to her face again, but only to hold her hair in the wind. I went back into the cabin.

12

FRANCESCA'S shop turned out to be fairly easy to find. I reached it, after my usual sticky breakfast, at around ten o'clock. It was between St. Mark's and the Fenice. I saw its big hanging sign with the simple legend FRANCESCA'S from the far end of the street. But it also turned out to be closed, with shutters over the windows. Then I remembered that a lot of shops are closed on Monday mornings.

I made my way to Busetto's shop since it was fairly near. That too was closed. It looked as if I'd done everything wrong this morning. (Even the cake I'd chosen—a thing called a cannolo, a tube of flaky pastry with cream oozing at each end—had turned out to be the classic fraud with a hollow middle.) I should have got up at dawn and gone for a run and then hung around outside the Danieli in order to follow Osgood's movements. By now I'd probably missed him. Well, I could always try phoning the hotel.

I did so from one of the phones outside the post office at the Bocca di Piazza. I was told that il Signor Osgood had gone to Asolo for the day, and would not return till that evening; he had

157

given instructions that any urgent message could be left at the Cipriani at Asolo, where he would be taking lunch and tea.

I put the phone down. Would there be any point in my going to Asolo and watching him have lunch—apart from the physical fascination of the spectacle? The only way I could do it would be to go straight to Piazzale Roma now and hire a car, since public transport would never get me there and back for my lecture. But car hiring was pretty expensive and the whole thing was likely to be a waste of time since I was fairly sure that he wasn't meeting Toni there. I had no well-founded reason for being sure of this, but it just seemed an unlikely place for him or Toni to choose: the Cipriani, for an ex-terrorist smuggler?

The only other move that came to mind was to try again at Busetto's home address. I started toward Cannaregio. Whatever else, these few days were proving marvelous exercise. When I rang his doorbell thirty-five minutes later, Busetto didn't reply.

The way things were going I'd have been surprised if he had.

Then I noticed the front door wasn't closed properly. It was just slightly ajar. I pushed it and it swung open. The hall revealed was unusually bright and new looking for Venice. I stepped inside. If anyone were to see me, I could just say that I'd found the door open, so I thought I'd run straight on up to my friend's flat. I pushed the door to but the latch was stiff; I didn't bother to give it the extra shove it needed, being nervous of the noise it might make. I started up the stairs. From the position of his bell outside I guessed that Busetto was on the second floor.

The staircase was new too. The whole place had clearly been recently restored. I reached the second floor, and there was Busetto's name on the door to the right. The flat opposite bore the name De Marchi. I approached Busetto's door. Was I really going to try to fiddle its lock with my credit card? Here, on a landing where people passed? And if not, why had I come on up? I knocked—but not so loudly that the De Marchis would hear. There was no answer of course. I knocked just a little louder—and the door swung a few degrees under my knuckles. I stared, then pushed it open and stepped in.

158

I was in darkness. The shutters were all closed. I gently pulled the front door shut behind me and stood still for a few seconds waiting for my eyes to adjust. The place was very warm. Then I thought, Why be in darkness? and I stretched my hand out to the wall beside the door. But before I touched it I stopped short, put my hand into my anorak pocket, and took out a pair of gloves and put them on. I was quite unaware of any specific premonition; this just seemed an appropriate precaution. My gloved fingers found the light switch. I turned it on—and at once drew in my breath in a sharp yelp.

There was a naked black man brandishing a club immediately in front of me.

Of course it was a candelabra—and he was brandishing a torch, not a club. Nonetheless, it was a rather threatening object to keep in one's hallway. I had a look at the door to see if the lock was broken. It didn't seem to be; again I just had to presume that it hadn't been pulled or pushed hard enough by the last person to go out or in. Out, I hoped. It crossed my mind that that person might have been nervous of making a noise too.

I stepped into the first room on my right and turned on the light. It was Busetto's shop.

Or at least it was exclusively and oppressively furnished from the shop. And if anything, it was more cluttered than the shop. Here too everything was looping-the-loop rococo, from the chairs and sofas and sideboards to the picture frames and the china and the chandelier. But there was more than just clutter: there was positive disorder. On the marble floor there were fragments of shattered china and glass and powdery heaps of ash. One of the chairs was lying on its side. I had a look at some of the ash; amid its powder were some blackened flakes of canvas: ancient canvas with still-distinguishable blobs of color. I couldn't of course recognize the style of the painter, but I thought I could that of the destroyer.

By now I had one hell of a premonition. There was a thumping inside my rib cage as if something was trying to get out.

I went behind the sofa and there he was.

He was lying belly down on the floor. I was standing at his head, which was twisted away from me. I was glad of that. His arms were tied behind his back, thus pulling his shoulders straighter than they ever had been in life. The simplified rigidity of his figure, in a dark suit, made it a kind of stark fact, in sharp-cut contrast with the rococo extravagances of the rest of the room—like a black X inked on a color photo. There was something else that made this dark shape that much simpler and starker and I didn't immediately realize what it was: then I realized, his hands had no fingers.

And then I realized too what the stickiness was that I felt my shoes slipping in. It spread out from these mutilated stumps in glistening tentacles. A rococo touch, just a little less obvious than elsewhere in the room.

"Jesus," I said—and it was more of a prayer than an imprecation. My eyes roamed over the floor and located a little clump of objects that might at first glance have been taken for spilled cigarettes. I found my own fingers curling as if protectively inside the gloves. I stepped to the other side of the body, the side his head was twisted toward. His forehead was a bloody mess, but the face was Busetto's. It had become too much of an object to talk of expression: all I can say is that his mouth and eyes were open and I found myself jerking back.

I forced my mind to act rationally. From the fact the blood was still definitely sticky, though not flowing, he couldn't have been dead for very long. The killers could even—and I suddenly looked round myself in alarm—they could even still be here.

I quickly moved out of the room and glanced over the rest of the flat: kitchen, two bedrooms, and bathroom. All crazily cluttered, but without killers as far as I could see. A mere glance was enough to show me that Busetto lived alone—*had* lived alone: one of the bedrooms was clearly never used (like, I guessed, most of the furniture and ornaments in the place) and the kitchen table only had one chair drawn up to it—the only chair in the whole flat, in fact, that looked any good for sitting on.

I went back to the sitting room and had another look at the disorder. Some of it could be explained by the idea of a struggle—the overturned chair, for example and perhaps some of the smashed glass. But the burned paintings suggested something else of course—and again I saw those obscene blank faces and the flickering of the cigarette-lighter flame. And those unflickering pale eyes. These people had wanted information from Busetto, and they had started trying to extract it by destroying his favorite objects. And then perhaps going on to his fingers. Unless the fingers had been a piece of bloody symbolism executed after death, as with the tongues.

There was something throbbingly compulsive trying to attract my attention: I realized it was the crazy tom-tom of my heartbeats, getting louder and more urgent. I had to get out of this place. And then, when I was safely away, I could think of the best course to follow. Like whether to phone the police or not.

Thump! Thump! Thump!

That was not my heart.

"Polizia, aprite!"

I glided out of the living room, with one last glance to check I hadn't left anything, and ran on tiptoe to the kitchen, which had been the only room with no shutters on the window. I could hear a confused burble of voices outside the front door, and then heard the great crash of a body against the door. The whole flat shook.

I opened the kitchen window and looked down. A canal. But a canal with a barge almost directly below me.

Twenty feet below.

I looked round the room, which vibrated with the shock of another great crash, then dashed into the first bedroom and pulled at the sheet.

Crash!

The sheet wouldn't come: Busetto had obviously been one of those who like to feel really tucked in. Cursing, I freed it from under the mattress on my side and then ran round and pulled from the other side.

Crash!

161

The sheet came free and I went back into the kitchen rustling it into a bundle as I ran. I looked around the room, wondering what the strange babbling noise I could hear was, and then realizing it was myself, repeating in rapid succession three fervent obscenities. I firmly closed my mouth.

Crash! And a nasty splintering noise too.

I could see nothing better to tie the sheet to than the handle of the window itself, a brass knob. I took my gloves off and knotted one end of the sheet around the spindle of the knob, noticing how the knob rattled rather unpleasantly. But then so did everything else in the kitchen. I thrust the sheet out, and it dangled to within about ten feet of the boat. I tugged the sheet and the knob didn't actually fly out, so I prepared myself for the descent. Then, on a last moment's thought, I snatched up a meat cleaver from the sideboard, wrapped it in a tea towel, and dropped it into the boat. It didn't smash straight through the bottom fortunately.

I was on the windowsill when the front door gave way: another great crash followed by a confused clattering and a babble of victorious voices. This sudden irruption of voices almost sent me straight over the edge—of the sill and perhaps sanity too. I managed to get a grip on myself, and then on the sheet, and I launched myself out and started sliding down, hand over hand. It was unpleasantly greasy to the touch, and I wondered how often Busetto changed his bed linen. *Had* changed it.

I was almost at the bottom when suddenly I was falling with the sheet coming after me: the knob or the knot had obviously given. I landed in the boat, which bucked wildly under the impact, and found myself staggering to one side, soaked in cold spray, and also fighting the sheet, which had wrapped itself around my head. I somehow managed to keep my balance, pulled the sheet off, and chucked it out of the boat; it could do with a wash after all. Then I grabbed the cleaver, freed it from the towel, and turned to the rope that tied the stern of the boat to a pole. I knew that there would be no time for fiddling with knots. It took me two sharp blows to free that end, and all the time I was listening to the open window above. The whole building in fact was buzzing with curious voices; fortunately no one as yet was looking out this way. All the same I pushed my scarf up to my nose, terrorist fashion. I ran unsteadily along the still-swaying boat to the pole at the prow. Three more blows and the barge was free.

I snatched up an oar from the bottom of the boat. I wasn't intending to row out into the lagoon or anything: not in a twenty-foot barge. I was making for an alleyway on the other side of the canal, and the oar was for pushing against the wall. I started by pushing with my hands, the oar tucked in my armpit, until the boat started moving sluggishly and still drunkenly out across the canal. Then, as the wall slipped out of reach, I used the oar. The boat was now drifting in a haphazard diagonal across the water.

"*Fermo o sparo!*" Stop or I shoot. This came from the kitchen window. There was a carabiniere standing there raising his gun to his shoulder.

I gave one more shove with the oar and then dropped it; I then ran along the wildly careering boat in a low crouching shuffle and leaped off the prow. As I leaped I heard the rattle of gunfire. I landed on the edge of the steps to the water and pitched forward out of sight. There was another burst of fire. Without showing myself I shouted at the top of my voice, "*Varemengo!*"

I didn't do it for the mere hell of it. This was Venetian for "Get lost" or "Go to hell," and I imagined that in the heat of the moment and at that distance nobody would notice an English accent in these four syllables.

Then I picked myself up and started running down the alley, blessedly dark and narrow. I remembered being once told that the Venetians called the back streets *le fodere*—the coat linings—and I'd thought at the time what an inappropriately cozy-sounding name. It felt just right then. This coat lining came out into another alley at the end of which I could see the Fondamenta della Sensa. I slowed down to a brisk walking pace as I came out

163

onto the *fondamenta,* where there were a few passersby. I took the first bridge over the canal and thus reached the Fondamenta della Misericordia. I was by no means so happy with the geography of this area of the city as I had been yesterday: these long *fondamente* left one very exposed. I could hear the siren of a police boat somewhere toward the Sacca della Misericordia, and the people along the *fondamenta* were all looking curiously in that direction. If the boat should come down this canal. . . .

I tried to look curious rather than panic-stricken myself, making for the nearest bridge at the same time. I wanted more of those snuggly *fodere.* Before I reached the bridge I heard the boat enter the canal, and it came tearing down, gashing a frantic V of wash. I thought: if I go running over this bridge now, I only attract attention to myself. I forced myself to keep walking toward the boat. It had now slowed down to a more suitable speed, and the carabinieri were standing at the sides, with their machine guns cocked, staring at every person on the Fonda-menta. Then, just before they reached me, they shouted to a bearded man on the point of entering an *osteria*: *"Documenti!"* He looked around and said in wild arm-throwing pantomime, for the benefit of friends inside the *osteria* I imagine, *"Chi, mi?"*

I took advantage of the moment and went lightly, casually over the bridge. There was another shout of *"Documenti!"* which might have been for me, but I didn't look. As soon as I was safely in the alley on the other side I started running again.

Four hours or so later I walked down toward Francesca's shop. It was open. It had large windows, and my first impression was of looking into a greenhouse; big-leaved plants and creepers sprawled and snaked over most of the window space: then amid this vegetation I saw very stylized wooden statues, placed like fetishes in jungle clearings—fetishes of some tribe that worshiped anorexic hermaphrodites with a taste for brightly patterned dresses and shirts. There was nothing so vulgar as a price tag anywhere to be seen, and indeed nothing to indicate whether it was the plants, the statues, or the clothes that were on sale.

I entered. "Spring" from Vivaldi's *Four Seasons* was playing from hidden speakers and I half expected to see real birds flitting among the plants. It was warm enough for summer however. A girl dressed in improbably high heels and impossibly tight trousers gave me a big toothy smile from where she was hanging dresses on a rack. *"Buongiorno."*

"Buongiorno. Could I see Frances—er, la Signorina Sambon—S, that is."

Her smile switched off. "I don't know if—"

Francesca's voice came from an inner room. "All right, Marina. I'm coming."

Marina returned to the rack of dresses with a slightly petulant swish of her behind. She bent to pick up a dress from a box and I watched with an interest that I have to confess was not purely technical to see whether her trousers would split.

Francesca came through a bead curtain, and I swiveled before I could verify the point. She was wearing a dark blue skirt and a frilly blouse with a light blue cardigan; not the exotic colors of the clothes on the racks and on the tribal fetishes in the window, more those of the serious businesswoman. Indeed, even in the simple sentence she'd addressed to Marina I'd been able to identify the definite tones of the employer: nothing peremptory or authoritarian, just a certain cool assurance. Very different from the voice I'd heard on the boat last night. And now she came forward smiling that *prosecco* smile I remembered from our first meeting. *"Ciao,* how are you?" she said in English.

"Fine thanks. And you?"

"Well, better than yesterday night. Shall we go and have a coffee?"

"That would be nice, but you're sure I'm not interrupting anything?"

"No, no." She turned to Marina and said, "I'll be back in ten minutes if anyone calls." Marina gave a sniff or a hmmph or possibly even a snort of assent, and Francesca went back behind the bead curtain and came out again with her sheepskin coat. We stepped straight out into the cold air and I said, "A nice-looking shop."

"Thank you. I'm sorry if this morning Marina isn't perhaps

165

quite—quite so—" We started walking in the direction of the Fenice.

"Well," I said, "it's probably difficult to keep smiling in those trousers. She did give me a nice smile when I came in."

"Oh, good. No, I am the one she's annoyed with. Because of those trousers in fact. I had to speak to her about them. And the shoes."

"Oh."

She looked up at me with those serious dark eyes. "I know, it sounds silly and—and interfering. Well, yes, it would be if I was the manager of a grocer's shop or a baker's. But it's one of those things I've always said, how can you expect that people buy your clothes—at least the kind we sell—if you yourself are dressed like a—like a—"

I wondered whether to offer her the word she was looking for or whether she knew it but just didn't want to say it. I said, "I get your point. Presumably Marina didn't like this."

"Well, it's difficult to criticize how someone dresses herself without offense. But it's a question of professionalism. And no matter what else, a new business has to show itself professional. I made this clear to the girls when I employed them."

There was no doubting her professionalism; it came out in her tone of quiet but well-thought-out commitment. I knew I could never talk about my work in quite the same way.

"She'll get over it," I said.

"I hope so. She's only on her trial period. But you didn't come to talk about my shop."

"No, but I'm interested all the same." I was in fact—and also I didn't want to start straight in on the role of interrogator. I'd prefer her to start talking on her own account. It would make me look that much less of a bully—and would help me to avoid making slips like talking in the past tense about Busetto—or his fingers. I doubted that she had heard of the murder; even if she had seen or heard the lunchtime news, the chances were the facts hadn't reached the studios yet. I went on in casual procrastination, "How's it doing?"

She put out her left hand, palm downward, and rocked it from side to side, as to say "so-so." "Of course it's early yet to say. We are only open since a few months. But I think the voice—the news is spreading."

"And what do your parents think?" I asked. "Are they proud?"

She almost winced. "Well, they—they are not so against it now. They didn't like the idea at first."

"Why not?"

"You may have seen that my mother is—is a rather old-fashioned lady. She didn't like the idea of me as a shopkeeper. Why don't you study? Do *economia e commercio* at Ca' Foscari, get a degree and a *good* job—but now they see I'm doing what I want to do, and what I'm good at. And"—she smiled—"I think they see it's not so very socially degrading. They just thought of it as serving in a shop, but I'm really a dress designer, a fashion designer. In fact sooner or later I hope to be able to put on a *sfilata*—a fashion parade somewhere."

"In Palazzo Sambon?"

She whistled, a rather surprising masculine whistle. "Ooh, that would be really—well, who knows? My mother might even like the idea after all."

I thought this quite possible. Fashion designers are definitely part of the new aristocracy in Italy.

She went on: "As I say, they're not against the shop now, and they're even going to help me financially, which is a great relief." She smiled as she said this. "So, who knows, *le sfilate di Palazzo Sambon* might not be such a ridiculous idea."

I said, "Well, I wouldn't do swimsuits in that big hall, not for a few months anyway."

"No." She gave a mock shiver. "Shall we have a coffee here?" We were at the Bar al Teatro, next to the Fenice.

"Yes, of course."

I ordered a coffee and she a cappuccino; I thought of saying that I'd never before seen an Italian take one after midday, but then decided it would be silly to prolong the small talk. I went to the cash desk and paid—it was my turn. We were both silent for a moment. Then she said, "Sorry about last night."

"I'm sorry I intruded."

"No, no. It was natural you should ask. I—I was not myself." She sipped her cappuccino, and put it down, a little line of froth clinging to her upper lip. "But how were you there?"

"I was following Osgood. I wanted to see who he might meet."

"I see. And you didn't expect me."

"No. I didn't even know you knew him."

"I didn't. It was another man I—"

"Busetto."

"That's right." She looked up at me with definite curiosity in her eyes. She hadn't heard of the murder, it was clear. Nor, it struck me only then, had she read the previous day's *Gazzettino*. She went on: "I had heard of this man Busetto through my bro—through Toni. I have even met him, I think, at some dinner or something. But only once. And yesterday afternoon he phoned to our house and asked to speak to me. He said he had some news about Toni, but I must not tell anyone in the family. He would give me the news at Harry's Bar." She paused, and then said, "You know, it's strange, I had never been there before."

"A place for tourists perhaps."

"No, there are Venetians who go there. My parents in fact."

"So what news did they have?"

"They didn't have news. They—oh, it's very complicated. You know who is Osgood, I suppose."

"Yes. He's the art dealer your brother is trying to sell the Cima to."

"And not only," she said, looking down sadly at the floor.

"And the Vivarini, I suppose."

She shrugged. "I don't know. Maybe. But not only them."

"Sorry?"

She looked back up at me. "No, of course you don't know this."

"What?"

She looked around the bar. There was nobody else in earshot. She said, "Well, I suppose you understood what is my mother's attitude to Toni."

"More or less," I said, in an effort to be tactful.

"And I said that you had to try to comprehend her. You remember."

"Yes."

"Well, I wasn't telling you the whole truth then. But now, *tanto vale,* I might as well tell all. It wasn't Toni's co-involvement with the terrorists and his jail sentence that really alienated my mother. She'd even found a way to pardon him for all that." After a pause she added, "Also my father," almost as an afterthought.

"Uh-huh," I said, remembering what that university colleague of Toni's had said about all being forgiven and forgotten in the Sambon family.

"No, it wasn't that. It was—well, first I must explain how important is the family to my mo—my parents. And how important is family pride, if I can put it like that. You might find it ridiculous"—and she looked so hard at me that I could only mumble something incoherent along the lines of "nonono" and feel a new twinge of guilt at my complete lack of family pride, and then she went on—"and maybe it is. But you must realize it is one of the few things left to them. It is one of the few things to which they can still attach importance; I mean the whole thing, our history, the palazzo, our possessions, et cetera. You maybe noticed this when you came to see the frescoes."

"Yes. Lovely frescoes of course," I said fatuously.

She gave me a quick and rather ironic smile and went on: "You see, it helps my mother in particular to feel she has some kind of—well, of identity. You do understand me?"

"Yes," I said, though wondering where all this was leading.

"So the worst thing any of us could do would be something against the Sambon name, something treacherous to the family. Is all that clear?"

Again I said, "Yes."

"Well, you may know that our family possesses two small paintings by Guardi."

"Yes." I suddenly remembered the icicles that had formed on the chandelier when I'd asked the contessa about these paintings.

"They're two small pictures of the lagoon, called simply *Morning* and *Evening*. They're very very beautiful. Well, when Toni came out of—out of prison—he came back to stay in the palazzo for a short period. My parents were as kind as they could be, but there was tension all the same. Or friction, if there is the word." She looked at me questioningly and I nodded. She continued, "I can understand why Toni felt he had to get away—well, not only from the family, from Venice too. And I think the police advised it too. But unfortunately, before leaving he had a big argument with my mother—a silly thing—in which he said they'd never tried to understand and she said she'd almost broken her heart trying to. Oh, it was terrible. And all so silly. But—well, when he finally left we found the painting of *Morning* had gone too." And suddenly her eyes were quivering.

I said, "Ah, I see. So he—"

She nodded. "Yes. I suppose it was an impulse. Maybe trying to—to react to my mother. *Una ritorsione.* Or maybe he just said to himself that at least the family could do one thing for him. Toni was always good at—at finding excuses for what he did. And I'm sure he believed in them too. As I said, he isn't really bad—he's just made some bad choices."

Like choosing to be bad, I thought but didn't say. Instead I said, "So that presumably was the unforgivable crime for your parents."

"Yes. My mother won't even allow his name to be mentioned now. I really don't think there's any way he could excuse himself—make it up."

"If he brought the painting back?"

She pondered this over another sip of cappuccino. She delicately licked her upper lip and then said, "I don't know. He

170

probably can't now anyway. And even if he could . . . Well, it would be difficult. My parents had pardoned him so much, to be rewarded like that was . . . I also can't understand it, in fact."

"Well, presumably he needed money," I said, a little crassly.

"Oh, I can see why, but not how—I don't mean physically how, because nothing could have been easier, the painting would have fitted into his smallest document case. No, I mean how he can have made himself to—to . . ."

I thought it better not to offer any answer myself. I said, "But why should Osgood and Busetto want to talk to you about this?"

She stirred the froth at the bottom of her cup with the spoon and stared into it. She said in a just controlled voice, "They want the other Guardi painting."

"What? They want you to give them it?"

"Well, the fat man wants this."

"And why does he think you would?"

"Because he says if I don't he can make Toni be arrested."

"What? For the first Guardi? But presumably your parents wouldn't press charges."

"No, of course not. But it was still a crime to take it out of the country. But that is not the real crime for which this fat man says he can make Toni be arrested. No, he says that Toni brought him here to buy some other paintings: the Cima and the Vivarini, I suppose, though he didn't want to say, and he could denounce him for those."

"I see. I suppose he came all this way in the interests of justice. So why shouldn't *you* denounce *him*?"

"That's what I said and he—he just smiled—a horrible benevolent smile—and said for what? I got so angry, and he just kept smiling. So I had to say I'd think about it. He said to ring him at the Danieli when I'd finished thinking."

"And what about Toni? Where is he?"

"He says he doesn't know at the moment. He's expecting a message from him too. I told him to tell Toni he must *leave* because it's not safe for him here now. And again he smiled."

"A jolly chap, I know."

"He's disgusting." This was in Italian, the last word (*"schifoso"*) being said with a sudden curled lip and wrinkled nose as if she'd discovered canal sludge below her cappuccino froth. "He said all this as if it was a simple business transaction between reasonable people."

"Well, this is the kind of business he does most of the time. And, er, Busetto, did he say anything?" I tried to keep my voice casual.

"He just sat and tried to look apologetic, as if it was nothing to do with him. But he is the one who must have told the fat man about the other Guardi, and about—well, about me. And our whole family. He knows my mother. And he knows Toni, and he must have heard that I have always been close to Toni."

"I see. Mind you, Osgood could have heard about the Guardi from some book on the subject. As I did. But when you say Busetto knew Toni, how did he know him?"

"I don't know. Toni had some friends he was—he was quiet about."

"Oh, yes?"

"I don't mean Busetto was like this—not necessarily."

"Like what?"

She looked up at me. "I think you understand."

"Ah." Well, now I did. Then I remembered something. "But when I asked you yesterday if he had any friends, you said—"

"I know. I wasn't lying. He had friends once. But I think you call them fair-weather friends. When he was in jail, not one of them went to visit him. Can you imagine?"

I could—only too well. But I didn't say so. "I see."

"So those two colleagues I told you about, the ones who live in Rome, they were the only friends who showed some—some sympathy."

I said, "You mustn't be too hard on people. It's kind of difficult for most people to—to enter a prison willingly. And anyway, aren't there usually limits to the number of visitors allowed?"

172

"What do you know about it?" she said with sudden bitterness—savagery almost.

I shrugged, turning my remarks into mere fatuity.

She went on: "These people didn't even ask if they could visit him. They didn't even write."

"I see. Sorry. But just because they didn't visit him in prison doesn't mean he can't be staying with them now."

"But if they wouldn't offer any help when he was lonely, do you think that they would look after him now? Now that he is perhaps a target for the terrorists?"

"Perhaps not, but you never know. Could you give me any names?"

"But truly I didn't know them. It was a whole aspect of Toni that we knew very little about. I think you understand."

"Yes." I didn't pursue the subject. I could see no particular point in trying to establish how Toni had first met Busetto. It would probably have been through a friend of a friend of a friend, or something equally unhelpful.

"Why is all this so important to you?" she said, those dark eyes fixed on mine. "Why do you disturb yourself so much?"

"I like Cima da Conegliano, I suppose."

"What do you do? I mean, what is your work?"

"Well, I'm an artist."

"I see. Are you successful?"

I wondered whether to say, "I was," but then thought that this might sound rather whining. And I felt she wasn't the sort of person who would fall for whining. I said, "I get by."

"You what?"

"I make a living. Not a very secure one. But then it's not a very secure profession."

"Does one exist?" she said, smiling.

"Isn't yours?" I said. "People always want good clothes."

"And do you know how many people are making them?"

"I'm sure you're going to be successful."

"Why do you say so?"

"You're obviously determined. And you seem a real businesswoman."

173

"That isn't always said as a compliment. Do you mean it to be one?"

"Shrewd question." I wasn't sure I could answer it.

She picked up her shoulder bag from the bar and said, "Let's go."

"Yes. I suppose you ought to be getting back to your shop."

"Not immediately. I think I would like a walk. Shall we go to San Stefano?"

"Yes, sure." I felt pleased that she should want just to stroll with me. We left the bar and started walking down the side of the Fenice. We were both silent for a moment. We could hear a soprano trilling up and down a scale inside the theater. Then Francesca said, "Are you going to tell me if you were flattering me?"

I said slowly and rather ponderously, "I admit the world of business is a closed book to me. But that doesn't mean I can't respect or admire a determined person in that world in the same way I admire, well, a singer, even though I know I'm never going to sing."

The soprano trilled again and Francesca said, "No, but you like music, I suppose." She shook her head. "I think it's silly to talk about 'business people' in the abstract. That's not how I think of myself. I'm a fashion designer—and of course I want to be a successful one. As you must want to be a successful artist."

"Yes, of course," I said. I'd be happy if I could just pay the bills. Well, and afford a holiday now and again—a real holiday.

"And to be successful means that one must know something about business—it means to be serious about what you do. And I'm serious about my work. I know that most men think that the world of fashion is something trivial—"

I was about to protest politely but she went on: "Well, I won't say it is so important as—as to save Venice from the floods or—or to find a cure for AIDS, but it does bring a little more beauty into the world and give much pleasure to many people—"

"And make an enormous amount of money," I couldn't resist putting in.

"Okay, and help the general economy." She smiled. "I know

174

I couldn't have chosen anything more alien to Toni's ideals, but I believe in it as much as he believed in his—his manifestos. I believe in beauty. It's one of the things we've always done well in Italy; I know we aren't on the same level as Titian or Bellini, but we do still make things that people admire all over the world, so why shouldn't I be proud of what I do?"

We came out of a *sottoportico* and up a bridge. She stopped at the top with me one step below her and looked at me, still smiling, her eyes on my level. "But you probably think me very silly, you as a real artist."

"No, not a bit." I could be quite sincere here. "Who's to say who's a real artist—just because I work on a canvas and you with a—well, whatever you work with." I wanted to say that I wished I had her certainty in what I did, but was stopped in time by that feeling that she was not a person to whine to. Instead I said, "But how serious is it to be out strolling with someone in shop hours?"

"Marina and the other girls work shop hours, as you say." She started down the bridge. "I work shop hours and more. But for something important I can take a break. And for me this walk is important."

"Thank you." She was looking straight ahead, deliberately I felt.

"But I want to know what is important to you."

"That's a big question," I began.

She broke in. "These paintings—they are important, no?"

"Yes." I felt a bit let down. I'd been ready to talk about quite other things.

"And you are angry with Toni then? Do you want that he gets punished for what he has done?"

"No." Then I added, "Well, I don't want to be hypocritical; I can't say I'll be heartbroken if he gets caught."

"No. *You* won't be."

"So will you be?"

"Toni has suffered enough now. All I ask you is that you don't involve the police."

"Nothing is further from my mind," I said quite sincerely.

Again she stopped at the top of the bridge we were climbing and turned and looked at me on the step below her. "Thank you. I trust you."

Her head was on my level, and her eyes were gazing fixedly into mine. I placed my left hand on her right, which was on the parapet, and she didn't draw it away. But she didn't give me her other one. She just said, "Martin . . ."

"Francesca." At this point I could have leaned forward to kiss her, and I'm sure she wouldn't have withdrawn. At least I felt sure of it at that moment. But something stopped me. I think it was the memories of the morning. I just had an instinctive and quite illogical gut feeling that you can't run from a corpse and then kiss a girl. I turned my tender hand touching into a mere reassuring squeeze. "I promise," I said, and withdrew my hand. The moment passed completely and, I thought with sudden regret, perhaps irrevocably.

"Thank you," she repeated with the same artificial sudden breeziness. She led the way down a dark side alley, and we walked in silence. Suddenly to our right we saw the almost frighteningly leaning tower of Santo Stefano. She said, *Impressionante, no? The most—come si dice, pendente?"*

"Leaning," I said.

"The most leaning in Venice."

"Ah."

We came out into the busy brightness of Campo Santo Stefano. I felt suddenly nervous about being in such an exposed place—and then thought that if I gave way to such feelings I'd end up a gibbering wreck. I returned to business. "Don't get in touch with Osgood just yet," I said.

"No? And if he does what he promises?"

"He won't. Not yet. And I think there will be developments."

"What do you mean?"

I said, "Give it a day or two. He'll wait." I wished I could tell her that he would be too terrified of getting mixed up in the murder to persecute her anymore. But I couldn't casually drop my knowledge of it now—and besides, it might not even be so. Osgood might feel perfectly safe. "If you want to get in touch with me, you could leave a message at the Britannia School."

"Why? Are you there?"

"I'm giving some talks there. One in about an hour in fact, if you want to come along. Mainly on Bellini."

"I'd love it, but I can't leave the shop the whole afternoon. That *would* be unserious. Give my best wishes to Mr. Crews. He was my teacher there when I was a child."

I vaguely knew George Crews, the oldest of the teachers in the language part of the Britannia School; always dressed in patched corduroy trousers and old pullovers, usually with red-wine stains. "So you learned your English there, did you?" I wasn't surprised. Mr. Robin didn't let any of the aristocratic families' children slip by him if he could help it. His class registers often read like a guide to the palazzi on the Grand Canal.

"Yes. And Toni too. Mr. Crews, he was funny. Well, I must go back." We had sauntered up toward the statue in the middle of the square. She now turned around.

"Thanks for the stroll," I said. "I'd never been round the back of the theater like that."

"I'm not a good guide, I think. I haven't told you anything about where we walked."

"Well, it wasn't supposed to be a guided tour." But I felt that whatever it had been supposed to be it had failed as. Something had been missed. And probably through my fault.

She said with a forcibly bright change of subject, "Do you know what we call this statue in Venice?"

"No." A pretty boring nineteenth-century one of someone called Tommaseo, a scholar whose studious habits are represented by a pile of books that rises behind his back to the level of his frock coat.

"*Cagalibri.*" The book-shitter.

I laughed. "I'm sure that's not in the guidebooks. I'll definitely hire you for my next tour."

"Thank you."

So we were finishing on a comic note. Better like that, I thought. Then she looked at me with those so-changeable dark eyes and said, "Someone said to me once that to be successful in business—to *sfondare, come si può dire*—to make it, you must be both careful and impulsive. The important is to have the instinct about when to be careful, and when to be impulsive."

"Ah."

"Ciao." She kissed me, but formally on both cheeks, and said, "Keep in touch." I watched her dark hair bouncing to her steps as she walked away.

13

ON my way to the Britannia School I suddenly realized I was nervous—nervous about giving my talk, of all things. It was crazy. I'd given these talks year after year, and had never felt anything more than a mild exhibitionistic pleasure in front of the students, who had always sat diligently taking notes (when the lights were on) and politely laughing at the appropriate points. So why this stage fright now? Well, maybe one insecurity triggers off another. If you're worried about possibly getting shot and/or mutilated, you're not likely to be in the best psychological conditions for standing up and being witty about Bellini.

I tried to convince myself that this was the explanation, but had a sneaking doubt that even if I were here in circumstances quite unrelated to terrorism, I'd be quaking. After all, I'd been nervous about going into that private view the other day.

And rightly, as it turned out.

But these are just students, I told myself. The same set of languorous youths with double-barrel names and Etonian voices that you've seen at the Britannia School every year.

179

And in fact, as I entered the now-dark campo where the school was situated I heard the familiar noise of high-spirited upper-class voices: those long braying vowels as two girls hailed each other all the way across the square. (In Italy you have to go to Naples to find such unembarrassed long-distance conversations.) "Hey, Charlotte!" "Oh, *ciao*, Belinda!" Wide fluffed-out skirts, green anoraks, long ruffled blond hair. Only the word *ciao* ("cheeow") showed any influence of the surroundings. I made toward the door of the school, listening in to their conversation as they met up in the middle of the square. (Well, I didn't exactly have to strain my ears.) "It's somebody on Bellini, isn't it?" "Yaah. They say he's been to prison." "No, go on, you're making it up." "No, honest. I got it from Piers. Something to do with drugs." "Gosh, what fun. Not the sort of thing you'd expect from old Christopher Robin, is it?"

I went on up the stairs. The *piano nobile* was already nearly full of students, sitting around and chatting and laughing and saying "Re-eally!" or "Re-eally?" They looked younger than ever. Mere babes. Though quite sexy babes, one or two of them. About two-thirds of them were female. Some of them had turned toward me as I crossed the room and I hastily looked away: if they caught me ogling, what would I be to them but a dirty old man? Lucy was standing at the back by the slide projector. She was wearing fairly tight black corduroy trousers and a white pullover; she looked good, I had to say. And so different from the pink-cheeked adolescents all around. When she saw me she came up to the front and said, "Hi. You can give me the slides. I'll operate the machine." Quick businesslike tone. Just the way I'd wanted things. So why did it irritate me so much?

"Okay," I said. "Have they been told who I am?"

"They know your name. And that you're an artist."

"Hadn't you better warn them not to accept any sweets from me?"

"Don't be silly." This was said quite neutrally as she took the boxes of slides from me. "You're sure they're all the right way round?"

"Well, if any of them comes out upside down, I'll tell them it's so we can study the color harmonies more objectively."

"I remember that one," she said, and smiled.

Professor Perkins pottered in from the staircase. Today he looked as if he were auditioning for a part in *Waiting for Godot*. He saw us with the slides and said, "Oh, thought it was Jones today."

"I'm substituting," I said.

"Ah, I see. Well, er, I'll see you later, no doubt." And he pottered back out.

Thank you very much, Professor, for the confidence boost.

The secretary's door opened and Mr. Robin peered out and beckoned me. "One word, please." He closed the door again.

I felt like a schoolboy summoned to the headmaster's study. I turned in puzzlement to Lucy and she said, "I think it's your fighting in the streets."

"My what? Oh, I see." I went into Luisa's office. She was sitting placidly reading the provincial pages of the *Gazzettino*. Mr. Robin was standing by the desk with his arms folded forbiddingly. Somehow he managed to make them look primly symmetrical nonetheless.

"Ah, Martin," Mr. Robin said.

"I'm ready to start if—"

"Yes, of course. But first I would like some clarification on something that appeared in yesterday's *Gazzettino*."

"How do you mean, 'clarification'?"

"Am I to understand you got involved in some kind of fight?"

"If you read the article properly, you'll see that the person mentioned slipped."

"We tried to phone this morning to find out what it was all about, but the hotel said you had moved."

Not, I noticed, to find out how I was. "Yes, I've moved to Santa Croce. People are less clumsy there."

"If you remember, I stated yesterday that we would appreciate it if you kept a low profile. This is not the kind of publicity that the Britannia School needs."

"The Britannia School didn't get mentioned."

"No, not yet. But who is to say in the next edition of the paper."

I hoped he hadn't caught my wince. I said, "I'll keep my head right down."

"It's a little late now," he said. "Martin, I think it would really be better if you limit yourself to just the one lecture. I have to think of the—"

"School's reputation, I know." Another nice prelecture confidence boost. "You're not going to give me another chance?" I realized how pathetic this sounded as I said it. And besides what was the point? The next day's newspapers would probably put paid to any such hope. The connection was bound to be made between Saturday's street fight and Monday's murder.

"I really don't think it would be in the interests of either of us."

"Speak for yourself" would be the only sensible answer to this. But that would be to assume that Mr. Robin's words were supposed to make sense. They were mere bureaucratic noises, issued at occasional intervals to assure the listener that steps were being taken, paths followed, procedures carried out. . . . So I shrugged and said, "Okay. Are you going to listen in to me?" In case I start a brawl.

"Yes, of course. Oh, and please do not overrun. The students are to be at the car park at seven to take a coach to Mantua." He walked to the door.

I looked at Luisa and she lifted her eyes from the *Gazzettino* and gave me a sympathetic hand-spreading shrug. I mouthed the word *stronzo* and she giggled. She said, "Give me the name of the hotel and we'll send your check there." I gave it to her and followed Mr. Robin out.

Well, at least this anger had killed the butterflies in my stomach, I thought. But then as I stood out in front of the sea of faces—well, more like a pink-pebbled beach really—listening to Mr. Robin's few words of introduction, those butterflies fluttered to life again and I found my hands hot and sweaty. Mr. Robin's

clichés pattered along—"very happy to have with us . . .";
"well-known artist in his own right . . ."; "the gift of the artist's
eye"; "could someone please close the shutters?"—and I tried to
pull myself together, promising myself that I'd so enthuse them
(wild cheering, waving of scarves, thunderous applause) that
Mr. Robin would just have to ask me back.

They listened with polite attention to my opening remarks,
laughing courteously but not uproariously at my comparison of
the Bellini family to other such prodigy families as the Jacksons
(I remembered I'd used the Osmonds in earlier years, but the
name would mean nothing to these kids), and when the lights
went down for the first slide, there wasn't the instant outbreak of
fumbling and fidgeting and possibly fondling that Professor
Perkins always had to put up with. So I calmed down and started
to enjoy myself. I suppose there was something reassuring about
just being a voice and a pointing rod in the semidarkness; it was
another cozy cocoon, like the fog (the fog as I'd yearned for it
yesterday morning, rather than the fog as I'd actually felt in on
Friday evening).

I was probably the only one to have a sudden intimation of
danger: well, of course I was the only one to need the intimation.
I had just said my fifth peremptory "next" and thus brought onto
the screen Bellini's Naples Transfiguration when I noticed the
door to the staircase, halfway down the right-hand wall, open a
few inches and then close again. Some student who'd missed a
boat or something, I thought, and was now embarrassed to come
in. I was the only one not facing the screen at that moment, so
the only one to notice this tiny movement. I turned back to the
screen ready to say something about the subtle play of light when
it suddenly struck me that there had been no irruption of light,
subtle or otherwise, from the doorway: why was the staircase in
darkness? The lights were usually never switched off until the
school closed.

I said, "Er, note the background buildings. I don't know if
you've been to Ravenna yet . . ." and my eyes wandered back to
the door. I found myself gripping the rod like a sword.

183

Suddenly the Transfiguration disappeared: one moment a silvery serene lucidity, and the next utter blackness. There was a quick silly scream from a girl at the back followed by laughter and a buzz of voices. I jumped away from where I had been standing and crouched with the rod held out: I dimly saw the door open—a flicker of gray amid the blackness—and a dark silhouette slip through.

Mr. Robin was saying, "All right, keep still everybody, it's obviously just a power cut. . . ." Luisa had come out of her office and was saying, *"Oh dio, ancora . . ."*

Then a hand grabbed my shoulder and made as if to spin me around. I have no doubt that if I hadn't been ready I'd have twirled like a top. As it was I twisted out of reach and lashed out with the rod at head height. It struck something and I heard, amid the hubbub of the rest of the room, a sharp intake of breath. *"Pezzo di merda, ti rovino la faccia,"* came a quick whispered sentence—"I'll ruin your face."

Why the hell was I fighting back in silence? "Help!" I suddenly shouted—and there was a momentary hush in the room, immediately broken by loud laughter and cheers and just one scream from the same girl at the back. Mr. Robin said, "Come along, that's enough nonsense. I'm going to get a torch."

I was aware that my assailant's eyes were more adjusted to the dark than mine and mere backing away was no use: he could no doubt see me. I smashed out with the rod again and it was snatched in midair. I leaped forward, taking advantage of the fact that his hand was thus occupied and made to grab his other arm. Something went swish in the air and I felt a hot searing pain on the back of my hand. I yelped, and jumped to the window. I managed to grab the handle of one of the shutters: I knew there was a lamppost almost directly outside the window. I felt my shoulder gripped again and suddenly there was something pricking at my cheek just below my eye. I kept my head dead still and at the same time jerked the handle of the shutter. A silver sliver of light sliced down to the floor and instantly I was released: I fell over and heard his footsteps run to the door; it was swiftly opened and shut again. I heard the faint noise of footsteps on the stairs.

Another shutter was opened at the back and I pulled myself to my feet in the gloom. I could feel a hot trickle down my cheek and on my hand. The voices in the room were still hearty, jolly, enjoying the unexpected diversion. Mr. Robin was halfway down the center aisle, picking his way past the students who had, I think, been deliberately stretching their legs out. He saw me getting to my feet and said, "Martin, whatever have you been doing?"

"I—I—nothing." I ran to the door and started down the staircase.

He called out to me, "The fuse box is at the bottom, by the cleaning cupboard."

I reached the door to the campo and stared out. There were just two old women with shopping bags in the far corner. I closed the door and went toward the fuse box. I pulled the switch and heard the satisfied "Ahs" from above. The staircase remained in darkness. I found the switch by the entrance, and in the light examined my hand. There was a cut halfway across, but not deep. The knife had obviously caught me glancingly. I put my fingers to my cheek and they came away with a dab of blood. But it was only one small laceration; a bandage should be enough.

At this point Mr. Robin came down the stairs and joined me, repeating, "Whatever were you doing?"

"I tripped over the wires," I said, "and got mixed up with the rod." I noticed, with a kind of paradoxically calm annoyance, that my voice was shaking as I spoke.

"The wires are at the back of the room," he said.

"Ah. Well, I must have tripped over something else. Shall I go on?" I took a handkerchief from my pocket and put it to my cheek.

"You don't look in any fit state to. Martin, have you been drinking?"

"No more than usual. I tell you I just fell over. It was pitch black, wasn't it?"

185

"So it was for all of us. Not drinking, you say. Have you been taking anything else?"

"A toasted sandwich and a coffee," I said. I had finally managed to get the tremble out of my voice. I started up the stairs—and found that the tremble had switched to my right hand. I made it grip the handrail firmly. As I entered the room there was a general "Ooh," and Luisa and Lucy both came forward solicitously. "It's all right," I said, "I just slipped."

Lucy said, "But what was going on? We heard you shouting 'Help.'"

"It was nothing," I said. I looked around at the students. They were curious, but not especially so. Mr. Robin was making quick officious gestures to get them to return to their seats. Could they really not have seen or heard anything? Well, there had been a great deal of noise and confusion. I said, "Did you see anybody go out the door?"

"Yes," Lucy said. "I thought it was somebody going for the lights."

"Ah," I said. "Probably." It was simplest to leave things like that.

Luisa gently took the hanky from my cheek and said in Italian, "You need a bandage. What did it?"

"It must have been the rod," I said, pointing.

Lucy said, "Come with me. I'll clean it up. There's a first-aid box in the bathroom upstairs."

"Okay," I said. I turned to Mr. Robin. "I'm just going to wash my face off, then I'll—"

"Oh, I think we'll make that a natural break," he said. "I'm sure you'd rather get over your—your unfortunate mishap. Thank you very much, we've all enjoyed the talk a great deal."

One or two of the students started a little ragged applause but most of them hadn't taken in what Mr. Robin had said and merely looked around bewildered. I wondered whether to make any closing remarks myself, but realized I was too irritated to say anything acceptable. I allowed myself to be led away by Lucy. She took me out onto the staircase and we started up to the next floor.

We heard Mr. Robin say, "Piazzale Roma at seven, and you are requested to be there on time as the coach will not wait . . . ," and then the rest of the sentence was drowned by the scraping of chairs and shuffling of feet and excited chatter as the students finally grasped that they could leave the building.

"Sometimes I'd like to throttle that man—or twist his tie, whichever he'd hate more."

Lucy said, "He can get on your nerves." Then, as we reached the door into the language-school part of the building, she said, "Martin, just what did happen down there?"

"I told you. I slipped and cut—"

"You didn't get those cuts from that stick thing. What is going on?"

"What do you mean, 'going on'?"

"Something is. Somebody came in and did that to you, didn't they?"

I opened the door and passed on into the hall without answering. It was only half as big as the one below, since a dividing wall had been put in to provide an extra classroom. The hall served as a waiting room, and Italian students sat around in ancient wicker chairs thumbing through copies of *Country Life* and *Homes and Gardens*, which were presumably supposed to provide them with an idea of everyday life in England. There were big posters of London on the wall, with red buses and smiling beefeaters and bobbies and punks. Through the wall I could hear George Crews's voice, "Present-perfect simple and present-perfect continuous: I've drunk three liters, I've been drinking all afternoon. Okay, let's repeat it." A slurred chorus of children's voices repeated the sentence; it sounded like the truth. I made toward the bathroom amid the startled looks of the people waiting. Lucy followed me in. She opened a cupboard above the sink and took out a blue box. I sat on the loo and she looked down at my face.

"Take that hanky away. Well, am I right?"

"What about?"

"Did someone do that to you? And is it anything to do with what happened the other day? Your falling in the canal?"

"Look, the person I was with slipped."

She dabbed at my cheek with wet cotton wool. "You too can be pretty exasperating, you know. You slipped. He slipped. Come on, Martin." Then in a rather gentler tone—which irritated me no end—she added, "I could see you were trembling when you came back in."

"Pretty cold in these big Venetian buildings."

She turned back to the sink. "Look, I'm not asking all these questions just because I want a bit of gossip to swap around; I can see you've been slashed at, possibly with a knife—and you're scared. So naturally I want to know why."

"You want to be of help."

"Yes. Simple as that." She looked straight at me.

"Well, that'll make a change."

I saw her flush a deep red and she turned back to the sink. "Okay. You win." She peeled free a bandage and bent down to place it on my cheek. Her face was now set hard and her eyes firmly avoided mine. "And your hand," she said. I stuck it out and she cleaned that too in silence.

I stood up and said, "Thanks. If I get desperate, I'll come running to you." A pause and I added, "But really desperate."

"Okay, okay. You've made your point." She turned to the cupboard and put the box back in and without turning back said, "Leave me, will you?"

"What? Oh sure, you want to be alone."

"I want to use the loo." She still didn't turn round to face me.

I crossed the waiting room, smiling bravely at the people there who stared at my bandages, and then went down the stairs feeling anything but brave. I opened the door onto the campo. In the far distance there were just two stray students ambling in the direction of Campo Santa Maria Formosa. The voice of one of them drifted across the square, "Well, Piers insists he must have been high on something. But I must say I thought he was rather nice."

I felt quite touched. Then the other one answered, just

188

before they left the campo, "But did you see that really awful anorak he had?"

The square now seemed empty. I walked in the opposite direction of the two students. I had no immediate aim in mind; I just wanted to get away from that area as quickly and as anonymously as possible. After a couple of turnings I was in the Calle del Fumo, a long straight alley always fairly busy with people going to and from the Fondamente Nuove and the boat stops for the islands. I walked halfway down it, listening to the brisk footsteps and occasional voices, and then before reaching the end, turned off left down a wide but empty alley. Some seconds later I heard footsteps enter the alley after me.

I started walking faster without turning around. I turned left again so that I was going back on myself. I heard the footsteps become hesitant and then enter the alley. I still didn't look round. I was now almost running, and I turned right. This was an area of narrow unfrequented alleys, quiet little squares, and *sottoportici*. Perhaps I'd made a mistake in not going back to the busy Calle del Fumo. But I suddenly realized the footsteps were no longer following me.

My first reaction of course was intense relief, but it was followed by a kind of anger mingled with curiosity. I wanted to see who the swine was who'd scared me into a cold sweat.

I made my tiptoeing way back to the end of the alley and, against all the rules of all private-detective and secret-agent handbooks, peered round. A small figure in a duffle coat (or Montgomery as the Italians call them—and this one looked as if it might have been through a few battles with the field marshal) was walking back the way he'd come—away from me.

And I started following him.

I suppose it was his size that decided me—and perhaps too the way the overlarge coat made him look like Dopey in *Snow White*. He just didn't seem dangerous.

He turned right into the alley that led back to Calle del Fumo. I hurried up close behind him: he obviously hadn't read the handbooks either. As soon as there were other people in sight, I clapped a hand on his shoulder.

He spun around with a sharp squeaky cry—this too was reassuring—and I recognized him. It was the bearded man I'd rescued from the ladder at the university.

14

"HELLO," I said.

"Er—hello—hello—hello." The bush-animal eyes were swiveling left and right, as if looking for a convenient bush—or to check that I was on my own.

"So you got down from that ladder all right," I said.

"That what? Oh, that, yes, of course. And I got the book. Em, would you mind letting go of me?"

"Yes, of course." I did so. "But would you mind telling me why you were following me?"

"*I* was? You were following *me*."

"Only because you followed me first," I said. "It was a kind of ricochet reaction, if you follow me."

"If I follow you? Ah, I see, yes. Well, perhaps I was a little."

"Yes, you were a little. But not very well."

"Em, let's go and have a drink and I'll explain."

"A drink?" This wasn't quite what I'd expected.

"Yes. Then we can both explain."

"And what have I got to explain?"

"Ah, well, rather a lot. That's why—well, that's why I was

following you. Because I was curious." He started walking down the alley with sudden leg-twinkling speed. As he walked he talked. "You see, I don't make a habit of following people around. Not even at the university, where some of the professors expect you to do so—with your tongue down—or out, if you see what I mean. But, well, I was curious. Well, more than curious. A little worried."

"Worried?"

"Yes. *Cioè*, my first reaction was to—to forget about it all, but then, well, I started to feel a little too worried."

"Forget what? Worried about what?" I was finding it hard to keep up with him, both in his walking and his talking.

"Well, I was made curious by certain things I read on the papers—*cioè*, in the papers—and things I heard at the radio—*cioè*, on the radio. Let me put them in order. On Friday an Englishman comes to me and asks me about my old colleague, Toni Sambon, an ex-terrorist—or at least, ex-*fiancheggiatore*—a supporter of the terrorists. Then the next day I read in the *Gazzettino* about an Englishman who falls in a canal, apparently pushed by a certain Signor Michele Busetto. Okay, so far nothing so special. Many Englishmen in this city—I don't even think about the two things. Then this afternoon, while I'm preparing to go to the university, I hear on the radio that this Signor Michele Busetto has been killed by terrorists. Now, I expect I'm not the only person to remember that this Busetto was the man in the paper the previous day. Also on the radio they say that he sold antiques. At the university an hour later I remember a little curious thing—the Englishman looking at Toni Sambon's horrible lamp—and I look at it myself, by chance you could say, without really thinking about it, and I see the name Busetto." He looked at me as we paused outside a bar—the first direct glance at my face. "Do you agree that these are too many coincidences?" He said it as apologetically as if he'd caused the coincidences.

"Yes," I said. "So why didn't you go to the police?"

He gave a half smile and a quick jerk of a shrug. He pushed opened the door of the bar. "What will you have?"

"*Un'ombra,*" I said, happy to get the chance of showing off a little Venetian.

He raised his eyebrows. "Very good. *Anca mi.*" He ordered two glasses of Refosco. When they were in our hands, he said, "Well, cheers, bottoms up." Obviously he too liked to show off his knowledge of not-always-appropriate idioms. We both moved a little away from the barman. "We might as well introduce ourselves properly, I'm Alvise. Alvise Ballarin. I already know your name." He thrust his hand out in a sudden jerk of a movement that had me jumping back. Then I understood and shook it, smiling rather foolishly.

"So why not the police?" I asked again.

He looked almost pained this time. "I—I well, I suppose you could say it's a typical Italian reluctance to get mixed up with the authorities if there are other paths to follow." He paused, then went on quickly: "And also there is the fact that this Englishman didn't seem to me to be a murderous type: I thought I'd prefer to speak to him and find out his version of the facts first."

"So why didn't you speak to me? Why all the secret-agent stuff?"

"The what? Oh, I see. Ah, well—" He looked into his wine in embarrassment and started twisting his finger in his beard. "Yes, sorry. I—I wanted to speak, but then I couldn't think what to say, so, well, I thought I'd just follow you and try and find out something about you. I was, well, I suppose I was a bit embarrassed."

"And how did you find me?"

"Well, I tried phoning the hotel they mentioned in the *Gazzettino* first, but they told me that you had left. So I thought a little. It struck me that if you were looking for Toni Sambon, a person you must surely have spoken to is his sister. I know her—not well but enough. I telephoned to her shop and asked her about this Englishman called Martin Phipps. And she told me you were teaching at the Britannia School. So I went there straightaway and I saw you walking away in the direction of the Fondamente Nuove. And then—well, then I started following you. Sorry."

"Did Francesca ask you why you were asking?"

"Of course. I told her, more or less. I asked her what she knew and she said you were looking for a picture. A painting by Cima da Conegliano. She hadn't heard about the murder of Busetto. She seemed quite—quite upset when I told her. Worried. For her brother, I think."

"Ah." And a teeny bit for me, I fondly and sneakingly hoped.

"But I didn't want to say too much on the phone."

"Ah," I said again.

"So you knew about this murder then?"

"Er—" Well, it was a bit late to clutch my hair and say a gaping "What?" I said, "Yes. I heard it on the radio." Then, after a pause: "At the hotel. I didn't get the details. It was the landlord's radio downstairs and I just caught a few words and I didn't want to call attention to myself by going down to listen in. It was the terrorists, wasn't it?"

"It would seem so." He darted one of his quick intent looks up at me and went on: "The police received a phone call with the usual message about *un porco borghese* having been *giustiziato* for his crimes against the people. And they found his fingers had been cut off. This makes them think it's the same people who committed the other murders."

I said, "Did they, er, see anyone?" I made this very casual.

"There was apparently someone still at the scene of the crime when they arrived, which made them suspect a trap, but he escaped. But now, em, shall we hear what you have to say about the whole thing? About these strange coincidences?"

I said, "It's a long story."

"I'm not in a hurry." He smiled. "We could have another drink. And who knows"—darting me another of his rare direct looks—"I may want to help."

I suddenly thought, Why not? I'd been on my own for too long. I felt a great need for a confidant and I trusted this man. There was something a little mysterious about him—occasional evasive looks and moments of embarrassed shiftiness—but overall I found it difficult to take seriously the idea of him as a

194

conspirator—not with that Dopey duffle coat and those big bush-baby eyes. If those eyes occasionally avoided looking at mine, and he perhaps avoided certain subjects, well, I suppose he was just of a naturally nervous disposition. So I said, "Okay. But not here. Let's go walking."

"Of course. Anywhere particularly?"

"Just not toward the center. I mean nowhere with too many people."

We left the bar, walked through a couple of small squares, along a porticoed *fondamenta,* and then around the cramped but picturesque apse of the Miracoli church, and I kept talking. I told him everything, my meeting with Toni, the visit I'd been paid by the two thugs, my investigations in Venice, my conversation with Busetto, and subsequent watery incident, my conversation with Zennaro, and the threatening letter at the hotel. Well, everything up to a point—up to the point of the murder: I halted before my discovery of the corpse. I suppose I just decided it was less complicated to stick to the story I'd given him so far—the story that made me look a little less of an outlaw than I actually was. He listened intently, turning and darting occasional quick looks at me and saying, *"Sì, sì, ho capito,"* and nodding like a toy dog in a car's back window. I finished by telling him òf the strange attack inside the school while I gave my lecture.

"I see, I see," he said when I'd obviously finished. We were now walking through Campo Santa Maria Formosa, which was fairly busy but big enough to feel safe. He'd moved on from toy-dog nods to sorrowful shakes, as if despite his questions he could in fact have done without knowing all this. "So—so now what?"

"How do you mean, 'now what?' "

"Well, there is obviously murder involved now. Do you still intend to keep away from, em, from the police?" He mentioned them with his usual apologetic note.

"Yes," I said. Then, realizing that this had come out far too quickly, I added, "I don't know anything that could be of any possible use to the police."

"Ah, ah." He was silent for a moment and then said. "You

realize that these killers probably got onto Busetto because they too read the *Gazzettino*. In London they torture you to find out what you know about where Toni is, and you tell them you don't know. Then a few days later they read you are in Venice fighting with an antique dealer."

"Yes," I said. "I've thought of that. And yes, it does make me feel pretty sick to think I was responsible for—"

"No, no," he interrupted. "That isn't what I wanted to say. Besides, I think that sooner or later they would have discovered something about Busetto and things probably would have finished in the same way for him. He was mixed up in a bad business, and, well . . ." He drew his finger along his throat in a gesture that expressed a kind of bloody inevitability. "*Povero bastardo*. No, I'm just saying that there is something you know about the motives of the killers."

"They're looking for Toni. I don't think that'll help the police very much. And besides I don't want to get Toni involved unless necessary."

"He is involved. You mean you don't want the police to know that. Toni made such a favorable impression on you then?"

I looked sharply at him. There had been just the faintest shade of irony in his voice. "Not exactly," I said. "He seemed a bit ineffectual, to tell the truth. But, well, I know Francesca doesn't want him mixed up with the police again."

"Ah. That is understandable. She has—she has great family loyalty." He smiled. "Please don't think I'm criticizing. I have no great desire to go to the police myself—as you see from my coming to you. But you have thought that the police will probably want to speak to the man Busetto pushed into a canal just two days before?"

"Yes. I'll wait till they do, though. I'm not going to offer myself voluntarily. I'm an Englishman on holiday. Of course I don't read the local newspapers."

"I suppose so," he said. "You can try this line." He sounded a little doubtful.

"I will." I didn't tell him that my worry was that they would then check with the English police about my background and get a confused story with a mention of drugs. I wondered if there was a Venetian proverb about not crossing bridges prematurely.

"And I suppose this Zennaro is not likely to go to the police himself."

"Hardly. He'll probably be packing his bags now. Like Osgood."

"Which will be a relief for Francesca."

"Yes."

"So we should all just keep quiet and pretend nothing has happened," he said.

"Well, for the moment."

"Ye-es. It's a nice idea—but . . ." He shook his head again. "I suppose my trouble is I just feel I have to understand things properly. I'm an academic, you know. Puzzles irritate me." He sounded apologetic as ever. "Shall we just try and resume the facts, to get them clear?"

"Okay," I said.

We were walking toward the Ruga Giuffa, one of the alleys out of the square, and it was rather too crowded and cramped for my liking. I swung him around toward the quiet Campiello Querini and he hardly noticed the change in direction. He scratched his head vigorously with both hands and started walking faster as if his legs supplied dynamo power for his brain. "Let's start with Toni. He and his companions were responsible in the 1970s for stealing three paintings, one of which turned up in England. Right?" His head jerked to me and I nodded. "These paintings had become, as far as they were concerned, the property of the Red Brigades—or the New Proletarian Front, or whatever they called themselves."

"Er, excuse a silly question," I said, "but isn't property theft?"

"Private property is theft. Everything belongs to the people, and the New Proletarian Front were the people, you see."

"Of course they were," I said. "Silly of me."

"Now they tried to ransom these paintings but no one was interested. And so maybe it was at this time that Toni made the acquaintance of Busetto, in order to find another way of making money on these paintings so that they shouldn't become mere pink elephants for them."

"Er, I think you mean white elephants."

"If you say so. Well, anyway, we can't know whether Toni was doing all this on his own account, or with the agreement of his companions. In theory, of course, the New Proletarian Front would not like to have dealings with the totally corrupt world of the art market—"

"Hang on," I said in vague protest.

"—but all terrorism is about the end justifying the means, so probably they didn't let this get in their way. But possibly, as I say, Toni may have arranged this on his own account—off his own wicket?"

"Off his own bat," I said.

"Indeed, if he did, it would suggest one reason for this murder, since Toni and Busetto could be considered as having jointly stolen the property of the New Proletarian Army, that is the people. And indeed that would seem to be the symbolism behind the cutting of his fingers. With the other murders we had tongues cut out because they were informers. Fingers suggest theft to me: it's even more precise and so more contemptuous than cutting off the hands."

"And harder work," I said.

"Yes, they must have been very keen on the precision of their symbolism." He could have been commenting on a verse from a Scottish ballad. I remembered the clump of stubbed-out cigarettelike objects to the side of the corpse and repressed what would have been a squirm rather than a mere shiver of revulsion.

He went on in a musing tone: "Of course in England he could have been an informer again. Don't you say that someone puts the fingers on his mates?"

This was a mere idiom-fondling parenthesis, and he returned to the subject.

"Now when Toni leaves prison, he needs money and he still knows where the other paintings are hidden. And this time he decides to go straight to Osgood. He must have realized that he could make far more money this way than if he went through Busetto again. I think that we can reject the hypothesis that he might have gone to London as an agent for Busetto, can't we?" He darted a quick look at me for confirmation and I nodded in thoughtful agreement, not having been aware that such a hypothesis existed. He went on: "After all, he had to ask you where Osgood could be found, which presumably Busetto would have informed him about if he had been acting for him."

"But," I said, "Busetto was involved in some way. Why did Osgood come here to see him?"

"Presumably Busetto is his regular contact in Venice. So when he comes to Venice, he naturally goes to see him. And we mustn't forget the business about the Guardi."

"Yes. I've been thinking about that," I said. "I suppose Toni stole it as something easily portable that he could take to Osgood to establish his credentials. And, as Francesca suggested, as a way of getting back at his mother. But how does Busetto come into it then?"

"It is possible that Toni stole it to take to Busetto in order to find out who Busetto's London contact was. Or, more simply, Toni took it to Osgood and Osgood knew that there were two Guardis and so, without telling Toni of course, he got in touch with Busetto to find out if there was a practical way of getting hold of the other one. And Busetto suggested the idea of putting pressure on Francesca. I think that was probably Busetto's idea. He knows—he knew the family vaguely. That's what Francesca says, no?"

"You're sure," I said, "that it couldn't just be a sneaky idea that Toni himself thought up? He could have told Osgood that his sister would be sure to hand over the picture if she thought that he would get into trouble otherwise."

Alvise winced. "In theory it is possible. But I think I know the limits of Toni's—em—badness. And if he had one virtue, it

199

was his fondness for his sister. He wouldn't do anything to hurt her." Then after a pause he added cautiously, "I think."

We were crossing the Rio della Paglia, and turning left, we could see five bridges over the canal, one of them the Bridge of Sighs. I stopped and looked at the view. With his usual tentative tone when offering a suggestion Alvise said, "Why don't we go and see Francesca? I think she would like to know the full story too."

"Okay." We started down the bridge. I said, "I'm getting a very confused idea of Toni. Let's face it, he was a terrorist."

"He was a *fiancheggiatore*. He was never what they call a *regolare*."

"I see," I said. "He never killed anyone, is that what you mean? Just cleaned the guns."

"You could put it like that. He was never in full-time *clandestinità*. Until the very end, of course, when he hid in that palazzo."

"Yes. That's something else I'd like to know about. How long was he there? And was he alone?"

"It was in 1979, I think. The column he belonged to had been completely smashed and he was one of the few who managed to get away. The police went to his house to arrest him, in the middle of the night, but he escaped. They only found him about a month later. They guessed that someone must have been helping him, supplying him with food, et cetera, possibly someone in the family, but they never asked any questions about that. As I say, family loyalty is very strong there. But, yes, Toni was alone in the building. Except for the rats, possibly."

"And he didn't have the paintings with him."

"They weren't found there. But it's true the police did find evidence that the building had been used to store other things that belonged to the terrorists. They found some arms and leaflets and other things. It was obviously useful for the terrorists to have an aristocrat with a key to an enormous empty palazzo."

"How does an aristocrat get tied up in left-wing terrorism? Especially a dreamy academic aristocrat, which is the picture everyone gives me of Toni."

"Just because he *was* a dreamy academic. It all depends what he dreamed about. When I was a student, at the same time as Toni, we were all dreamers. We were always protesting, marching et cetera. I can't always remember what about. Sometimes for concrete things, sometimes just as part of the Great March, as Kundera says. And Toni and his *compagni* dreamed about the revolution. And it was just a dream: you had to be pretty far from reality to believe that the Italian working class were going to take up arms for communism, which was the only belief that made any kind of sense of their actions. And nobody is farther from reality than an academic, particularly a modern academic."

"Excuse me," I said, "what's your job?"

"Ah, yes, I know." He gave a quick nervous smile. "For my sins, that's what I am too. But the important thing is not to let the university limit you—which is not easy. You see, one of the effects of university life seems to be to turn one into either an alcoholic or a—a monomaniac. I'm still choosing. The people at the top at Ca' Foscari are all monomaniacs. On the whole the alcoholics are nicer. And Toni was a monomaniac. He was really very intelligent in a way, but also very very stupid. That is, he only knew what he knew, and didn't know—"

"What he didn't know," I concluded.

"Exactly. He was interested in his subject, which was the popular ballad in Italy and England, and he knew loads on this, and could say intelligent things on it. But he was quite amazingly ignorant about things outside this subject. I told you about the lamp, no? Well, he knew nothing about painting or music or history. Nothing. Zilch. His politics were limited to slogans about the people, and the people's power, et cetera. If you read about terrorists or ex-terrorists, they say they were always talking about politics together, but they must always have been reiterating the same few fixed ideas, because when you see them on television explaining their vision, they're obviously incapable of taking in anything new. I think you call it tunnel or funnel vision. Funnel is perhaps better, for not only can they see nothing outside their fixed ideas, these ideas become narrower and

201

narrower—they become blinder, until it comes to seem logical that they must kill for these ideas. For their beautiful dream. *Terroristi pentiti* often talk about their having been closed in a certain *logica*—a way of thinking. Closed in it like a box."

"So," I said, "beware the dreamers."

"Beware those who have only their dream. Because if you don't fit into their dream, then it's, well, it's hard cheese on you."

"It's what? Oh, yes, I see. And on your tongue too."

"Ah, that . . ." He was suddenly and unexpectedly at a loss for words. He let his face and hands state his disgust.

We came out into St. Mark's Square, and I found my nervousness about open spaces and people evaporate in its frosty marble splendor. How could the drawing room of Europe intimidate? We crossed it in silence.

When we got to the shop, Marina was showing a customer a selection of blouses. She hadn't changed her trousers, I was interested to note, and they hadn't split yet either. She turned her toothy smile on us and then recognized me. "If you want Francesca," she said, "she went out a few minutes ago with a girl." She managed to suggest the words "yet again" by her tone.

I said, "She'll be coming back?"

"I suppose so. But if you want her now you could try the Bar al Teatro. That's where she usually goes."

"Okay."

We went on to the bar, and through the glass door I saw Francesca holding a drink next to the counter and listening seriously to Lucy. Lucy was talking with quick animation. She too was holding a drink, but her other hand was gesturing freely. Alvise and I entered and Lucy caught sight of me and flushed in that sudden way of hers. I said, "*Ciao*. I didn't know you two knew each other."

"I don't," Lucy said. "That is, I didn't. She rang the school just a minute or so after you left, asking for you."

Francesca nodded. "This is true. I wanted to speak to you."

"And so?" I said to Lucy. "What made you drop everything and come running out here?"

202

"Francesca sounded a bit upset on the phone when she asked for you, and I simply asked what the matter was. She asked me who I was and I said—I said—"

"She said she was a friend," Francesca put in.

"Oh, really?" I said. I looked at Lucy with my eyebrows raised.

She said, "All right, let's just say I want to bloody know what's going on." There was always something awkward about Lucy's swear words: they were too deliberate and often unnaturally placed. "Francesca said she had to get in touch with you, and it sounded urgent, so I said, quite openly and honestly, that I was worried about what you were mixed up in, and could she tell me anything about it. And so she told me where to come and see her. That's all. I was just telling her about what happened at the school and I told her about you getting pushed in the canal—"

"I didn't know that," Francesca said to me. "By Busetto, no?"

"Yes," I said. "What have you told her?"

"Nothing yet," Francesca said. "Lucy had just started to tell me these things."

"Right. Well, thanks, Lucy, that'll save me a little time. Have you paid for that drink?"

"What do you mean?" Lucy said.

"Well, I still owe you one, don't I? I'll pay for it and then we'll be quits and you can go."

"Are you ordering me out of the place?"

"Well, I'm just hoping you'll take a gentle hint."

Francesca opened her mouth as if to say something, but then thought better. Alvise had simply stepped back a few paces and was examining the magazines on sale in the corner of the bar. Lucy said, "Martin, why do you have to—" She stopped and shrugged. "Well, all right, I suppose it's your life. Okay, *ciao*, Francesca." She finished her drink and walked out.

After this there was naturally a rather awkward pause, which I bridged by saying sorry, it was all a private matter, and then getting Alvise to explain our theory about Busetto's murder.

"Why did Toni come back?" Francesca said at the end, shaking her head.

"Well," I said, "now he might decide that things are too hot and clear out. It all depends how much he wants that money."

"And," Alvise put in, "Mr. Osgood might decide this too, in which case Toni will have to give up whether he wants to or not."

I said, "The only thing I can suggest is we try and convince Osgood to clear out."

"Yes," Alvise said, "by now you surely know enough about his—his business to frighten him, if Busetto's death hasn't already done that."

Francesca gave an involuntary shiver. "That man—he frightens me."

"*Oh, dio,*" said Alvise. We both turned and looked at him and he gestured toward the door. Two carabinieri were coming into the bar. Machine guns hung on their shoulders and their hands were caressing the triggers.

15

"*DOCUMENTI,*" the first one said. It was an announcement to the whole bar, almost as if he were selling them. Apart from ourselves and the barman, there were only a couple of businessmen and three youths. The latter raised a protesting grumble as they fumbled in their pockets. I was pleased to note their tattered jeans, the earring of one of them, the long hair of another. They looked just the sort to attract all the attention of the carabinieri. I reached inside my anorak and discovered with relief that I had my passport with me; I could feel a sullen tom-tom starting up in my temples and only hoped it wasn't visible.

The two carabinieri did no more than glance at the identity cards proffered by the businessmen and then moved on to the group of youths. The youths were disappointingly meek at this point, one of them merely asking, "What's all this about?" He wasn't answered and he didn't insist. What a wimp. One of the carabinieri stayed with his gun covering the group while the other examined the documents. He looked from card to face, from face to card, and then passed on to the next. He had a thin southern face, with what looked like a very first attempt at a mustache. He couldn't have been any older, I thought, than the students I'd taught that afternoon: but he did have a machine gun.

He moved on to us. His colleague stayed a few steps back, with his gun leveled. The one with the mustache looked at Alvise's tattered card in silence, and then at Francesca's. I handed my passport over, hoping to see a look of suitable awe as he took in the lion and the unicorn and the crown. He just flipped it until he came to the photo. "Peeps."

"Phipps," I said. My voice was a raucous whisper. I repeated it.

"Do you speak Italian?"

"Yes."

"Where are you staying?"

I told him the name of the hotel. "I'm on holiday," I said unnecessarily.

He tapped the passport in his hand for a second or two, then went over to his colleague. I could feel sweat forming on my forehead and the tom-tom pulsing faster. I glanced at Alvise, who merely gave a tiny shrug and a tic of a smile. Francesca was looking at the two carabinieri as if she were about to throw herself at their feet. The two carabinieri spoke rapidly in an incomprehensible southern dialect, then the first one beckoned me over. I went forward slowly, holding my arms out from my body so the carabinieri wouldn't have any excuse for making any foolish mistakes. The one with my passport said, "English, yes?"

"Yes."

"My colleague wants to know what it means 'groovy keend of love.' "

"Kind," his colleague corrected him.

"Ah, oh," I said. I translated it as best as I could: "*Un tipo di amore,* um, in the groove, *cioè, quello giusto, un po' speciale.*"

They nodded with a kind of official acceptance of this version, then he gave me back the passport and they left.

As soon as my voice was under control again I said, "I should have called them fascist brutes and refused to comply, I suppose."

206

"Oh, no," said Francesca, with big serious eyes, "you mustn't do anything that can provoke."

I looked at Alvise, expecting some quip. I suddenly noticed his left cheek was twitching. He caught my eye on him and forced a smile to his face. "Too many memories of my merry student days in the seventies. When there were riot policemen outside the university every other day." His voice was level but sounded forced, as if he were fighting to keep a tremor out of it.

I tried to defuse things a little. "I could do with another drink."

"Not for me, thank you," Francesca said. "I should get back to the shop." She picked up her scarf from the counter and wrapped it around herself. "So you will go to see this Mr. Osgood then?"

I said, "I suppose so, though I can't guarantee anything. There's a chance that he might simply laugh and say what proof have you got?" And he might say a word or two as well about the credibility of evidence gathered together by me. "He's apparently away at Asolo today, but tomorrow morning, first thing, I'll be at the Danieli. After all, we'll surely be able to get witnesses together that he was with Busetto at Harry's Bar."

"And with me," Francesca put in gently.

"Ah," I said. "I suppose you'd prefer to be kept out of it."

She gave a half smile. "Otherwise we might as well go straight to the police and tell them about Toni."

"Yes," I said. "I see what you mean. Well, I won't insist on that point."

Alvise said, "Isn't it possible that someone will remember seeing Busetto there anyway?" His voice sounded more natural and the twitch had died down.

She shook her head, frowning. "I don't think so. Mr. Osgood, yes, of course. Nobody could forget him. But Busetto: well, he'd obviously never been there before and nobody knew him, and, em, he wasn't the kind of person you notice."

"All the same," I said, "I'm sure I can persuade him that the risk just isn't worth it, whether we've got anything definite on him or not."

"I wish you luck," Francesca said. "I don't want ever to have to see him again. Bye-bye."

" 'Bye," I said. "Give our best wishes to Marina."

"Oh, that girl," she said, rolling her eyes to heaven. She gave us a final, rather wan smile and left.

"Do you want another drink?" I said to Alvise.

"I won't, thank you. I think I should go home. I have a mountain of theses to read."

"Okay. Which way are you going?"

"Toward the Accademia. I live by San Nicolò dei Mendicoli."

"Oh, yes?" I said. "I like that area. That's where the house with the monkeys is, isn't it?"

"That's right. I live just round the corner, on the *fondamenta* going—" He stopped suddenly, as if he saw no point in explaining. "Round there anyway. Goodbye."

"Well, I'll come as far as Campo Santo Stefano," I said.

"Oh, yes, of course."

We left the bar and started walking along the route that Francesca had shown me that morning. We were both silent, and after a while I felt the silence was an awkward one. Maybe Alvise hadn't wanted me to come with him. Maybe he still had a bit of quiet twitching to do. I said, "So—er . . ."

"So?"

"So thanks."

"What for?"

"Well, for not going to the police." I looked sideways at him, with a rather stupid curiosity to see whether the word would start him shaking again. He remained impassive and I went on, "And for talking through the whole thing with me. I think you saved me from going mad."

"Good. I'm glad my academic love for a puzzle has served some good purpose."

We were silent again and I could feel the big question "What next?" hanging over us both. Then, as we crossed the little square behind the Fenice, he said, "So the best of luck."

"Ah, yes, thanks."

"I might as well tell you I don't want to get any more involved."

"No, of course not." In fact I felt a sudden crashing disappointment. The thought of having an ally had greatly cheered me. But I knew I had no right to expect anything else.

"You see," he went on, "I've satisfied my curiosity and I've appeased my conscience about the need or not to go to the police. That is what counts. For the rest, well, I can only say that in all matters to do with politics I have a sort of Swiss attitude of noninvolvement. I am a complete *menefreghista*." (This word can only be translated by something like "a couldn't-care-less-person.") "At least I have been since about 1978. It seemed to be the safest thing to do at the time. It was either that or end up hurting people. Or being hurt."

"I see," I said. Then I added, "Not a complete one, or you wouldn't have bothered to come looking for me."

"Well, you know, the temptation just to forget about your visit to the university was very strong, but then . . ." He gave one of his quick jerky shrugs. "Well, let's just say I had good reasons for not giving into this temptation."

"Oh," I said, and waited for him to go on. But he didn't. So I went on myself, "Well, as I say, thanks for your—your help and, er—sometime you'll have to tell me all about Scottish literature . . ."

"Start by reading *Waverley;* that's all about the dangers of getting mixed up in other people's business. So—so good-bye." We'd come out into Campo Santo Stefano and that was as far as I'd said I'd accompany him, so his obligation to go on talking to me ended there: this was what his attitude seemed to say.

I said, "Right, I take your point. 'Bye then." I put my hand out and he shook it in his village-pump fashion, gave me a last quick smile, and scuttered off.

It was a little after nine when I reached Rio Marin, the canal on which my hotel stood. The two *fondamente* on each side of the canal were empty and the canal lay still, the bridges forming almost perfect unwavering circles with their reflections. Only my footsteps echoed clickingly castanetlike on the cold pavement. I was looking forward to being in bed, far from all terrorists (well, and all carabinieri too). I would curl up in luxurious snugness and enjoy the end of my Dick Francis novel, with its pleasantly distant dangers and thrills (the only horses in Venice, after all, were of bronze or marble) and its guaranteed happy ending.

I was about ten yards from the hotel's front door when two men came out of a *sottoportico* directly in front of me. There was no mistaking their intentions, not even for a second: one blocked me from the front and the other slipped around behind me. Something hard was jabbed into my back. My mouth opened—probably to scream—but no sound came out. The one in front then stepped to my side, his left hand firmly gripping my arm. He was taller than me, in a dark coat; a black beard and glasses were about all I took in of his facial appearance. The other one serpented round to my side as well: the gun scraped around my middle but was not withdrawn.

"Keep walking," the one on the right said in Italian, "and don't say a word."

I kept walking. I suppose all that anyone would think on seeing the three of us was that I was being helped home by solicitous friends after a merry evening. I glanced at the man on the other side; smaller, also bearded, and with long fair hair. The gun was rammed in harder and the blond man whispered, "Look straight ahead."

"What do you want with me?" I managed to get out at last. I was trying to work out whether they were policemen or terrorists; I was afraid they were the latter.

They said nothing. After just ten paces down the *fondamenta*, the man on my right, the one without the gun, released my arm and dropped into a boat that was loosely moored to a pole. The gun was pushed with even greater force into my side, as if to brand me. The man in the boat flicked the rope free and started up the outboard motor. The boat was entirely empty, with just bare wet boards.

At this point we heard a tune being whistled farther down the *fondamenta.* We all turned but there was no one in sight. The two men looked at each other and the one in the boat said, "Okay, let's move." The man with the gun prodded me and said, "Jump."

I suddenly realized I recognized the tune: it was *Celeste Aïda.* I looked down the *fondamenta* again and at that moment Lucy came into sight from an alley off to the right. She had her hands in her pockets and was walking in our direction. Her air was that of one taking a casual evening stroll and she didn't seem to be looking at us. I had one moment of desperate confusion. Was she in with these men? Was it she who'd led them to my hotel? But the two terrorists were now paying her no more than wary attention, and I realized that that tune could be a message only to me.

I halted at the very edge of the *fondamenta;* the gun was still pushing me, and the man moved in closer to hide it. "Jump," he hissed. (The word does have an *s* in Italian.) The man in the boat, however, made a pacifying gesture with his hand and said quietly, "Wait." He didn't want any signs of struggling in front of a witness. He fiddled with the rope so as to give some kind of explanation for our frozen tableau on the edge of the *fondamenta.*

Lucy was now just a few feet away and I saw she had a cigarette in her hand. She was holding it a couple of inches from her mouth. She said in Italian to the man who was gripping me, "Have you got a light?"

He turned for just one half second, the gun withdrawing from the crater it had delved into my innards. I acted instantly, jerking away and jabbing my left elbow back hard. At almost the same moment Lucy must have struck him: I didn't actually see this, but suddenly he was falling into the boat. I saw his colleague rearing back, his hand halfway inside his coat reaching for a gun. Then he was knocked overboard.

Even before the splash Lucy and I had started running. A couple of seconds later I heard the boat roar into life behind us, which presumably meant that the man who'd fallen into the boat was not bothering to rescue the man he'd knocked out of it. Well, if that was the way he treated his *friend,* getting caught by him seemed like a very bad idea. The engine noise grew louder, and the canal water swished and swirled against the banks and the moored vessels all creaked against their poles. Just as the boat came level with us we reached an alley off to the left and we turned into it, our shoes skidding and our hands grabbing at the stone angle to steady ourselves. Lucy was just two few paces ahead of me, and my hand momentarily touched hers on the wall. I glanced around and saw the man in the boat looking back down the canal to his friend. He put the boat in reverse, obviously deciding the chase wasn't worth the while. I kept running, however.

"Let's cross the canal," Lucy gasped. She presumably meant crossing the Grand Canal by the bridge near the station.

"Why?" I said. Now we were slowing down to a side-clutching stagger—at least I was clutching and staggering; she was just slowing down.

"We can go to my hotel there."

"And if they see us on the bridge?"

"They'll be getting out of the area—won't they?" The last two words were added with sudden doubt and a glance at me.

"All right, let's hope so."

We were both walking now. Ahead of us we could see the green dome of San Simeone Piccolo, the church that stands on the Grand Canal opposite the station. Neither of us spoke for a few seconds, we just panted. We thought of all the hundred things there were to say—and to ask.

Eventually I said, "I didn't know you smoked."

"You didn't know I—" This slow sentence of disbelief turned into a sudden laugh. "Oh, Martin."

I said, "Look, don't think I'm not grateful—but as I expect you can imagine, I'm just a bit confused."

"Nothing like as much as I am, I can assure you."

"But how did you come to be there?"

"And how did those two come to be there?" she came back.

"Oh, God, I can see we've got one hell of a question-and-answer session to come."

"But you're going to answer them, are you?" She was looking at me hard as she said this.

"Least I can do, I suppose."

"Yes, I'd say it is."

"Right."

"Are you going to say anything else?" she said. She'd stopping walking and stood staring at me hard; her fists weren't exactly set on her hips, but there was a general suggestion of the akimbo about her.

"Like what?"

"Like sorry."

"Well, I don't want to confuse a momentary feeling of gratitude with a feeling of repentance that's not really there."

Wham.

That was her open hand on my face. And it stung.

"Go on," she said. "I've seen all the films. Now you smash me back."

"Won't be necessary," I said, rubbing my cheek. My head was still reeling. "I probably deserved that. For phrasing things pompously, if nothing else."

"Yes," she said, "I won't argue with that assessment of the state of affairs."

I looked hard at her. "That, I imagine, is a parody." There was even the hint of a smile, a rather twisted smile, at the corners of her mouth.

"You've got it."

We started walking again. We came out on the Grand Canal. There were a few people around the brightly lit station and a vaporetto pulling away from the stop opposite us. But there was no sign of my would-be kidnappers' boat. We walked briskly up and over the bridge, again not talking by unstated assent. When we were walking down the Lista di Spagna, we breathed more easily again and she said, "Right, you start, and first off I want a good reason why I shouldn't—why *we* shouldn't go to the police."

There was going to be a touch of *déjà entendu* about this conversation, I felt—for me at any rate.

213

"Please," I said, "just tell me how you came to be strolling along Rio Marin at this time of night."

"Because I'm a bloody fool, I suppose. A bloody fool who believes in such things as—as old times' sake. . . . No, this isn't the right way to tell this story. Sorry, I'll start again."

"No hurry," I said.

"All right. When I left that bar earlier, I was pretty annoyed. That's putting things mildly. I was—I was—well, you can imagine, I suppose. That was the point, no doubt."

She turned and stared hard at me. I gave a noncommittal shrug.

"But I was still worried," she went on. "I'd seen that cut on your face and hand. I knew someone had come in to the school and attacked you—and I knew you were mixed up in something—something dangerous. All right, emotional logic told me I should just shrug my shoulders and say, well, if that's his attitude let him get carved up, that's his business. . . . But, well . . . I couldn't convince myself that I cared that little."

"Really," I said.

"You're a real swine," she said at once.

"I just said really."

"I know what you said. And I know what you meant. And—and. . . . Oh hell, I suppose you even have a point."

I jerked around at this. She was staring straight ahead and refused to look at me.

She went on: "Let's talk that through later. So when I left that bar I was furious, but scared for you, and I was really wondering whether I should be going to the police or something. I just couldn't shake off the thought of how I'd feel if you got killed and I hadn't lifted a finger. So I decided I'd go along to your hotel and at least see if you got safely back—and perhaps try and have another word—if—if it didn't prove too demeaning for me. Luisa told me where you were staying. I went along. I wasn't going to hang around in the streets all evening of course, but I felt I ought to make some kind of effort—maybe just for the sake of my conscience, I really don't know. And then I discovered

214

that there was a restaurant there which had a good view of the canal and *fondamenta*. So I ate there. I had nothing else to do."

She took a breath here. We crossed the large square of San Geremia and a drunk hailed us from one corner. We ignored him and he shouted something about "*foresti maledetti*"—bloody foreigners—and went back to his bottle.

Lucy returned to her story as we crossed the high bridge over the Cannaregio Canal. "I had a table by the window. I'd been there about ten minutes when those two men came in and sat by the window too, and I noticed they were keeping an eye on the canal as well. So at this point I knew I just had to hang around. I thought of going to the police again, but then realized how stupid I could be made to look. I mean what could I say to them? So I played the part of a pretty gormless tourist and just ate and watched. I even got out my map of Venice to add to the effect. They left eventually, and I was pretty sure they hadn't really noticed me. I saw them going to that boat and checking the rope or something, then they went into that alley by the hotel. Well, I had a look at my map, a real look this time, and I saw how I could go round to that alley by the back and so I did. I saw them there, just standing at the corner and watching, and obviously not wanting to be noticed. So I went to the other end of the *fondamenta* and waited in an alley there. About ten minutes later you came along." She paused. "I was terrified."

"I wasn't too cool either," I said.

She was obviously still thinking back. After a few seconds she said, "Since you're interested, it wasn't a cigarette, just a bit of paper wrapped round the top of a pen."

"Well, that's a relief. Lucy smoking, whatever next, I thought."

"And you can say thank you again now," she said.

"Thank you." I'm not sure how I was intending it to sound. Polite but ungushing? Dry and ironic even? I was in fact generally confused about my own feelings, and this probably showed. She made no comment on my tone.

She had started walking down the side of the Cannaregio

Canal. I was about to ask her where her hotel was when I heard a boat turn into the canal from the Grand Canal. I grabbed her hand and pulled her with me into a side alley. We stood there flat against the wall as the boat chugged on past. We saw it to be a taxi and our two breaths were let out in simultaneous explosion.

"Sorry about the panic," I said.

"Quite understandable," she said with a smile.

We both realized we were still holding hands. I made as if to withdraw mine, but she squeezed it hard and said, "You're a stubborn bastard but—" and she moved around in front of me. I found my arms wrapping around her.

Some seconds later our mouths disengaged and she said, "This is very odd."

"Yes," I said.

"But nice."

"Mm."

"Don't you think?"

"Yes," I said again. "I suppose so."

"Oh, Martin," she said in her usual mock despair at my tone. Then she laughed. "This is definitely the last thing I thought the evening had in store for me."

"Well, shared danger can have funny effects on one's feelings."

"You're still trying to reason your way out of it, aren't you?" Her lips closed in on mine again. My attempt to be cool and objective in my reaction lasted about a quarter of a second this time.

"Now," she said about half a minute later, "go on, tell me what the psychological aberration behind that was."

I gave as much of a shrug as our close-bound circumstances permitted. "I don't know," I said. "I need to think. Abstinence perhaps."

"Well, you certainly don't seem to have forgotten anything."

"And the suggestion of the surroundings," I said.

"Yes. It takes you back, doesn't it? Kissing in side alleys, with one eye out for the other students or Derek Robin."

216

"That's the trouble with this city," I said. "It just naturally soaks up memories: you can't do anything here without remembering other times, or other people doing it like Byron or Casanova or Fred Astaire."

"Oh, Martin, don't you go all gushy over Venice as well; is there any other city where people spend so much time talking rubbish about the place?"

"New York," I said.

"Possibly," she said. "But they've been talking rubbish about Venice for longer. So you're going to say it was all because of the moonlight on the water and the gondolier singing in the distance, right?" She had stepped half a pace back and her hands were just loosely touching my sides now. Her eyes were still closely engaged, however.

"No," I said. "Not entirely, but—well, Venice doesn't inspire cool rationality, does she?"

"When people start calling Venice 'she,' I know all hope is lost. But look, don't let's get sidetracked, fun though it might be. You've got an explanation to give to me."

"Let's get moving," I said. "I still feel a bit nervous out in the open."

"Okay," she said, "you can tell me the whole thing when we get to the hotel. I've got a bottle of wine we can open. And there's a phone there if you decide to call the police." She paused. "Or if I decide to." She stepped out onto the *fondamenta* again and stretched her hand out to mine. I hung back for half a second, then took it. We walked in silence. There was no doubt that her hand in mine felt right—for the moment.

I hardly noticed where we were going—and then suddenly I realized we were in the square where the old Palazzo Sambon stood. I said, "Look, wait a moment. . . ."

"What?"

"Where are you taking me?"

"That's the hotel," she said, pointing to the building next to the palazzo.

"No," I said, "no, I don't—I don't believe it." I had dropped her hand. A hideous and quite illogical doubt had gripped me. "Why are you staying there?" I was looking around the square as I spoke. There was nobody in sight, not even a pigeon. The houses were all shuttered; even the hotel had no lights showing.

"Why shouldn't I? What's the matter with it?"

"It's nothing, I just—I was just surprised." Surprised and suspicious.

She looked hard at me. "You've obviously got a lot to tell me. Come on."

"Who else is there?"

"Well, nobody for the moment. That's why you can come without creating any problems. We've booked up the whole hotel for the course, and all the students have gone to Mantua for two days. Derek thought someone should stay, just to keep an eye on the rooms—check the woman doesn't start subletting them, which I wouldn't put past her."

"I see." I was thinking hard; there was no reason why they shouldn't be staying here. It was just a hotel. "Look, maybe I'd better not be seen by the people at the desk." I doubted that the woman I'd spoken to would remember me, but there was no point in risking it. And if I could sleep there without handing in a passport, so much the better.

"If you're thinking of my reputation, I can only say thanks—but I suppose you've other things on your mind."

"Well, is it possible?"

"Yes. The desk is on the first floor, but there's nobody there permanently. A bell rings when the front door's opened, so the woman looks out of her kitchen. You just hang around in the entrance, and when you hear me whistle, come on up. Just keep going on up the stairs. I'll wait for you on the second floor. She's usually got the television on, so she shouldn't hear."

"Okay. *Celeste Aïda*, of course."

"Of course."

This worked easily enough. Lucy had her own key to the hotel's front door. I hung around in the entrance, heard her say "*Buonasera*, signora," and then a few seconds later *Celeste Aïda*

218

started up. I walked nimbly and quietly up, past the murmur of a soap opera, and joined Lucy on the staircase. "Top floor, I'm afraid," Lucy said. "I've got the only single room."

Top floor was the fourth floor. The room was rigorously single in its furniture: one bed, one bedside table, one chair, one light bulb, one sink, one wardrobe, one picture of the Rialto Bridge. Lucy had used her own belongings to give the place a rather more welcoming air of multiplicity. There was a row of books on top of the wardrobe, various postcards of paintings propped up on the table, some blouses and skirts spread along the foot of the bed and the chair, and an array of shoes under the sink. She went over to the radiator and put her hands on it. "It's on," she said with relief. "I thought she might have decided . . ." She took her coat off and tossed it on the bed. I did the same.

I glanced at the books: Hugh Honour's *Companion Guide* to the city, various modern novels, *Middlemarch,* a book on Palladio,and two novels by Calvino in Italian. She saw me looking at them. "Go on then," she said.

"Go on what?"

"Let's have the usual sneer at my tastes in literature."

"Did I do that?"

"Yes, always."

"Just disguised guilt," I said, "because I read nothing but rubbish, as you know. No, I'm impressed."

"And there's no need to patronize."

"We have gone back, haven't we?" I said. This semiserious bickering was almost more pregnant with memories than anything that had happened so far. I saw her tugging at the corkscrew and thought back to twenty such evenings in an almost identical hotel room elsewhere in the city. And, as almost invariably on those occasions, she gave up and handed me the bottle. "You prove your manhood."

I pulled the cork out without rupturing anything. She poured into two glasses she'd taken from a cupboard by the door. I took one and went over to the window. I opened it and looked out. It's impossible to resist any elevated view in Venice.

I tried to identify the bell towers I could see across the rooftops and chimneys and aerials. Then I looked down to the canal, which was full of moored boats, unmoving in the rippleless water. Leaning out, I could see the patchy white facade of Palazzo Sambon directly to my right.

"Hey," she said, "it's getting cold."

"Sorry." I brought my head back in and closed the window. I went and sat on the bed.

"Sorry about the lack of chairs," she said.

"I've been in worse places."

"Yes, I suppose so."

This dried up conversation on both sides. She was obviously thinking hard and carefully about what to say.

I said, "You don't have to pretend it never happened, you know."

"I don't mean to. I want you to tell me about it. Among other things. I want you to tell me everything."

"Why did you never—oh, hell." I took a great swig of wine.

"Never what?"

"Never ask me then. About anything."

She stared into her glass and turned it slowly in her hands. "I think we were both really silly."

"Silly." I put my glass down on the bedside table. "Extremely silly of me to go to jail. Should have escaped at once, of course."

"Now you really are being silly. But no, I was probably the stupider one then. And I had no excuses. But it all just goes to show what—what balls it is when people say that perfect love means understanding. Love means never having to say you're sorry, and all the rest of the rubbish. I don't think anybody ever loved anybody like I loved you, and vice versa I'm sure, but we could still both make the stupidest mistakes about each other and what the other was thinking."

"Go on, tell me. What was my mistake?"

"Well, you remember how things were just before you got arrested? You'd had that row with my father—"

"Hardly row. I'd just asked how it was that the Vatican

always seemed to be involved in shady financial dealings. I hadn't brought the subject up either."

"It was your tone, Martin, and you know it. That God-save-me-from-the-dirty-business-world tone."

I winced a little. Well, at least she hadn't categorized it, as she might have done with equal fairness, as greasy chapel piety. Certain things stick, even when you think you've shaken them off completely.

"But anyway," she went on, "you remember how I defended my father to you afterward."

"Yes. And I didn't criticize you for doing so, did I?"

"Not directly. But you managed to give the idea that you'd decided we were all a Mafia—and that I had to choose between them and you."

"I never said that."

"I know, I know. It was all along the lines of, 'Well, of course if that's what Daddy says, that's what you must do.' Day in, day out. Your stupid bloody Jimmy Porter stance."

I said nothing. It was all too fair a description. Me as anachronistic as ever, Looking Back In Petty Peevishness.

She went on. "Then you got arrested, and when I saw you before the trial you—you—" She faltered. She was obviously thinking back to something she'd thought back to many many times. "Well, you were all kind of stiff and formal with me. It'll sound stupid, but it really did seem from the way you spoke that you almost welcomed what had happened as a way of breaking things off. . . ."

"I what? But I—" I thought back too. "Oh, Lucy." A slow sad headshake, learned from Adrian. "It must have been nervous reaction. Desperation even. You know I get more *antipatico* when I'm in the shit."

"I know. I know *now*. But then . . . well, I suppose I needed—I hoped for—for just one sign that you wanted or needed help from me. Just one tiny sign, of any sort. And you didn't give it. And I was too stupid to realize just how far your bloody inverted snobbery or pride could go."

I was silent for a few seconds. "Yes, it was that too."

I remembered even making some stupid joke about how nice of her to come and see how the other half lived. And she hadn't laughed. Well, my tone probably hadn't been particularly jocular.

"Sorry," I said eventually.

"Idiot," she said at once. "You can say sorry for this afternoon, but for *then,* well, as I say it was me who was the—the insensitive swine then. And when I did think better about it all, you'd been sentenced and—well, it just seemed too late for anything. I'd screwed things up and probably you wouldn't want to hear from me again, and quite rightly too. So I just let things ride."

"I see," I said.

"Though if we're going for total honesty, I suppose I should add that all these feelings and decisions were probably helped by the fact that they were the easiest ones to take, family pressure being what it was. And that's what makes me feel guiltiest of all."

"What'll you tell Daddy now then?"

"Look, Martin, I'll take anything from you now but cracks about Daddy. Okay?"

"Sorry. Just call me Jimmy Porter when I do it and that's guaranteed to stop me. Come here."

She didn't move. She said, "I bet all this time you've been thinking of yourself as Rick in *Casablanca.*"

"What?"

"You know: 'a guy with a silly expression on his face because his insides have just been kicked out.' " The imitation of Humphrey Bogart wouldn't have won any prizes, but I recognized it.

"You're right," I said. "You do know me too bloody well. Come here."

"And you'll kees me as eef it were the last time?" She came and sat next to me. Well, she started off sitting anyway.

222

16

"YOU still haven't told me anything about yourself and this evening," she said sometime later. She was sitting up against the pillow, her hair in great spreading disarray.

"Sorry," I said. "Things seemed pressing. I wanted to get in before your usual religious doubts did."

"Get in," she said. "How delightfully you put things. Pour yourself some more wine."

"Thanks, I will." I got out of bed and shivered. The radiator was not exactly a furnace. I put my trousers and a sweater on. I poured out two glasses and handed her one. She sat right up with the sheet and blankets pulled around for warmth. I said, "So what do you know about the whole thing?"

"Just what I read in the paper. How you and that man, whatever his name was, fell into the canal."

"No, unfortunately it was only me. Well, I'd better start from the beginning." So for the second time that day I told the story. And this time I really did get that sense of overwhelming relief and liberation that I'd hoped for when I'd started talking to Alvise, because this time I really did tell everything. It was as much a confession as a narrative. I realized I hadn't talked so

223

freely to anyone since I came out of prison. I found myself pacing up and down the room and gesturing with my glass. At one point I even mimed my falling into the canal. She listened with her usual responsive attention, her eyes widening and narrowing, her mouth opening and closing (though not necessarily in synchrony). She didn't interrupt too much, however. She leaped out of bed at one point to hold me tight when I told of the picture burning, and this threatened to lead into an extended digression, but then she sat back down again and I continued. The only thing I did hold back was that vague urge I'd had to kiss Francesca: it hardly seemed essential to the story. At the end I poured out the rest of the wine and she said, "You do get yourself into some right messes, don't you?"

"Yes, miss."

"So what now?"

"A long sleep, I reckon. Will any of your charges have left a pair of pajamas, do you think?"

"Be serious."

"Are you going to start bludgeoning now?" I asked. "What about the police and my duty as a citizen and all the rest of it?"

"Look, I understand your—your reluctance, but you can't be more scared of the police than you are of those thugs tonight."

"Let's say it's a toss-up," I said.

"One thing I don't understand," she said, frowning. "That attack in the school was obviously just to scare you, right?"

"Yes, I suppose so. Like the note in the hotel."

"So what made them suddenly change tactics and try and kidnap you?"

"They may have thought that I don't scare so easily. Wish it were true."

"Maybe. It just seems odd to me. And then how had they found out where you were staying?"

"I've thought of that. I suppose they knew the category of hotel I'd left and they just phoned round all the other hotels in Venice of that category as being where I'd most likely move to. It wouldn't take them that long."

224

"I suppose not. But are you sure that's how it was? I mean, what about this Elvis guy?"

"Alvise," I said. "It's a common name in Venice, though I've never come across it anywhere else."

"Never mind about the name. You say he got you to tell him the whole story and then just suddenly upped and offed."

"I know what you're thinking. But I find it hard to believe. He seemed—well, a nice guy. A bit nervous—particularly of the police, but—"

"Of the police. Well, then."

"That doesn't mean anything necessarily. I'm nervous of them—and so probably is anyone who went through the seventies as a student here. Though he did seem very scared. . . . Well, I don't know, I reserve judgment. Because as I say, there are plenty of ways they could have found out where I was staying without it being anything to do with him."

"I suppose so," she said, still doubtfully. She changed the subject. "So the next thing you have to do is speak to Osgood, right?"

"Right."

"He sounds a character," she said.

"He's poison," I said at once.

She looked surprised. "That sounded really bitter."

"Don't tell me, I'm supposed to have a soft spot for the lovable old rogue, because after all we're all in the same business, right? Con artists together."

"Martin," she said, "come here."

I obeyed, lying out beside her. She stroked my forehead, which I discovered with surprise was what I really needed at that moment, and she said, "Don't get twisted up inside."

After a pause I said, "You do know why I got involved in all this, don't you?"

"Go on, tell me."

"It's because I really care about that painting—those paintings. . . ."

"Cima is the tops," she murmured.

"Right. I mean it's not one of the greatest paintings in the

225

world, its rediscovery isn't going to set the bells ringing much outside Treganzi, but its loss is going to make the world that one bit poorer. In some ways I care for it so much *because* it's a minor work. I sometimes think it's the wonderful smaller treasures that you find in remote places that make Italy special: the fact that every little one-horse hamlet has its jewel. And it's because of bastards like Osgood that the paintings get pinched or have to be moved to museums, where they just become one more Madonna and Child. With careful catalog notes by Professor Perkins probably. Because it's not a question of sneak thieves; it's a very professional business, in which Osgood and his kind are essential elements. Your average sneak thief would be wasting his time pinching a sixteenth-century painting, because who's he going to sell it to? He's not going to know the sort of lunatic aesthete who's prepared to pay thousands for something he's going to have to gloat over in secret. But Osgood does know these people. And there seem to be more of them than one would think possible, judging by the number of works that disappear every year. And to my mind every painting that disappears is another victory for barbarism."

"Martin, you've convinced me. Okay, I see you care: you're a lone knight against the forces of barbarism."

"Sorry, sorry," I said. "I reckon prison must have brought out my latent chapel sanctimony."

"Don't worry," she said. "I suppose I'm just not used to seeing you so—so worked up about anything. You really do care, don't you?"

"Well, it's something to keep me going," I said with a shrug.

"Ah good, that's more like the laid-back Martin I remember. So long as it's not all just a clever way of putting off painting again."

"What?" I stared at her.

"Well, I always remember how you'd fiddle around for ages between every new painting—saying you had to clean the studio first, or get new brushes, or even just tidy the house. Anything."

"Well, only if I was going to try something new."

"Exactly. And I bet the one thing you don't want to do now is paint the same old things all over again."

"No," I said after a moment's thought. "I can't think of anything that would depress me more. The same bloody gimmicks."

I poured myself another glass of wine and went over to the window to change the subject. "Hey, why don't I go in and have a look at Palazzo Sambon?"

"What, now?"

"When better? Have you got a torch?"

"Yes, but if you think I'm coming . . ."

"No, of course you needn't."

"And what do you expect to find but rats?"

"I don't know. But it just seems silly to be so close and not go and have a look." I opened the window and leaned out again. I looked at the nearest window of Palazzo Sambon. It was on a slightly higher level than the one where we were and had a protruding marble sill resting on corbels. "You know," I said, "I could probably step across to the window there, and the shutters don't look all that strong."

"I forbid you," she said. She got out of bed and took a dressing gown from behind the door and joined me.

"I'd only fall in the canal and I'm probably immune to everything now."

"And how do I explain things to the coroner? I'd probably lose my job. You know what Derek's like."

"Yes," I said. "Okay, I'll spare your reputation. There's a loose shutter on the ground floor actually."

"Good. I know you like to pretend you're Indiana Jones, but I'm quite happy to keep you as a boring old artist who—"

"Plays safe."

She was taken aback by my tone. "Martin, have I touched another sore spot?"

"Sorry, I'm covered in them."

We kissed. It seemed the easiest way to conclude the momentary embarrassment. Then we just stood by the window gazing out, listening to the faint sloshing of the boats below, with their ropes squeaking against the poles. No other noise at all.

"What was that?" she said suddenly.

"What?"

"Listen."

And I heard it too—a yelp or bellow, apparently from next door. From Palazzo Sambon. It was a male voice and it was impossible to interpret the emotion behind it beyond the fact that it seemed to be uttering the protracted *e* sound of the English word *help*.

We both leaned out as far as possible, but could see nothing. And then there was a flicker of light apparently from one of the windows—as if a swirling torch beam had momentarily stabbed through a chink in the shutters —perhaps.

"It's from there," she said, "isn't it?"

"Yes. We'd better—"

"What?"

"Go and see."

"You're not going to climb out—"

"No, of course not," I said, already turning from the window. "I'll go down to that loose shutter in the alleyway." I put my anorak on. "Where's that torch?"

She took it from a drawer in the bedside table. I said, "Thanks. I won't do anything silly," though I wondered whether going to see was in itself silly. I picked up the front-door key and slid out of the room before she could make any further protest. I went down the stairs on tiptoes, and when I reached the first floor, I took a glove from my pocket and stuffed it between the bell and the clapper. I didn't want any more attention called to myself than necessary. When I opened the front door onto the square, I was pleased to note that there was no tinkle, even muffled, from above.

The square outside was deserted, a cool windless expanse. I ran alongside the front of Palazzo Sambon, staring up at its stained white facade. The windows were, as ever, shuttered and silent. I turned left down the alley that ran along the side of the palazzo toward the canal. I reached the window with the loose shutter. The shutter was in fact pushed wide open.

I stared into the black silent interior. I switched the torch on and its beam prodded a few yards into the damp gloom. There was nothing to see—or to hear.

Suddenly there were footsteps from the campo and I spun around guiltily. I recognized Lucy almost immediately—but that *almost* meant a split second in which my heart was pounding at my teeth.

"What the—" I started in a hoarse whisper.

"Did you think I was going to let you go in there alone?" she whispered back.

She'd gotten dressed in absolutely record time. I could see her black cords below the big gray coat. She peered through the window. Still no noise, no movement. She took hold of my arm, which saved me from grabbing hold of hers. "You sure we should go in?"

Of course I wasn't. It was the last thing I wanted to do, but I'd said it now. "You wait here." I put the torch in my pocket and placed my hands on the sill.

"Don't be stupid. Of course I'm coming too."

I didn't argue with her. I swung myself up and over in two reasonably graceful actions. I then stood by to help her over: she did it in one extremely graceful action. I got the torch out and played it around the room. It was a small side room and an empty doorway opposite gave onto the main entrance hall.

We stood still and listened again. Still there was nothing.

"Turn the torch off," she whispered.

"Why?" I said, doing so and plunging ourselves into complete blackness.

"You don't want to warn them—"

"Don't I? Who?"

"I don't know."

"Maybe the voice wasn't from here anyway," I said.

"You know it was."

I started toward the doorway and she let out a whispered scream. "Where are you?"

"Here." I stretched my hand out and took hers.

"Don't leave me, whatever you do."

"No," I said, and added rather foolishly, "never."

We passed through into the entrance hall and I switched the torch back on again, turning its beam to the left in the direction of the entrance door from the square, and then to the right toward the watergate. There was nothing to be seen, and only the sloshing of the water at the steps to be heard. In the opposite wall was the arched entrance to the stairway.

"We're not going up there, are we?" she said.

"You can wait here if you like."

"On my own? You don't think we should—we should call the police. . . ."

"Well, not now we've come in," I said, as if my only concern was not to look inconsistent to some unseen observer. And I started firmly toward the staircase. I was even on the point of saying something encouraging or comforting when she whispered, "You're crushing my fingers."

"Oh, sorry." We paused at the foot of the stairs and I played the beam up their gray dusty extent and tried not to think of *Psycho*. We started slowly upward. This was possibly the stupidest thing I'd done so far, I suddenly thought, and then thought, So why not stop now?

Because that would be even stupider.

We kept walking, and I felt our hands getting damply glued together, as if they were trying to blend in with the building's atmosphere.

We reached the big arched doorway to the first floor and the torchlight revealed gray stucco work and flickering frescoes: dynasties of Sambons, I imagined, staring down at us with hostility. As we passed through the doorway someone—an only dimly seen dark shape —leaped at me, striking at the torch with one hand. Lucy screamed—and so did I probably, I can't really remember. The torch fell to the ground, swirling shadows around the room like great Dracula cloaks. I was turning to this figure when a fist—presumably his—smashed into my jaw and I lost my footing. I rolled over and stared confusedly back up to where Lucy was struggling with the assailant. The torch was pointing across the floor in the opposite direction, so all I could see were the squirming dark shapes of their two grappling bodies in the doorway. Lucy's voice came breathily clear: "Let go, let me go—" The other person was saying nothing. I was just rising when all movement stopped and a new voice whispered in Italian, "Don't move or I slit her throat."

My eyes worked out that he was standing behind her with something held to her throat. It wasn't actually glinting in the torchlight, but I was prepared to believe that it would if I turned the light on it. Lucy's arms were both pulled behind her back.

"Oh, my God," Lucy said, and her voice sounded merely tired.

"Don't move," the voice whispered again. It was male and Veneto and slightly muffled. I didn't recognize it. I couldn't make out the features of the man, just that he had a scarf pushed up to the level of his eyes.

We didn't move. For five seconds. Then I said, "Look, how long—"

"Shut up. Take hold of the torch—slowly—and turn it off."

I realized those five seconds hadn't been merely a terror tactic. He'd been trying to work out what to do. I obeyed his instructions, and thought with an almost sick feeling how infinitely more horrible this sudden darkness must be for Lucy than for me.

"Now throw it across the room. And no tricks. I've still got this knife at your friend's throat. Go on, throw it."

I was trying to think if I had anything else on me that would convincingly sound like a torch thrown, but all I had was a packet of paper hankies. With an underarm lob I sent the torch skidding as undestructively as possible across the floor. I heard it clunk into the opposite wall.

Then suddenly Lucy let out a gasp and I heard her stagger forward and fall. The man's footsteps clattered down the stairs.

"You okay?" I said, slithering toward her.

231

"Yes, yes, yes," she said in three gasps that weren't quite sobs.

I reached her. She was kneeling up and we clung to each other in that position. She breathed short and hard against me but didn't burst into tears. Neither did I, for that matter.

"Who was it?" she said after a few seconds.

"God knows."

"Get the torch."

"Yes." All this, rather pointlessly perhaps, was still in a whisper.

I got to my feet and moved to where I thought the torch must have landed. I groped around on the cold dusty marble. After a few seconds Lucy said in a hoarse whisper, "Where *are* you?" and the question was taken up by the Sambons all around the big chilly room. I found it and switched it on, illuminating Lucy, still kneeling with her hands clasped tight, like a pious Victorian painting. She stood up and I walked toward her.

"He wasn't the person we heard yelling," Lucy said.

"No," I said. Our voices were just a little less tense, though not much louder. It was as if we thought that the place couldn't have any worse surprises. "Let's check the rooms out here," I went on.

We moved to the nearest one, Lucy again holding on to my arm, though lightly, not desperately. I shone the torch through the doorway, and before I'd even seen anything I felt her fingers crook from touch to clutch.

And then I saw too. It was only because she'd been to my left that she'd seen it sooner than I had, not because it was in any way difficult to see. Osgood couldn't be that, alive or dead. Now he was dead.

He lay flat on the floor—well, not flat of course, but supine. His swelling hill of a belly had two great wounds from which blood was still flowing, and his forehead was blown away. It was difficult in the torchlight to see where his red scarf ended and the blood began.

232

"Look at the hands," Lucy said. I straightaway knew what to expect. And I was right. I shifted the torchlight and found the soggy heap of fingers some inches away. There was a stained meat hatchet lying with them. I left the light on them till Lucy said, "Stop it, stop it."

I played the torch quickly over the rest of the room: cobwebby walls and grimy marble floor. A spider scuttled across the floor and hid beneath a large pistol on the floor. I kept the torch on it. It had what looked like a telephoto lens for a barrel. I guessed it was a silencer.

"Don't touch it," Lucy said.

"I'm not going to," I said. "There's a spider. I mean—" I found myself giving a stupid nervous laugh. I forced myself to speak calmly. "I suppose he forgot it in the panic."

"He must have put it down to—to do that with the fingers. God, it's sick." She was still clutching deep into my arm—as if to assure herself that I was still there. Or that her fingers were.

"Yes. You feel all right?"

"I'm not going to *be* sick, if that's what you mean. It's Osgood, isn't it?"

"Yes."

"God, it's sick. Come on, let's get out."

"Yes, of course."

We went back down the stairs in silence and across the empty hall. There was still no sound but the swirling and sloshing at the watergate steps. We found the shutters still wide open. I peered out; there was no one in the alley. I climbed out and then gave Lucy an unnecessary hand. "Let's go straight to the hotel," I said, "where we can think about what to do."

"What do you mean, think? It's obvious, isn't it? We call the police."

"Please, let's get out of the open first and then we can discuss."

"There's nothing to discuss. All right, I'm coming."

We entered the hotel and tiptoed on up the stairs. We could hear the television on in the signora's room: she was having to put up with a Neapolitan comedian. I removed my glove from the bell.

As soon as we were in the bedroom I said, "Look, Lucy, it's not so easy as all that."

"This is bloody murder, Martin. And bloody bloody murder." I noticed how bloodless *she* was. She sat on the bed and I saw her hands were shaking.

"I know."

"Look, every moment you put off going to the phone, you're giving that bastard extra time to escape."

"Yes, but—" I stopped. "Listen."

The distant sound of a motorboat could be heard. I went to the window and opened it. It wasn't in this canal, which was too congested with parked boats to permit any movement anyway. Around the corner in the next canal I could hear the boat coming to a stop and a hubbub of voices. I went and opened the door onto the corridor. We could now hear voices and running footsteps in the campo. A voice shouted, *"Fermi, polizia!"*

"I don't think there's any urgency for us to intervene," I said.

"Yes, but—but we've got to tell them what we saw."

"Why? Could you describe the man who attacked you?"

"That's not the point."

"What is the point then?"

"You tell them the whole truth. All of it."

"We've been through all this. Look, I'm not going to the police. Do you know how long people wait in prison in this country just to get put on trial? And terrorist suspects don't get kid-glove treatment either."

"Look, Martin—"

"There's no look about it. You haven't been to prison and I have. And I know I don't ever want to go back again."

"Okay, okay. What about earlier this evening? Those men who attacked you. I saw them. I could tell the police about them."

"Go on, describe them."

"They—they both had beards, dark hair—er, big coats. One had tinted glasses. Um . . ."

"False beards, wigs, and fake glasses. Before going into action, these guys disguise themselves. Did you see their features at all?"

"Well, they were turned away from me in the restaurant and—and outside it was dark."

"So you've got nothing to tell the police of any use. Take my advice, keep your head down." I went to the window and listened. I could hear the sound of distant shouting voices and clumping feet.

"This is bloody irresponsible," she said, her voice shaking as well as her hands now.

"Well, that's the way I am," I said. I was forcing my voice to remain calm, and it came out more sarcastic than I intended.

"And suppose they come in here to question people in the hotel?"

"Don't worry. I'll clear out, spare you all possible embarrassment. Okay?"

"You can't—where are you going to go?"

"Don't let it bother you. Just forget you've ever seen me."

"Martin, don't be such a bloody fool, you—"

"Look, just face it. I *am* a bloody fool and I *am* bloody irresponsible and that's all there bloody well is to it. Okay?" I was mainly scared and flustered by that point, but it was easier to express myself in anger. Why couldn't she understand what the thought of jail meant to me?

"How are you going to get out anyway? There'll be policemen all over the square."

"I'll go down to the canal and make my way along the boats to the bridge."

"You're mad—they'll catch you."

"Well, if they do, I'll confess everything this time. Unless you'd prefer me to keep your name out of things. I don't want to screw your job up."

"Just my whole bloody emotional life. Go on then. Get out. I don't want to hear any more sarcastic cracks."

I picked up my shoulder bag and slung it around my neck and then went to the door, my eyes glancing around the room to see if I'd forgotten anything. As I opened it she said, "Martin—" Her voice had a sudden pleading note, and I looked and saw her hands stretched out in a vague gesture of conciliation.

I stood there for half a second and felt a great urge to chuck my bag down and just bury myself in her arms. Then there was another cry of *"Polizia!"* from next door and I gave a quick resolute headshake. *"Ciao,"* I said. "It was good . . ." and I pulled the door to. Again I didn't know what I meant by this exit line, but I suppose it was meant as final. What possible point could there be in trying to make things up at that moment? Better to accept the clean break.

I reached the first floor and heard the television still on; she was watching a film with two Sicilian comedians now; maybe it was some kind of penitential rite for her. I tiptoed on down to the ground floor. I made my way to the back of the dark entrance hall, where a small window gave onto the canal. It refused to open at my first pull; it was rusted into place. Another tug and it jerked open with a sharp grating noise. I stood rigidly silent—except for my heart—and listened to the policemen's voices and the Sicilian comedians. There was no other noise; no laughter from the signora and no sign of perturbation either. I brushed off my anorak the little rush of rust that had fallen there and pulled myself onto the sill. There wasn't any sign of life from Palazzo Sambon; no shutters had been opened as far as I could see, and only faint voices could be heard. I looked at the building opposite and saw that all its shutters were closed as well. It seemed I would be unobserved.

I lowered myself down to the boat below the window, which rocked under my weight. There was a bridge about twenty yards beyond Palazzo Sambon, and as far as I could see there were boats tied up all the way down the canal. Obviously the tricky part of my trip would be passing in front of the palazzo:

if they were to open a shutter at that moment, or the watergate itself, I would find it hard to explain myself.

I started my progress, clambering from boat to boat, getting my feet wet in some of them, where the owner hadn't bothered to bail out. I passed below the windows of Palazzo Sambon, glancing up and seeing the dark shutters all still in place. Then, just as I was stepping into a small rickety canoe moored in front of the palazzo's seaweedy steps I heard voices on the other side of the door: "Open that door."

Any precipitate movement on my part would set the boat sloshing wildly, sending giveaway slobbers of spray into the palazzo itself. And yet only precipitate action would get me away. I could see tiny stabs of light at the crack at the foot of the door, showing they were carrying torches. The moment the door was opened I'd be caught like a rabbit in car headlights. I couldn't even curl up at the bottom of the boat, it was so small. I looked desperately around while I heard fiddling and scraping at the other side of the door.

"Sorry, sir, it's locked," said a southern voice.

"Oh, leave it then. They didn't get out that way obviously."

"No, sir." Footsteps moved away.

I breathed out, thanking whatever instinct it had been that had prevented me from making a wild leap into the next boat: incapacitating fear, probably. I started my splashy clambering progress again. I reached the bridge and had a moment of panic strangely mingled with dull resignation when it seemed it was too high for me to climb up to. Then I saw the holes in the brickwork in the nearest building. (Never sneer when people talk about the magic of Venice: how else do buildings with foundations like moldy Gruyère stay up?) I pushed my shoulder bag around to my back and climbed up, my fingers finding holds in gritty damp cracks and my feet in slimy caverns. I made it onto the bridge and glanced down the alley. There was no one around. I gave one look back at Palazzo Sambon, which was still in shuttered darkness. Beyond I saw the light from a window at the top of the hotel and the dark shape of a head leaning out. I gave

237

a quick wave and a hand fluttered back. Then I set off down the bridge, my heart suddenly feeling like Gruyère cheese itself: heavy but with gaping holes.

And that tom-tom in my temples was back, surprise surprise.

I went in the direction of the station, refusing to think about what had happened between Lucy and me, and just concentrating on the immediate future. I'd decided that I would get a couchette train down to Rome: it was the only way I could think of getting a night's sleep without having to hand my passport over. Unless the timetables had changed, there should be one around midnight.

I made my way through the Ghetto, and along the side of the Cannaregio Canal, not glancing at that alley where we had kissed, but passing straight over the bridge. When I reached the open space below the station, I saw policemen at the top of the steps with machine guns. I stopped where I was, though not too noticeably. I thought of trying the side entrance, which takes one straight to platform one, but then guessed there would be just as many inside the station as well.

For all its great beauty, Venice does have the disadvantage of being the easiest city in the world to bottle off. Stop the cars at Piazzale Roma and the trains at the station and then scatter a few fast boats around the lagoon, and you've got your terrorists trapped. And your innocent but unfortunately-rather-guilty-looking terrorist suspects too.

I turned back and crossed the bridge over the Grand Canal, thinking hard. I could go back to my original hotel on Rio Marin. The terrorists weren't likely to make another try at me there. Not with the police out in full force like this.

So maybe the police would come for me there.

This required even harder thinking—and my brain was already staggering. I couldn't take much more of this—by which I meant just about everything: the latest confusing murder, the police everywhere, the terrorists everywhere, and Lucy mad at me: or was it me mad at Lucy? I was already unable to remember

238

exactly how our latest little altercation had gone. The tom-tom prevented any really concrete thinking.

So maybe I'd just have to bed down in some boat for the night. Unless . . . I suddenly thought of Alvise. This wasn't exactly the usual time to drop in, but I felt he owed me an explanation. (He didn't of course, but at that moment I felt he did: I felt the whole world owed me one right then.) He'd said he lived on a *fondamenta* by San Nicolò dei Mendicoli; well, that was conveniently near, and there weren't that many *fondamente* around there. I should be able to find the place. Maybe I could even drop in on the hotel on the way and pick up my stuff. I'd tell them I was taking a train to Rome. I'd have to pay for the night all the same, but then I'd have had to do that anyway.

And what if Alvise was with the terrorists? Well, this would be one way of finding out for sure. It might be one way of getting killed for sure too, but at least I'd die with one question the fewer on my mind. Yes, I had to find out what was behind his twitching and stammering.

So I entered the hotel and explained my change of plans. They looked a little surprised but not actually suspicious. Why should they? I set off down the *fondamenta* ten minutes later with my kit bag on my back but my troubles all in a knot somewhere at the top of my head.

17

THE area around San Nicolò was very quiet. I'd once read that this part of the city had its own doge, and it has something of the feel of a separate little fishing village. Maybe I'd retire there.

I tried the *fondamenta* leading toward the church. The doors to the houses were not on the *fondamenta* I discovered, but in the alley behind. I found Alvise's name on a bell push together with the name Chiara Bortolo. For some reason I hadn't thought of his not living on his own. Well, I hadn't thought, full stop.

Their names were on the middle of three bell pushes. I looked up at the house and saw that there were lights on behind the shutters of the middle flat. So I wouldn't actually be waking them up.

No, but all the same . . .

The rucksack got heavier by the second. Well, I could always go away again if I was obviously unwelcome. And I did want to know just where Alvise stood in all this business. I rang the bell and stood back and cringed.

"*Chi xè 'o?*" Alvise's voice said from the grille.

"*Son mi,*" I said. "Martin."

"What?" From the fact that he spoke in English I gathered that he'd understood.

"Can I come in?"

"But, but . . ." Then the door clicked open.

I stepped in and started toward the steps. Then, with a second's thought, I took the rucksack off my back and put it down in the narrow hallway next to a pram. This, I thought, was what was known as breaking things gently.

I could also make a quicker getaway if he confronted me with a machine gun.

As I walked up the steps I heard a baby crying. And the closer I got to the open door on the middle floor the more obvious it got that the crying was coming from there. This made the machine gun seem rather less likely—and the chances of a hearty welcome.

Alvise was standing in the doorway. I was glad to note that he was fully dressed. He had both hands deeply embedded in his beard and looked rather as he'd looked when I'd first put my hand on his shoulder in the alley.

"What—what—what's the matter?"

"Hello," I said. "I hope I didn't wake the baby."

"No, no, but what's—what's—"

A woman's voice called out in Venetian from the flat. "Let him come in, and then you can ask the questions."

Alvise stepped aside and removed a hand from his beard to usher me in. It returned straight to his beard.

The flat was obviously very small. The room I walked straight into functioned as dining room and living room, but most noticeably as library. The walls were mainly books, as were most of the horizontal surfaces, with the clearly begrudged exception of two of the four chairs, half of the dining table, and some of the floor. In one of the book-free chairs a plump but pretty woman of about thirty was rocking a six-or seven-month-old baby to and fro. The baby seemed mostly an enormous mouth, from which an appropriately enormous noise was coming.

"Ah, er, piacere," I said.

The plump woman smiled in a surprisingly unharassed way in my direction, almost as if she assumed I'd come to baby-sit. *"Ciao,"* she called out above the noise, and then in English, "I'm Chiara, Alvise's wife."

"Ah, I'm Martin."

"Yes. Alvise told me about you. And this is Federica, our daughter. Say *ciao,* Federica."

Federica said it: the vowel part of the word anyway. Chiara said, "Alvise's just warming the bottle for her."

"Yes, yes," Alvise said, and disappeared into the kitchen. I followed him with my eyes. The kitchen looked fairly ordered but I could see a Pisan tower of dirty plates by the sink. I turned to Chiara and tried to convey by my general pose and attitude that if the baby noise had permitted I'd be making profuse apologies and explanations for my arrival at that hour. She smiled back and concentrated on the baby. Then Alvise emerged holding the feeding bottle, which was thrust into that huge opening, which immediately closed tight on it: there was sudden snuffling peace.

Chiara said, "Sit down. Have a glass of wine." Her English was rather more heavily accented than his.

Alvise was still hovering in an agitated fashion. I said, "Look, I'm sorry, what I've done is unforgivable. I shouldn't even have thought of coming round. I'm going. Just forget I came." I turned to the door; I think I really meant it. It was the sheer domesticity of the scene that had decided me.

Chiara said, "No. First tell us why you came, why not?"

Alvise said, "Yes, yes . . ." but without much conviction I felt.

"Thanks," I said, "you're very kind."

"Have a glass of wine," Chiara said again.

"Okay. But I promise I'll go at once." I sat down at the table but tried to make my pose look provisional. I accepted the glass of red wine that Alvise poured for me. I said to him, "You've told Chiara about me, have you?"

"Roughly."

Chiara looked toward me. "I don't think I've understood everything."

"Why did you come here?" Alvise said.

"If you want to know the real truth, because two men tried to kidnap me outside my hotel this evening." I drank some wine, hoping to take the melodrama out of this statement by the cool gesture.

"What?" Chiara said. Her tone was of polite wonder, and she didn't move the bottle in her hand one millimeter.

Alvise lifted both hands to his beard again and twisted it. "Go on."

"That's it. They tried to chuck me into a boat, but I managed to run for it. I thought of jumping on a train out of the city, but the station turned out to be full of policemen."

"So you came here," he said.

"Sorry, it was a stupid thing to do. I was just—well, I just felt so tired." I took another sip.

"Get the spare mattress out," Chiara said in Italian.

Alvise looked at her. "You're sure?"

"Don't be silly. Of course. You'll have to sleep in the room with Federica," she said to me. "Don't worry, she doesn't usually wake up."

"Thanks, that's marvelous. So long as Federica doesn't mind. I'll leave straightaway tomorrow morning, I swear."

"Yes, you will," Alvise said. "I'm sorry, but you must."

"Alvise, don't exaggerate," Chiara said. "I know it's for my sake you say this, but things aren't so tragic."

I was obviously looking a bit puzzled. Alvise said suddenly. "I suppose you must have asked yourself why I left you so suddenly this evening."

"Well, er, I did wonder a little. . . ."

"I told you that I've become a complete *menefreghista* in all things to do with politics, no?"

"Yes. Is it true?"

He gave his nervous shrug. "It's true enough. I've learned the importance of keeping my head down. And when the carabinieri came round, I felt my head was up a little too high."

"When he says he's learned this," Chiara said in Italian, "what he means is that I have taught him this."

"Ah."

She spoke placidly and easily, with a rather more marked Venetian accent than he had. "You see, I learned this on my own. I went to jail."

"Oh." And I didn't add, "That brings us close."

Alvise said, "It was all so stupid, she had nothing to do with anything, they merely got names wrong, and because she had been involved with some political groups—" He was walking quickly up and down the tiny bit of free floor space tying his beard into the most complicated knots.

"*Caro,* I'm telling the story, aren't I?"

"Yes, of course, of course, I was just explaining. . . ."

"You see," she went on, "when I was studying, I belonged to a political group on the left, and we were fairly active in the university—organizing protests and strikes. All the usual things: but unfortunately there was a woman called Clara Bortoli who was a member of a Red Brigade column in Milan, and her name was mentioned by a *pentito.* I was the nearest thing to be found, so they took me in."

"It was crazy, completely crazy," Alvise said, "because first they wouldn't say why she'd been arrested, what the evidence was, and then they just said her name had been given, without telling us by whom, and when we did find out, we could show that Chiara had never lived anywhere near Milan, but then they just said the *pentito* must have got some details wrong, but that didn't change anything, and then—"

Chiara's voice came in calmly over her husband's. "I was in jail for a year and a half, waiting for my trial. In that time they even arrested Clara Bortoli, but it took them a few months after her arrest to make the connection."

"A year and a half," I said. I couldn't say snap to that.

"Yes." She took the bottle out of the baby's mouth and swung her onto her shoulder and patted her back. A Falstaffian belch was produced. *"Brava, brava."* She put the baby back on her lap and dabbed at her mouth.

"So," Alvise said, "you see why I thought it best not to get involved in your story. It's the old old story. Chiara was declared completely innocent, but she's still the girl who was arrested as a BR suspect. That is still how she must figure in the police files. And with many of the neighbors too."

"Yes," I said. "I see your point." And how. "I'm sorry I came round at all. I mean the last thing I want is for you to get into any trouble. . . ."

"It's the last thing we want too," Alvise said. "But you're here now, it hardly matters."

"Yes, of course you must stay," Chiara said.

"So who were these people?" Alvise asked.

"I didn't stop to ask them, but they didn't look like the police." I recounted briefly how they'd waited for me. I told the story without any mention of Lucy, saying that I'd simply spotted them before they came at me and so managed to run for it.

"And you're still not going to the police," Alvise said.

"Well, not tonight at any rate."

"Okay. I suppose I'm hardly one to lecture you on civic duties."

"Well," I said, "you did come looking for me when it would have been much easier just to forget you'd seen me."

"Yes," Alvise said, "yes, much easier. But . . ." He gave another jerky shrug. "Once in the past I did the same thing and, well, the result wasn't—wasn't so good." He suddenly turned and took the baby from Chiara and swung her in the air above himself.

"Remember she's just finished eating," Chiara said.

"Ah yes," he said, bringing her to a more conventional cradled position.

He didn't seem ready to go on with what he'd been saying, so I thought maybe I should get in the usual baby questions: her age, her sleeping habits, whom she resembled most. Chiara

245

answered all these questions as she washed out the bottle while Alvise did the fond-father bit, allowing her to tug his beard, which she did with even more savagery than he did himself. Then he said, over his daughter's gurgles, "Maybe I should tell you about what happened in the past. It's connected with Toni, so you might be interested."

"Yes, of course."

"One of Toni's closest friends was another *ricercatore* at the university, a guy called Padoan, Giulio Padoan."

"I've heard that name."

"Oh, yes? I may have mentioned him to you myself. Anyway, he taught history. I believe he specialized in Byzantine studies. I never knew him well, but one day not long after Chiara's arrest Toni took me round to Padoan's flat on the Giudecca for dinner. There were just the three of us. Padoan had a small flat, very neat, clean, and he prepared quite a good meal. Naturally they asked about Chiara. I'd only just started going with her. Well, all I could say was that there must have been a mistake. I didn't know any more than they did, except that she must be innocent. Anyway this got us onto the subject of the Red Brigades and I remember Padoan saying that he never knew why they refused the name of terrorists: they would always call themselves *combattenti per il comunismo*, or armed revolutionaries, or whatever. Padoan said that as far as he was concerned 'terrorist' was a name to be proud of."

Chiara said, "I'll put Federica to bed."

When she had left us, Alvise resumed. "Terror, Padoan said, was a weapon that the state had always used against the proletariat—the workers were kept in terror of the law, of the bosses, of unemployment. Well, finally the proletariat had learned that terror was one of the few weapons they had at their disposal too. They should be proud of having taken it up against their oppressors."

"Not nice," I said as Alvise paused, and then wished I'd said something less fatuous.

"Not, not nice at all. And you have to remember the

246

context. It was in a period when you heard every other day that a newspaper editor or a union leader or some *povero Cristo* had been shot in the legs. *Gambizzato*—they even had to invent a new verb for it. I can describe only the climate at the university, as that was the world I knew; it was worst at Padova perhaps: there was shooting, but that was only—the top of the iceberg."

"Tip."

"Tip. Tip top, whatever. The iceberg was made up of the whole atmosphere that you could sense everywhere. People whose ideas weren't on the 'right lines' found threats against them sprayed on the walls, received threats by phone, their cars were blown up, their front doors set on fire. . . . It was one hell of a time." He made a gesture of disgust, which, since he'd just taken up a glass of wine, spattered the tablecloth.

"So what did you say to Padoan?"

"Well, we talked it over, and I tried not to take it too seriously: but I remember his—his thin voice explaining this point of view so reasonably, so care- fully over the sweet course. And he then praised a recent Red Brigade action in which a factory owner had been *gambizzato* despite his bodyguard. Efficiency, he said—the proletariat had to show himself to be organized and efficient, if he wanted to achieve maximum terror."

"Why all this to you?" I asked.

"Well, it was obvious to me afterward that Padoan must have been taken in by the arrest of Chiara. He must have thought that I was a possible new recruit—or perhaps I was already part of the movement. You see there were so many subversive groups that nobody could keep track of all of them. Anyway, I think the general idea was to sound me out, if that is the expression. To test my reactions. Of course at the time, as I say, I just tried to convince myself it was mere academic chatchit, with nothing behind it. After all, the real terrorists, I told myself, were in *clandestinità* and did nothing that might expose themselves. Well, a little later I said I had to go, and just before leaving I went to the—the john?"

"Yes."

"When I came out Padoan was showing Toni something in a cupboard. I caught a glimpse of what looked like a machine gun. Well, now I wonder if I wasn't in fact deliberately supposed to see this, but at the time this didn't strike me. They closed the cupboard and I said nothing, and I left the place alone. When I next saw Toni I never mentioned the gun."

"Didn't you tell anyone about it?"

"No. This, you see, is the point of the story. If I thought of doing anything at all it was something vague on the lines of, um, have another—another wag chin with Padoan about the whole business, try and, well, persuade him of the foolishness of the whole armed struggle. . . . I mean, very vague ideas. Stupid ideas in fact. And these didn't come to anything of course. But as for going to the police, well, it hardly occurred to me. I mean, one might not agree with the terrorists, but one wasn't an informer either. This was the climate. And particularly I didn't feel any loyalty or warmth to the system after Chiara's arrest."

"I see."

"And then two weeks later there was a raid on an arms depot near Mestre in which two carabinieri were killed. And it was then that Padoan disappeared and evidence was found that showed he was involved. More than involved in fact: he'd probably planned the whole thing. And planned it most—most cold-bloodedly. The two carabinieri were killed deliberately: they were carefully eliminated before the terrorists moved in on the store. As he would have put it, it was *una questione di efficienza.*"

"What?" I said so sharply that Alvise jumped in his chair, spilling more wine.

"*Una questione di efficienza,*" he repeated, in a prissy tone, obviously an imitation of Padoan's.

"That's just what the little bastard who burned my paintings said to me." I was staring at a bound thesis on "river imagery" in *Waverley* on the table but I was seeing that obscene unmoving white mask and hearing that quiet uninflected voice come from beneath it.

248

"Little, you say?"

"Yes. I suppose a bit—well, just a big bigger than you. And yes, a quiet, sort of precise voice, like—like the one you just used. And pale eyes that never moved."

"Yes—yes. That is Padoan. Well, I can't say it surprises me. This whole business is exactly Padoan's style. Particularly since there is no attempt to disguise the fact that the aim behind the killings is to intimidate—to create terror." He finished his wine. "Which was obviously part of what they intended in killing the two carabinieri in Mestre. And of course I couldn't get the murder of those two men off my conscience. I kept telling myself that I could have spoken about what I'd seen in Padoan's flat."

I didn't say anything for a while, and then thought that my silence might seem accusatory, so said, "What about Toni? What did you do about him?"

"I spoke to him and he swore that he wasn't involved at all: he'd merely flirted with the idea of getting involved. And I believed him. That innocent ineffectual look of his which you mentioned—well, it convinced me. I was the ingenuous one there, the right sucker."

"So this Padoan was never caught," I said.

"No. There was a rumor that he had gone to Africa and got involved in some little revolution there, but nothing certain was discovered. He's collected prison sentences for hundreds of years over here, so, well, he'd have to be pretty crazy to come back. But then he probably is crazy: you should have seen him talking about spreading terror. . . ."

"Thank you, I've seen him spreading it."

"Yes . . . yes, you probably have. These people . . ." He shook his head—not a slow sad headshake, more like a dog after a swim.

Chiara emerged from the bedroom. "Let's talk just a little more quietly," she said. She shifted the books from one of the chairs onto the floor and sat down with us.

Alvise said, "Martin probably has had the pleasure of meeting Padoan."

She gave a melodramatic shiver. "I've only heard of him

from Alvise, but that was enough." She spoke in English again. She obviously wasn't as fluent as Alvise, but she spoke with a natural confidence.

"But I just don't get what's in these people's minds," I said. "I mean, who do they think they're going to win over like this?"

"It's useless expecting any idea of rational behavior from them," Alvise said. "You only have to see the faces of the *irreducibili* in court to see that they're obsessed people. Winning people over doesn't come into their schemes of things."

"But they must want some kind of solidarity from the working classes; otherwise—"

"You've obviously got a very old-fashioned view of them: Che Guevara and all that. Power to the people. But these people have stopped looking outward like that completely. This was obvious when they killed Guido Rossa, no?"

"Was it? I mean, er, who was he?"

"He worked for Italsider in Genova and he informed the police about a fellow worker who was mixed up with the Red Brigades. Put the finger on him, right? This must have been 1978 or 1979—about the time of the Moro kidnapping. So they killed him. And that was the end of their Robin Hood image. I mean, you'd have thought that, well, a little elementary common sense would tell them that the way to conquer the workers' hearts was not by assassinating workers." He did another wet-dog shake. "And in fact there was a big reaction against them, with many more denunciations everywhere—but did they learn? Oh, no, they went right on with their tactics of punishing the informers, even taking it out on people's relatives when they couldn't reach the real people. Like the Nazis."

"Or the Mafia," I said.

"Right," he said. "Exactly right. And now, since they are completely isolated, with nobody at all believing in communism, they've ended up like all secret societies—obsessed with the enemy in their middle—"

"In their what?"

"Inside them—"

250

"In their midst."

"Exactly. So now the few believers left are trying to create and enforce a code of secrecy like that of the Mafia—to suppress the phenomenon of *pentitismo* which was what broke them." He took another glass of wine, having scattered half the contents of the one he was holding as he talked.

"They're crazy," Chiara said simply. "*Ecco tutto*. Would you like some coffee or something?"

"Oh, er, no, nothing thanks." I found it difficult to switch from the Red Brigades/Nazis/Mafia to coffee. "Actually what I'd really like if you've got it is an aspirin. I've got a bit of a headache."

Alvise stood up, but Chiara said, "No, I know where they are: you'll be looking in the fridge or the oven. You get the mattress out—and that's under our bed."

Alvise and I made up a bed in darkness in Federica's room. He told me that if she were to cry, one of them would come in, since an unknown face probably wouldn't be much comfort. At that moment she sounded as if nothing would wake her. Chiara gave me the aspirin, which I knocked back with a glass of water. I then went down to the hall for my rucksack. When I came back up, I thanked them both again and said that I would crash out; my head was now feeling as if the drummer of some heavy-metal group were doing his solo inside it. I had a quick wash in their minuscule bathroom and then retired. They went to bed too, and I heard them talking quietly there, Alvise the usual babbling torrent, and Chiara's voice damming him with occasional slow calm comments. I couldn't hear what they were saying, but presumably I came into it.

I lay there listening to the baby's rhythmical breathing and finding some kind of illogical sense of security in it. It, and presumably the aspirin too, brought my drummer to the end of his solo and I slept.

Some hours later, however, he came back for an encore, and he'd brought a support band with him who started up a jam session in my stomach. I lay there, my head throbbing savagely, my stomach queasily playing along, and fans stomping to the beat in every muscle: my throat felt as Rod Stewart's must after a concert. I threw off the blankets and twisted and turned, then decided I needed them, then threw them off again, sweating and shivering in rhythmic alternation.

Well, not to go into too many distasteful details, the night was hell from then on. I vomited three times, fortunately each time into the toilet bowl. In between these bouts I got occasional snatches of sleep, but no raveled sleeves were knitted up by it. It played with my cares in fact like a kitten with a ball of wool. Most of the time I was back in jail, at one point trying to paint a Madonna with the face of Lucy, which kept turning into a white mask and mouthing the word *efficiency,* at another point throwing my slop bucket over a huge bonfire stoked by tongue-less aliens who then became an audience of merchant bankers in Adrians' gallery who wouldn't let me speak above their public-school chatter, in the midst of which I kept hearing the word *gimmick,* each time followed by manic giggling.

Nothing, of course, is more boring than other people's dreams: the point was I didn't enjoy the night.

When Federica finally started up a little plaintive wailing at around half-past seven, Alvise came in and I croaked, "Good morning."

"Are you all right?" he asked. "You look a bit behind the weather."

"I feel awful," I said. "Sorry. I must have eaten or drunk something." I had of course thought of my bath of two days earlier, though wondered whether it could have taken so long to have its effect.

He picked up Federica, who started gurgling happily, and said, "I think it'll be the Mongolian—or the Chinese or Russian, whichever it is this year."

"You mean flu?"

"Yes."

"Oh, God, I've brought you that, have I?"

"No." He smiled. "You've caught it off us. We both had it

last week. Federica fortunately didn't get it, but maybe we'd better move her cot into our bedroom."

"Well, look, I can't possibly stay here. You're not a hospital." I also knew I couldn't possibly get up.

"Don't worry. No trouble. It won't even be expensive for us, because if you feel like we felt, I know you won't want to eat anything."

I just made a noise of revulsion by way of answer to this.

My temperature was taken and discovered to be forty or something: luckily I remembered that thermometers are not put under the tongue in Italy, and so not necessarily washed. Chiara was a great nurse, taking things entirely in her stride, and continuing to reassure me that there was no problem, an assurance I found it convenient to pretend to myself that I believed.

Thus began four rather surreal days. The first day was particularly so, since I could hardly get my throbbing brain to concentrate on anything for longer than a few seconds. So when Alvise came in to tell me that he'd just heard on the radio of the death of Osgood I was able to present a convincingly bewildered reaction, because it was almost impossible for me to make any connections between yesterday and today. I had a vague feeling that I ought to be asking questions about just what they'd said on the radio, but this got no further than a feeling, and Alvise obviously realized it was useless to attempt any conversation on the matter. So I lay in the darkened room, listening to the pair of them as they talked in the kitchen, listening to the radio that Chiara had on as she did housework, listening to Federica's intermittent complaints, listening to the occasional boat passing along the canal outside—or rather hearing all these things but taking in none of them. So the day passed, with my throbbing diminishing in intensity, the vomiting bouts stopping altogether, and even a little peckishness coming on toward evening.

The next day I was able to sit up and read the papers. Alvise had bought *La Repubblica* and *La Nuova Venezia,* both of which had front-page headlines on the latest atrocities. NIGHT OF

TERROR IN VENICE announced *La Repubblica*. I glanced quickly down the page, feeling terrorized myself by the possibility of seeing my name. I didn't, so was able to start again at the top with a touch more calm. "Three deaths in twenty-four hours" was the lower-case headline, which surprised me. The night apparently hadn't ended with the death of Osgood: to discover what had happened I skipped to the end of the article and read that an hour after the police entered Palazzo Sambon, a police boat had signaled to a boat in the Giudecca Canal to pull up for a check. The boat had at once driven off at top speed, at which point the police had opened fire, killing the man inside. He was carrying false documents, but had nonetheless been identified as Simone Gerosa, a terrorist who till that moment had been thought to be living in France. He was wearing a wig and false beard; another wig was found in the bottom of the boat, sopping wet. No explanation for this last detail had been found; there had been nothing in Palazzo Sambon to indicate that anyone had entered in wet clothes, or had left by the canal, since all the windows and doors onto the canal were shuttered and locked, and in any case the witness the police had talked to had seen them enter by the side alley.

At this mention of a witness the paper almost dropped from my hands. I jumped back to the middle section of the article, which dealt with the second murder, that of the English art dealer Harry Osgood.

> Marina Berton, a housewife, lives on the first floor of a building that is separated from Palazzo Sambon by a narrow alley. On the evening in question she had opened the window onto the alley in order to close the shutters when she saw what she describes as "a very fat man" in the act of climbing into Palazzo Sambon. Her husband, Giuseppe Berton, was in the room with her, and when she told him what she had seen he suggested she keep watching. Signora Berton remained at the window, watching the alley, with the lights turned off in their flat in order to escape observation. The husband and wife had not forgotten the palazzo's links with terrorism. Only one

254

minute later Signora Berton saw a younger man come down the alley and enter by the same window. Unfortunately the alley has no lighting and she was not able to distinguish any features of the man, beyond the fact that he had a long coat. To her immense surprise only two or three minutes later a man and a woman came down the alley and entered the palazzo. Again she could distinguish nothing beyond the fact that the woman had hair of average length and was wearing trousers. It was at this point that Signor Berton decided to call the police. A minute or so later the first young man came out by the window and ran off down the alley, to be followed after another minute or so by the couple.

The police, though commending i Signori Berton for their action, regret that they did not think to contact them earlier, since greater promptness might not only have helped to prevent the latest atrocious murder but also resulted in the capture of the three assassins. Nonetheless the police claim they have elements in their possession now that may lead to arrests very soon.

This was probably the usual police line, I thought hopefully. Osgood was simply described as an art dealer, in Venice on business. Mention was made of past investigations into his activity and of a possible connection with the antique dealer Busetto, although no definite link had been established as yet. The identity of the two victims had induced the police to toy with the idea that the murderers might in fact have nothing to do with terrorism at all, but simply have used the outward trappings of the recent crimes by way of confusion; however this line had been conclusively disproved, not only by the fact that the terrorists themselves had not disclaimed the murders, but also by the discovery that the gun left at the scene of the crime had been definitely identified as one stolen by terrorists in a raid on an arms store in Mestre in the 1970s.

There was much theorizing in both newspapers over the possible motives: the link was made between the two men and the paintings that had disappeared some ten years' before, and question marks were scattered liberally at the end of the articles. What had happened to Antonio Sambon? How was it that this ex-terrorist had been allowed to leave the country so easily, without any supervision? Could he have anything to do with the death in the building where he had once hidden himself? Why had Osgood been entering the building in the first place? Did he have an appointment with Toni Sambon? Was it possible, despite the denials of the police, that the paintings were still hidden there somewhere?

I was even induced to ask Alvise, "Could we all be totally wrong about Toni, and in fact he's behind the whole thing?"

"What, the murders?"

"Yes. I mean, everyone keeps telling me how good he was at taking people in—"

"Yes, this is true, but are you saying that perhaps he's working with Padoan?"

"Well, perhaps."

"Padoan, whom he put the finger on, who must hate him as a complete traitor to the cause . . ."

"Well, perhaps it was a bluff."

"And when Padoan came asking you about Toni, was that a bluff?"

"All right, I'll think it through a little more carefully."

I read with interest the full background to the Busetto murder. The police had been summoned by an anonymous phone call from the terrorists themselves; a disguised but northern voice had simply said something about the people's justice having been carried out on the pig Busetto, and the address had been given. Later a communiqué had been left, as was customary, in a rubbish bin near the offices of *Il Gazzettino*. The explanation in the communiqué was rather confused, referring to Busetto's involvement in the world of international art dealing, a parasitical world of class enemies and thieves from the people. However, the newspaper said, medical evidence had revealed that it was possible that Busetto's death had been an accident; his weak heart might have given way under the stress of interrogation (or whatever it was the terrorists had been doing with him), and the subsequent shooting had thus been a disguise. The communiqué's confusion merely showed the terrorists' embarrassment at having to concoct a reasonable-sounding excuse for his "execution" by the tribunal of the people.

The fact that one of the killers was still at the scene of the crime when the police arrived, although they'd been summoned by the terrorists themselves, was generally considered very puzzling. The only explanation the police could come up with was that he must have gone back for something incriminating that he'd left there. After all, that same evening they managed to leave the gun behind. The description of this man was comfortingly vague, and referred to his probable Veneto origins. I wished I could boast about my linguistic accomplishment to someone.

The communiqué for Osgood's death, left the next day in a bin near St. Mark's Square, contained more or less the same concepts as the Busetto communiqué in a more or less equally confused fashion, ending with the words, "Thieves and parasites, beware!" A further message had been phoned to the *Gazzettino*, proclaiming *"Onore al Compagno Morto,"* and promising that Gerosa's death would be avenged.

So these surreal days went by. I progressed from my mattress to the armchair, from bowls of müesli to pasta dishes, from occasional scatty exchanges to proper conversations. Alvise was at home much of the time: an Italian academic's timetable was not exactly backbreaking, I gathered. He spent hours reading on a kitchen chair, occasionally asking me words, which were never the Scottish dialect grunts I feared; hours were spent reading through theses, and he would break off to swear and read aloud the worst bits of jargon ("Thus we can establish the main semantic isotopies of the macro-text"), adding his comments on the colleague who was behind each particular piece of verbal lunacy. I got to know most of the *professori* in the department, together with their unofficial titles of windbag, buffoon, pompous idiot, cretin. . . . Both he and Chiara were scrupulously careful in not bugging the invalid with too many

257

policemanlike questions, Alvise merely supplying me with newspapers, and discussing the articles with me if I felt like it. He pointed out a reference in *La Nuova* to the Englishman who'd had an altercation with Busetto, and with whom the police would like a word, but made no further comment. Neither did I.

I don't think I'd read papers so thoroughly since my trial, and this time I could do it without the anger—just the worries. And even the worries began to die down—at least the tom-tom in my temples did—as I became more and more domesticated. I did the washing-up and some cleaning and, by the end of my convalescent period, even helped to change nappies (well, I handed Alvise cotton wool while he did the dirty work). I could feel myself winding down.

In my more meditative moments I naturally thought of Lucy and what had happened between us. Another triumph for Phippsian tact and gentleness in personal relations there. Well, in addition to silliness and irresponsibility, prison had obviously added excessive touchiness to my list of qualities. I'd just have to accept that that was the way I was. Lucy and the postprison version of Martin Phipps were not destined to make it together, and to try to pretend otherwise would be, well, silly and irresponsible—and unfair on her.

It was a pity this left me still feeling as if my insides had been kicked out.

On the Thursday evening we had supper together, and I was dressed for the first time; I had actually been intending to go out for my first walk that afternoon, but had then stayed in to baby-sit while Chiara did some shopping. Federica was sitting in her high chair, with Chiara alternating mouthfuls of *pappa* for her and mouthfuls of pasta for herself. I announced that I would finally leave them the next day and Alvise said, "So what are you going to do?"

"Get out of the city," I said.

"And go home?" Chiara asked.

"Well, I'll have a few days' holiday first," I said. "Somewhere."

258

"So you're just going to forget all about the paintings," Alvise said.

"Isn't that what you said I should do?" I asked.

"Oh, yes. But I didn't think you'd take my advice."

"Why not?"

"I don't know. Maybe I'm just not used to people taking my advice. And then you seemed to have some kind of special—special mission with regard to these paintings. Or am I wrong?"

"Well, I like them a lot."

"But why must it be you to discover them? Yes, I know, you don't want to get other people into trouble, like Francesca and Toni. Yes, Francesca is *simpatica* but I don't know if her brother is worth so much trouble. Poor little confused Toni, remember, was able to fool everyone around him for years with his innocent looks. And now he wants those paintings for money, nothing else. No?"

"Yes, well, I never said I was particularly brimming over with sympathy for Toni."

"So why this refusal to have anything to do with the police?"

I glanced across at Chiara and she caught my glance and turned straight to Federica. What had I been expecting? Instant understanding from a fellow ex-con? I said, "I've been to prison too."

Chiara looked up again. Alvise said, "Ah." Then, after a pause: "Sorry."

"So was I."

"How long?" Chiara asked.

"Six months," I said. "Nothing compared with you. Oh, and I was guilty too."

"Yes. That makes a difference," she said.

"Okay," Alvise said, "we'll say no more about the police and such things. Maybe you're right; just go and have a holiday."

"Yes."

They both tactfully asked no further questions. Alvise changed the subject and told us about the recent inauguration of the academic year at the university, a ceremony the students had not been allowed to attend. "You should have seen how happy most of the professors were. I think they'd prefer it if the students weren't allowed into the university at all."

At that moment the doorbell rang.

It wasn't the first time that callers had come, but this didn't mean I'd gotten blasé about it. The other times I'd retired to the bedroom, a quivering mass, while Alvise had gone downstairs to explain that he had a lot of work to do; fortunately the callers, not being terrorists or policemen, had accepted this and left. On each occasion I'd felt that even if I were to offer to change Federica for the rest of her nappy-wearing life, I wouldn't really repay my debt as a guest. And yet they made no complaints. Now Chiara merely raised her eyebrows in good-humored resignation and Alvise moved toward the answer phone. I rose from the table, swallowing a last strand of spaghetti and opened the bedroom door. I heard Alvise ask in Italian, then in English, "Who?" I stopped in the doorway and looked around. He said, "Lucy who?"

"Oh, my God," I said.

He raised his shoulders questioningly toward me, one hand twisting his beard. I shrugged back and he said, "Come on up, first floor," pressing the button that opened the front door.

"You're sure it's her?" Chiara said calmly as she shoved another spoonful into Federica's mouth.

"*Oh, dio,*" said Alvise, looking suddenly worried. He didn't open the door.

We all looked at one another in a rather hopeless way, except for Federica, who just screamed for another mouthful. Then there was a timid knock.

"Who is it?" Alvise called.

"It's me," Lucy's voice said.

"That's her," I said.

The door was opened and she looked in, a little puzzled. Her eyes lit on me and her face at once expressed relief.

"*Ciao,*" she said to me, and then to Alvise, "Sorry about the time."

260

"Come in," he said.

Introductions were made, and further apologies given about disturbing the meal, and she refused anything to eat but accepted a glass of wine, and asked about Federica's age, etc., and then she said, "Martin, I've been so worried."

"Well, I'm all right. I had the flu." Now don't be silly and irresponsible, I cautioned myself. Keep a sensible distance.

"Ah."

"Possibly it was coming on when I left you, I don't know."

"I see."

"So if I was exceptionally rude, put it down to that."

"Nobody apologizes quite like you."

Alvise was looking puzzled. "When did you leave her?" Of course as far as he was aware, she had left us at the Bar al Teatro that evening.

"We met the night I came here."

"We met?" Lucy said. Her voice was dry, ironic.

I gave one of my all-purpose shrugs. "How did you track me down?"

"I didn't know you were here. I just thought Alvise might know where you were, and I got his address from the university."

"But how did you know about me?" he asked. "We met that one time, but I didn't tell you my name."

"I was told about you." She looked at me. "You keep things secret, do you? Is that for the sake of my reputation or what?"

"I couldn't see any point in dragging you into things," I said. "Anyway, I'm leaving tomorrow."

"Where are you going?" she asked.

"Back home."

"You decided that two seconds ago. Or possibly three."

"Yes, but better late than never." I changed the subject. "Have you had trouble from the police?"

"No, though Derek wanted us to change hotels."

"Well, of course, what *would* the parents say?" I said in a fair imitation of Mr. Robin's voice.

"Exactly. But then he realized he'd paid in advance." She

looked at Alvise and Chiara. "I'm sorry, this is all very rude. But you do understand I've been out of my mind with worry."

They both made not very convincing gestures of comprehension.

She said to me, "You've seen the bit about you in the paper?"

"No," I said. "And that's the story I'm going to stick to."

She shrugged. "Okay," she said, "if that's the way you've decided to play it. Well, look, there's no need for us to inflict our bickering on Alvise and Chiara. I'm glad I found you still alive. Anyway you know where to find me if you change your mind." She picked up her glass, and I noticed that for all her pose of cool self-possession her hand had a nervous—or perhaps angry—quiver as she took it. She finished the wine, said good-bye warmly to Alvise and Chiara, and left.

"*Mi no go capìo un casso,*" said Alvise. "I haven't understood bugger all."

"*Gnanca mi,*" said Chiara. "Me neither."

"Never mind," I said. "It doesn't really matter." I wished it were true.

About half an hour later the phone rang.

"Pronto," said Alvise. "Ah, hello. You want to speak to Martin again, yes?"

At that moment I was lying on the floor holding Federica above my head and saying something along the lines of "Wheeee, you're an airplane." I brought her to land on the carpet, and she at once squirmed over to an inviting pile of books, and I got up and took the receiver from Alvise's hand.

"Hello?"

"Hello," said Lucy's voice. "Look, I'd like to speak to you but in private."

"What do you mean?" I heard the *thunk* in the background of the books going over, and Alvise's stern, "No!"

"Well, I thought it best not to say anything in front of the others," she said. "I mean, I'm still not sure of Alvise's role." Her voice sounded strained, as if speaking to me was a duty.

262

"What do you want to say?" I raised my voice over Federica's wail of complaint.

"Well, could I see you?"

"What, now?"

"If possible. I mean, you looked better to me."

"Well, yes I am, but what's it about?"

"I've got a line on Toni."

"What?"

"Look, I can't tell you over the phone. You come here. I'm in a bar on the Zattere, by the San Basegio boat stop." That was about five minutes' walk away.

"Okay," I said slowly. "I'll be along."

"And, um, I'll sing our song."

"You'll what?"

She whistled a few bars of *Celeste Aïda* and then put the phone down. I was left extremely puzzled. Was she going to be in disguise?

I explained to Alvise and Chiara—at the top of my voice, as Federica was explaining her point of view at the same time—and then I put my coat on and left the house.

My first breath of fresh air. It wasn't the most welcoming weather for a postconvalescent walk—cold and misty—but I was relieved to be outside again all the same. Just to stretch my legs I walked all the way around the church of San Nicolò. Behind the church there's a house with a garden covered by netting where someone keeps monkeys, but very sensibly they were inside, no doubt watching television. I walked on down the *fondamenta* and crossed the first bridge. To the right was a piece of scrubby waste ground with a diagonal path across it: it was probably, I thought, a shortcut to the Zattere. I set out along the path, and as I walked felt lonelier and lonelier. I suddenly stopped and listened: there were footsteps behind me. There was, of course, no reason why there shouldn't be, but nonetheless I speeded up, wishing I'd chosen a more frequented route. I glanced around but saw only mist.

I reached a long wide alley with blocks of houses to my left and a high wall to the right. I hoped I was right and this alley was going to come out by the bridge near Campo San Basegio, and not turn out to be a dead end.

No, I was lucky: the bridge appeared before me. I felt a sudden surge of relief. Then I saw there was a man standing at the top, looking into the canal. I had a second sudden surge—of fear. He turned and looked down at me: black beard, glasses, beret. I turned around myself: the footsteps were close and another man appeared from the mist—another dark-clothed, dark-bearded figure. He was holding a gun. I opened my mouth to shout, and suddenly heard the man jumping down from the bridge. I swiveled and saw something raised high above my head: and then it came down.

18

I SUPPOSE I must have blacked out for a second or two. The next thing I was aware of was pain—a pulsing supernova at the back of my head. Beyond this conflagration I had a dim realization that somebody was being lowered like a sack of potatoes into a boat. Quite probably the somebody was me, but I wouldn't have bet on it. Then the same somebody was being trussed with his arms behind his back and shoved facedown onto the damp boards. He made a vague groggy noise of protest and a wad of cloth was thrust into his mouth, and another cloth tied around his eyes. Then an oily tarpaulin was thrown over him. There: now he could go to sleep.

Gradually, in this damp, gagged darkness, the somebody and I merged, and I became aware enough to feel sudden and total panic. This was *me* in the shit! I gave a thrash of a protest with my legs—and something hard whammed into the pit of my stomach.

"Keep still, we'll tell you when to move," a voice said in Italian.

I kept still. There was the noise of an engine, and the boat started to move.

I have no idea how long the journey lasted: forty minutes, four hours, four days. . . . A long time, which I spent trying to work out ways not to go mad with fear. This meant hosing down all my powers of reasoning and logic, which at that moment were dancing in the flames of my brain's supernova. I lay there and tried to deduce as many things as possible from the tactile and aural evidence I had about me.

First, the speed of the boat—or what the throbbing of the engine and the juddering of the floor suggested was the speed—seemed to indicate that we were out in the lagoon, not in the canals of the city. This also made sense of the journey's length. At the beginning of the journey I heard the occasional noise of other engines, and once or twice the mournful hoot of a fog siren, but after a while these died away completely.

Second, I had been expertly tied and gagged, and apart from the bash on the head and that one kick in the stomach hadn't been physically maltreated. They were quite enough, however. I desperately wanted to touch the back of my head—just to check that it was intact.

Third, there were two people in the boat with me. They exchanged occasional words, mainly about the direction to go in and the need for care in the fog. Their accents were Veneto. I didn't know whether I'd heard them before. Presumably they were the two who'd attacked me. One of them never completed a sentence, confining himself mainly to grunts and occasional imprecations. The other spoke rapidly, but not very clearly. I imagined the grunter as large and oxlike, and the other as squat but wiry. I was basing my guesses on the voices and on the dark glimpses I'd had of my attackers and was probably quite wrong, of course.

I passed on to wider questions, like what was Lucy's part in all this? She couldn't be in with them, could she? Could she?

And even as I asked myself the question I knew she couldn't. I knew that I knew Lucy as I knew no one else in the world, and if there was one thing she wasn't, that was treacherous. So presumably she had been coerced into making that phone call. Maybe that line about *Celeste Aïda* had been her desperate attempt to get a warning across to me: it had become our danger signal as well as our song—and I'd been too dumb to realize it. But why hadn't she kept away from me in the first place? It was obvious no good could come from it.

And then I realized that she must be their prisoner too and I felt instant crushing guilt at these peevish thoughts. Oh, hell. I had definitely not been good for her.

The engine juddered to a halt. The tarpaulin was lifted and somebody hauled at my shoulders. I was pulled to a standing position while the boat rocked. The supernova became more frantic, more intense, and suddenly I knew my head was going to explode. Well, that would show them, I thought, and I crumpled gently at the knees. I was jerked to attention again. I heard a woman's voice, and then hands grasped my side and lifted me bodily out of the boat. There must have been two people doing this. They might have been the woman and one of the two men from the boat; I couldn't be sure. I was plonked down onto muddy ground and left to stand there; cold gunge seeped over the top of my shoes. I started to crumple again.

"Move," the woman said, and I was prodded in the back. I started hesitantly walking, having to pull my feet up from the heavy sucking mud at each step. Somebody guided me with a hand on my arm. Then I felt firm ground underfoot, and there was a haze of light through my blindfold.

"Sit him on the floor over there." It was the woman again. Her voice was hard and biting.

A pair of hands pushed me down by the shoulders. I went down uncertainly to a squatting position, then toppled over sideways and was unable of course to use my arms to right myself. The same hands pulled me up and arranged me against a brick wall. I leaned back against it, my knees hunched up in front of me.

The woman said, "Did he make any trouble?" Her accent was Milanese, I thought.

"No. Just lay there." This was the quicker-talking man; the squat one, as I imagined him.

"What about the girl? Where's she?"

"Bruno and Lucio are bringing her."

I made a muffled noise from behind my gag. It was torn away and I said, "What have you done to Lucy?" I had to have two goes at this sentence before I could get my tongue to coordinate with my brain.

The woman said, "She's been taken hostage as well."

"Let her go. She's nothing to do with all this."

"You're in no position to give us orders. Now keep quiet."

"Give me some water." I wondered whether to add "please," but decided it would be superfluous.

She instructed someone to get water, and a plastic cup was put to my mouth. I drank some, but much of it went coldly spilling down my chin and coat front.

"Where am I?" I said.

"I said keep quiet."

"Look, I want to know what you want with me—"

"Silence." I could almost feel the spray of saliva as she spat the z and t of this word (*zitto*).

"But look—"

Something hard hacked at my shin: it could have been anyone, but I imagined it as her sharp pointed shoe, and I suddenly thought of Rosa Klebb in James Bond. I felt a sudden plummeting inside, as if my innards had dropped down a lift shaft. I was in for a rough time—and I wasn't going to be able to see it coming. My innards came back, but definitely travel-worn. I said, "Excuse me, I'm going to vomit." I don't know which language I used. I twisted sideways and started retching. Somebody was already there with a bucket. A few seconds later I sat back weakly and asked for more water. It was given to me.

Well, my head was no better, but I felt just a little stronger. I said, "Who are you?"

"We're the New Front of the Proletariat." Again it was the woman speaking, and you'd have guessed from the way she pronounced the word she thought the proletariat were scum.

I said, "You don't sound like the proletariat."

"What is that supposed to mean? You don't expect the proletariat to be articulate?"

268

"Forget it. It was just a—just a remark."

"A typically patronizing one. You expect submission and deference from the working classes."

"Look, my father was a housepainter."

"The worst oppressors in the class war are those who boast of their humble backgrounds." Her answers came back like ricochets. "Now silence."

"But don't you want me to talk? What did you kidnap me for?"

"We're waiting for our group leader. He is going to question you."

She gave instructions to the men who'd brought me here to keep their guns at the ready and not to let me make a single move. Then she said, "I'll go and see if Bruno and Lucio are coming."

"I hope they find the place in this fog," the "squat" man said. "It's getting thicker." She made no answer. I heard her footsteps moving away, and imagined her poisoned steel caps killing the grass she walked through. Then there was silence. My guards occasionally shifted. It sounded as if they were sitting on the ground, and I heard the rustle of newspapers. I guessed we were in some kind of barn, a fairly ancient one, judging from the brickwork behind my back. There seemed to be no door, so the fog could sneak in and wrap us up clammily. I began to feel cold. After a while I said so, and one of them threw a blanket over me. It was my bottom that was coldest, however, and my wet feet. They were the farthest from the fierce glow inside my head. This was just what a flu convalescent needed, I thought bitterly. I twisted my hands inside the rope, but uselessly.

Eventually the noise of a boat was heard, and the men scrambled up. I had worked out that there were just the two of them, the pair who'd brought me over. "I'll go," said the squat man, and the other grunted assent, moving quickly toward me. He shoved a cloth into my mouth and then I felt the cold hard impress of metal against my temple—fortunately not against my bruise. I stopped feeling cold.

Then we heard the sound of voices in the distance, in the

269

midst of which the piranha-teeth consonants of the Milanese woman. The gun was removed from my head and the cloth pulled out. I started breathing again—in fact it was only then that I discovered that I'd stopped. The voices got nearer, but I couldn't hear Lucy. Possibly she was gagged. I wondered if it was worth shouting to her, but couldn't think of anything to shout. *Sorry* might have been the most appropriate. The voices moved away again, and finally were inaudible.

Then I heard the woman coming back with the man who'd left. As she entered the barn she announced, "Emanuele won't be coming tonight."

I said, "Who's Emanuele?"

"Silence," she said automatically, but the squat man had already replied unthinkingly, "The group leader."

"So," she went on, "we'll leave the interrogation of both prisoners till tomorrow."

"Am I supposed to sleep like this?" I said.

"You're supposed to keep still. Whether you sleep or not doesn't interest us. There are thousands in Italy with worse beds."

I rather doubted there were thousands sitting with their hands tied behind their backs. I said, "My friends will have got onto the police, you know."

"I don't think so. Your girlfriend phoned them and told them you'd decided to spend the night with her."

"Ah." I wondered whether they'd believe it. If they didn't, it put them in a nice dilemma: though perhaps less of a one than I was in. But mine was my own fault. "I couldn't have another blanket? And one for underneath. I mean if you want me to be still alive tomorrow."

"As it seems necessary that you should be so, we'll give you a sleeping bag."

"Can't I speak to my friend?"

"No."

There seemed to be no point in trying to argue with this. I said, "Remember she's nothing to do with the whole thing."

270

"I heard you. Now silence. We'll bring the sleeping bag. If
you need to piss or shit, say so." She spat out these activities, as
if these too were filthy habits of the *borghesia*.

"I—I—well, where . . . ?"

"Outside, of course."

One of the men pulled me up, and my head screamed like
fingernails on a blackboard as I rose. I was escorted outside for
a pee. My hands were freed for this; it obviously seemed the least
distasteful solution. But the knowledge that there were certainly
guns trained on me didn't help with the relaxation of the bladder
muscles. Eventually I did what I had to do, and wondered briefly
if I should now make a sudden run for it, before they retied me.
But blindfolded, with my fly down . . . maybe not. I was shoved
back into the barn. My coat was removed. Then, instead of the
rope, a pair of handcuffs was produced. My hands were linked in
front now, and a chain ran from the cuffs to somewhere in the
wall. I was made to sit down again and my shoes were removed.
I was then fed into the sleeping bag. "Remember," the woman
said, "there will be someone on watch all night. So don't think
of trying anything clever."

I said, "Can I have something to rest my head on? It's
extremely painful."

The blanket was folded, and I brought my head down
delicately on it. I lay on my side, with my hands in a praying
position, so that the chain wasn't taut and rubbing against my
face. A groundsheet had been lain down, but the ground was
hard and cold under me all the same. My head sang, but not a
lullaby. At least, I thought, the sleeping bag was warm. I could
feel my socks drying.

I didn't even attempt to go to sleep for some time, but lay
there listening, hoping to catch words that might tell me their
intentions. But they left the barn whenever they wanted to talk,
and conducted the conversation in low mutters, among which I
could nonetheless distinguish the venomously salivating voice
of the woman. The one thing I kept repeating to myself was
they wouldn't keep me blindfolded if they weren't thinking of

271

releasing me sooner or later. Then the thought struck me that that might merely be what they wanted me to believe, just to make sure I cooperated—and I wished I hadn't thought of this.

I thought of Lucy and tried by thought transference to communicate my sincere apology to her. I could have done with her company.

I must have got some sleep that night. But it wasn't the sort you wake from with a luxurious yawn and stretch—particularly if you're handcuffed. It came in crumbly bits, like Parmesan cheese. I was often aware of the squat man walking around, rubbing his hands and stamping his feet, and this was at least a tiny consolation. At some point in the night I heard him waking the other man to change guard, and this too—the more-porcine-than-usual "What, what?" followed by a resigned imprecation— was a meager source of satisfaction. I noticed the extreme silence otherwise: not the faintest noise of engines, nor any sheep or cows. I guessed we must be in some particularly remote island of the lagoon—and if the fog kept up, there was little chance of our being discovered here: certainly there would be no helicopter search.

I noticed grayish light through my blindfold and stirred. I was reminded of my head at once—and then of almost every bone and muscle in my body, each one making its little protest at this unwarranted disturbance. The exposed part of my face tingled with cold and damp. I brought my right hand up to scratch my nose, and was reminded of the handcuffs. I scratched with both hands and pushed my hair up from the blindfold; the hair and the blindfold were clammy. I listened to the world. I could hear the crackly voice of a newsreader on a tiny transistor radio. Somebody said, "Ssh," not to me, and I realized they were all awake, gathered around the radio.

The newsreader was saying: ". . . two of the carabinieri are seriously injured, while three others escaped with minor cuts and wounds. The carabinieri are taking seriously the phone call that came just twenty minutes after the explosion, in which the New

Front of the Proletariat claimed responsibility for the bomb as a direct reprisal for the death of the terrorist Simone Gerosa five days ago. This is the first action of the group in Padua, and perhaps indicates a shift of the terrorists' attention from the lagoon city, which is at the moment preparing itself for the first weekend of Carnival. Messages of firm condemnation and . . ." The voice was drowned as the listeners set up cries of "They did it!" and cheers. Another "ssh" was issued—with so much saliva I had no difficulty in identifying the woman. The newsreader read out the messages of condemnation and revulsion from various politicians, which were greeted with a chorus of jeers and raspberries. Only the woman, as far as I could tell, did not join in. I had by now a picture of her, her face set in a permanent cold sneer, with spittle hanging from the corner of thin lips—or perhaps blood. The newsreader went on to talk of the roadblocks and the searches in the surrounding area and then said, "Meanwhile in Venice, the authorities remain firm in their decision not to call off any of the manifestations for Carnival. It is not possible, they say, to disappoint the enormous number of people involved, and to do so would be to give in to the criminal plans of the terrorists. . . ."

"You'll give in soon enough," the squat man said.

When the topic changed to the Middle East, the radio was turned off. The squat man said, "With the roadblocks and all that they might not be here for some time. They didn't say they were going to do it in Padua."

"The point is to take attention from Venice," the woman said. "We have to make it clear we're active in the whole of the Veneto."

"So are we going to wait here all day for them?"

"Why not? With this fog it's the perfect place."

"To get rheumatism," said the grunter, and followed it with a routine imprecation.

"You know we can't go back to that flat on the Lido. Any moment now somebody's going to remember seeing Marco there."

Marco was presumably the "battle name" of the dead terrorist, Simone Gerosa.

"Well, the sooner we leave Venice the better, as far as I'm concerned."

"When we get that stuff—and Toni Sambon." I thought that I'd never like to hear my own name pronounced with such venom. I'd probably curl up and die of my own accord. She went on: "Go and tell Bruno and Lucio the news. And see if the girl's awake. He is." She was presumably gesturing in my direction.

I saw no reason for sitting up. There seemed nothing outside the sleeping bag that was worth leaving it for: it was unlikely we were going to have a jolly breakfast around a campfire.

I lay still, therefore, until a boot prodded me and I was asked if I wanted another pee. Well, that was one possible reason for moving. The chain was removed from the cuffs and I was escorted outside, as on the previous evening, and I shivered in the clinging fog. The handcuffs were then removed so I could put my coat on; they were clicked back on and I was given a stale brioche and made to sit back against the wall. I ate my breakfast, feeling rather like a hamster, with both hands clumsily raised to my mouth. All my attempts at conversation were rebutted with the same hissed *"Zitto"* from the woman, and the promise that I'd be given all the chance I wanted to talk when Emanuele got here. I began to wonder if this building up of Emanuele was a deliberate ploy. Every so often she said something on the lines of, "With Emanuele you'll talk, whether you like it or not." Well, if it was intended as a terror tactic, it worked all too well.

As the day wore on they got a little more careless about chatting in front of me, or at least within earshot. I had now put names to the male voices. The squat man was Luca and the grunter Piero. Both were undoubtedly assumed names—possibly just for this operation. (At one point Piero took a few seconds to answer to his name.) The little pictures I had made of them got more detailed. The woman, of course, was by now a full-length portrait: Rosa Klebb with a touch of Cruella DeVille, painted by Fuseli. Luca I saw as a minor but active demon from a medieval fresco, with a leathery leering face, and Piero was a cross

274

between a Leonardo grotesque and Sylvester Stallone. They made little small talk. The radio was turned on every so often to catch the latest news, which after their initial display of triumph was now commented on only briefly. They all seemed quite content to spend the day doing nothing. I occasionally heard newspapers being turned, and at one point Luca and Piero engaged in a little desultory conversation about the chances of Inter in the following day's match. The woman did not join in.

One fragment of conversation that did catch my attention began with the woman talking about the filth of the water. A few predictable comments were made on the responsibility of the pigs in charge of Montedison (the chemical company on the shores of the lagoon) and Piero put in one of his rare complete sentences: "Of course you haven't had to drink it like me."

The woman's voice kept the contempt it had had while talking about Montedison: "Only because you allowed yourself to be caught off guard—and by an unarmed woman."

"It was Marco got caught. I was in the boat."

So it had been Piero and the dead "Marco" who had tried to kidnap me the other night. I gathered that Piero had been taken back to their hideout on the Lido after the accident, and Marco (Simone Gerosa) had then gone out again on his own. It explained why the terrorist who had followed Osgood into the building had been on his own. But at this point they realized I was listening and changed the subject.

I asked twice about Lucy and was each time answered by the woman and told to shut up. When the woman left us for a few minutes, I asked again and Luca said, "She's all right, but if you keep asking . . ." He said no more, and I imagined him standing there preparing to jab me—or Lucy—with his three-pronged fork. I shut up.

There was one moment when a boat was heard in the distance, and I was regagged. The gun was put to my temple again. But the engine noise died away. It had probably been several hundred yards away, and quite invisible in the fog.

I was given a cheese sandwich and an apple for lunch. I did my little hamster act again, eating more from boredom than hunger. I had never realized before that it is possible to feel both bored and terrified. The thought of Emanuele's arrival was a permanent sick dread at the forefront of my mind and the pit of my stomach, but at the same time there was a tiny part of me that looked forward to his arrival, as being at least an event. An infinitesimally tiny part, mind you.

And when the boat was finally heard, this tiny part got completely washed away by the wave of blind terror that swelled up nauseatingly inside me. This was helped, of course, by the usual routine of gag and gun. Then the boat came to a stop, voices were heard, and the gag and gun were removed. I could feel my heart pounding, five times as quick as their plashy footsteps.

Luca was continuing to say *"Bravi"* with reference to the Padua bomb. I had already gathered that Emanuele had placed the bomb together with an accomplice, and they had presumably both arrived. The woman said, "No trouble in getting away?"

"We drove off in the direction of Bologna," replied a new voice. I recognized at once the cold precise tones of the man who'd burned my paintings. Padoan.

Irrationally I imagined him standing there wearing that white mask. My heartbeats got even faster.

He went on: "Then we got a train at Rovigo. It was full of people coming up for Carnival."

"There were no deaths," said the woman.

"It's the message that counts," Padoan said. "It was clear enough." His voice was quite level, in contrast with the vicious stressed tones of the woman.

Another voice spoke. "You should have seen the chaos, though. I mean we really put the shit up them." I recognized the voice as that of the other man who'd visited me that night in London: Alfredo. This recognition had nothing like the effect that Padoan's had had on me. Another thug, that was all.

Padoan said, "The important thing is to make it clear that we aren't indiscriminate like those fascist pigs. We hit the people we want to hit. They didn't die this time, but they know that next time they probably will."

There was a murmur of agreement. He hadn't said anything particularly brilliant but it was clear that he had them under his thumb—even the woman. I suppose it was the calm certainty with which he spoke that did it.

The woman said, "There's the painter guy. The woman's in the other barn."

"Okay. Well, I'll begin with him."

"Do you want him sitting up?"

"Not for the moment."

I heard him walking toward me. I said, "Now, look here. . . ." And then a foot hacked hard against my shin. In blind rage I thrashed back, but hit nothing.

"Martin Phipps."

"Yes."

"You're a fool." He spoke in Italian.

"Okay, I'm a fool. So let me go."

"You know what we want from you. You didn't give it to us in London, but now that you've been so stupid as to come here, you'll give it to us here."

"What are you going to burn this time?" I knew it was a stupid question as soon as I'd said it.

"You. Or perhaps your friend. But only if necessary."

"Look, she's got nothing to do with all this."

"I suspect you may be right. But that doesn't matter. She could prove useful in helping to convince you to collaborate."

I couldn't think of what to say other than "You bastard," so I said that.

"I told you in London that I have no love of causing pain for its own sake. For me it is purely a matter of the most efficient means to an end. Now let it be quite clear that there is no point in your persisting in the line you used in London. It is clear from the fact that you're here in Venice that you know something about Sambon, and it is clear from your past that you are not new to trafficking in art."

There it was: the albatross of my past. I said, "So you know about me. Which means you presumably know I've been to jail.

Well, don't you think that I might be as angry as you about things?"

"Are you telling me that you wish to join the armed struggle?"

"Well, you tell me about it, and who knows . . . ?"

From a little farther off I heard the woman splutter, "This is a waste of time. He's typical *borghese* filth."

"We must never show reluctance to state our position on things," Padoan said. "It might be mistaken by fools for uncertainty."

"What is your position?" I asked. "What are you hoping to achieve?"

"The overthrow of the capitalist system. I think you know that."

"Um, tomorrow?"

There was another sharp jab at my shin. He answered so immediately and so unmovedly, that I guessed he hadn't been the one to administer the kick. "It will occur when the social forces needed for the change have been prepared and made sufficiently aware politically. This will not happen overnight. At the moment the capitalist-controlled press and media have done their best to instill a general belief that the armed struggle is a lost hope. Even ex-fighters for the cause have been bribed or coerced into the spreading of this defeatist line. Our immediate task is to make it clear to the people that the present political and socioeconomic system is not an unshakable, permanent reality, but can be destabilized. We first have to create a climate of uncertainty, and demonstrate our determination to win and our extreme efficiency."

"Show how good you are at killing people."

"That is part of it. The first phase, if you like. The *pentiti* are to be wiped out completely. It must be made clear that the choice of the armed struggle is one that cannot be gone back on. He who betrays his *compagni* is a traitor to the proletariat as a whole."

"Excuse me, but have you asked the proletariat as a whole?"

278

"These facile comments are the typical sneers of the *borghesi*, convinced that the masses have been so duped by the paternalistic propaganda of the exploiting classes as to be happy under their oppression."

"Ah," I said. "You may be right. But have you actually been into any bar and listened to what the oppressed masses think about your killings?"

"We're not television stars, trying to win a popularity competition." There was never any hesitation or uncertainty in his replies: they came back at me without any pause for reflection, in a flat but completely secure voice. I could imagine his unmoved, unmoving eyes. "Our task at the moment is to prove to the masses that we can win. We have to overcome the crisis of confidence that followed the mass arrests of the eighties. And a display of determination is the way to do this. Our killings are designed to make maximum impact on public awareness. The so-called barbaric mutilations are highly charged symbolic messages to the masses, telling them that victory will be theirs if they have total commitment to the cause; and, as I say, total commitment means denying the possibility of ever going back."

"I see." I would have liked to be able to think he was raving mad, but his voice was too controlled, too calmly logical in its exposition, to permit such a comforting diagnosis. In the background I could hear the others shifting around, impatient with the time being wasted on me, but none of them daring to protest. "And where do poor old Busetto and Osgood come into all this?"

"They were mere parasites who stood in the way. Their deaths were not an integral part of our strategy, but nonetheless have served to reinforce the message of our determination."

"And what was Osgood doing in the palazzo?" I asked.

"That we want to know from you."

"From me?"

"You heard me."

"Well, you're the ones who followed him in there."

"It was our *compagno* Marco who did so. And as he got killed by the so-called *forze dell'ordine* immediately afterward we don't know the exact sequence of events. We presume that he must have seen Osgood somewhere near the palazzo and started following him. The execution inside the building may have been—"

"A balls-up," I said.

Another sharp jab at my shin. I thought I recognized the Rosa Klebb steel caps.

Padoan said, "It might have been excess of zeal on the part of our *compagno*. But what we want to know from you is whether those paintings are in the build- ing. And whether you know anything about what happened that night." So they didn't know we were the ones who'd entered the palazzo—or weren't sure, at any rate.

"Before I answer any questions I want a guarantee you'll let Lucy go."

"We're not going to bargain with you. You will answer our questions whether you like it or not."

I knew I wasn't going to like it at all. I wasn't liking any of it already. "I don't know anything," I said feebly.

"You will hardly expect us to believe that line now. Where are the paintings, and where is Toni Sambon." There were no question marks in the way he said this. His questions were as secure as his opinions.

"I came to Venice to look for him like you. Why do you think I got mixed up with Busetto as I did? And anyway, how can these paintings possibly be so important to you? You'll get better money by robbing a bank."

"Those paintings have already been appropriated in action by the Front of the Proletariat. We do not intend to give them up—particularly not so that a parasitic traitor like Sambon can enrich himself."

"So what are you going to do with them? Hang them on the walls of your hideouts?"

"We have no interest in these pictures as such, as I'm sure you're aware. We have a buyer for them."

"Who?"

"I see no reason not to tell you. A functionary high up in the government of a certain African state who obviously wishes to improve his cultural standing. He has agreed to pay us in arms."

I felt a sudden rise of spirit and burst out in English. "Don't you think it's kind of ironic that for all your talk of the people, here you are stealing from the people one of the most popular forms of art ever practiced?"

"What sort of relevance has it for the proletariat today? An art form practiced at the orders of an oppressive institution and now the interest of decadent academics and aesthetes."

"I suppose the people who go into the churches don't count. How can old ladies be the people? The people are those chin-thrusting Herculeses holding banners that you see on communist posters, right? And that's the crappy level of art we'll have with your new order." I was surprised at my own vehemence. It wasn't at all what the rational part of my brain was suggesting as the most suitable line to follow.

"Isn't it typically pathetic that your judgment of a socio-economic and political system is based entirely on what kind of pretty pictures it produces. But all this is irrelevant. Where are the paintings?"

I recognized the uselessness of arguing. After all, these were people whose whole way of life was a negation of argument: you didn't try and talk to people you disagreed with, you kneecapped them or shot them—or tore their tongues out. I said slowly, "In Palazzo Sambon."

"Where?"

"In the attic."

"Where in the attic? Remember we have already searched there."

"Really? When?"

"Some weeks back."

I remembered the hotel lady's reference to nocturnal noise from the building. "There's a false wall where the roof slopes down. It's on the side of the palazzo by the alley." I wasn't sure what I hoped to gain by these lies, other than time. I rather doubted that he'd say thank you and release me at once. But I remembered how unwilling he had been in London to accept the idea that I really didn't know anything.

"How is this false wall constructed?" he asked.

"It—it's just planks. I haven't been there myself. That's what Toni told me."

"When?"

"In London."

"And where is Sambon now?"

"Didn't Busetto tell you?"

"He said he hadn't seen him since he went to jail."

"Well, he was lying obviously."

"I hardly think so. We were extremely persuasive. Too much so, it turned out."

"Well, if you believe that he didn't know, why don't you believe me?"

"You are clearly a more stubborn type than Busetto. I wish to know the full story of your relationship with Sambon."

I started a rambling story of how I'd met Toni in a picture gallery and how he'd told me about the paintings and I'd agreed to meet him in Venice and help him swing the deal with Osgood. Halfway through, I did wonder if this story was any more convincing than the truth would have been, but I felt I could hardly start all over again. By the end I was merely repeating, "It's the truth, you've got to believe it, you've got to." I had switched back to English, and I didn't know when I'd done so.

"So where is he?"

"I don't know. He came to Venice and then he must have heard of these—of your strategy with the *pentiti* and he went into hiding."

"You don't know." He repeated this in the flattest of tones. There was a contemptuous noise from the woman.

"No."

"We will now go and question your friend."

"She doesn't know anything."

"We will see." He snapped out orders to Luca and Piero to keep me under surveillance and left, with sharp decisive footsteps. Obviously it was part of the image that everything should be done with the minimum of hesitation. I heard Alfredo saying as he tagged along, "We could have been a bit more persuasive," and Padoan's reply, "All in good time."

Piero and Luca made no conversation and I sat there in an agony of apprehension, praying that the next sound wouldn't be a female scream of pain. Five or ten minutes went past and then I heard voices approaching again, among them Lucy's, "Not so fast."

Padoan said, "Put her by the wall there."

There was a bit of confused scuttering here, concluded by a bump and "Ouch" from Lucy. Well, it was better than a scream.

"Their blindfolds can be removed now," Padoan said. "I think sight will only render our interrogation methods more effective. And we can try out the Carnival masks that our *compagno* here bought for us."

"Hope you like them," Alfredo said, with an obviously humorous note. There was a rustling sound of a bag or something being opened.

"You're not going to win any prizes for imagination," Luca said.

"What, they're all the same?" Piero grunted.

"Obviously," Padoan said. "We may need to establish quick identification in a crowd."

There was a little sniggering as the masks were put on. I wondered how funny Lucy and I were going to find them. Their voices became muffled. This didn't take any of the arrogant security out of Padoan's, however, as he gave the order for our blindfolds to be taken off.

I blinked in the sudden light. At first my eyes were hit just by the white haze of the fog at the building's open end, and then the dark silhouettes against this haze filled in with gray, and gradually colored details. Seven figures in coats, wearing cheap Mickey Mouse masks. I didn't have even a momentary urge to snigger. The guns in the hands of most of them put a damper on the joke.

I looked over to the wall on the right and saw Lucy leaning

back, her hands tied in front of her. Her eyes were screwed up and they turned and came to slow focus on me. She forced a smile to her face—not a very convincing one, but nonetheless a lot more cheering than the Mickey Mouse grins. "Hi," she said. Her voice had a slight tremor, even in this one word.

"Hi. Er, sorry."

"Think nothing of it."

"Silence." Padoan's voice came from a slight figure in the center, wearing a large ski jacket. He wasn't holding a gun and his arms were folded. The pale eyes were fixed on me. I glanced around them all, trying to work out who was who: I could only recognize the woman; she had a belted coat that showed a slim and undeniably attractive figure: more Cruella DeVille than Rosa Klebb.

I looked around the room. We were in what at first sight seemed like an empty barn with rough, ancient brick walls, and a floor partly of stone, partly of bare earth—both equally hard and cold. But a second glance suggested it was more probably a ruined chapel of a rudimentary sort: there were a couple of rough niches in the side walls where statues of saints might have stood, and the three windows—one in each of the standing walls—had pointed arches; they all had ancient wrought-iron grilles, and the chain attached to my handcuffs was linked to a bar in one of these grilles in the window opposite the entrance. It was the open end of the building that suggested a barn, but the jagged remains of the wall there could be seen on both sides. I just trusted the roof was well enough supported all the same.

There were a couple of camp stools, a camp table, three rucksacks, and three rolled sleeping bags lined up against one of the walls. The table had a water container, a couple of bulging plastic bags and knives. Everything suggested tidy habits—or readiness for a quick getaway. By the entrance was a sagging pile of old fishing nets—presumably nothing to do with the terrorists. Looking to the open end of the chapel, I could see uncultivated scrubs and undergrowth outside, and beyond that only fog.

Padoan said to me, "Your friend insists she knows nothing. Well, this may be the truth. I feel, however, she must have had some idea that something was going on to have waited that night outside the hotel." The moment I caught sight of those pale fixed eyes, the mask suddenly seemed irrelevant.

"I just wanted to speak to my friend," she said. Her Italian was hesitant, but probably her English would have been as well at that moment.

"But this has little importance," Padoan said. "We need to know just one thing: where is Toni Sambon?"

Lucy turned to me, her face a picture of weariness. I said, "I don't know. Why do you think I got fighting with Busetto?"

"Why did you?"

"Because he wouldn't tell me where Sambon was."

"Give the signorina a tap with your gun. On the shin."

"Stop!" I yelled as one of the bigger Mickey Mouses (Mice?) stepped forward, his pistol held by the barrel. Lucy drew her knees up and hunched forward, staring at the man and then at me. Her mouth opened imploringly but no words came out. The masks were never less funny.

The gun stopped in midswing. Padoan said, "Proceed." The gun lifted again and slammed down with a nasty crack. I guessed it was Alfredo behind that particular mask. Lucy drew her breath in—a quick sharp whistling intake—while I let mine out together with a stream of the foulest curses I knew, in both English and Italian.

Padoan waited till I'd stopped. "Why waste your breath in this way? You know perfectly well that your insults are not going to have any effect."

He was right of course; and the unchanging plastic grins on their faces made this all the more obvious. You don't know the meaning of futility till you've spent thirty seconds vituperating against a bunch of people in Mickey Mouse masks.

Padoan said, "We are going to go on until you tell us what we want to know."

"But I don't—"

"Martin," Lucy's voice came in in English. "Tell them—it can't matter."

"But Lucy, you know—"

"Tell them what you told me—about Zennaro."

"About what?" Had the blow affected her brain?

"You know," she said. "Toni and Zennaro."

I looked at her. Her eyes were fixed full on mine, pleading. I thought, Well, I can lose nothing by playing along—and she could lose a hell of lot by my not doing so . . . starting with intact bones and teeth and fingernails. I turned my expression to one of resigned anger. "You tell them," I said.

"Who is Zennaro?" Padoan said.

"He's a painter," I said—at exactly the same time as Lucy. Well, that was convincing if anything was.

"And so?"

Lucy said, "I don't know much about this whole thing, but I know Martin said he had to get in touch with this Zennaro because he was looking after a friend." She said all this in English still.

Padoan's upturned black nose swiveled around to me—and the eyes, of course. "Where is this Zennaro?"

I opened my mouth—but Padoan suddenly added, "No, don't tell me. Write it. And you too," turning and nodding at Lucy.

"But I've never been there," Lucy said. "I just think—"

"Silence. Write."

I was given a pen and a torn-off piece of newspaper. I wrote, with my left hand dragging along in the ink's wake, "Far end of Via Garibaldi." Lucy wrote something on another bit of newspaper. Padoan looked at the two scraps. "Good. They agree. So why all these lies about not knowing?"

I shrugged. "I don't approve of murder, I suppose."

"What we are doing is justice: the justice of the people."

"Yeah, you and Li Peng and Hitler and Ceausescu and—"

"Silence." My remarks hadn't angered him in the slightest, though I could hear some of the others stirring and the woman snorting into her mask. Well, I hoped she drowned in her own spittle.

"Zennaro doesn't have anything to do with the paintings," I said.

286

"We will deal with him justly, have no fear."

Oh, my God. Had I sentenced him to death? "Look, I mean it—he—he—he isn't anything—"

Lucy came in. "Zennaro's just a poor painter for the tourists from what I hear. You mustn't touch him—"

"We will decide. What is the exact address?" The eyes were staring down at me.

I told him, thinking there was no point in trying to go back on it now.

With his usual quick decisiveness he announced, "We will pick him up at once."

"And the paintings?" one of them said: a new voice, presumably Bruno or Lucio.

"We will get the information from Sambon about them."

"While he's still got his tongue," Luca said, and there was a snigger from behind two or three of the masks.

"Exactly," Padoan said, with no trace of humor. Why laugh at an accurate statement of fact?

Plans were immediately made over a map of the city, which was spread out on the camp table. Two of them stayed with their guns pointing down at us. I looked at Lucy and she looked at me. I tried by a little raising of the eyebrows and a shrug to get across the message, "So what about Zennaro then? And what do we do when they find out Toni's not there? Invent another painter?" She gave a faint smile back, which, I felt, suggested she hadn't fully grasped the subtleties of my questions.

It was decided that only one of them would be left to guard us, and after a certain amount of argument the woman was chosen. The others would set off in two boats, three in each of them. Cruella DeVille clearly rather looked forward to the idea of having us both under her sole control. I could imagine a little serpent tongue flickering around thin lips behind the mask's toothy grin.

"Put them together," Luca said. "They'll like that." His mask seemed to curl into a sneer as he said it.

We were both made to stand by the window opposite the entrance and Lucy's wrists were untied, the rope having been

287

judged inadequate. As they only had the one pair of handcuffs (and how does one obtain such things, I found myself wondering, what sort of shop sells them?) they did for both of us. They were clicked onto my right wrist, passed around one of the bars in the window's grille (which was first tested for solidity), and clicked onto Lucy's left wrist. We were thus forced to a standing position with our arms raised, but we did at least have one arm free. I used it to touch the back of my head—and at once wished I hadn't.

They checked their guns, clicking them open, loading them, snapping them shut, thrusting them into holsters and adjusting their coats over them; the masks looked pretty silly at this point—but even so, I still felt no urge to laugh. Padoan left first, saying nothing; one or two of the others made some remark to the effect, "We'll be back," and the woman lifted her rifle in salutation, her Mickey Mouse nose held arrogantly up, and she said, "Good hunting, *compagni*." It was, of course, typical that amid all the horror of what was being here prepared, I should be struck by the kitsch of the scene. Well, that's the decadent kind of elitist I am.

The woman gazed out at the fog, which was gathering thicker and darker, and then swiveled to face us, her rifle leveled. "I shoot first and ask questions afterward," she said. "So no foolishness." Clichéd kitsch again: but I felt the real import of it this time: a sick dread in the pit of my stomach.

19

"CAN we talk?" Lucy asked.

"Go ahead and screw if you want. But any suspicious move will be your last."

She should obviously get a job at Hollywood. I turned to Lucy and said, "Sorry."

She said nothing, just curled her upraised hand into mine. I held it tight and then brought my free arm around her. I said, "Funny the ways we get brought together."

"A scream."

"But look, Zennaro—"

"Zennaren't you going to keep your mouth a little more carefully buttoned?" Here eyes merely flickered to her left by way of gesture. The woman was sitting on one of the camp stools, the rifle on her lap. We were talking in low voices but she could have exceptional hearing. Lucy suddenly switched to a caricature Scottish accent. "Och, at least make your gab a wee bit tough to crack, will ye no'?"

"Hoots," was all I could think of saying. Then: "Gotcha." I went on with a broad West Country accent. "And old Zennarrr, what'll be of 'ee, then?"

"Och, the puir wee man has done a bunk."

"And how d'ye ken that?" I switched dialect.

"Because I tried to get a butcher's at him meself, dinneye? I went round there Wednesday-like, and the li'l old lidy told me 'e'd slung his hook, scarpered, wiv all his stuff. She dinno why."

"Wotcher go there for?"

"I bin all over, trying to get a line on you."

"I see." So they'd find an empty flat, which could mean anything—even that we'd been telling the truth, as far as we knew it. But I wished the empty flat had been a bit farther away. They'd probably be back within an hour and a half.

I let go of Lucy and glanced over at the woman. She hadn't budged. She was still sitting upright on that stool, not even leaning against the wall, and the rifle was still across her lap. There was of course no way of seeing if she'd been following our conversation; the mask gave no indication of puzzlement and certainly she hadn't scratched the big round ears.

"Does it hurt?" I said, gesturing down at Lucy's leg.

"There'll be a bruise, I guess. Could have been worse."

"Well, that's always true." We'd both settled down to fairly sloppy cockney; the other accents were too much like hard work, and we hadn't even been getting any amusement out of them. Lucy's cockney, I noticed, was really quite convincing; a lot better than mine, at any rate. "How'd they get you?"

"Moved in on me when I come out of the flat. They said if I din call yer, they'd go in after yer, and there was a biby, so . . ."

"Yes, yes, I see."

"They'd been following me for a bit, though. I'd had a bit of an idea they were, but couldn't be sure. Reckon they got onter me when I went round to your hotel asking about yer—yer know, the di after they tried to nab you there. I went along to see if you'd gawn back there and they were keeping tabs on the plice, and they must have recognized me."

Another pause, and then I said again, "Sorry."

She let a quick smile flicker up and said, "Well, can't be helped—spilt milk and all that."

Some clichés are more effective than others, I thought.

"That's enough talking," the woman cut in here. "If you want to say anything, say it aloud. In Italian."

"Where are we?" Lucy asked in Italian.

"No stupid questions."

"So what's an intelligent question?" I asked.

"None you're likely to ask. You probably haven't asked a real question all your life."

"And what's a real question?" I said.

"One that challenges the system, one that isn't intended just to reinforce it, and your position within it."

"Oh, yes, my position within it. My great position down at the slammer."

She made no reaction to this; nothing that indicated whether she'd understood the idiom or not.

We remained silent for twenty minutes or so. The woman never moved once. We continued to shift our upraised and shackled arms, trying to find a comfortable position. (There wasn't one, but we kept trying.)

I looked at the iron bars in the window once or twice. On closer examination they didn't actually form a grille; they were simple vertical bars with ornamental flourishes added at top and bottom—rough curls on either side of each bar. There had obviously been four bars at one time but the one on the far right had disappeared, together with some of the stonework at top and bottom. This made me look at the other bars with some hope, but I soon saw that they were solidly embedded at both ends—or at least solidly enough for any surreptitious fiddling or scraping to be of no use whatsoever.

I looked out of the window; this meant twisting around, with my head crooked over my shoulder; all I could see were bushes and trees, indistinct shapes hulking in the mist.

The woman glanced at her watch: her first movement. She got up and moved over to the table. As she did so I put my head closer to the bars, almost cricking my neck in the process, and I peered out in the hope of seeing anything that might give a clue to where we were. But there was nothing. I dropped my eyes down to the ground below the window: in the dank vegetation I saw something long and straight—too straight to be a twig or branch.

A voice suddenly said, "—direct from our studio in Rome." My head spun around. She'd turned on the radio. She was watching me carefully: at least the mask was pointing in my direction. The radio went on to announce the evening's programs.

I wasn't listening: I was wondering whether the object outside could be the other bar from the window. I didn't want to call attention to myself—or to it—by having another look. I calmed myself, saying, Well, even if it were, I couldn't reach it, and even if I could reach it, what use would it be against a gun?

I suddenly realized the news was being read: they were talking about the bomb in Padua. The condition of the two hospitalized carabinieri remained critical. The police were still taking seriously the phone call from the so-called New Front of the Proletariat. Roadblocks were still in force. "And in Venice—"

We all leaned in closer: I could have sworn the Mickey Mouse ears pricked up.

"—the police this afternoon raided the flat of a man suspected of having been a partner of Michele Busetto. Michele Busetto, who was murdered earlier in the week by the New Front of the Proletariat, is known to have trafficked extensively in stolen works of art, and the man whose flat was raided this afternoon, Fabio Zennaro—"

There was a general intake of breath here.

"—is a painter who the police believe may have helped disguise works in order to facilitate their transport abroad. Zennaro had already abandoned the flat, but the police say they have clues that may lead to a speedy arrest.

"Meanwhile Carnival continues apparently unaffected by the recent events. The inflow of visitors to the city, this first weekend of the celebrations, is said in fact to be considerably up

292

from last year. People are being advised not to try to arrive by car, but to use the specially provided car parks on the mainland, since holdups are likely on the causeway into the city, owing to the numbers of visitors.

"In Israel this afternoon—"

The woman turned the volume down and said, "I'm sure my *compagni* will have listened to this news on their radios in the boat."

I thought I detected some uncertainty in this statement—or even wishful thinking—but then thought there was probably more wishful thinking in my own detection of it. It was nice to imagine them walking unawares into a flat full of armed carabinieri—or at least nicer than imagining them coming back here. But I remembered that during the day they had apparently not missed a single news bulletin, so if they had radios with them, they probably wouldn't have missed this one either.

The woman turned the volume back up. There was no more relevant news. She turned toward the building's open end and looked out into the fog. I looked out of the window again, squinting down at the ground. In the gathering gloom I could only just make out the bar. At one end I thought I saw the ornamental curls still attached.

"Lucy," I said quietly, "we've got to get her away from the building for a few seconds."

"Why?" Her voice was dull, as were her eyes. The prospect of a speedy return pleased her no more than it did me.

"Too complicated to explain. Have you got anything we can throw out into the bushes? Quickly."

She put her free hand into her coat pocket and came out with some coins and a notebook. I took the coins, keeping my eye on the woman, who was still gazing out at the fog. I then swiveled around to face Lucy and with my free hand flung them out over her shoulder. I drew my hand back in and dropped it to Lucy's waist even before they landed. There was the faintest of distant scuffling noises. Nothing else. The woman turned around and came back in. She probably hadn't heard anything, and the rain of gold hadn't awakened any scurrying little animals, as I'd hoped. I broke away from Lucy as if embarrassed at the intimate pose we'd been discovered in.

Lucy looked at me and shrugged. We waited another five minutes or so during which the woman lit a gas lamp. Then she moved again to the entrance and stared out. I took the notebook; it was solidly bound and satisfyingly heavy. Once again I moved around to Lucy's side. I threw it, upward, outward, and to the side. My hand was at her waist again before we heard it hit the bushes: a few seconds' threshing of leaves, even a tiny crack of a twig, and then a little thud. The woman definitely heard this. I heard her turn and I glanced over my shoulder and saw her with the gun raised and pointing at us. We broke free again with another display of embarrassment, raising our free arms at the same time, but she was already turning to stare around the side of the chapel. She made a few steps in that direction—stopped— and then a few more, disappearing around the side.

I pulled a pen and a pencil from my pockets and threw those. More faint pattering noises and we now heard the woman moving farther from the building.

My hand dropped to my trouser belt and started fiddling at the buckle. "Help me undo it," I whispered.

Lucy's face was a picture of surprise and puzzlement. Fortunately she wasted no time in asking questions but put her fingers to the buckle and helped me flip the tongue from the hole. I then tugged at the belt to free it: as ever it snagged halfway around, and as ever I told myself, More haste, less speed, while continuing nonetheless to tug savagely. It came away with a sudden jerk that suggested a loop on the trousers had given.

I stood there holding the belt in one hand and listening to the woman outside: just a faint rustling of distant leaves and an occasional squelch, which I hoped meant her feet were getting soaked.

I said to Lucy, "I'm going to try and fish something up from outside." I'm quite sure she had no idea what I meant, but I felt I had to say something before my next action. Which was to close in on her again—but really crushing her this time as I dangled the belt out over her shoulder, the buckle hanging down to the grass. There was a moment's desperation when I was sure it wouldn't reach, but Lucy somehow made herself yet smaller and I felt the belt brushing against grass: I couldn't see anything unfortunately. Then there was a tiny dull clink as the buckle touched something metal. I slowly trailed it up the bar, my arm stretching to its full length, and Lucy obligingly managing to lose one of her dimensions. It caught on something and I guessed I'd reached the end where the loop was attached. I gently jiggled my arm until I thought I could feel the buckle actually slipping over the end of the curl and snagging on it.

I was now reduced to two senses: tactile and aural. Every quiver and every extra tug of tension in the belt transmitted itself up my arm: the bar, belt, and arm became one thing. And my ear was tuned in to every tiny noise outside the barn as the woman continued to poke around in the bushes. I started lifting—gently, gently—and I felt the extra weight of something coming up with the belt. I continued to lift my arm.

Suddenly the woman's cautious padding became a decisive thrashing: she'd given up and was coming back. As I realized this I jerked my arm upward with the panicky intention of catching the bar in midtoss. I merely succeeded in jerking it off the buckle. It dropped with a clatter back to earth. I only just managed to stop myself swearing.

The woman's returning footsteps stopped at this noise and suddenly she was moving away again.

I restarted the process. By now I'd completely forgotten Lucy's existence: her body was a mere irritating obstacle, one that wasn't as reducible in size as I would have liked.

The buckle snagged again, I pulled upward, and seconds later I had the whole thing off the ground, hanging from the buckle. I suddenly thought, And suppose the woman comes round to this window now, and tried not to let the agitation communicate itself to my arm again. In another three seconds my handcuffed hand had grasped the rough metal of the bar. I dropped the belt and transferred the bar to my free hand.

I stepped away from Lucy and she let out a relieved "Phew";

295

it relieved me too—I hadn't actually crushed her to death. Then she saw the bar, and a smile transformed her face.

Perhaps a bit prematurely: it was a metal bar, not a Kalashnikov.

There was an ornamental loop only at one end, the other one clearly having come away. This made it possible to slip it up my coat sleeve; it was a little shorter than my arm and I was just about able to conceal the protruding loop in my curled hand.

"And now?" Lucy said.

"We wait for an opportunity." I said.

"Don't waste it."

"No." It was of course by no means certain that I would get a chance to use it; what *was* certain was that I wouldn't get two chances.

We heard the woman coming back, probably having decided that what she'd heard had been animals. I looked at Lucy and said, "Just pray my trousers don't fall down." She gave another quick smile.

The woman came back in, adjusting her mask as she did so. She had presumably removed it for her search.

"I'd like a glass of water," Lucy said.

"Wait."

This was merely an automatic refusal in order to show who was boss. Some seconds later she went over to the water container and, with her rifle tucked under her arm, slopped some water into a plastic cup. She put the rifle down on a stool and took a handgun from inside her coat. Then, with the gun in one hand and the cup in the other, she came forward. She held the cup out to Lucy, while the gun unwaveringly pointed at Lucy's heart. Lucy took the cup and sipped.

There was just the noise of Lucy's eager swallows; otherwise a dead-still, dead-quiet tableau, all centered, as far as I was concerned, on the dark circle of the gun's barrel.

Then Lucy lowered the cup. As she held it out to the woman I said suddenly, "Hey!" and there was a moment's fumbling and the cup fell to the ground. "Idiot," said the woman—a sibilant spray of consonants that must have soaked her mask.

296

"But listen," I said. And in the next moment's hush we all heard the faint far-off noise of a boat's engine.

The woman nodded slowly. She stepped back a little and bent down to retrieve the cup. At that moment I let the bar drop down from my sleeve, catching it by its jagged end and, in one sudden circular movement, swung it around and down on her head. The crack coincided with a gasp from Lucy for which I was glad, and the woman pitched straight forward, cracking the plastic nose of her mask. She lay still, the gun a foot or so from her hand.

"Now let's hope she's got the keys to these cuffs," I said.

Lucy said nothing, just nodded. She thrust her handcuffed arm as far around the window bar as she could so that I could bend down to the body. I had to drag the woman closer, tugging at the nearest leg. She scraped across the ground, and the mask cracked further and slipped up her face. I could hear her hard, heavy breathing. "She's not . . ." Lucy said in relief. I guessed the unstated word "dead."

I felt in her pockets: a purse, a notebook, a packet of paper handkerchiefs (to wipe off spittle?), and a set of keys—but none of them small enough for the handcuffs.

"They're not there," I said.

"They must be—"

We could both hear the engine getting louder. They'd be mooring within seconds.

"The gun!" Lucy said suddenly.

She was right. We could try shooting through the chain. I bent down: it lay a foot or so from my outstretched fingers.

"Use the bar," she said.

I nodded. We could hear the engine noise change to a low rumble as the boat slowed down. I picked up the bar and managed to drag the gun across the ground. My fingers closed on it and I straightened up.

"Okay, stand clear." I held the nozzle just above one of the links in the chain and squeezed the trigger. The noise and kickback were terrific: the gun leaped out of my hand—almost *through* my hand—and we both staggered sideways.

There was a sudden babble of voices from the boat.

The link was shattered, however. We both broke free. Lucy picked up the gun and I ran toward the rifle. We could hear urgent squelching footsteps from outside now. I turned off the gas lamp.

"Shall we use her as a hostage?" Lucy said.

"And suppose they don't give a damn?" I couldn't imagine anyone caring about her. "Let's just run for it."

"This is probably an island, Martin."

"Let's get out of here, anyway." I made toward the open end of the building, but halted by the pile of old fishing nets. With vague thoughts of Roman gladiators I picked up a tangle of the stuff and bundled it under my arm. It was knotted, torn, and slimy and obviously useless—as a fishing net at any rate. With another "Come on" to Lucy I ran around the side of the building and she followed me. We flattened ourselves against the wall and peered out into the fog.

The footsteps had become cautious now, and I could just see one blurry dark shape among the bushes, moving forward with slow crouching caution. Presumably they'd separated, fanning out in true military fashion.

I raised my rifle and fired. I aimed close to the figure and he dived to earth, rolling behind a clump of vegetation.

"Come on, let's make for the boat," I said.

There was a shot from the bushes.

"Too obvious," Lucy said. "Let's go the other way round the building."

"Okay."

I picked up the bundle of netting, which had fallen to earth when I'd fired, and we ran as quietly as possible along the wall and around the corner. I stopped there, tapping Lucy on the shoulder. "Give me a leg up to the roof." I propped the rifle against the wall and dropped the netting.

Again she didn't waste time asking questions. She thrust the pistol into her pocket, cupped her hands, and I stepped into them and grabbed the ancient stone guttering. A second's heaving and rolling and I was lying on the sloping wet tiles. Lucy had understood what was wanted and was already handing me up a corner of the fishing net. I pulled it up, and it came away, leaving her holding a separate section. She then flattened herself against the wall. We could hear somebody approaching the side of the chapel with quick stealthy footsteps. One of the terrorists had entered the building, and I could hear exhortatory remarks being made, presumably to the stunned woman.

I swiveled so that I was facing out over the side of the building, and I lay there with a length of slimy net between my hands, praying that the man would not look up, and the roof would not give way.

The figure appeared, without, I noticed, the distorting features of the mask: dark hair, pale face. His gun was held out before him in both hands as if it were trying to get away, and he was moving in a crouching run. Seconds later he was below me and I threw the net. He became a mere distorted struggling shape, all wild bulges and grunting. I swung my legs around and dropped down, my feet aimed at the head. It was a brain-staggering blow and he reeled to the ground, where Lucy delivered another crack with the butt of her gun. I only heard this, as I too had gone sprawling. When I got to my feet he had ceased wriggling. We both ran back around the corner again.

I grabbed the other section of netting Lucy had dropped and thrust it under my arm again, and in the same action snatched up the rifle.

Lucy was standing flat next to the window—the one we'd been manacled to—preparing to look in, but I signaled to her not to. They could be waiting for that, with a gun ready.

I indicated we should go on around the other side and she nodded. We tiptoed on, through rough undergrowth and sucking mud. Lucy was leading the way.

Suddenly a figure appeared around the corner, and almost before I'd noticed him Lucy fired. He was flung backward and let out a sharp yelp as he fell.

"My God!" I said. "You—"

"I just got him in the shoulder," she said. "Come on."

We were now running without any caution at all. We stepped past the man who'd been shot. He lay there cursing, his right hand clutching at his left shoulder. He had no mask on either, and we saw his features twisted in pain and fury. Lucy bent and picked up his gun, another pistol. We reached the end of the building. In its dark depths we could just make out the woman sitting against the wall, her face dead white.

"I think only one of the boats has come in," I said. "We'd better get to it before the other one turns up."

"Don't worry, I wasn't going to start making bandages."

We ran down the rough path that led to the mooring place. As there had been three terrorists in each boat and we'd knocked out two just now, there was presumably one still left there, guarding the boat.

"Who goes there?" came an uncertain voice through the fog: Luca's, I think. We could now see the end of the vegetation, and the mist hanging in drifting tendrils over the blackness of the lagoon. Under our feet the ground was getting squelchier. We made no answer to his cry and we heard the engine being started and the water churning. The boat was moving out slowly.

We reached the end of the path and saw the boat, with a crouching figure, some feet out in the water. Lucy stuffed one of her pistols into her coat pocket and took double-handed aim with the other. I watched, the tiniest touch appalled, but mostly fascinated.

The shot resounded and the man in the boat was hurled back in exactly the way his companion had been; he fell overboard in a whirl of limbs.

I dropped the net and rifle and waded out. He was kneeling in the water, which had already gone a darker color with blood from his shoulder. I hauled at his good arm and dragged him to shore, laying him down on the mud. He was gasping some words that I couldn't make out, but I don't think they were of forgiveness. Lucy was also in the water, clutching at the boat, which was revolving in a threshing wash of foam.

300

I picked up the rifle and net and joined her. We clambered aboard. It was a simple *sandalo*, with an outboard motor. Lucy settled herself by the motor. A little farther along the shore another boat was moored to a pole. "Move us over to that," I told her.

We chugged toward it. I stood up and raised my rifle and fired into its bottom. I prepared to fire again.

"Give me the gun," Lucy said.

"What?" I handed it to her, and she pulled a catch or something and the spent cartridge flipped out. She handed it back. I fired again. Water started bubbling up through the holes. She backed us out into the lagoon.

"Now where?" she said.

"God knows," I said. I saw a lamp at the bottom of the boat. I picked it up and played its beam in a slow circle: there was nothing but thick drifting mist in all directions.

"Just move," I said. "The farther we get from here the better." I didn't say anything about the other boat probably being on its way: we were all too aware of that. I found a notch the lamp attached to at the front of the boat and fixed it there. We chugged forward through the fog.

After a few minutes we saw low spongy marshlands ahead—*barene*, as they call them in the lagoon—and we swung around and coasted by them. Lucy kept our speed down: much of the lagoon is under a meter in depth, and it gives way to marshes and mudflats almost imperceptibly in places; it would be annoying, if not actually suicidal, to foul up our propeller through careless speed.

"Listen," Lucy said, quietening our own engine. We both strained our ears and through the fog we heard the distant rumble of a boat. She cut our engine completely and I switched off the lamp.

The dark and the fog pressed in clammily on us as we sat there, waiting, listening. I moved back and put my arm around her; the boat rocked drunkenly.

The engine was getting louder and we could now see a fuzzy

glow somewhere ahead to our right. All we could do was sit tight and pray that they passed us unseeingly; it didn't cross my mind that it might not be Them: who else would be chugging around these remote waters on a night like this?

Louder, and louder—and brighter and brighter. It was almost impossible not to feel the boat was aiming deliberately at us. And there was nothing we could do. . . .

So I thought, until Lucy stooped and picked up the rifle. She raised it and sat there carefully aiming. And then, when it was clear that they would see us within seconds, if they hadn't in fact already done so, she fired.

A tinkle of glass and sudden blackness. She started our engine up and we suddenly leaped forward. There were confused voices from the other boat, and then the cutting clarity of Padoan's voice: "Fire, you fool."

Somebody fired. We could hear the thrashing and whirling of water as their boat swiveled to follow us. We were still showing no lights but the white gash of our wash would show up, even in this fog.

It was clear that their boat was the more powerful. Their motor was now roaring, and as I looked back I could see the shape of their upraised prow, rearing and swooping on the water like snapping jaws.

"Slow down," I said to Lucy. She glanced at me, and I brought my hands up close to her face to show her the net I'd taken up from the floor. She nodded, reducing power.

I turned around and leaned out, beyond the motor; I threw the net, using both hands to cast it over as wide a surface area as possible. Lucy pressed down again and we shot forward. Their boat must have reached the net just seconds later and there was a sudden spluttering and then a wild churning as their propeller tangled itself. Whoever was driving was clearly trying brute force to break free, and was fouling things up even more.

I let out a whoop of victory as we surged forward; almost immediately Lucy slowed down and said, "Turn the light on." I lurched to my feet and suddenly something slammed into my shoulder—something hot and sharp and noisy. The shoulder was smashed into smithereens—or so at least it seemed to me. When I came to my senses—two seconds later—I was lying on the boards, in a twisted position, with my right hand clutching at my shoulder, which was still there but already felt sticky through the coat—and extremely painful. Lucy was saying, "Martin! Martin!" but was sensibly continuing to drive forward.

I found myself repeating three short words, spitting them out one after another like retaliatory bullets. It helped a bit: I managed, with their propulsion and that of my legs, to get to the front of the boat, where I was able to kneel up. I removed my hand from the shoulder and clutched at the lamp, coating it with gore, but managing to switch it on. Then I rolled over to a sitting position, noticing with surprise that my arm hadn't dropped off. I wasn't actually relieved about this: it felt to me as if that would have been the most comfortable solution.

Half a minute later Lucy brought us to a halt; there was no sound of pursuit. She came carefully forward and removed the lamp from its notch to examine me.

"Oh, my God," she said.

"Sorry."

"This is one thing you needn't apologize for. We'd better stop the bleeding."

"Yes. Or we'll drown."

Thirty seconds later my coat, pullover, and shirt were off: they aren't thirty seconds I particularly like to recall. Enough to say that the one thing I didn't notice was the cold as I sat there bare-chested, watching her try to tear my shirt into strips. She managed it eventually with a little help from her teeth, and she wrapped the largest one around and around my armpit and shoulder, pulling tight each time.

"I suppose the bullet's still in there," she said.

"Yes." I wouldn't have been surprised to be told there was a Cruise missile in there.

"You need a sling really." And she immediately took off her own coat and pullover and blouse. We would have made a curious picture had anyone happened by. She converted her blouse into a sling, and then, before redressing herself, helped me into my pullover and coat.

As she started the motor up again I said, "So you did end up making bandages."

"Yes. How do you feel?"

"Well, I'd sooner be in bed, but I'll survive."

We chugged along between *barene;* the occasional sea gull shrieked and flapped off into the mist, its belly flashing white with reflected light. There was no other sound. I started to notice the cold again, particularly around my feet, which were soaking of course. This, I suppose, was a good sign, but on the whole I would have preferred to have no sign and warm feet. After a while I said, "Where did you learn that kind of shooting?"

"My father used to take me shooting in Scotland."

"I'll never make another crack about him in my life."

"Well, that will be a change."

"Protestants, proletarians, or just pheasants?"

"Three seconds that promise lasted. Jimmy Porter."

"You're right. Sorry, sorry." I let a wincing gasp into my voice as I said this, guaranteed to win her over: the hero, wisecracking through his pain. "You were brilliant."

"Thanks. We were both pretty good." After a pause she said, "I've never shot anyone before."

"Well, no, I suppose not. I've never been shot, come to that."

"Where are we?" she said, shivering.

"God knows. The Depths of the Seven Dead Men, maybe."

"The what?"

"It's the name of a part of the lagoon. I once noticed it on a map: *I Fondi dei sette morti.*"

"Great." She wrapped her coat closer around herself. "Thanks for telling me."

"Or maybe we're somewhere near the bone island," I said.

"The what?"

"Sant'Ariano I think it's called. Where they dump everyone's bones after they've had a few years on the cemetery isle."

"Right, thank you, thank you, Martin."

"Just trying to be informative."

"If we bump into it, we'll just get out and lie down, shall we?"

"I will. You go on." I probably would have too. I was becoming more and more convinced I was on the way out, and I didn't even hear Lucy's next remark, let alone answer it.

It was another few minutes before I realized we were passing along the side of a proper island; I twisted around and through the mist made out the faint but definite shape of a square tower.

"Torcello!" I said.

"I think so," she said. "Shall we try and find someone?"

"Burano," I said. This one-word answer was intended to convey the meaning, "Torcello's got a tiny population and won't have any hospital facilities; we might as well go on to Burano, which is just over the way from Torcello and which will certainly have facilities of some kind." She nodded; she was getting better at catching my meaning.

I went through the next quarter of an hour in a kind of painful daze. I somehow managed to get the message across to Lucy that she should go around to the back of the church on Burano, since there was a mooring place there very close to the central square—and very close to the carabinieri station as well, as I remembered. (I think I grunted the words "behind the church"—and waved my good arm.) Then from the cold darkness of the lagoon we passed to the cheerful noise and illuminations of carnivalesque Burano: people clustered around our boat, helped us both out; awed voices commented on my wound, on the guns at the bottom of the boat. We were escorted into piazza Galuppi, which was strung with colored lights; young people in masks and animal costumes were dancing to the sound of Beatles songs. Questions in dialect came at us from multicolored faces, from plastic and rubber animal masks—fortunately none of them Mickey Mouse. Lucy kept repeating, *"I terroristi, i terroristi,"* and this word spread around the square, mixing into the music.

Then there was neon-lit cleanliness and hush as I was laid down on a plastic-covered bed; a white-coated man with a big black mustache (which seems to be obligatory for male Buranelli) asked Lucy questions as he undid my bandages. The Beatles were a faint pulsing noise in the distance. I thought, Well, where better to drip blood than on colorful melodramatic Burano?

I faded out on this happy thought.

20

I CAME to with a sense of sudden panic, looking for the animal or vampire that had sunk its teeth into my shoulder. My eyes came to slow focus on a tiny dim-lit room in which I was the only person lying down. A man in a white coat and a carabiniere were sitting on a bench a foot from my bed. I realized I must be pretty groggy since the whole room seemed to be throbbing and bouncing—and then I realized that we were in a boat.

"Where am I?" I said. It seemed the most appropriate question, but came out as a mere croak. I said it again, and this time, after a moment's thought, in Italian.

"We're taking you to Venice. You're going to spend the night in the hospital there." It was the man in the white coat who answered. He had no mustache—obviously not a Buranello.

"Where's Lucy—the girl—"

"She's answering questions. As you will be when we get to Venice."

"Why couldn't I stay there?"

"There are no proper hospital facilities on Burano. And besides, too many people knew you were there."

So I had to be kept hidden. I lay back and pondered this not very cheering thought. The man in the white coat spoke up again to tell me they'd removed the bullet and no serious damage had been done: I'd just have to keep my arm in a sling for a week or two.

And keep out of the way of any other bullets, I added to myself. Aloud I said, "Thank you."

There was no further conversation. I wondered what had happened to my clothes: I seemed to be wearing some kind of nightgown. I couldn't work up enough energy to ask, however. My arm was in a tight sling now, and the pain at my shoulder was somewhere below a padding of bandages. The handcuff had also been removed, I was pleased to notice.

The ambulance boat came to a stop; I was helped out of the cabin; I felt slightly dizzy but was capable of walking. We had driven up to a landing stage inside the hospital building itself, and I was guided up the steps to where two policemen and a man in a gray suit were standing next to a wheelchair. The policemen were both carrying guns: were they expecting me to make a break for it? A sudden dive and a one-armed swim for freedom perhaps.

I sat in the wheelchair as that seemed to be what was expected of me, and I looked at the man in the gray suit. I thought I recognized him: he was either Edward G. Robinson or the investigating magistrate whose photo had appeared in the papers—Menegazzi. The latter, more probably. He was carrying a small briefcase.

He walked alongside the wheelchair, which was pushed by one of the ambulance men. We rose in a lift and I was then pushed along a marble corridor to a private ward. I was helped into bed by a nurse and then left alone with Menegazzi. Through the door's glass panel, however, I could see one of the policemen standing in the corridor.

Menegazzi sat down on one of the two chairs near the bed. He opened his briefcase and drew out a small tape recorder. He started it recording and put it on my bedside table. Then he took out a cigarette and put it in his mouth, but after looking around the room and shrugging, he took it out again. He didn't put it away, merely refrained from lighting it. For the rest of our conversation it stayed in his hand, as a kind of indication of how much he'd like to get the interview over and done with. Finally he spoke. "Martin Phipps."

"Yes."

"Artist, jailed for forgery, regular visitor to Italy." They all three sounded like accusations.

"Yes."

"You've been on the move here in Venice. Never two nights in the same hotel." His accent was Veneto, but not Venetian.

"No, well, you see—"

"Never mind about that. We've had quite a long statement from your girlfriend, and from a certain Alvise Ballarin."

"Ah. So he—"

"He came to us this morning."

"He's got nothing to do with any of this business."

"So he kept saying. We believe him. I gave him a good bawling out all the same. Idiots, all of you."

I suppose I should have felt a sudden wave of relief at this point, but Menegazzi's tone didn't encourage it. It wasn't one of avuncular tolerance for our scampish escapades; it rather suggested that he would like to see idiocy as a jailable offense.

He went on: "I now want the whole of your story."

"What about the terrorists—that island—"

"I told you; your girlfriend gave us a statement. We sent boats out. Found the two who'd got shot and the two who'd been bashed on the head."

"What—you caught them?"

"They made no resistance. All declared themselves political prisoners and refused to speak."

"Were they badly hurt?"

"More than you. That bother you?"

"No."

"Good. Wouldn't have believed you if you'd said yes." At

309

this discovery that I was as callous as he was, there was the faintest hint in his voice of a mellowing toward me, as if he wasn't going to set the electrodes under my testicles just yet. "Your friend is going to identify them."

"And the others?"

"No trace."

"Okay. So what do you want to know?" This news definitely helped my position: whatever my precedents were, I had contributed to the arrest of four terrorists. Maybe they'd give me a medal.

"The whole story of your cretinous interfering."

Well, maybe not a medal. "I suppose it started when I met Toni Sambon." There now: that was the end of my protective reticence. I went on talking. I kept Francesca out of my account and, on a sudden rush of generosity, Mr. Robin and his school: but I withheld no detail of my own actions, even the most truly cretinous ones—like my entering of Busetto's flat. Menegazzi let out a snort as I told him this part and I said a definitive bye-bye to the medal. He didn't even look faintly impressed when I described my trick with the iron bar on the island. He put in occasional questions, using his cigarette as an extra admonitory finger. I picked up snippets of information from his questions, such as the fact that Osgood's business was being looked into in England, and Zennaro was still in hiding.

At the end he said, "It ties together. Most of it." But he didn't look satisfied. He stuck the cigarette in his mouth and rolled it around there, as if he really was putting in for an Edward G. Robinson look-alike competition. Then he said, with the cigarette still there, "But there are too many coincidences."

"Yes, well—"

"Never mind." He took the cigarette out again. "You'll stay the night here. That's our decision. As far as the doctors are concerned you could walk out now. We'll keep a couple of our men on guard and tomorrow we'll probably come and ask some more questions."

"Where's Lucy?"

310

"She's safe."

"Can I contact anyone?"

"Who?"

"Well, Alvise Ballarin for example."

"Wait." He switched the recorder off and put it back in his case. Then he got up and left with no more than a nod. He was already fishing out his lighter. I was left with a hundred and one other questions—like, where were my clothes?

Was I under arrest or just being protected for my own good? This was the question I went to sleep with, and woke up with. The policeman outside the room made no objections to my walking down the corridor for a pee, and certainly didn't come and stand guard outside the loo door. But then he probably guessed I wasn't likely to make a run for it in a nightgown.

Well, at least I didn't have to piss in a bucket, I told myself.

I took stock of my room: I had a view of the lagoon, with the cemetery isle just visible through the mist. (I'd often thought what a cheery sight this must be for all the wards on the lagoon side of the hospital.) There was a pair of cheap but wearable slippers under the bed, a chest of drawers that contained sheets and a rather tatty but quite warm dressing gown. I suppose I wasn't the first patient who'd turned up with nothing.

As far as the nurses were concerned I was just another patient. One of them came and took my temperature—normal— and checked the bandages and plumped up the pillows. I was given a cappuccino and a soggy croissant: I thought of my breakfasts over the previous week with nostalgia. I asked for and was given a copy of the *Gazzettino*. There wasn't a word about me or Lucy in it, nor about the arrests: presumably they'd happened too late at night. (Or the editor had been in a bar on the other side of town.) I read the general news and then lay back on the pillows listening to the Sunday-morning bells of the surrounding churches and thinking.

At around midday Lucy called: the policeman on guard had a word in his walkie-talkie and was told he could let her through.

311

She walked in, her hands in the pockets of her gray coat, her face serene and smiling. She came straight over and kissed me.

"Hi," I said. I looked through the door's glass panel. "I think that kiss is just getting clearance." The policeman was talking into his radio again. "You might have been passing me the secret microfilm in your tooth."

"Oh." She drew away a little, her cheeks flushing. "How are you?"

"Fine. I apparently have only 'soft-tissue injuries.' No bones or ligaments affected."

"Good."

"Well, it's a lot better than I'd ever have thought judging by how I felt. Anyway, where are you being held?"

"I'm not. I was questioned most of the night at Burano and then at the Questura here, and then they told me I could go. I had to leave my passport, mind you."

"Well, I've had to leave my clothes. Where did you sleep?"

"They fixed up a room in a pensione near the Questura and told me not to go out too much. But then I thought, seeing it's Carnival, I could put a mask on." She pulled a simple spangled mask out of her pocket.

"Ah yes. But how did you get on to me here?"

"I just asked down at reception."

"Oh, great," I said. "And they told you just like that."

"Well, they asked for identification and then phoned someone or other. Aren't you glad to see me?"

"Yes, yes. Just imagining Padoan down there asking."

"Oh, he wouldn't dare."

"No, of course not. Great big hospital receptionist, probably on a hot line to NATO headquarters."

She laughed. "I expect Padoan's halfway to Africa now."

"Do you really think so?"

She thought for a second or two and shook her head. "I don't know. Listen, have you really got no clothes?"

"Just what you can see."

"Well, I could go and fetch something from Alvise's."

"Thanks. That would be a help." I suddenly remembered I had a set of clothes still at the laundry near Via Garibaldi. Well, there was no reason why Lucy should have to go there as well. "You couldn't lend me some money? Just so I can buy a paper and make a phone call and things."

"Of course. Ten thousand enough?"

"Plenty. Thanks. So what did they ask you?" I said.

She told me what she'd told them: as she talked I noticed the lines of strain around her mouth and eyes, and a new nervous habit of pushing at her hair. It struck me that I'd been the lucky one—just going to sleep at the end of the whole business, while she'd had to put up with hours of interrogation—bright lights and hard faces and Menegazzi no doubt blowing smoke into her eyes. It was probably worth a bullet to have got out of that.

"I told them all about you," she said. "Mind you, they already knew a lot; but I told them what a romantic idiot you were."

"What a what?"

"Oh, you know—you and Cima da Conegliano."

"Oh, yeah. Me and him." Well, it was a nicer coupling than me and Osgood, or me and Zennaro.

"You know: how you're obviously out to—to redeem yourself."

"I see. And how did a roomful of antiterrorist cops take this?"

"Well, the chief one—Menega . . . Menegallo?"

"Menegazzi."

"Yes, him. He nodded and smiled."

"Smiled?"

"Yes. Quite a nice smile."

"You obviously have to be blue-eyed and feminine to get that from him. So he believed it?"

"I think so. He said it all—'quadrava.' Tied together, I suppose. I did get a bit confused at the beginning because I couldn't remember all the names: well, I got Busetto and Zennaro mixed up."

"Ah. You're never very brilliant with names, are you?" This little fact suddenly tickled my mind, like a loose dangling thread that I knew led somewhere, but as I tried to follow it through it flicked out of my mind's grasp.

She was saying, "And then I had to identify the four of them that they caught, but of course I'd only had glimpses of them without their masks. Still, it was only a formality."

"How did they look?"

"Heroic and defiant: you know, martyrs to the cause." She paused. "Bastards."

"Yes. Except I suppose they think of themselves as romantic idiots. Them and Che Guevara, me and Cima."

"Don't talk rubbish. They're killers. You're just a dreamy fool."

"My God. And all this time I've been thinking of myself as a hard-bitten ex-con."

"Exactly—just like Rick in *Casablanca*. Romantic underneath it all."

"I hope you didn't say that to Menegazzi." I sat up straighter in bed. "Did he mention coincidences to you?"

"No."

"Ah. Well, he did to me, and I've been thinking hard. Also about loose ends. Like, how you said the terrorists got on to you."

"What about it?"

"Well, they didn't know about you working for the Britannia School, did they?"

"No," she said, obviously thinking hard. "At least not then."

"Another thing. Why does the Britannia School course choose that hotel?"

"They've always gone there. When I did the course myself, most of the students were there."

"Well, you weren't."

"No, but only because there were so many that year that some of us had to overflow to another place. I think the hotel offers Mr. Robin special prices."

"Why?"

"I don't know. I've never asked. I think it was just a promotion deal when the hotel opened."

I remembered that the woman had told me she hadn't been there very long. "I see," I said. "Have you got in touch with Mr. Robin?"

"Not yet. But it was a weekend off for me anyway. There's no reason why I should have been missed."

"So you're just going to go back to your job tomorrow, without saying a word."

"I don't know. Not if the police say I'm still in danger here."

"So back to London?"

"Martin, give me a moment or two. And yourself?"

"I've still got to redeem myself, haven't I? That Cima's not been found yet."

"Oh, God." She got up and kissed me again. "Well, I suppose I love you for what you are, not despite it. Which probably makes me a romantic fool too."

"Well, a fool, after all I've put you through."

"I won't say I've loved every minute of it—but it was worth it." Her eyes had lost their tiredness.

I suddenly felt better than I'd felt for several days: a crazy wave of optimism had gone rushing through my veins—for the first time I felt there were good things ahead. Nothing definite—no pictures of domestic peace in a country cottage, or my pictures winning prizes at the Biennale—just a general feeling that there was light at the end of the tunnel: and not the oncoming train, or a cigarette lighter poised against my paintings, but real daylight—like the glow in her eyes.

Well, she'd said I was a romantic idiot. "Thanks," I said. It wasn't a brilliant speech, but I followed it up well.

The door opened and we broke apart again, Lucy flaring away like a traffic signal. It was my lunch being brought in by a woman in white. "Visiting time is over," she announced.

"Okay. I'll come back this afternoon, Martin. With clothes. Four o'clock okay?"

"Yes. I'll try and fit you in."

Lucy looked at the woman who was standing there, expressionless, with the tray in her hands, and she obviously decided she couldn't face giving me another kiss under that gaze, so merely flicked her right hand in a wave and left.

After lunch I lay back and kept thinking. Then at around two-fifteen I got out of bed and, with a preliminary glance at the door, took the pillowcase off the pillow. I folded it and tucked it carefully into the loop of my sling. I put on the slippers and the dressing gown and took one of the spare sheets from the drawer; it wouldn't fit inside the sling, so I stuffed it inside the dressing gown, letting the latter hang a little loose. I opened the door and gave a nod to the policeman (who was far more interested at that moment in the retreating rear view of two nurses) and set off down the corridor to the loo.

I closed and locked the door and then took out my hidden booty. I draped the pillowcase over the sink and then shook the sheet open and draped that on top of the pillowcase. Then, with a touch of forethought, I had a pee. I closed the loo seat and pulled the chain. That morning I had scratched my hand on the broken link at the end of the rather old-fashioned chain, and it was that fact that had given me the idea for this little Carnival caper.

I reached up with my free hand and managed to work the top link of the chain free. Then with the jagged end of the broken link at the other end I tore a hole in the center of the sheet. With both hands (my left hand, though not very mobile, was perfectly usable) I enlarged this hole until it was wide enough for my head to fit through. I used the chain to make two small holes in the pillowcase, a couple of inches apart: I tried to enlarge these with my fingers but merely succeeded in creating one long gash; well, it didn't really matter.

I folded the sheet again, though in the cramped space and with only one hand probably not quite as Florence Nightingale would have done, and stuffed it inside my dressing gown; I did the same with the pillowcase, and on a sudden thought, with the loo chain too.

I opened the window. The fog had cleared a little and in the milky sunshine I could see the great proud bulk of SS Giovanni e Paolo rising up in front of me: I remembered that there was a Cima da Conegliano in the right transept of the church (a rather feeble one, to tell the truth), and I said, "I'm doing this for you." I was probably getting just a touch cracked.

The loo looked out onto the flat roof of what seemed to be a small ground-floor extension to the building. Just a few yards away, at the end of the roof, was a simple metal fire escape coming down the side of the main building. Nothing could be easier.

Before clambering out, I unlocked the loo door: there would thus be no proof that I'd actually made a surreptitious exit. I was sure the policeman would not be able to swear that his eyes hadn't moved from the door—not if there were nurses around. I wasn't intending to be away for very long, so on my return I would stroll brazenly along the corridor: "Why," I'd say, if questioned, "nobody told me I was under arrest. I just thought I'd go for a walk."

I stepped onto the loo seat and then, with a one-handed hoist, got myself to a sitting position on the windowsill. I swung my legs up and over and I was on the roof. I walked briskly but unsurreptitiously to the fire escape. The important thing was to look completely casual.

Despite the sunshine, a cotton nightgown, dressing gown, and slippers were pretty inadequate outdoor clothes: luckily I didn't have far to go—and at that moment I was thinking too hard of what I was doing to pay much attention to the temperature.

I went down the fire escape to the ground. I then walked briskly to my left, in the direction of the Fondamente Nuove. I remembered there was a simple gate in the wall there, near a vaporetto stop. I was less likely to be noticed leaving there than by the great monumental entrance next to SS Giovanni e Paolo. I passed a couple of doctors in white coats who did no more than glance at me. I could see the gate in the wall now; next to it was a little wooden booth with a concierge behind a window. He was reading a paper, but would doubtless notice me as I left. Maybe now was the time to don my Carnival finery. I stepped into a doorway and pulled out the sheet, pillowcase, and chain. When I'd put the sheet over my head, I discovered it hung right down to the ground, so I tucked it into the cord of my dressing gown as best as I could. Then I slipped the pillowcase over my head and adjusted it so that my eyes peered out of the gash. I draped the chain around my neck: there I was—a traditional house ghost.

I went toward the gate, and as I passed the concierge I flapped my sheet and rattled the chain and let out a ghostly groan. His eyes looked up from the paper, rolled heavenward, and dropped straight back down.

There was no better way of escaping notice today than by making myself noticeable.

I walked down the Fondamente Nuove: said like that it sounds easy, but it was far from being so. I had only one hand free, and it had to do triple business in plucking up the sheet from under my feet, in pulling back the pillowcase, which kept slipping down and blinding me, and in occasionally rattling my chain as the occasion demanded. There weren't many people around until I reached the boat stops to the islands; here there were clusters of people, many of them in costume. Six cardinals and an unshaven pope were studying the timetable and arguing about it in French, and a couple of nuns with fishnet stockings under their miniskirts were swinging provocative handbags. A rather weedy Superman was standing outside a bar talking to a much tougher-looking winged fairy. Nobody paid any attention to me, apart from a couple of teenagers in painted faces who feigned extreme terror. I gave them a few of my best groans and then turned left down the Calle del Fumo, which led toward the Britannia School.

The calle was busy with people; Walt Disney characters, clowns, pirates, and cloaked devils jostled with aged Venetians making venomous comments about bloody Carnival turning the city into a funfair. Halfway down the alley all traffic was held up

318

by a woman in hooped skirts so wide that no more than one person could pass at a time. She seemed supremely content with this result and even posed for photographs.

I made my way through the Corti and Campielli at the alley's end. There was a steady pulsing noise that got louder and louder as I approached the square where the Britannia School stood. Most people seemed to be making in the same direction as me, which surprised me: the square is usually a quiet little backwater.

It was, however, transformed today. A small bandstand had been set up opposite the Britannia School and a heavy-rock group, wearing denims that had been through a gas explosion and Dennis the Menace hairstyles were bashing out a version of Led Zeppelin's "Black Dog," arranged for drums, drums, drums, out-of-tune electric guitars, nails-on-blackboard voice, and drums. People in costume were jumping up and down to the beat, as if determined to bring about Venice's final collapse. A banner above the bandstand read PREGANZIOL'S SATANIC VERSERS. I watched a couple in eighteenth-century costume who were taking such care not to ruffle their clothes as they danced that the music might have been Vivaldi. A tourist photographed them and they stopped and moved away: they'd achieved what they wanted there.

I crossed the square to the Britannia School door and rang the top bell: Mr. Robin's flat.

After a while his voice came through the little grille: "*Chi è?*"

"Guardia di Finanza," I shouted. I drew in closer to the door so that he wouldn't be able to see me from the window.

"Is this a joke?" he said at once.

"No," I said, as categorically as possible.

"But today's Sunday," he protested.

"It doesn't matter. We must speak to you immediately." I felt sure that the intercom and the Satanic Versers would serve to cover up my English accent.

"It's not very convenient."

"Do you want us to come back with a warrant to search the entire premises?"

"All right." The door clicked open. I entered, closed the door, and ran up the stairs as quickly as possible, hoisting my sheet up high around my legs. I ran on up, past the *piano nobile,* past the second-floor schoolrooms, and met him on the staircase to his own flat.

"Oh, my God," he said.

I adjusted my pillowcase so that I could see him. He was standing with one hand at his tie, his mouth slightly open. I imagined it was surprise rather than terror: despite my slippers and the noise outside, my ascent had been solid enough to dispel any idea that I might be a creature of mere ectoplasm.

He adjusted his tie and straightened up. I had counted on the fact that he would probably pause before a mirror before leaving the flat, so I'd be able to meet him so near his private premises. *"Ma chi è lei?"* he said. *"Che scherzo è questo?* What joke is this?"

"No joke," I said in English, removing the pillow.

"Martin. What on earth—"

"I want to come into your flat," I said.

"You what?" It really was a pretty unheard-of suggestion.

I repeated my words. "I want to come into your flat. I know you're hiding Antonio Sambon in there."

"Who?"

"There's no point in pretending anymore. I *know* he's there."

"This is quite ridiculous. You oblige me to express myself in terms—" He had moved to the cozy realms of bureaucratic language, where he obviously felt securer.

I cut in, with the simplest, briefest of words: "Let me in or I'll call the police."

"No!"

This was not Mr. Robin—he had never used an exclamation mark in his life. The voice came from the top of the stairs. At the doorway stood Antonio Sambon, in jeans and pullover. In his hand he was holding a small gun. It was pointed at me.

"Put it down," I said.

"Er, yes," Mr. Robin said, nervously. "There's no point—"

"Silence," he said.

"Toni," I said, "what do you think you're going to do with that? Suppose you kill me—then what do you do? Kill him as well as a witness?"

"I don't want to kill anyone," he said. "But I don't want the police."

"Right," I said. "Let's all go up and talk this through like sensible people. It's obvious that if I'd wanted, I could have sent the police round myself, and I didn't. So—"

"All right," he said after a few seconds' thought. "Come up."

We went up, Mr. Robin first so as to make it quite clear that I wasn't being ushered in as a welcome guest.

Like most top floors in Venice, the flat was full of curious angles, sloping ceilings, brain-bashing beams, and inaccessible corners, all of which had obviously presented Mr. Robin with a major challenge in his attempt to give the place a look of rationality and seriousness; but at first glance he seemed to have succeeded: the sitting room he led us into had all the coziness and domesticity of a filing cabinet. Gray office chairs were arranged around a rectangular white table. The irregularities of the room's angles were masked by metal bookcases; the books, of course, were uniform editions in rows of military precision: if he ever took one out, I'm sure, he had a dummy copy to place in the gap. The white walls had no pictures, merely a calendar (with no picture) and a copy of the school timetable. The two windows had thick lace curtains that prevented any clear view of the crazy skyline outside, with its tottering chimney pots and television aerials and jumbled rooftops.

But nonetheless, after a minute or two in the room I could feel that Venice was having the last word: the room's dark corners and beckoning crannies could be masked but not hidden. One knew they were there. Rather like the secret nooks of Mr. Robin's own character, behind the geometrical neatness of his facade.

321

Now he motioned us to sit around the table, as if we were going to have a business meeting: the school director, the terrorist-in-hiding, and the artist-dressed-as-ghost. I sat down at one end and Toni Sambon took the other end. We were both, I suppose, trying to be head of the table. Mr. Robin sat carefully in the middle of one side; not just for the sake of symmetry this time, I thought: he was hedging his bets.

The music pulsed away outside: no tune could be heard, just a regular throb-throb-throbbing.

Toni Sambon spoke. "Why have you come here?" He laid the gun on the table, in front of himself.

"Because I want those paintings."

"You want them?" His tone was contemptuous.

"I want them to go back where they came from."

"There is no need for that."

"There's what?" I said.

"No need. They don't need those paintings."

"What a nice easy way to decide things," I said. "I suppose you *do* need them, right?"

"You know my situation. I'm in danger of my life—because I decided to help the cause of justice. I *need* money to protect myself. Just to keep living." His voice was quick and urgent and even pleading, but there was an undercurrent of self-assurance that really irritated me: he'd long ago thought these things out and thus justified himself.

"So you don't want the paintings, but the money. Which is the major reason why those churches should have them back. They want the paintings." I looked at Mr. Robin. "What the hell do you organize art courses for, if you don't give a damn about what happens to real paintings?"

He put his fingers together. "One has to consider individual cases on their merits," he began.

"Balls. This is simple money-grubbing theft, and there's no other excuse for it."

"Martin, I don't like to cast slurs, but you hardly seem to me to be—"

322

"So I went to jail for forgery. So I seem a hypocrite. Well, maybe. I'm not going to argue the case, but I'm not going to let your friend slip off with those paintings either."

Toni spoke up, quietly, fiercely. "So it's all right for you when you wanted some money, but not for me, when I *need* it. Do you know what it means to be all on your own, frightened, against the world, do you know what—"

"I know that the first thing you terrorists learn is how to justify any action you take, however mean."

"I am *not* a terrorist."

"Well, what was that attack you made on me supposed to do, if not terrify me? You know—assaulting me in the dark, with a knife."

He shrugged; he had the grace to look a little ashamed. "That was only—only a means. I didn't intend to hurt you. Only frighten you so you would go away."

"I knew nothing about it," Mr. Robin said quickly. "I had no idea he was planning to do anything of the sort. Indeed, I spoke severely to him afterward."

"Yes, but you used it happily enough to get rid of me, didn't you?" I imitated his tone: " 'Martin, I think perhaps we'll make that a natural break.' "

"Yes, but as you know I'd already taken the decision to—to break off your temporary contract. I'd already told you we didn't require your lectures any further."

"What I can't understand is why you let me lecture at all. You can't have been pleased to see me."

"Well, in the circumstances, your presence was a little, em, embarrassing, it's true. But I felt, in all fairness to Antonio, that I had to find out why you had come to Venice, and the best thing seemed to be to let you give a lecture or two so I could make discreet inquiries. So do I now understand that you knew all along where Antonio was?"

"No," I said. "It was that stupid attack of his that gave it away."

Mr. Robin shook his head. "Antonio, I told you—"

"But you refused to do anything," Toni said, "and all the time he was here, asking questions, speaking to Busetto and to other people—getting into the newspapers. I had to protect myself."

"Well," I said, "you gave yourself away. I imagine I was supposed to think that your—your *ex-compagni* were onto me. Well, they didn't know I had anything to do with the Britannia School. Why should they? I mean, the papers hadn't said anything about the school, and the police didn't know I was there. And then, what a place to choose for an attack like that: I mean, the risk with all those people—someone might have had a torch, someone might have blocked your exit route, you could have run into someone on the stairs. . . . No, the only person who would have run all those risks was someone who had no choice—who had to attack me there or nowhere."

Toni muttered, "It was an impulse. I was scared of you and your questions. I had to do something."

I went on with my own thoughts. "And that only made sense if there was someone hiding in the building: which meant someone being hidden by you." I nodded to Mr. Robin.

"It was merely an act of compassion on my part," he said.

"Oh, yeah? And was that what it was ten years back when Toni was hiding out in Palazzo Sambon?"

"How do you know about that?" Mr. Robin said.

"I don't know. I'm working things out—trying to clear up some of the coincidences. I've heard that the Britannia School used to be somewhere the other end of Cannaregio, and now I've found out that you get special rates for your students at that hotel next to Palazzo Sambon—the other end of Cannaregio. So it struck me—"

"It was a businesslike arrangement," he said. "When I moved the school, I had some contact with the new proprietors of the building who told me they were opening a hotel, so I—"

"I'm not accusing you of any sharp practice there," I said. "I'm sure it was all aboveboard. No. The only interesting fact I'm pointing to is that when Toni was hiding out in that palazzo,

324

the next-door neighbor was you. And probably you heard noises at night. The woman in the hotel told me she heard noises herself through the walls, when Toni's *ex-compagni* went through the building a few days back. I suppose that there, like here, you had a top-floor flat over the school, so you'd hear things at night."

"It was quite by chance," he said. "I had heard noises and wondered, and then one evening as I was closing my shutters before going to bed I saw Antonio leaning out of the window."

"And you recognized him, right?"

"Well, yes. He had studied at the school for some years."

"Yes, I know. So did his sister. She told me."

"My sister mustn't be involved," Toni broke in. "Why do you bother her?"

"I didn't bother her. I just asked her some questions. She's very worried about you."

"You must leave her alone. She has nothing to do with this story."

"Okay." I turned back to Mr. Robin. "So you recognized him. And you knew he was on the run from the police."

"Yes, I knew that. But sometimes personal feelings can take precedence over—"

"You mean he looked at you with big eyes and said, 'Don't give me away,' and you were bowled over."

His voice was very stiff as he replied, "I was naturally moved by his predicament."

"Because after all he was a count's son." I was sure that this had been the deciding element in Mr. Robin's choice of action. A member of one of the leading families of the city, who would thus be eternally grateful to him. . . . Who knew what invitations might ensue? And, of course, it couldn't be ignored that Toni was, by all accounts, a lad who knew how to switch on and off the charm: on that occasion he had presumably switched and left it on. I decided not to probe too deeply into this side of the matter, since it could be of no importance now, and Mr. Robin certainly wouldn't care to discuss it.

"I knew the family well," Mr. Robin continued, "since they

had decided to patronize the school, and this naturally imposes a certain sense of obligation."

"Okay. If that's how you like to put it. So what did you do—just keep him in food?"

"It was Antonio's idea. He said that after a week or two he would leave for somewhere abroad. So all I had to do was pass him provisions at night. I could scarcely refuse such a simple request."

"But there must have been another request as well: 'Would you mind looking after one or two paintings for me while I'm away?' No?"

"Well, yes. They weren't, as far as I knew, of inordinate value, but would doubtless be of great use to Antonio. I felt it would be churlish to refuse."

"So in the middle of the night," I said, "he passed them from one window to another, right?"

"It wasn't difficult. They weren't very big. And after midnight the windows in the house opposite were always shuttered."

"And when Toni got arrested, didn't it strike you that it might be quite a good idea to mention that you knew where they were?"

"Now, how could I do such a thing, when Antonio had gone to such lengths in court to deny that he knew anything about their whereabouts? It would—"

"Don't tell me—it would be churlish. Perhaps even caddish. So you hung on to them all that time for when Toni came out, right?"

"Yes. After all, I had no idea of how one might set about selling them."

"You being so upright in all your dealings."

"Well, with the exception of this one, em, compassionate peccadillo, I think you will find that I have always abided strictly by the letter and spirit of the law. This was a special case."

"And Toni came out having decided he wouldn't bother selling through his old friend Busetto, right?"

Toni said, "He was no great friend; he had merely helped the organization. We'd sold a few paintings to him."

"But you were the only person in the organization who knew him."

"Yes. But so what? We all had our special duties assigned to us. I was responsible for funds at that time."

"But then after prison, when you weren't thinking about the organization but yourself, it struck you that you'd get more money if you went direct to his buyer, Osgood."

"Yes. Busetto mentioned me his name once."

"And that brings us to the next big coincidence: or was it one?"

"You mean Toni's meeting you?" Mr. Robin said.

"Yes."

"Well, no. Toni went to London, as he'd told me he would, to see this man Osgood, and discovered that he was no longer at the address Toni had. Apparently he wasn't in the phone book either, and Toni was nervous about going round asking people, since he didn't wish to call attention to himself. It so happened that Professor Perkins had just told me that you were then having an exhibition in London, so I suggested to Toni he should go along and get in touch with you."

"Me being the sort of shady character who'd know about someone like Osgood."

"Well, it struck me that after your little, em, mishap, you probably wouldn't feel in a position to ask possibly embarrassing questions of Antonio."

"I see. Unlike Professor Perkins, who would want to know everything. So Toni went along to my gallery, found out I'd be there for a private view, and got into 'casual' conversation with me. And I upset the whole thing by being so shamelessly insensitive about my moral status as to persist in asking embarrassing questions. As I am still doing now. Where are the paintings?"

"Now really, Martin, try and see other sides to the question—"

"You try and see the people of Treganzi's side—"

"Come now, a few superstitious old women—"

I could merely stare stupefied at the patronizing arrogance of this remark. Then, deciding it was hardly worth replying to, I said, "Anyway, now that Busetto and Osgood are both dead, what are you planning to do with the pictures?"

Mr. Robin said, "I don't know what Toni's decided, and I've decided I don't want to know. I've merely told him he must remove them from these premises. He's been waiting till Carnival to be able to do it unobserved."

I detected a rather belated attempt to distance himself in these words. "I see," I said. "So I've come just in time."

"Well, of course Antonio had hoped to conclude things more quickly, but when these murders started, he felt he'd better stay hidden here until Carnival."

Outside the music came to a crashing end—as if the whole band and the loudspeakers had fallen through the platform. The cheering that followed rather seemed to confirm this hypothesis.

Toni said, "It was your interfering that caused the deaths of Busetto and Osgood, you know, don't you?"

"I'd feel really hurt by that if I didn't know that all you're thinking of is the damage to your pocket."

"You complacent *borghese* pig—"

"Now you really do sound like your old *compagni*, Padoan and his friends."

He stared at me. "Who told you about Padoan?" The silence outside added to the sudden sense of tension in the room.

"I've met him—and heard what he intends doing to you." I was instantly sorry I'd said this, which sounded like mere gloating. "But don't worry, he's far from invincible."

Suddenly Mr. Robin raised his right index finger—in a flawlessly vertical gesture of course. "Ssh." He was listening, his head leaning in the direction of the flat's entrance door.

We all listened: there were footsteps on the stairs.

"Did you close the door?" he said, turning to me.

"Yes," I said. I was sure of this.

328

He got up and moved out of the room into the corridor; Toni and I followed him. Outside, the music started up again: maybe they were performing live from hell now.

Mr. Robin put his eye to a little spy hole in the front door; at the same time he took a key from his pocket and double-locked the door. He straightened up and looked at me. "Did you bring them here?" he said in a hoarse whisper.

"What?" I shouldered him out of the way and looked through the spy hole myself. It was one of those holes with a lens that gives you a slightly distorted but wide view of what's outside the door: I could see two people coming up the flight of stairs; they were both carrying guns and both wearing Donald Duck masks.

The imagination of these people.

21

"OH, my God," I said. I could hear Toni asking, "Who is it? Who is it?" I kept looking. Neither of them was small enough to be Padoan: so they had to be Alfredo and Piero, the grunter. They reached the landing.

"What do you want?" I yelled in Italian before they could knock—or fire.

"That's Pheeps, isn't it?"

"And so?"

"We followed you from the hospital."

I suppose it must have been the shoulder that had given me away. Even below the sheet, the immobility of my arm must have been noticeable: or perhaps they'd even spotted me in the hospital, putting the costume on.

The voice went on: "We want those paintings. And Toni Sambon."

I said to Mr. Robin quietly, "Go and phone the police. There's no choice."

"We've cut your telephone lines," the voice went on— Alfredo's, I thought. "Just be intelligent and open the door."

I was fairly sure I didn't agree with their definition of

330

intelligence. Mr. Robin had gone to the telephone on a little stand in the hallway, and was doing that useless little act people do if they've seen too many old films: tapping the receiver stand and repeating "Hello? Hello?" Toni was standing with his hands close-wrapped around his gun; his face had gone dead white and was twitching like the skin of milk coming to the boil. "No no no no," he repeated in a low moan.

"Give me the gun," I said. "You go and shout out the window for help."

"It isn't loaded," he replied in Italian.

"All right, let's all go and shout for help," I said, running into the nearest room, which had windows overlooking the square. Behind me I heard Toni saying, "And who'll hear with this noise?"

He was, unfortunately, right. When I opened the window and yelled, I was competing on far from equal terms with the lead singer whose yell was being broadcast by two twelve-foot-high speakers—not to mention with the drummer, the guitarists, and the stomping crowd. And, I suppose, even if anybody were to see us waving our arms, they'd only think we were joining in the fun—or complaining about the noise. Mr. Robin's flat was also much higher than any of the surrounding buildings, so we couldn't try to contact the neighbors.

"We'll give you fifteen seconds," said the voice, "and then we start breaking the door."

I came back to the door. In the corridor I saw Mr. Robin putting the phone down and plucking at his tie—obviously his eternal resource in any emergency. Toni had gone back to the living room and was opening the window there, which gave onto the canal.

"Ten seconds," said the voice.

"Antonio," said Mr. Robin. "What on earth—"

I looked around and saw Toni hoisting himself up to the sill.

"Five seconds."

Then he was gone—I imagined I heard the faint splash through the music.

"Hey!" I shouted through the door.

"What?"

"We can't give you Toni."

"Why not?"

Oh, my God, I thought, with sudden sick realization, I can't give him away like this, just to save our own skins. I said, rather feebly, "Because he's not here."

"Don't lie."

"He isn't," I said. "There's nobody here—"

Mr. Robin pushed me aside. "He's just jumped into the canal," he said in his precise Italian.

"Tell them to hurry," I muttered, "or they'll miss him."

He ignored me. "If you don't believe me," he went on addressing the door, "go down to the next landing and look out of the window."

I pushed Mr. Robin aside (it was getting a bit like Punch and Judy, in fact) and put my eye to the spy hole. I could see one of them standing with his gun trained on the door and the other leaping down the stairs. When this second one reached the landing, he turned out of my line of vision. Moments later he yelled. "It's true."

The man outside the door cursed and ran down to join him. I ran to the living room and stared down; some yards down the canal, Toni was hoisting himself out where a small alley ended in the canal. Seconds later he had disappeared.

I stepped away from the window. "So what happened to your sense of bloody obligation?"

"We had to take some decisive action," Mr. Robin said behind me. "You surely can't have wanted them to break in."

"They'll still want the pictures."

"Well, I'll give them to them. No painting is worth bloodshed. I'm sure you'll agree."

I shrugged. "That doesn't seem to be their opinion."

"You don't think it's possible they might, em, concentrate their attention on Antonio now?" he said, with a note of hope.

"Not with the crowds as they are. Bird in the hand and all that. The pictures are secure, but not if they leave us. They'll be back."

He stroked his beard. "I think you're probably right."

"Where are the pictures?"

He moved to one of the bookcases and reached into an alcove behind it. He pulled out two narrow cardboard cases, each about waist height and four feet wide.

I said to Mr. Robin, "Are they on canvas or panel?" It was fairly typical of my slapdash approach to the whole case that I couldn't remember—or had never known this.

"I've no idea," he said. "I've never really looked at them."

I couldn't think of anything to say to this. Anyway, it was good to know that if they were on canvas, they clearly hadn't been rolled; careless rolling can cause a good deal of damage. Presumably the terrorists had just lifted them off the church walls as they were, frames and all. It's been known for paintings to go like that during High Mass.

The boxes were sealed all round with packing tape; this was clearly not the moment to check up on the paintings. It struck me, however, that it would be very irritating to get killed without having had one little peep at the Cima.

Well, I'd just have to do my damnedest not to get killed.

There was a thump at the door. They had come back. A voice called out: "We still want the pictures."

I said, "You can't have them. And by the way, the people next door are phoning the police."

"That is a lie."

"Wait and see," I said in what I hoped was a tone of calm complacency.

Mr. Robin broke in, "If you go down the stairs, we'll put the paintings outside the door. Then you can take them and just go away."

There was a moment's discussion: at least I presume they were discussing the proposal—the music didn't allow us to hear any noise quieter then a yell. Then the same voice said, "We agree. We'll go down the stairs now and come up again in one minute's time."

I couldn't think of any more stalling tactics and even helped Mr. Robin carry the paintings to the door. I was wondering

333

whether we couldn't fob them off with something else, but a map of Venice or a photo of Mr. Robin would hardly be very convincing. I checked through the spy hole: there was nobody to be seen on the landing or the stairs. I nodded and Mr. Robin turned the key and opened the door. I shoved the two boxes outside with a sense of furious frustration—and treachery. Mr. Robin slammed the door and turned the key again.

I watched the two Donald Ducks come up the stairs. It struck me that if they were to pick up a painting each, then might be the moment to try a counterattack: but of course they weren't so stupid. One of them stayed with his gun cocked and the other heaved one of the cases up and set off down the stairs, his beak pointing to the ceiling. The one with the gun stayed on the landing.

A couple of minutes later the "porter" returned. He didn't suggest an exchange of roles, which surprised me: maybe he felt he had to prove what a he-man he was, even without a gun. He heaved up the other case and I wondered forlornly, uselessly, whether it was Cima or Alvise Vivarini. He started down the stairs, followed by his colleague, who made his way crabwise down the stairs, the gun still pointed in our direction.

When they'd disappeared I turned back to Mr. Robin. I caught him rolling his tie around his finger; he instantly removed the finger and pulled his tie straight. "So now what?" he said. "Have they gone?"

"Well, let's see." I made my way back into his bedroom and leaned out of the window. The rock band had just started a more or less combined assault on a Bruce Springsteen number, the words of which were being savaged by the singer's Preganziol accent ("wee wenna down toody reeva . . ."). A group of youths were throwing beer cans at the stage, whether in jubilation or criticism it was difficult to tell; the action seemed fairly in keeping with the spirit of the performance. All this was easy enough to see. Unfortunately, however, the wide windowsill made it impossible for me to make out what was happening directly below, at the entrance to the palazzo. I grabbed a chair and clambered up, sitting on the sill and leaning out as far as I dared. I now saw the two figures with their Donald Duck masks leave the palazzo, carrying one of the two cases between them. Their guns had been put away inside their coats. The one at the rear pulled the door to behind himself.

So, I thought, they've already carried off the first painting. They walked along the front of the building; as I watched them it suddenly struck me that the one at the front seemed shorter than either of them had done when seen through the spy hole. I couldn't be sure, however—the spy hole, after all, rather distorted things—and the coat and jeans were indistinguishable.

I kept watching. They turned into the first alley off right, which led to the canal—not, however, a stretch of canal that could be seen from the flat. I stepped off the chair and turned around and looked at Mr. Robin. He was studying the photographs on the wall—Mr. Robin shaking hands with the mayor of Venice, Mr. Robin shaking hands with the Patriarch of Venice, Mr. Robin shaking hands with Gianni De Michelis, Mr. Robin shaking hands with Sir Ashley Clarke, Mr. Robin shaking hands with John Julius Norwich. . . . Remembering happier times, no doubt. I said, "There's one of them still in the building."

"What?"

"Well, think about it: they're not going to want us to go straight off and tell the police. And they've got a score to settle with me."

"Oh, my God. Why *did* you come here?"

"I wouldn't have done if you hadn't been harboring the paintings." But even so, he seemed to have a point. My little Carnival escapade didn't seem to be turning out very happily. "Listen," I said, "he won't imagine that we've guessed he's there. If I can take him by surprise from the back, we might have a chance."

"How?" He seemed to have lost all the poise and self-satisfaction that his perfect clothes usually gave him: the clothes were still faultless but he was definitely rumpled inside them.

"If I can get down to the floor below without him seeing.

Climb down—using sheets or something." It would be quite a spectacle: a sheeted ghost, shinning down its own ectoplasm.

"You only have one functional arm."

"True." I noticed that he didn't make the obvious offer. Well, he wouldn't want his suit rumpled as well as his soul.

After a few seconds he said, "There is of course the lift hatch."

"The what?"

"Didn't you know about it?"

"No, I didn't—tell me about it."

"I don't know when it was put in. It goes from this flat down to the storeroom on the second and first floors. We hardly ever use it, except for transporting books. I suppose it was used to go down to the kitchens in the old days."

"So where is it?"

"But of course you realize it's not intended to take people. That's not its function."

"Where is it?" I repeated, not bothering to point out that its function was to make life easier, and it wouldn't be able to do that for him if he were dead.

He frowned but led me into a room that was furnished entirely in filing cabinets: I suppose it was to save him having to go all the way down to his office on the first floor when he wanted to hold secret communion with his soul. He opened what looked like a cupboard in one wall, revealing the hatch.

"It's a bit small," I said, "but I suppose we could take out that central tray."

"Well, I—that is—"

I had already started examining the tray. "Yes," I said. "If we unscrew here." Then before he could start talking about intentions and functions I said, "Get a screwdriver." And he went and got one.

Half a minute later I was inside the hatch, squashed-squatting like a fetus and wondering for the first time about the strength of the thing's bottom—after all this wasn't what it was intended to do; it wasn't its function. I was now wearing just the dressing gown—rather more practical then the ghost outfit—and clutching a wooden rolling pin, which I suppose Mr. Robin used as a mangle: I couldn't actually imagine him in an apron, covered with flour.

He pressed the button and I started to descend. The oblong view to my left slid away and I whirred down into blackness. I wondered if this was how it had been inside the womb, but decided it must have all been a bit softer. The position wasn't doing any good at all to my injured shoulder, and I couldn't wait to arrive.

I suddenly realized that for the first time the music outside sounded quite faint, and I had a moment's despair in which I thought that the man down below couldn't fail to hear the whirring of the machinery. I suddenly found I *could* wait to arrive: indeed I was now dreading the moment when the oblong of light would slide up on my left: the next sensation might be the impact of bullets.

But the aperture appeared, and the hatch juddered to a halt, and no gun was fired. I eased myself out onto the ground, resisting a propulsive force that threatened to shoot me across the room like a nut from a cracker. I straightened myself, nursed my arm and shoulder, and looked around the room. It was a small airless storeroom with sagging bookshelves all around. I listened hard, trying to block out the thunder of the music, and to pick up the footsteps or heartbeats of the enemy.

I could hear nothing (inside the building, that is). After a few seconds I opened the door, which gave onto a little corridor. At the end of the corridor was the main hall of that floor. There were the usual chairs, cupboards, and tables bearing copies of *Country Life* and *Punch*, but not a sign of a killer.

He was almost certainly waiting at the staircase, ready for the first noise from above.

I padded across to the door that gave onto the stairs and started inching it open. Before I'd seen anything I heard a noise of sudden movement—the nervous jerk and flurry as of someone swiveling around—and I slammed it shut, dropping the rolling pin. There was a sudden *bang* and a bit of the door leaped out at me. I threw myself to one side and slithered along the marble floor to the door of the nearest classroom.

Well, so much for taking him by surprise.

I pushed the door but didn't pass through it, instead diving to cover behind a bookcase to one side of the door. An old, old trick—but I had no new ones. And no weapon now either.

I heard the door to the stairs open suddenly and the thump and run of his flying entrance. I imagined him crouching there, sweeping the room with outstretched gun and beak. Then he must have caught sight of the door I'd pushed, as it swung back shut, and he came running over. I blessed Mr. Robin for his forethought in providing the school with slow-closing doors.

I peeped around the corner of my bookcase and saw what I had hoped to see. He was gripping the gun with both hands and his right foot was rising slowly as he prepared for his Chuck Norris–style flying kick at the door. He had removed his mask: I saw a pale face with set mouth and eyes.

I gave him another three-quarters of a second, by which time his right foot was raised some two feet above the ground and was quivering like a pointing dog and his body was tilted backward like a taut catapult: and I leaped.

I was aware of his face and gun—both round and gaping— swinging around at me but then my hand smashed into his shoulder. He had time for just one grunt of surprise before I hit him, but the grunt was enough for me to recognize Piero. I had hoped with my one free hand to grab him by the neck from behind and pull him down, but he had turned too quickly; nonetheless my frontal smash served the same purpose. He fell straight back, his head cracking on the marble floor. There was an explosion in my ear, but a second later, as I found myself kneeling astride him, I realized I was still alive. My hand was tugging at the gun. I saw his face working in fury as he struggled to get his finger to the trigger again.

The blow to his head hadn't actually knocked him out but it had obviously dulled him, since he made no attempt to smash at my injured shoulder, an action that would certainly have affected my grip on the gun. After that half second of swift violent action our struggle became quiet, intense, and almost motionless—a question of white-knuckled hands and fingers, clenched teeth and hissing breath. That invisible vampire had sunk his fangs into my shoulder again, as my body twisted and turned, and the music outside was rising to some sort of fatuous crescendo as if in mockery of our fight—and of my pain. And then the gun was in my hands.

Even without thinking, and in a continuation of the movement with which I had jerked it from his grasp, I lifted it by the barrel and brought it down on his head.

He ceased struggling.

There was an avalanche of applause outside and I felt suddenly sick. I knelt back on my haunches and his belly and waited for my shoulder to explode: but gradually the lacerating pains subsided, and I found myself repeating, "Bastards, bastards," and I didn't know whether I meant the terrorists, the applauding crowd, or the Preganziol Satanic Versers. All of them, probably.

Half a minute later Mr. Robin was standing by my side looking down at the stunned figure. I was removing the man's greatcoat, as best I could with one hand.

"What are you doing?" Mr. Robin said.

"Help me. I want to put his clothes on." I had got his right arm out of the sleeve and thus revealed the shoulder holster.

"His what?" Mr. Robin's incredulity was plain as he stared down at the man's faded jeans, old pullover, and shabby greatcoat.

"Help me," I repeated, pulling at the other arm.

He bent down and with some distaste started undoing the trouser belt. The man groaned a little, which I didn't allow to bother me. I merely talked over it: "I'm going out after them—just to try and hold them up if they're still around. You call the police and explain everything. Put this bloke in a cupboard or something and then go straight to a phone. Clear?"

"Well, yes, but—"

"Do it. These are killers."

"Are you sure that what you're intending to do is a good idea?" He pulled the trousers off and handed them to me.

"Of course I'm not. But I can't think of anything else. They're not going to get away with those pictures."

I struggled into the clothes. The trousers were wide but the belt held them up, the shoes were just about right, and the pullover large. I had removed my arm from my sling to put on the pullover, and this action in itself, as my shoulder was now letting me know, had not been a good idea, so the pullover's floppiness was fortunate. I thought if I could keep my left hand in the coat pocket, there was a good chance my shoulder wouldn't actually disintegrate. I put the coat on and picked up the gun. I hadn't put the holster on, so slipped it straight into my pocket, which was fortunately deep. Then, on a sudden thought, I took it out and checked if there was a safety catch; there was, of course, and it was off. I flipped it on.

"Do be careful," Mr. Robin said as I did this. He presumably didn't want his floors chipped.

I ran to the stairway and there found the Donald Duck mask. I strapped it on and started down the stairs with one last shout to Mr. Robin: "The police, remember."

As I ran down, the beak flapping playfully in front of my eyes, I wondered what the hell I was doing. I had no strategy: all I wanted was to get as close to the other two bastards as possible—if they were still hanging around—in order to do something, anything, that might stop them getting away. An indication of my half-crazed state was that I was really hoping that they would still be there, waiting for their companion—for me.

Well, Carnival is a time of folly.

I left the building, without stopping to see how they had forced the lock. I paid no attention either to the Satanic Versers' version of "All Right Now" and took the alley I'd seen the two terrorists go down. And at the end of the alley I saw a boat with one Donald Duck sitting by the tiller and holding on to a pole, and another one sitting toward the front. Their beaks swiveled around at me and one of them said, *"Fatto?"* Have you done it?

I gave a thumbs-up sign and let out a quick assenting grunt, which, I was fairly sure, was how Piero would have reported two successful killings to his companions. I looked at the two cases, leaning against either side of the boat.

"Get in then," Padoan said from the front.

I had had one moment of fierce flaring exultation on seeing the boat and then suddenly reason had flooded back—ice-cold drenching reason—and as Padoan said this I felt—well, very silly. And very very scared.

I had no choice, however, but to go on with the masquerade, so I stepped into the boat. I tried to do it as casually as possible, so that my left hand's fixity in its pocket would seem nonchalant self-assurance, but unfortunately I came down harder than I had hoped and set the boat rocking wildly. *"Attento,"* said the one behind me, and I grunted again and sat down with a thump on the middle bench just behind the two paintings, and in between the two terrorists. My back had to be turned to one of them. I was facing Padoan, at the front of the boat.

We chugged off down the canal. Padoan continued to face me, which seemed unnatural; any normal person would twist around to see where the boat was going. I could see those pale eyes on me. Inside the mask my face was running with sweat, and I would have given anything to remove it and wipe myself clean. Well, anything except my life.

"How many shots?" Padoan suddenly asked.

I grunted, *"Due,"* holding up two fingers—inoffensively. If I could stick to answers of that kind, I might be safe.

The boat turned into another canal. I realized that I was losing track of where we were. I knew my way around Venice's alleys and streets; the canals were a completely new map to me, one that I had never learned. I caught glimpses down alleys of squares and buildings that I knew, I recognized bridges, but I could only make the wildest guess at what the next turn in the canal would reveal. Then I saw the bridge of Santi Apostoli ahead, crowded with people: we passed underneath, and a few people took photos of us.

We swung into the Grand Canal, turning right in the direction of the station and Piazzale Roma. With the kind of crazy irrelevance that my mind seemed capable of, I was struck by how beautiful it was in the hazy sunlight, which softened the scene, subduing the colors; the palazzi hovered over the water, seemingly insubstantial, like a pageant seen behind a theatrical gauze, and in the distance they faded into a misty monochrome. My eyes filled with tears, adding to the shimmering indistinctiveness of the picture—and to the mushy discomfort behind my mask.

Was this how I was destined to end—weeping behind a Donald Duck mask in the middle of the Grand Canal? What a mixture of the pathetic, the sublime, and the really bloody ridiculous.

As the view did its unreal water dance beyond my yellow beak I suddenly knew I wanted to paint it; I wanted to catch that golden-gray light, get that transitory effect of the sun and the mist onto canvas. And I felt sure I could do it—I could even imagine the exact mixtures of paint I'd need. I could imagine myself standing there in front of the easel, the brush firm and comforting in my hand.

I had to paint it. I had to.

But to do this it was pretty essential that I lived.

I slid my right hand into my pocket and eased the safety catch off the gun. I grasped it—firm and comforting in my hand. There now: I could shoot my foot off if I wanted.

Padoan spoke: "I don't think we'd better stay on the Grand Canal. It's too public." His voice was, as ever, decisive, final.

"Sorry," said the man behind me. "It just seemed the obvious route. We can go off right by San Felice and then go around by the lagoon to the Tronchetto."

The Tronchetto is an artificial island beyond the station, with a huge car park. I couldn't afford to postpone my action—whatever it was going to be—any longer. Once we left the Grand

Canal—and Rio San Felice was only another twenty yards or so—I'd lose the advantage of witnesses.

But what *was* I going to do?

I shifted on my seat, glancing around at the man at the tiller. I grunted, "My legs," making them understand that they were too cramped by the paintings. I swung them over to the other side so that I was facing backward, and in continuation of this movement rose, took one step forward, and sat down next to the driver. I pulled the gun out of my pocket and pressed it into his side.

I spoke to Padoan at the front. "Take your hands out of your pockets—empty."

He had obviously grasped the situation at once. "Why?"

"Because I'll blow a hole through your friend's stomach if you don't." His friend was still driving us forward, but had gone rigid with shock.

Padoan brought out only his left hand and laid it on his knee; his right hand, instead, lifted inside his pocket until the pocket was pointing at me—in the shape of a gun. "He may be my friend," he said, "but first and foremost he is a fighter for the revolution and he knows perfectly well that my first duty is to the cause." His voice was steady and reasoning.

I found myself going cold with horror. "Ask him," I said. The man at the tiller still said nothing.

"Even if he were to plead with me," Padoan said, "which I feel sure he won't, my duty would still be to the cause. Indeed, if he were to plead, it would be quite clear that he isn't worth saving. Lucio, turn right down Rio San Felice as programmed."

Lucio gave a trembling nod.

"And when we are away from general observation," Padoan said, "we will see. . . ." The trail of menacing dots at the end of the sentence were almost audible.

My hand gave a tiny preliminary shift, as if I were about to swivel my gun. Padoan said, "The merest millimeter in my direction and I shoot. My gun is aimed directly at your heart. My suggestion is that you drop your gun."

I said, "No."

343

"Very well. I am not going to fire here in the Grand Canal unless obliged to, so we will continue this tableau until we are a little more secluded."

I said, trying not to let desperation sound in my voice, "You must know that you're defeated—that your revolution isn't going to happen. Two of you, stealing pictures—what's the point?"

"We are only defeated when we admit we're defeated."

I recognized this as his central creed: presumably the moment he acknowledged failure, he'd cease to have any reason for existence. His funnel vision, to use Alvise's term, had a mere pinhole for its final aperture, and everything in his being—his powers of reason, his emotions—had to be forced through that pinhole, and in the process got compressed into one laserlike ray of destruction. Despite the outward appearance of calm reasoning, he was in fact obsessed to the point of madness.

"That is why the admission of defeat," he went on, "is the greatest crime a true revolutionary can commit. And why Sambon must suffer."

There was a new note in his voice: something more than contempt. Toni's escape had obviously hit him hard. The eyes were as unmoving as ever, but I suddenly felt I saw something frenzied in their fixity.

"Why the obsession with Sambon?" I said. "He's only one of the many *pentiti*." I was trying to keep him talking—hoping, rather feebly, to distract him.

"Sambon betrayed the cause, betrayed the proletariat movement, betrayed his *compagni*—"

"Betrayed you," I said. There had to be something personal in this obsession: could Padoan and Sambon have had a relationship that went beyond mere "comradeship"? Or was this just the teacher enraged at the treachery of a former model pupil? Whatever it was, it made it clear that the recovery of the paintings had a significance for Padoan far beyond their mere commercial value.

"*Basta*," said Padoan. "There is no point in further conversation." His voice was conclusive; maybe he realized he'd given away the fact that he too had feelings.

We passed a couple of gondolas bearing French tourists in eighteenth-century costume who cheered our masks. One of them made Donald Duck noises. We none of us acknowledged them. Nobody could see my gun, as I was pressed in close to Lucio—and even if they had been able to, I suppose they would just have taken it for another piece of Carnival jollity.

Bloody Carnival, I thought, along with half the Venetian population.

Then I saw a small carabiniere boat, coming around the bend in the Grand Canal, by the Fontego dei Turchi. It was about fifty yards away—and we were going to turn off right in another few seconds. I looked at it and said suddenly with a forced note of triumph, "Carabinieri!"

Padoan didn't swivel around, as I'd rather forlornly hoped—though not expected. He said to Lucio, "True?"

"Yes, but we're turning now." And he began to swing the boat into the side canal.

Padoan now gave the merest flicker of a glance aside—the beak wobbled to one side. As he did so his left hand made the slightest of movements on his knee as if he were about to lift it; the right hand stayed rigidly raised and pointing inside the pocket.

And as he made this tiny movement I suddenly saw a clear picture in my mind: I saw him in my studio in Acton, standing by the easel and flicking a cigarette lighter—with his left hand.

I knew I had to take the biggest gamble in my life—in the next half second.

I shoved Lucio viciously with my gun hand and my shoulder, and, even before he hit the water, swiveled the gun in Padoan's direction: he froze, his left hand halfway inside his coat, where it had lunged for his holster under the right armpit, and his right hand outside his pocket—empty.

"Hands up," I said. "Slowly."

The boat was rocking wildly of course, but even so, for one

second I had the sensation that he and I were locked more fixedly than ever in a frozen tableau—it was Venice that was swirling and swooping. His eyes stared into mine, but for the first time they must have received a message and not just transmitted one: he must have seen in my eyes my absolute determination, because during that split second I knew—*knew*, beyond a shadow of doubt—that at the first sign of swift movement I would kill him. His hand came slowly out from his coat, empty. He raised both hands.

As he did so I became aware of the thousand things that were happening around us: the crazy rocking of the boat, the gabble of excited French and Italian and Venetian, the thrashing and splashing of Lucio, the vaporetto with a hundred faces turned in our direction, the carabiniere boat speeding toward us—and the perfection of the Grand Canal—completely unaffected by our little squabble. Well, what else would one expect of the Serenissima?

I found myself smiling. I was going to get to paint it after all.

22

"YOU must have all looked very silly," Lucy said.

"What?" I was thrown for a moment. "Oh, well, yes, I suppose so. Right then I didn't actually think of that. Er, is that all you're going to say?"

"Oh, no, of course, you were wonderful. A real hero." And she leaned across the table to kiss me.

"Well, I wasn't bad, actually," I said. "though I says it meself. Excuse a smirk or two."

"I bet Menegazzi didn't let you do much smirking."

"No, that's why I want to indulge myself with you."

We were eating at a restaurant not far from Lucy's hotel and the old Palazzo Sambon. (There being no apparent reason for further anonymity, she was going back there, to her pajamas and her job.) The only other customers were a French couple who'd obviously had a row and were drinking cappuccinos in a sullen silence that made their clown costumes and makeup look a trifle incongruous. The place had probably been full earlier on, but it was now almost midnight, and indeed it was only because the waiter knew Lucy that we'd been given a table—for a quick

347

pasta dish and wine. We'd finished the pasta and were now killing the bottle—or rather the jug, which bore the Venetian slogan, "*Magna, bevi e tasi*. Eat, drink, and shut up." For most of the meal we'd obeyed this injunction, having been too weary and hungry to do otherwise.

I'd spent the last seven or eight hours in the Questura, answering questions—mostly the same questions, asked by different people—dictating declarations, explaining things, and even, for two crazy minutes, being photographed by the press, an experience that had woken many less happy memories: Menegazzi had been by my side and fielded all the questions for me; I'd limited myself to an occasional "I'm very relieved it's over," "I'm happy to have helped save the paintings," "Yes, I was very frightened." Later I'd looked out of the window of the Questura and seen a police boat come rushing up the canal and then get sent back by the television reporters, whose cameras hadn't been focused properly at that moment; an interview with an unshaven English painter was okay for a few seconds or so but the viewers would want their license money's worth of action as well.

"And he didn't mellow at all?" Lucy asked about Menegazzi.

"Well, I'm not in jail for destruction of hospital property and sheer idiocy, so I suppose by his lights he mellowed. And in fact, after a bit of a lecture about vigilantes and people taking justice into their own hands, he said something along the lines of: Well, at least it worked out all right."

"He talked about vigilantes?"

"Yes. I kept pointing out that I wasn't Charles Bronson out to clean up the streets: all I'd wanted to do was save the paintings."

She looked at me with her glass to her lips and said, "But tell me, did you—" She stopped.

"Did I what?"

"Well, did you feel just the slightest temptation to pull that trigger?"

"Yes."

"Ah."

"I suppose what held me back was just the thought that it would—it would make a beautiful moment ugly."

"Get blood on the paintings, you mean."

"Well, yes." I sipped my wine. "Maybe I haven't got a morality, just a sense of aesthetic fitness. Like the Borgias. At that moment I was really feeling things like—well, like a painter. I mean, it was my painter's eye that had saved me—that visual memory of Padoan's left-handedness; and it was a determination to live to paint again that kept my nerves steady. And it was, well, it was the thought of Cima and the perfection of his work that kept me from blowing Padoan's guts out."

"I see. Another of those miracle-working paintings. And you didn't even get to see it—them."

"No. Only on television. They let me watch the news in a back room. Menegazzi standing next to the pictures and saying something about my rather foolish but fortunately successful action. And the rest was all, 'Brilliant operation by the antiterrorist forces,' et cetera, et cetera." I paused. "Still the Cima looked good."

"And what about Padoan? How did he look, once the, er, mask was off?" She put these last three words in quotation marks.

"A boring little academic. Which was apparently what he once had been."

"And he didn't make any last desperate move, or anything like that?"

"No. I suppose he was never one for useless risks. Perhaps when he's studied the whole situation in a completely rational way, he might hang himself in his cell. In a completely rational way, of course."

"Anyway," she said, "you're redeemed, right?" She poured me another glass of wine. "You've proved you're on the side of civilization."

"Well," I said, "I like to think so—but probably, in a year's time, all anyone will remember is that that junkie forger was mixed up in art smuggling and terrorism as well."

"Don't be so cynical. You know you don't really believe that."

"Well, do you remember that headline in *The Star* when it came out that I'd forged a Renoir nude: 'Experts fooled by nude in playboy drug case.' Sheer genius that, to get so much spice into eight words."

"I remember. You a playboy. I wondered if they'd ever seen how you dressed."

I smiled. "All Italy did this evening: baggy terrorist trousers and sweater. They didn't send anyone round to the hospital for the clothes you'd taken there until about eight o'clock."

"With your apologies for the sheets, I suppose."

"Yes. But as I said to Menegazzi, I couldn't think of any other way of making a discreet exit from the hospital—and I'd known Mr. Robin for years: I had to get to see him personally. I couldn't just send the police round. I had to check I was right, and hear his version of the facts."

"Poor Derek."

"Yes. This is one scandal he's not going to be able to get around by sacking the person responsible."

"Well, he's not actually under arrest at the moment, is he?"

"No. He's in *libertà provvisoria*—on bail. Paid for, I imagine, by the Britannia School. I suppose at bottom I feel sorry for him too—which is probably more than he ever did for me." I finished the glass and looked out of the window. "Funny."

"What?"

"That's the third time I've seen that man go past."

"What man?"

"Well, I presume it's the same man: a big cloak and a black mask."

"Oh, come on, Martin. Haven't you had enough melodrama for one day?"

"For a lifetime. Sorry. It was just an observation. I expect he's just a lost tourist. I've probably gone paranoid." I turned back to her. "Anyway where does Mr. Robin's dilemma leave you?"

"Out of work I suppose. Still, as I told you, I never thought of this as being my career."

"So back to acting?" I looked out of the window again.

"I hope I'm not boring you," she said with gentle sarcasm.

"Sorry, but there he goes again."

"Go and ask him what he wants."

She was probably still being sarcastic, but I said, "I think I will." I got up and told the waiter to prepare the bill—to his obvious relief. The French couple had finished their cappuccinos and were now drinking *digestivi*, which perhaps partly explained the new looks of disgust and fury beneath their painted smiles. With an explanatory murmur to the waiter ("I think there's a friend outside . . .") I stepped out into the alley. The cloaked man was a few yards away; he turned around as I came out, but instead of a face presented a mere black blur. I was suddenly aware of the silence and emptiness of the alley, even though the restaurant door was just behind me.

"Excuse me," I said in Italian, "but are you lost?"

"No. I want to speak to you." The voice was a hoarse whisper. It brought to mind uncheering notions, such as a worm-eaten face behind the mask, or a mere empty skull. . . .

I forced myself to ask a reasonable question. "Who are you?"

"Come out with your girlfriend and I'll tell you. I want to speak to both of you."

"Why don't you come inside?"

"It's better outside."

"Martin, can I help?" It was Lucy. She was standing by the cash desk, paying the bill, and had leaned over and opened the door to ask this question.

"He wants to speak to both of us."

"Who is he?"

"He won't tell."

"I'm not coming out unless he takes off that mask."

I turned back to the black figure and said, "Did you understand?" I translated what Lucy had said.

"I don't intend any harm."

I suddenly recognized the voice. "Zennaro."

"What?" He was caught off guard and spoke in his normal voice, at once "correcting" himself with a hoarse whisper of the same word. I could now see the mask; it was of black plaster, with a mouth slit and eyeholes. With the hood of his cloak over his head, the effect was of total darkness.

"I think you can come out," I said to Lucy. "He's safe enough."

"You *think*?" she said.

I said to Zennaro, "Is there any point in keeping the mask on now?"

"If I want to I will," he said, almost sulkily, and making only the feeblest attempt at a hoarse whisper now.

"I really don't think you need to worry," I said to Lucy.

"Who is he?"

"He's Zennaro—you remember: the man in Busetto's pay."

"Signorina!" This was the waiter's voice, complaining— reasonably enough—about Lucy's holding the door open.

"Hang on," I said to Zennaro. I slipped inside the restaurant and got my coat. Lucy put hers on too. She said, "Look, what the hell does he want?"

"I don't know. To talk to us. I'm sure he's not dangerous. And anyway there are two of us."

She frowned but said, "Okay."

We said good night to the waiter and joined Zennaro in the alley. "How did you know where to find me?" I asked as we started walking in the direction of the hotel. He walked by my side, forcing Lucy to tag along a few steps behind. It was surprising how his appearance had lost all its suggestions of the sinister the moment I'd recognized his voice: even as masked mystery man he was a washout.

"I saw you on television," he said, "and they said you worked for the Britannia School. I know the Britannia School has people staying in the hotel here, so I came and asked for you and they told me you might have come here with this lady."

"Who told you?" I said.

"Some English girls."

Lucy said, "Well, I didn't tell them."

"Never mind," I said. "They probably married us off the moment you took me upstairs to wash my face." I turned back to Zennaro. "And why the urgency to see me?"

"I want to know what you're up to."

"Wasn't that clear from the news? I was looking for those paintings."

Lucy suddenly pulled me away from Zennaro. "Martin, be careful."

"What?"

"The voice."

"What do you mean?"

"His voice."

"What about—oh, no. Put it down." From inside his cloak Zennaro had pulled out his flick knife. He stood against the wall in that vague crouching stance I remembered from his studio. He had either understood what Lucy had said, or had been put on his guard by her attitude and tone of voice. Or maybe he just liked pulling knives out. At any rate the cloak and mask had suddenly reacquired a few suggestions of the sinister.

"Don't you see?" Lucy said. "He's the man who was in the palazzo that night."

"What?" I was still watching that gently circling blade, which caught the nearby lamplight.

"It was him—that voice—that knife."

Lucy had been speaking English. I said in Italian, "Was it you that night in Palazzo Sambon?"

He said, "Yes—and what were you doing there?"

"Look, why don't you put that knife down?"

"I want to know what you were doing there."

"And I want to know what you were doing there."

"Oh, this is ridiculous," Lucy said. She put her hand out and said in sudden stern Italian: "Give me that knife."

The next moment it was in her hand. She didn't exactly

snatch it and he didn't exactly hand it over, but somehow she ended up holding it. She clicked the blade closed and put the knife behind her back. He said, "But—but—" and then shut up, realizing that he would only make himself look sillier.

I said, "Is that how you talk to the students?"

She said, "When I have to."

"A bit riskier with a murderer."

"Well, it suddenly seemed to me he couldn't be one. Not the way he was holding that knife."

"Oh," I said. Then: "It looked good enough to me."

"Film stuff. Not for real."

"I see," I said. "And so you decided he wasn't a real murderer."

"I took a gamble which paid off."

Zennaro broke in rather plaintively. "What are you saying?"

I said, "Did you kill Osgood?"

"The fat man? No."

"But it was you, not a terrorist, that we met in the palazzo that night?"

"Yes. But I didn't kill him. He was already dead when I got there."

"So why did you attack us?" I said.

"I didn't know who you were. I just wanted to get out."

"So why were you there?"

"Why were you there?"

"Oh, God," said Lucy. Then, in her stern voice again: "We heard noises in the palazzo from our hotel, so went to see what was going on. All right?"

"Er, yes," he said nervously. I half expected him to add, "Sorry, miss," and touch his hood. He said, "Let's walk on a bit." I suppose it wasn't such a good idea to keep talking under the same windows. We proceeded down the alley, with Zennaro now walking between the two of us, which was just about possible without our actually rubbing shoulders.

He went on: "I'd been following that fat man."

"Why?" I asked.

"What else could I do?"

354

"What do you mean?"

"Well, I heard about Busetto getting killed, and I didn't know where that left me. I mean, if the police started looking into Busetto's affairs . . ."

"Yes, I see," I said.

"And he hadn't paid me, so I was really in the shit. I mean, I couldn't afford to clear out, even if I wanted to. And then I remembered you telling me that the man behind Busetto was staying at the Danieli Hotel, so I thought maybe I could go and have a word with him."

"What sort of word?"

"Well, point out my situation, and, you know . . . ask for a bit of help."

"Very reasonable," I said.

"So I went along there, and when I asked at the desk, they told me he'd just that minute gone out, but they told me I couldn't miss him, he was a really fat man in a summer suit. So I went out and saw him going toward the piazza. I followed him to a restaurant, and I kept meaning to go in and have a word, but then thought it was a bit too public, so maybe I should wait till he came out. So I hung around while he ate."

"You make a habit of hanging around outside restaurants then," Lucy said.

"I didn't have any choice, did I? Then when he came out he didn't start going back in the direction of the hotel, so I thought, Well, I'll just follow him, see where he's going, and he went to the Rialto and got on a vaporetto going toward the station. I thought, Well, I can't speak to him here, on the vaporetto, and anyway by now I was really curious. I mean, what was he doing wandering around Venice in the middle of the night? He got off at San Marcuola and made his way up here, through Cannaregio, looking at a map. And then I saw him go down that alley by the side of the palazzo." He said this pointing at the alley in question, as we had just come out into the square. The hotel had several windows lit up tonight; presumably the students kept late hours.

"So," he continued, "I kept following him. I mean, a great fat man like that, climbing through windows."

"It must have been quite a sight," I agreed.

"Weren't you scared?" Lucy said.

"Well, a bit. But mostly I thought it would be great to take him by surprise in there. I mean, that would really give me the—the advantage."

I said, "And instead . . ." and let the sentence trail away. We had all stopped in the middle of the square and were looking up through the gathering mist at the cracked elegance of Palazzo Sambon. We could hear the sound of chatter from the hotel—jolly public-school vowel sounds drifting through the mist.

"Well, I'd gone up the stairs, feeling my way, and was sort of groping around on the first floor, and then I heard a scream—I mean, a really horrible scream—and gunshots . . . with a silencer, but gunshots all the same. Then somebody comes running out at me and swipes at me with the gun. I fall over and lie there for a bit, feeling sick. I don't know how long for. When I get up I want to go back down the stairs, but I go in the wrong direction and I find Osgood's body. So then I make for the stairs as quickly as possible—but bump into you. Well, I didn't know it was you until I heard you speak. But all I wanted was to get out."

"I see," I said again.

"Anyway, after that I decided it was best to clear out of my flat and go and lie low for a bit. So I went and stayed with a friend of mine in—" He stopped, obviously deciding it was better not to say where. "And then tonight I'm watching the news and I see you. And I decide I've got to find out where I stand: what's been going on—and who the hell are you." He went silent. The whole account had come out in his usual plaintive, half-sulky tones, as of a child explaining just why he'd been forced to steal his younger brother's lollipop.

"You'd better go along and tell the police all this," I said.

"Oh, yeah? And they're going to believe me?"

"Why shouldn't they?"

He ignored this question. "And anyway what's the point, seeing as they know the guy who did it's dead?"

"Gerosa?"

"Yes, that terrorist the police shot."

356

I said, "So why did you tell us all this if you don't want to tell the police?"

"Well, I didn't come along meaning to tell you all this. I wanted to get an explanation—to see where I stood."

"What do you mean, where you stood?"

"Well, I wanted to check out—to check out if you'd recognized me or not that night. I was going to ask sort of discreet questions. But when she suddenly jumped away like that, I realized she'd recognized my voice."

"Well, it was pretty silly to whisper in exactly the same way you'd done that night," Lucy said—a schoolmistress reprimanding a silly boy with chalk on his hands after writing a rude word on the blackboard.

He immediately went on the whining defensive. "But I wasn't—I was doing a hoarse one this time. At least that's what I meant it to be. And I was speaking with a Ciosoto accent."

"Ciosoto?" Lucy said.

"From Chioggia," I informed her. I said to him, "Well, maybe that was just a bit oversubtle for us."

"But anyway," he said, "once you'd recognized me I just wanted to make it clear that I didn't have anything to do with the murder."

Lucy said in English, "Martin, we've got to let the police know this."

"Yes, I know. Persuade him, though."

She turned to him. "Come into the hotel with us and we'll talk it all through."

"Oh, no," he said. "I'm not stupid."

This was too stupid to be argued with. I said, "Look, you can't stay on the run forever."

"Why? Are you going to give me away?"

"These are things the police have to know."

"Well, not from me."

"Okay then, from us."

"But then you'll have to tell them you were there too," he said with a note of triumph.

"We already have done," I said.

"What?" His triumph took a nosedive. "But—but—" Clearly he'd been basing this whole encounter on the assumption that we had things to hide as well. He said, "I don't believe you." But his voice was uncertain.

"That's up to you. But I expect the newspapers will tell you so tomorrow."

"Look, I—look, I'd better go—that is—see you—" He backed away from us, still blathering. Then he halted and said, "Er, my knife . . ." It was a plea, not an order.

I half expected Lucy to say she was confiscating it permanently, but she tossed it to him. Of course he missed it and had to go groping on the ground, nearly tripping over his cloak in the process. Then he ran off into the mist.

"Not quite Al Capone," Lucy said.

I said, "This is serious."

"Yes, I know. But does it change anything right now? Can't it wait till the morning?"

"Well, probably." You can't beat good old procrastination.

A light went off in the hotel. I said, "Let's walk around a bit, shall we? Wait until they've all gone to bed."

"Martin, it's cold."

"Well, we'll walk quickly. Let's just go down the side of Palazzo Sambon."

"Have you gone completely mad?"

"No. I just have a—well, I suppose it's what you call a hunch."

"What about?"

"I don't know. Various things."

"About what—what's-his-name was saying?"

"What's his name?"

"Yes, him."

"No, go on Lucy, tell me his name."

"But you know it."

"Yes, but do you?" I had turned and placed my good hand on her shoulder as I said this.

"Does it matter? He's Busetto—no, Zanaldo."

"Zennaro. Zennaro. Busetto was the one who was paying him, the one who got killed."

"Yes, I remember. Martin, what's the matter with you?"

"Come with me." I took her by the hand and led her down that narrow alley toward the canal. She made a token attempt to draw back, but then resigned herself to my madness. The window at the end of the alley by which we'd entered had a new shutter, which was firmly closed. But I walked on past it to the edge of the canal.

"Listen," I said.

We said nothing for a few seconds. All was as quiet as only nocturnal Venice can be. We couldn't even hear any *oh really*s from the hotel.

"I can't hear anything," she said after a while.

"Exactly."

"Martin, if you don't tell me what you're talking about—or not talking about—I am going to push you into the canal."

I told her.

23

IT must have been about two hours later that I was woken by the slightest of noises—but a noise I had obviously been unconsciously waiting for: I heard the gentle sloshing of the canal water and the squeaking of ropes against poles. Just what we'd heard the evening of the murder, before Osgood's death scream.

I slipped out of bed and padded over to the window. I opened it and leaned out. There was nothing to see: just the faint rocking of the boats and the broken surface of the water.

"What's up?" Lucy had sat up in bed.

"Listen."

She listened. "Can you see anything?"

"No."

"So what do you think . . .?"

"I think Toni's probably in there."

"Why?"

"I don't know. I just have a feeling. He has to have gone somewhere."

"But here? After all that's happened—"

"Exactly. The last place anyone would think of." I was getting dressed as I spoke, in my one-handed way.

"So what are you going to do?"

"Go down and see."

"Martin, you really are mad. Look, why not call the police now?"

"Maybe there isn't time."

"What do you mean?"

"It's another bloody hunch. Look, you get onto the police. I want to get down there and check—"

"Oh, my God, you mean that wasn't him that entered just now."

"No, he's in there already."

"So it was her."

"Exactly."

"Martin, don't—"

"You call the police," I said, and closed the door. I ran down the stairs to the little room on the ground floor with the window onto the canal. I pulled open the window, not worrying about the grating noise this time. As I only had one useful arm, I used a chair to climb onto the sill. I swiveled and dropped down to the boat below with a heavy thump, which set it rocking crazily.

I made my clambering way, just as I had that other evening, from boat to boat. I reached the seaweedy steps of Palazzo Sambon and stepped out onto them, clutching at the nearest pole in order not to slip. I pushed at the door and it scraped open.

I stared into the black emptiness of the entrance hall. Then I stepped into it.

Listening hard, I could hear footsteps going up the stairs to the right. They didn't pause or hesitate, so I presumably hadn't been heard. I ran on tiptoes across the hall and started up the stairs myself.

I'd reached the first landing when I heard voices above me, on the first floor. Furtive voices, which nonetheless started a whispery echo around the dark spaces of the building. I kept running, as quietly as possible. I could now see torchlight ahead of me, issuing from the big hall of the *piano nobile*.

Francesca Sambon's voice said in Venetian, "Maybe we'd better turn the flashlight off, in case it gets seen outside."

361

At this point I yelled, "Toni, don't trust her!"

There was an immediate flurry of movement while the echoes took up my cry. The torch beam stabbed out to the stairs.

"Who's that?" Francesca's voice said, and the beam swiveled and hit me full in the face. "Oh, you."

"Toni," I said, trying to squint past the dazzle, but failing of course, "don't trust your sister."

"What do you mean?" His voice came from somewhere behind the light, with a touch of uncertainty.

"Get away from her."

"Come up the stairs," Francesca said, speaking in English now. "Slowly, I have a gun pointed at you."

"Francesca," said Toni, "what the—"

"Shut up." She addressed him in Venetian. "*Tasi.*"

"Toni, don't let her do this. . . ." I hadn't moved on the stairs.

"Francesca, have you gone mad?" Toni said.

"Shut up." Then in English to me: "Come up the stairs."

I didn't move. She said to Toni, "You go and join him on the stairs."

"What?"

"Move." She must have shoved him: the torch beam wavered, and amid the swirling of shadows Toni came pitching down the stairs, letting out a sharp cry of alarm. One flailing arm struck me in the face and then he was a dazed bundle on the landing. I jumped down beside him and he dragged himself up to a figure two: just as I'd seen him in Kensington that evening—and just as bewildered and scared. "Francesca," he said, dully. I put my good hand on his shoulder, and he repeated the name. He seemed not to have broken anything.

The light held us both unwaveringly. I squinted up and said, "There's no point in killing us, you know. My friend Lucy is calling the police at this moment." I spoke in English. I felt securer in that language.

"Kill us?" Toni said.

"Why else do you think she came alone to see you in the middle of the night with a gun?"

"Francesca?" They were like the questions of a little boy.

"I don't believe you," Francesca said. "You're on your own."

"Francesca!" Toni's voice was now the plea of a little boy begging to be told that the ghost story wasn't true. The cry echoed around the building, dynasties of plaintive Sambons.

"Shut up," she said. Then to me: "You're bluffing." It was the confident decided tone of the businesswoman—but she wasn't certain enough to pull the trigger.

I said, "And anyway the police know all about you."

"Don't lie."

"I told them this evening the whole thing about you. The Guardi pictures. You and Osgood." I just had to keep talking, eroding her certainty, like the canal water slobbering away toothlessly but remorselessly at the foundations of the palazzo. Because, like Padoan, she was one who killed for certainties—the certainty that murder was the most efficient way of furthering her plans. She was a businesswoman after all, not a mere sadist.

"How did you—" she said, and halted. I'd definitely caught her off guard here.

"You gave yourself away with a tiny lie when I saw you with Lucy. That got me suspicious at once," I lied myself.

"What?" The waves of doubt were swirling stronger, sucking away at her assurance. She had to hear what I said before she dared pull that trigger.

"Lucy said she'd just told you about my being pushed in the canal, and you said, 'I didn't know that—it was Busetto, wasn't it?' Well, Lucy certainly hadn't mentioned Busetto's name, since she didn't know anything about him, and she hasn't got a great memory for names anyway. The only way you could have known the name was by having read the *Gazzettino* the previous day—and yet when I'd called on you that morning you hadn't asked any questions about my—my row with Busetto, even though we'd been talking about him."

"And so? What does this mean?"

"Well, nothing by itself. It just seemed odd. All I could think was that you must have had some reason for not wanting me to know you'd read the paper. And the only reason that came into my mind was that perhaps you'd been the one to leave that threatening message at my hotel on Sunday morning. Because I hadn't told you where I was staying."

Toni was slowly getting up. "Francesca," he said again, "what is all this?"

"Silence," she said to him. Then to me: "But that proved nothing by itself."

"Well, just that you didn't like me looking into the whole business. You tried to get me to go off down to Rome by mentioning friends of Toni down there, and then when I didn't do that, you did your best to—to make up to me, presumably so that you could keep a close eye on what I'd found out."

"Make up to you?" She didn't know this idiom.

"You tried to pull your charm on me. Which nearly worked, I have to admit." Then, thinking this might restore too much of her confidence, I added, "But something held me back—I had a kind of inner feeling that something was rotten at bottom." I even wondered, as I said this, if it might not be true.

"What is all this?" Toni repeated, now to me. "What didn't she want you to find out?"

I said to him, without turning from the glare of the torch beam, "She was afraid that I might stumble onto the fact that *she* had stolen the Guardi painting, not you."

"What painting?" he said. "You mean our Guardis at home?"

"Oh, you didn't know anything about this?"

"About what?"

"About the fact that you were supposed to have taken a Guardi painting of *Morning* with you when you left the house, after your row with your mother."

"What?"

"Which is why your mother wouldn't forgive you."

"Francesca!" Again that pleading note: Please, say it's not true.

Instead she said, "I needed the money, Toni." It wasn't an

364

apology, merely an explanation. "I was going to write and tell you."

"So Mother thinks I'm a thief, on top of everything."

It wasn't the time to point out that he was of course a thief—merely not a thief from his own family. I said to him, "Your sister was opening up her shop, without your parents' support, which must have been a fairly expensive venture, and your departure like that made it very easy for her. She even knew, through you, of a crooked dealer she could go to in Venice. So the whole thing was perfect. What was it you said, Francesca? To be successful you need to know when to be careful and when to be impulsive, and this was a moment to be impulsive, I suppose."

"And you gave me the blame," Toni said.

"They were already furious with you, it hardly seemed to matter," she said with a touch of impatience.

"So then," I went on, "Busetto must have got in touch with Osgood about the Guardi painting, who presumably had just heard from Toni himself about the Cima and the Vivarini. I suppose Osgood knew the provenance of the Guardi—"

"So that's why he asked me all those questions about the family," Toni said, in dull remembrance.

"And this gave him a double reason for visiting Venice: firstly to get hold of the Cima and Vivarini, and secondly to persuade you"—I was addressing Francesca now—"to hand over the other Guardi. Your story of him blackmailing you about your brother didn't make much sense. It was you yourself who was being blackmailed—and a pretty powerful blackmail, given the fact that your parents were now supporting your venture financially. It wasn't just a question of having to face angry parents if they found out the true story, but perhaps of going bust."

"I'd put years of work into that shop," she said. "I wasn't going to fail for such a foolish reason."

"So when there seemed a risk of Osgood getting publicly involved over Busetto's murder, you were terrified of course that the true story might come out. And when I told you that I'd speak to him about the whole business, you took another impulsive decision: he'd have to die. Again a question of knowing how to use the moment—and what better moment than during a spate of terrorist killings?"

"He was no loss to anyone."

"Is that what you're going to say about killing us?"

"No!" Toni almost screamed. The idea had only just got through to him.

"Silence."

It was terrible not being able to see her: I could only imagine her, standing there, small but firm, her finger on the trigger. I spoke in Italian now, to make sure my words got across: "Francesca, it'll serve no purpose. You're not going to get away with it."

Toni said, "Francesca, no, no, no . . ." He was almost whimpering.

I felt if anything was going to persuade her to shoot, it was going to be that kind of noise. I said, "The police know it wasn't the terrorists who killed Osgood."

She answered me in Italian now. "They can't know. The terrorists claimed the killing."

"But now that the terrorists are under arrest they know that that was merely confusion on the terrorists' part—a mere freak bit of luck for you, with one of them getting killed on the night of the killing, and the others assuming he'd done the murder. But that's all been cleared up now."

"How?" Her voice was challenging—but the waves were beating in fast now, swirling around her supports, smashing at them.

"The police know that the man who followed Osgood into the building wasn't anything to do with the terrorists—and wasn't the killer either: so the killer must have entered the palazzo by another entrance. Which can only mean the watergate. And the only people who could use that entrance are the people with keys to it: the owners of the building."

366

"And what about the gun?" she said—but the challenging tone had almost totally given way to desperation now.

"Yes, it was a gun known to have been stolen by terrorists: presumably you found it in some secret cache of Toni's at your house when you were look- ing for places to store your stuff for your shop. But leaving it near the corpse was too much of a giveaway: nobody would be that distracted. It could only have been left by someone wanting to give a false trail to the police."

Her voice suddenly took on a new tone of cold fury: it struck me that I wouldn't like to be her employee. The words came out sharp and biting: "Everything would have gone smoothly if you hadn't started pushing your nose in. You know *Amica* magazine was going to do a feature on my shop? Business was really going to take off."

"I'm sorry," I said. Then, feeling that probably wasn't quite enough to make her throw down the gun: "But shooting us isn't going to solve anything."

"If I don't shoot you I'm in the shit—and maybe if I shoot you I'm in the shit too. But at least I'll have had the satisfaction."

The first thing that shocked me in these words was the crude language: it was so unexpected from her lips. Then the message got across. I couldn't think of anything to say but, "Don't do it. . . ."

She said just one word—"*Stronzo*"—but got a world of emotion into it, nearly all of it hatred, some desperation. I'd broken too many of her supports, and she wasn't going to go down gracefully, harmlessly, like the Campanile of San Marco, but take as many victims as she could with her.

Toni's voice sounded like the cracked bells of the campanile as he said once more, "Francesca . . ."

And then a shot sounded.

We both of us leaped to one side—and at once realized that the torch beam had swirled up to the ceiling, revealing in a mad sweep grimy stucco work. I stared up the stairs and saw a confused shadowy struggle. Then an arm was raised and came down with a crack on some hard surface. One of the bodies fell to the ground and Lucy's voice said, "There." It sounded like a prayer.

I ran up the stairs to where she was standing over the inert body of Francesca. She leaned on the marble balustrade and I took hold of her with my one good arm. "I hope the bloody evening's over now," she said, and fainted.

24

"I LOVE Burano," Lucy said, "it's pure Cav and Pag."

"It's what?"

"*Cavalleria Rusticana* and *Pagliacci*."

"This is more opera talk, I suppose." We were walking along the side of one of the canals of Burano. The sun and washing were out—a satisfactory combination both from the utilitarian and aesthetic point of view. The houses themselves, in their irregular shapes and cheerful colors, were reflected in the water, like another, even brighter row of washing—Sunday best perhaps. The male inhabitants seemed more luxuriously musta-chioed than usual and the female ones just more luxurious. Mind you, my eye was possibly being selective.

"Oh, come on, Martin. Even you've heard of them."

"Heard *of* them. Never heard them. Hum me the good bits."

"I'll play them both to you back in London. But honestly, don't those houses just look as if they're about to be whisked away for a chorus of dancing peasants to come on?"

"Dancing fishermen you mean—or more likely dancing souvenir sellers. Close your eyes."

"What?"

"Go on, close them and just listen."

She did so. "Wow," she said, "the birds agree with me. It's the opening chorus from *Cav*."

"Yes," I said. "You'd think we were in the middle of a wood."

"An aviary more like. They're all in cages." Every other house seemed to have put their canary out on the windowsill to enjoy the sun.

"I chose the right place for an outing then," I said. "I thought somewhere cheerful and unreal might be a good idea."

"Because Venice is real?"

"Well, it makes everywhere else seem unreal while you're there, whereas Burano is just—just brazenly theatrical."

"So this trip is to forget, right?"

"Well, at least to feel fairly distant from it all."

She took my hand and said, "You chose absolutely right. It's perfect."

We came out into a little open grassy space by the lagoon. Sheets were hanging out on lines—colored sheets of course. Across the water to our left lay the island of San Francesco del Deserto. To the right was Mazzorbo. A few yards out a gondola was moored—a bright blue gondola. "I don't know why Zennaro doesn't come here," I said. "Then he wouldn't have to invent the colors."

"I gather he doesn't rely on your exciting browns and grays."

"Colors aren't exciting. It's what you do with them."

"Yes," she said, "I know. I'm sorry. Like rubbish dumps and gasworks."

"Let's enjoy the view," I said.

She smiled and looked over toward San Francesco. "That's the kind of place I could understand becoming a monk to live in."

"I don't think they'd let you."

We stood in silence and gazed for a while. Eventually she

said. "One of the nicest things about these lagoon views is that they're completely horizontal."

After a pause I said, "You're thinking about—"

"Yes."

She had come upon Francesca from the back that night because she'd done what I had nonseriously suggested some evenings before: she had climbed from the hotel window to the window of Palazzo Sambon. "I couldn't bear the thought of you there on your own," she had said afterward, "and I thought it might be a good idea to come in by another way." Well, there was no doubt it had been, but her faint had been delayed reaction to those moments of vertical fear on the windowsill.

"It's a pity about the bell towers then," I said.

"No, they set off the flatness nicely." We strolled over to a bench and sat down. She said, "The other nice thing about Burano is that there are no sights to feel guilty about not seeing. No museums or galleries."

"A great Tiepolo in the church," I said.

"You go. I'm just going to sit here and soak up the horizontal lines."

"The Tiepolo can wait," I said. We sat and watched a lone boat chug across the lagoon, which was otherwise completely undisturbed—a sheet of taut tinfoil aglow in the sun. After a while she said, "Mind you, some things I'm not going to forget: like Francesca killing herself."

"No." This had happened when the police had arrived. She had managed to grab the gun that Lucy had wrested from her and which, after Lucy's faint, had lain forgotten at the top of the stairs; she had simply put it into her mouth and pulled the trigger. Her final businesswoman's impulse.

"Horrible." Lucy shivered. "Poor Toni. His own sister."

"Do you mean poor Toni, seeing her dying—or poor Toni finding out what she'd been planning?"

"Well, both. I mean, my brother makes me angry sometimes but . . ." She shook her head. "When do you think she decided on the murder?"

"Well, I suppose when he phoned her, dripping wet—"

"No," she said. "You've forgotten that poor Frenchman." In his account to the police, Toni had told how, after pulling himself out of the canal, he had assaulted a tourist and stolen his Carnival costume. He had then phoned his sister, who had told him to meet her in a bar in Cannaregio. As soon as it was dark enough she had taken him to the old Palazzo Sambon, letting him in by the water entrance and promising to return with a complete change of clothes and some money.

"Well," I said, "I suppose as soon as she heard from him she decided that he'd have to die. I imagine that was in her mind when she suggested he should go to the old palazzo. She must have thought it would look a credible place for him to commit suicide."

"And she had another of his guns to suicide him with."

"Yes, she must have come across quite a little cache in the house when she was looking for places to stow all her stuff for her shop. You know, when she told me that, about not having said anything to her parents until the place opened, it did make me wonder a little. I mean, she had to have pretty good powers of—well, dissimulation."

"Which means lying."

"Yes. Okay, we most of us have to tell little ones now and again, but this must have meant concealing all her activities for months—and this just didn't seem to fit her image, which seemed based on her oh-so-honest look-you-in-the-face eyes. And that magic smile. Well, as I say, it made me wonder."

" 'She deceived her father in marrying you. . . .' That kind of thing."

"Exactly. There was always some tiny little detail that didn't click in her 'niceness.' It made me wonder a bit when I saw one of her employees who was still on a trial period being, well, dead-grumpy with Francesca; not even bothering to hide her feelings. I only had to think about how deferential I got with Mr. Robin when I was angling for a job to find it a bit odd. I mean, you might be naturally boot-faced, but when your job's at stake,

372

you make some kind of effort to smile—unless your boss really is the pits. I didn't consciously follow these thoughts through at the time, but they must have lodged in my mind somewhere, and I suppose helped in my overall picture of her as—as—"

"A wrong 'un."

"Exactly. The only thing she was really sincere about was wanting Toni to get out of Venice. I suppose she'd meant to let him know sooner or later about what she'd done—the Guardi picture business—probably relying on his big-brotherly feelings toward her. I mean, I'd seen how protective he could be toward her—he wouldn't even let me mention her name, and she must have come to accept that as her due. But even she would have realized that just then, with the killings et cetera, wouldn't have been a tactful moment to add to his problems."

We fell silent. After a while Lucy said, "Well, so much for forgetting it all."

"I said, feeling remote from it, not forgetting."

A boat came slowly toward us and the man in it called out, "San Francesco?"

"What?" I said.

"I don't think he's taken you for him," Lucy said. "Do we want to visit San Francesco?"

"Well, why not?" I said, and stood up. "Can monks marry you?"

"What?"

"Oh, nothing."

"Repeat what you said. Slowly. Clearly."

"It was just an idea."

"Repeat it or I shove you in the water."

"Okay, under duress . . ." I repeated the words, and to the boatman's tolerant surprise Lucy flung herself into my arms and kissed me passionately. She broke free seconds later when I managed to get out the words, "Mind my shoulder," and she said to the boatman, "We're going to get married."

"*Bravi,*" he said indulgently.

As we sat on opposite sides of the boat watching the

cypresses of the island monastery approach she said, "Admit it, it's just the thought of a gondola wedding that put the idea into your head."

"That and the thought of your father's expression when I first call him Pop."

She rose impulsively and kissed me, causing the boat to sway wildly. (It was her rising rather than the actual kiss that did it.) "Ueeh, signorina!" the boatman protested. She smiled an apology back at him, then said to me, "I want to go back now and tell everyone—shout it to everyone. All over London."

"Well, I'm intending to stick around a bit here."

"In Venice?"

"Yes. You know there was a reward for the paintings. Enough to keep me here for a few weeks. I want to do some work."

"Paint?"

"Yes."

"You mean Mestre or the oil refineries at Marghera?"

"No." I patted the bag I'd brought with me. "I'm going to do some sketches of Burano today—and San Francesco, why not?"

"Burano?"

"Yes."

"You?"

"Me. And one or two views of the Grand Canal tomorrow."

"And perhaps a gondola wedding or two—with a sunset behind the Salute?"

"Why not?" I said offhandedly.

"You're joking."

"No."

She realized I was serious. "This is pretty daring, isn't it?"

I was immensely glad that despite the smile as she said this, she wasn't being ironic. "It seems worth a try," I said.

"And I thought back there you didn't want to think of work for the moment."

"Well, I'll probably spend an hour or so turning the paper

round before I make the first stroke, but—well, you keep pushing."

"It's going to be a bit of a surprise for quite a lot of people, isn't it? Phipps goes picturesque."

"My gallerist for a start. But it's going to be good."

"Are you certain?" she said. Her eyes, it struck me, were dancing with light just like the lagoon: something else I could try and paint.

"No," I said. "But I've been rather put off certainty over the last few days. Padoan was certain. And Francesca."

"God save wobblers," she said.

"Yes," I said. "It's probably why I like Venice so much."

"What do you mean?"

"I'm not going to say it." I looked around the lagoon, with its uncertain horizons, its uncertain blend of sun and haze, its uncertain divisions between land and water. . . . "I'll paint it for you."